Mile High

Rebecca Chance is the pseudonym under which Lauren Henderson writes bonkbusters. Under her own name, she has written seven detective novels in her Sam Jones mystery series and three romantic comedies. Her non-fiction book *Jane Austen's Guide to Dating* has been optioned as a feature film, and her four-book young adult mystery series, published in the US, is Anthony-nominated. As Rebecca Chance, she has written the *Sunday Times* bestselling bonkbusters *Divas*, *Bad Girls*, *Bad Sisters*, *Killer Heels*, *Bad Angels*, *Killer Queens*, *Bad Brides*, *Mile High*, *Killer Diamonds* and now *Killer Affair*, which feature her signature mix of social satire, racy sex and rollercoaster thriller plots. Rebecca also writes for many major publications, including the *Telegraph*, the *Guardian*, *Cosmopolitan* and *Grazia*.

Born in London, she has lived in Tuscany and New York, and she travels extensively to research glamorous locations for the books. She is now settled in London, where she lives with her husband. Her website is www.rebeccachance.co.uk. She has a devoted following on social media: you can find her on Facebook as Rebecca.Chance.Author, and on Twitter and Instagram as @MsRebeccaChance. Her interests include cocktail-drinking, men's gymnastics and the Real Housewives series.

By Rebecca Chance

Mile High
REBECCA
CHANCE

PAN BOOKS

First published 2015 by Pan Books

This edition published 2017 by Pan Books
an imprint of Pan Macmillan
20 New Wharf Road, London N1 9RR
Associated companies throughout the world
www.panmacmillan.com

ISBN   978-1-5098-5256-7

1 3 5 7 9 8 6 4 2

A CIP catalogue record for this book is available from the British Library.

Typeset by Palimpsest Book Production Ltd, Falkirk, Sterlingshire
Printed and bound by CPI Group (UK) Ltd, Croydon, CR0 4YY

Visit www.panmacmillan.com to read more about all our books
and to buy them. You will also find features, author interviews and
news of any author events, and you can sign up for e-newsletters
so that you're always first to hear about our new releases.

To all the flight attendants who take such great care of me in the friendly skies, with extra-special thanks to the chap from British Airways who insisted on giving me a miniature of vodka with the tomato juice I had ordered on an 8 a.m. flight because 'You might find yourself needing it'. You were damn right, Mr BA. I did.

And to my flight attendant friends, Karl Frost, Greg Herren and Brian Levett, who all answered copious questions and shared outrageous anecdotes with me over a large number of alcoholic beverages . . . *not*, of course, the nights before they were on the roster to fly . . .

Two crime-writer friends of mine, Laura Lippman and Greg Herren, were hanging out at the New Orleans Jazz Fest a couple of years ago. Laura's daughter, then aged three, and getting sick of the crowds, yelled loudly: 'I HATE PEOPLE!'

Greg, who worked as a flight attendant for a while, leaned down to her and quipped: 'You should be an air hostess when you grow up.'

Prologue

*Are you ready to join the mile-high club? I've been
waiting so patiently for so long for us to be together
. . . you know how good I've been, how slow I've
taken things. But now, finally, it's time . . .*

Pen in hand, the stalker considered these words. Did they
fully convey the excitement that was flooding through the
stalker's body, the heady, dizzy thrill of closing in, at long
last, on the object of their desire?

The fantasy had always been extremely particular, extremely specific. Luckily, the stalker was not only a very patient
person, but a born planner. Waiting had never been an issue;
in fact, it had been a highly pleasurable part of the game.
The slow, long-range task of putting all the pieces in place
had been enormously satisfying. All the obstacles had been
cleared, one by one, until every circumstance slotted perfectly
together, the anticipation building month by month, year by
year, until it culminated in this exquisite moment.

Finally, they were so close, the stalker and the target: Catalina, one of the few celebrities so famous that she was known

simply by her first name. It was an accolade reserved only for singers; mere actors never had that privilege, no matter how many Oscars they won. She was a global star. There wasn't a country in the world where a mention of Catalina would not spark instant recognition, prompt someone to hum a chorus of one of her ridiculously catchy songs. Her schedule was tightly controlled, her public appearances planned out far in advance, including, naturally, the one on which she was about to embark.

This was where the stalker's meticulous organization skills had been so crucial. They had schemed and plotted and planned like a general positioning troops on a tactics board, moving the central piece, Catalina, to exactly this point, bringing her and her stalker together in the same airport terminal, about to board the same plane, where they would share the same air, the same space.

And then they would join the mile-high club together.

There was no doubt in the stalker's mind that once this had happened, everything would change. That had been their conviction, right from the beginning. Once the eagerly anticipated physical connection with Catalina had been established, the whole world would crack and reform, reshape itself into an entirely new, glittering creation. It was fanciful, the stalker acknowledged with a little smile, but the image that symbolized this transformation so vividly for them was the scene in the first *Superman* film, where Christopher Reeve, alone in an icy, desolate polar landscape, places a single crystal into the snow and watches in dazzled wonder as the bleak white wastes explode into a riot of diamond-bright shards of glass, shooting up to form an ice palace fit for a queen.

Fit even for Catalina. Beautiful, enchanting, magical

2

Catalina. The stalker drew in a long breath, thinking of how close they were to their own personal queen; the hand holding the pen trembled. Only a few hours until the Pure Air LuxeLiner was slicing through the cold skies over the Atlantic, heading for a midnight landing at Los Angeles International. And before its wheels touched down on the ·LAX runway, the dream the stalker had been nursing for so very long would have come to pass. Catalina would have been seduced and conquered by the sheer, unstoppable force of the stalker's love for her.

The stalker's eyes, which had been filmed over with desire, refocused on the words printed neatly on the paper of the notebook. The pen lowered, made some excisions: the message should be simpler and more concise. Catalina would have drunk some champagne at the launch, possibly taken a sleeping pill when she boarded the plane. Rumour had it that she was withdrawn at the moment, her usual vivacious, bubbly, outgoing personality – for which she was beloved by her multitude of fans throughout the world – oddly subdued. Because Catalina was always positive, always smiling, always joyous, just like her music.

For the last few months, however, she had barely been on the media radar, and was emerging from seclusion only because of a long-standing professional obligation to sing at the upcoming Oscars. She had just completed the British leg of the pre-publicity tour and was now heading for LA, the Dolby Theatre and her performance of 'Forever is Now', the song she had written for the latest Disney animated blockbuster.

To the stalker, that title was the perfect omen, the symbol of the future into which the newly minted couple were about to walk, entwined, beaming, madly in love. It was as if Catalina had known, somehow, what was in store for her, whom she was destined to meet on her journey to sing that song live before a TV audience of forty million people. As if she had predicted her own imminent happiness when she composed those lyrics.

The stalker drew in a long, slow breath of sheer pleasure. Inside their skull, Catalina was singing 'Forever is Now', every note, every inflection, every flourish and modulation exquisitely familiar to the stalker. That song belonged to the two of them already. It was their theme tune, their love ballad. They would hold hands and listen to it together, over and over again, smiling into each other's eyes with sheer delight that finally they had found each other, and their life as a couple had begun.

There must be no opportunity for Catalina to misunderstand this note; it was by far the most important communication that the stalker had written to her. With further careful consideration, a few more words were pared away until the stalker nodded in satisfaction at the edit. It was copied onto a fresh page of the notebook, torn out and folded away neatly, slipped into a pocket, ready to be delivered at just the right psychological moment, containing only the essential message. Really, what more was there to say than this?

Are you ready to join the mile-high club? It's time.

And it was signed, like all of the previous messages had been:

Cat

Is

Mine

Chapter One

Fog over London, swirling like grey wraiths across the Thames and twining around the bridges, sweeping around the great bend in the river, clouding up the mirrored facades of Canary Wharf's jagged skyscrapers. Rising up from the murky water of King George V Dock over the single runway of City airport, trailing such thick, opaque curls of mist across the equally grey asphalt that, even without the storm clouds looming, so heavy that they almost touched the mist below, every plane at the airport would inevitably be grounded.

Buses lined up in front of the glass sliding doors, ferrying frustrated passengers to larger London airports; flights were swiftly cancelled or rescheduled, and Heathrow and Gatwick, already at high capacity, swelled like balloons about to burst. Travellers crammed into departure lounges, occupying every seat in the pubs and bistros, spending money they didn't have on duty-free perfume and chocolate they didn't need. Bookstores and newsagents did a roaring trade; smokers prayed in thanks to the god of nicotine for e-cigarettes; parents surreptitiously dosed their wailing children with extra Calpol. Airline employees worked frantically behind the scenes to cope with the flood of additional travellers, desperate to get them boarded before lengthy delays meant that they could start claiming food vouchers and compensation.

The view from the walkway above the airside of Heathrow's Terminal 5 departures area showed a seething, barely contained mob besieging the information desk. Much preferable, from the airport's point of view, were the passengers who self-medicated with tranquillizers before their flights and were slumped in Diazepam hazes on the seats facing the departures board, trying to keep their eyes open enough so they didn't miss the eventual call for their flights.

And yet, just a wall away from the crush of people, but a world apart in every other respect, a select cluster of VIP passengers were clinking champagne glasses and nibbling canapés at the launch party to celebrate the maiden flight of Pure Air's LuxeLiner to Los Angeles, quite unaware of the adverse effects of the bad weather on lesser mortals. Their celebrity status cocooned them from any mundane worries as if they were perpetually swaddled in silk and mink; concerns about being bumped from flights or having to crash overnight on uncomfortable airport floors were for people infinitely lower down the hierarchy of fame and fortune.

However, the woman whose job it was to make this launch, both metaphorically and literally, a soaring success, was by no means immune from pressing concerns about Pure Air 111 taking off on time.

'Fog! Dammit! I *said* February was a bloody stupid month to launch the LAX service!' snapped Vanessa Jenkins, the publicity director of Pure Air, staring grimly out of the floor-to-ceiling windows of the most exclusive lounge in not only Terminal 5, but the whole of Heathrow airport.

This was the Marlborough Suite, where true VIPs were hosted – no check-in queues or waiting at passport control for A-list celebrities. First-class passengers might have their own dedicated security areas, but the Marlborough Suite was the only port of call VIPs ever saw when travelling. Their limousines would pull up outside its discreet doors and the passengers would step out to be welcomed by the waiting concierge; their baggage would be carried in and stored as the concierge led them to their own private lounge, where they would be checked in by airline staff and have their passports verified. They would be served refreshments and left to relax before being chauffeured in due course to an equally discreet door next to their boarding gate and personally escorted onto their flights, the first to board.

Upon arriving at Heathrow from an international flight, the process was followed in reverse. Passengers would be met at the air bridge by a member of the VIP team and chauffeured to the Marlborough Suite, their bags collected and loaded into their waiting limo while a passport officer personally visited them in their private lounge. While hoi polloi were still queuing up for the automatic passport machines to scan their identity documents, the VIPs were already on their way out of the Marlborough Suite, a phalanx of staff trailing behind them like the wisps of fog outside the plate-glass windows. And though the concierge politely wished them a pleasant stay in London, those parting words were almost always ignored by the VIPs, as unimportant to them as the damp mists of February, which barely touched their slim, expensively dressed bodies as they moved from the carpeted, glassed-in entrance area to the soft leather interior of their limousine.

The Marlborough Suite offered not just whisper-smooth transitions from one mode of luxury travel to another, but the opportunity to celebrate one's A-list status with fellow VIPs. Its centre was a large, lavishly decorated lounge area, hung with colourful but inoffensive paintings that alternated with flat-screen TVs, a chrome bar at its centre offering waiter service. At the far end, slightly apart from the whirl of excited, bustling activity, Vanessa stood, looking out of the window in the hope of seeing the usual stream of planes taking off and landing. However, the Marlborough Suite, not being airside, had no view of the runways, and the fog meant that she could barely make out a lone plane taking off over the terminal building, a pale white streak whose purple and orange lettering and jaunty tail fin were only visible for a brief moment as it crested the mist before disappearing into the grey clouds above.

'FedEx,' Vanessa muttered to herself. 'Bloody bastards, why give *them* priority? They don't have passengers to shift!'

She rounded abruptly on the director of the Marlborough Suite, who was standing nervously at her side, doing his best to maintain his customary professional poker face. Functioning as the liaison between the VIP guests and the airport authorities, he was accustomed to all kinds of demands from imperious and spoiled celebrities, but Vanessa in full flight was infinitely more menacing than an entitled film star who had pre-ordered a cheese canapé selection and then, suddenly deciding they had gone dairy-free, was demanding yellowtail sashimi with jalapeno vinaigrette plus spicy tuna rolls, to be provided immediately.

'We'd better be keeping our scheduled departure slot to the *minute*,' Vanessa hissed at the director, her voice lowered to avoid attracting the attention of the many journalists present. 'No excuses. This is the biggest event at the entire airport this fucking *month*, if not *year*, and if there's *one* flight that makes it out on time, it's ours. Got it? I don't care how many other flights the airport has to push back to make it happen.'

'Lord Tony just told me—' the airport employee made the mistake of saying, glancing over at the Pure Air CEO and figurehead. Dressed in a cobalt suit and matching silk tie, the Pure Air signature colour, his golden hair brushed back from his high forehead, Lord Tony Moore looked like a Viking who had been reincarnated as an air steward. He beamed over the heads of the assembled journalists, his teeth flashing as white as the starched collar of his shirt, his eyes as blue and bright and clear as a Ken doll's; the Pure Air cobalt had been personally chosen by him to match exactly the same shade of blue as his irises.

'Lord Tony tells people anything they want to hear,' Vanessa said tartly. 'That's why he pays me a fortune to schlep along behind him, cleaning up the mess. Remember that big hurricane in Mexico last July? Planes grounded for almost a week? All those holidaymakers stranded?'

'Of course,' the Marlborough Suite director said, grimacing at the memory of the disruption it had caused.

'We had *swathes* of tourists over there with Pure Air Holidays,' Vanessa continued. 'Stranded, running out of water at the resorts, some of them even in storm bunkers.' She huffed out a laugh. 'One poor guy came out of the bunker to carry out the pee bucket, apparently, and the wind blew it right back in his face. All over his clothes. And then he had to go back down into the bunker again, stinking of everyone's pee and coated in sand, too, from the wind. Stayed there ponging up the place for three more days. God knows what they were doing visiting Mexico in July anyway. Fucking idiots.'

She fixed the director with a basilisk-like stare.

'Remember what Bayes and Cocker did?' she asked, naming one of Britain's biggest package holiday companies. 'They sent over all these BA jets to rescue their lot. Seven jumbo jets, landing one after the other at Cancun airport. Looked fantastic. Tons of publicity. Got onto the *News at Ten*, everything. Tony was begging me to organize a stunt to match that, but I told him no, we'd wait it out and do sweet FA till our own planes could fly. Got everyone out eventually. And guess what?'

The director knew much better than to hazard an answer.

'We did surveys afterwards, our lot versus the Bayes and Cocker travellers,' Vanessa said triumphantly. 'Both sets were equally pissed off. Blamed the travel companies for them being stupid enough to go to Mexico in hurricane season, whinged their heads off, yadda yadda yadda, the usual. But Bayes and Cocker didn't get *any* credit for spending an absolute fucking fortune on showing off with their BA jumbos. None at all. We got just the same customer satisfaction rating as they did. I was bloody right not to lift a finger to help them.'

She smiled triumphantly. Someone picturing a highly paid head of corporate communications might expect the stereotypical image of a high-flying career woman, slim and sleek-haired in a dark crêpe Stella McCartney business suit and Tory Burch pumps, the designer version of the handful of elegant, groomed Pure Air stewardesses who had been selected to attend the launch. Vanessa Jenkins, however, was the type of woman who people sometimes, unwisely, describe as 'maternal'. Comfortably built, with an extra roll of padding at neck, wrists and waist, she favoured loose peasant-style blouses with drawstring necks, and wide-legged trousers to balance her substantial derriere. Her hair was cut in a short shaggy style, her fringe sticking to a forehead that was perpetually sweaty, and her brown eyes, set in little puffy casings like grilled button mushrooms in miniature vol-au-vents, had a perpetually cosy expression that lured her opponents into a false sense of security.

'So what's the moral of this little story, I hear you ask yourself?' she concluded, her slightly gappy teeth giving her smile a crocodile aspect of which she was very well aware. 'Here it is: *no one* ever rewards you for being nice. *Ever.* There is no fucking benefit in the travel industry to being nice. Which is why I'm telling you, not nicely at all, that if *you* don't tell BAA that our LuxeLiner'll be pulling back from the gate bang on time, I'll have their fucking guts for garters, as my old granddad used to say. I don't care if they have to fucking bump *royalty* to make it happen.'

The director of the Marlborough Suite, duly briefed, shot off across the wood-panelled floor so quickly that he caught the toe of his shiny brogue in a rug, tripped and did a hop, a skip and a jump to save himself. Vanessa, her smile even wider for the benefit of all the media present, headed over to the group of journalists and entertainment TV crews who were gathered waiting for the most A-list of the celebrities who would be travelling on the first-ever LuxeLiner flight.

'She won't be much longer, will she?' a journalist asked Vanessa, who shook her head just as confidently as if she knew that Catalina was about to emerge from her private room off the main lounge.

'She's usually bang on time,' another chimed in, eliciting nods of agreement from the rest of the press pack. 'Could set your watch by her.'

'If she's not out in five minutes, I'll go and chivvy her along,' Vanessa promised, very aware that interview time was limited by the scheduled departure of Pure Air 111, and that it was crucial for the media to get decent quotes and footage from the one true superstar on the flight.

The term 'superstar' was often overused, but there was no doubt it applied to Catalina, who would be classified as A+ on any current celebrity scale. She had been an internationally famous singer and songwriter since she was fifteen, first conquering Latin America, then the English-speaking world with her crossover album, *Heart/Corazón*, which had been available in both English and Spanish. A phenomenal success, partly because a significant percentage of her fans eagerly purchased both versions, it had put her on the map: famous musicians had promptly lined up to collaborate and co-write with her, attracted not only by her talent but the entry she offered into the huge Spanish-language market.

Catalina was a triple threat, a singer, writer and performer who could literally dance rings round any of her peers. She had been onstage since eight years old as a child star in her native Argentina, and she was nothing if not a trouper. Her latest album, *Chasing Midnight*, had been a huge international success; the title song, of the same name, had gone to number 1 in almost every country in the world; she had just completed a sold-out worldwide; and the icing on the cake was 'Forever is Now' being nominated for Best Original Song at the Oscars, the bookies' favourite to win.

It was a dizzyingly high peak in Catalina's career even by her own extraordinarily successful standards. Unfortunately, this professional triumph coincided with the lowest ever point in her personal life. A few months before, she had simultaneously suffered not only a terrible heartbreak, but the worst betrayal of her life, and since then, she had been virtually a recluse, holed up in her beach house in Punta del Este with her personal assistant, Latisha, crying, grieving, and writing songs that were so depressive and miserable that the executives at her label were becoming seriously worried about the direction of her next album.

She had also dropped weight that she definitely could not afford to lose. Almost all stars are much smaller in real life than one expects, but Catalina was positively miniature, with the whip-thin, ectomorph build of a dancer that looked even tinier in proportion to the great mane of dark, curly hair that cascaded down her back. Curled up on one of the sofas in the private lounge that had been assigned to her in the Marlborough Suite, she could have been a cartoon version of herself, or one of those frighteningly unrealistic dolls made to appeal to pre-pubescent girls. Like the heroines of *Frozen,* her eyes seemed too large for her face, her waist and wrists and ankles so narrow that it was hard to see how those fragile bones could support even her minimal weight.

The resemblance to a doll was emphasized by her ridiculously lush hair, which cascaded around her face so luxuriantly that a little girl's fingers would have itched to brush and plait it, and it earned her a small fortune in styling product endorsements. Right now, however, it made her face appear narrow, even pinched, by comparison, and her body as thin and easily snapped as a daisy stem.

'Uh, hon, we need to get going,' Latisha said for the umpteenth time. She was sitting on the sofa facing her boss, doing her absolute best to remain calm and not jump up and start pacing the room impatiently. Catalina had done a big press call that morning, but since then had barely spoken, allowing Latisha to shepherd her in and out of hotels and limos, organize their mounds of luggage, while Catalina followed along in mute acquiescence. Now, however, she was required to reactivate her personality, participate in another lively press conference, and not only did she seem completely unwilling to say a word, Latisha was becoming increasingly worried that Catalina might not even get up from the sofa in time to board the plane.

'Hon, the clock's ticking,' Latisha said gently. 'We should be getting out there and schmoozing the press.'

She shot a glance at her employer, who had taken her mass of hair out of the loose chignon in which it had been pinned that morning by the London stylist and was hiding behind it as if it were a veil.

'I really think you should pull back your hair, hon,' she

suggested. 'It swamps you when it's down like that, unless it's properly done. And people want to see your face. I can do a nice braid if you want. That always looks good.'

Catalina drew her full lips into a straight line, pinching them together, a silent gesture that rejected Latisha's words.

'Or, uh, a ponytail?' Latisha suggested, although she knew perfectly well that the hairstyle suggestion was not what Catalina was refusing.

There was no response to this, not even a grimace. The only sound in the room was the soft, generic instrumental music piped through the overhead speakers, versions of pop ballads revamped for easy listening background music. One of Catalina's own love songs had been featured earlier, the hugely famous '*Corazón*', but to Latisha's great relief, Catalina had not seemed to notice it. She was liable to start crying at the slightest thing, and there was a mournful, yearning element to some of the verses that might have set her off, even if she could only hear the melody.

'Cat, look,' Latisha tried again, only to tail off as Catalina raised her head, shaking back her mane of hair, and fixed Latisha with her huge dark eyes.

'I don't want to get on a plane today,' she said softly, her English perfect, but lightly tinged with her native Argentinian Spanish accent. 'I don't want to go back to LA.'

Over the last few months, Latisha had been functioning more as Catalina's on-site therapist than an actual personal assistant, and one thing she had learnt was that Catalina talking was more positive than Catalina silent. A taciturn Catalina could not be encouraged to do anything at all: eat, sleep, take some exercise. She just sat or lay wherever she was, near comatose, her increasingly skinny limbs wound into a ball, seeming not to hear any words that were being addressed to her. Food and drink left on a bedside or coffee table were completely ignored: tea had got cold, water had got warm, snacks had gone stale.

But once Catalina started to communicate, Latisha knew her boss so well that she could usually find a way through to her. She leaned forward encouragingly, trying not to panic at what Catalina had just said.

'Hon, we gotta go back to LA,' she said reasonably. 'You're singing at the Oscars! I love you – I'd do anything to look after you – I'd get you out of anything I could! But this one is *so* not optional.'

She paused, very aware of the reason behind Catalina's resistance to returning to LA. It was there that Catalina had briefly been so blissfully happy before her life had been catastrophically turned upside down, there that she had lost the love of her life. Catalina now associated her beautiful house in the Hills with heartbreak and grief. She had fled it the terrible day of the showdown and never returned, holing up in a suite at the Roosevelt Hotel until she had finished her last shows in LA and been able to escape to Uruguay and the seclusion of Punta del Este.

'We've got a great suite all booked in at the Four Seasons,' Latisha commented. Worried that Catalina would baulk at returning to the Roosevelt, where she had mostly spent her stay lying on the carpet, crying and squeezing pillows to her narrow chest, Latisha had sensibly chosen a different hotel for their return visit.

'And hon,' she added, 'we kinda need to get there sooner

rather than later, you know? You have rehearsals scheduled, you need to get over the jet lag, you've got final fittings for your outfit, I have a whole bunch of beauty treatments booked in for you, and you *know* how busy it gets in Oscar week! There's no way any of those can be moved – they've been set in stone for months now.'

'I could get another flight,' Catalina said in a tiny voice. 'One where I don't have to do interviews and all this media stuff, so I could just board in a hoodie and keep my head down and not talk to anyone.'

Latisha closed her eyes briefly – safe to do so, as Catalina wasn't looking in her direction – and embarked silently on a long prayer that began *Lord Jesus, I'm begging you here . . .*

Catalina's presence on this Pure Air maiden flight had been on her calendar for as long as the various facials, hair treatments, styling and skin-brightening appointments booked in for the pre-Oscar beautifying week. It had been a stroke of genius for both Pure Air and Catalina's PR teams. The airline was able to garner superb press coverage from the fact that it had such a major celebrity on-board, while Catalina's squad of publicists at her record companies around the world rejoiced in the extra boost of this triumphant return to public notice after the months she had spent completely off the radar. Latisha had played a crucial role in organizing her employer's presence on this flight, and the mere thought that Catalina might baulk at the last moment and refuse to get on-board sent shivers down her spine. Pure Air would be livid if Catalina pulled out, and the fallout from the negative publicity would be huge.

But no one became the right-hand woman to one of the most famous stars on the planet by allowing themselves to panic – at least not visibly. Latisha's face remained as calm as ever, her high forehead smooth and unruffled, and when she responded, it was in the most easy-going tone possible, as if it made no difference to her at all that Catalina might be about to torpedo something that Latisha had spent countless hours and much painstaking effort organizing.

'Yeah, you totally could,' Latisha said casually. '*We* could. It's just that we're here now, and our cases are all on-board . . .'

'You could get them taken off,' Catalina said to her lap. 'Book us onto another flight.'

'Oh sure, no problem,' Latisha said just as easily as before. 'It's just that there isn't another LA flight out this evening. That's why Pure Air's making such a big deal about this one – the time slot. It's the only night flight. They're really pushing the whole landing-at-LAX-at-midnight thing. So we'd have to schlep back to London now, or crash in an airport Hilton till tomorrow. The morning flights don't start till at least 10 a.m.' She shrugged as nonchalantly as if it didn't matter a hoot to her. 'I mean, we're here now . . . But hey, if you want to head out and hit an airport hotel for the night, that's fine with me. I can start making calls.'

Latisha didn't reach for her phone, however. Instead, she picked up her glass of wine – sorely needed; thank God for these luxury airport lounges that laid on hot and cold everything without you even having to ask. She had meant to take just a sip, but she ended up sinking half the contents in one swig. The prospect of Catalina pulling out of the flight at the last minute, with all the mess and fuss of the consequences, the negative publicity, the torpedoing of such very carefully laid plans, made Latisha look very longingly at the Chardonnay remaining in the glass.

Catalina's head was still lowered, watching her slender fingers fold the hem of her sweater over and over in a series of tiny little pleats. Latisha settled back on the sofa and forced herself to count down from twenty to one, as slowly as she could bear. Then she shifted a little, fixed her eyes on Catalina's face, and said more firmly, 'So? Shall I phone for a car? I can tell Vanessa and make all the calls about hotel and flights as we go.'

She held her breath. So very much depended on this, for all sorts of reasons. Catalina needed to pull herself together, get back on track. Yes, she had been terribly disillusioned about the man she loved: no one knew that better than Latisha, who had broken the awful news to her boss. But Catalina had made a series of professional commitments around this Oscar nomination, and if she started allowing herself to break any, it would be a terrible sign. This was the kind of behaviour for which lesser stars were notorious: partying too hard, say, and pulling out of shows claiming exhaustion or dehydration and tweeting photos of themselves in a hospital bed with an IV drip in their arm. Or turning up late for a flight, holding up all the other passengers while they strolled nonchalantly on-board, neglecting even to apologize for having made the plane miss its take-off slot.

But Catalina had never behaved like that kind of entitled celebrity. She worked hard, didn't party, was always, as the journalist waiting outside for her had commented, a hundred per cent reliable. It was one of the reasons for her immense success, and it was a crucial part of Latisha's job to keep her boss punctual and on track. Catalina's management team would rip Latisha a new one if Catalina pulled out of this promotional opportunity at the last minute. For these, and all sorts of other very pressing reasons, Catalina could not be allowed to let herself and Pure Air down, *had* to land in LA at the scheduled time to keep all her appointments, *needed*, unequivocally and imperatively, to get up from the sofa right now, plaster a smile on her face, walk into the Marlborough Suite's main room to answer questions from the media and then *get on the goddamn plane . . .*

Latisha realized that her fists were involuntarily clenched in tension, her elaborately decorated nails digging into her palms. She couldn't have reached for her phone even if she'd wanted to. Finally Catalina stirred and raised her head, those huge dark eyes meeting Latisha's in a look of silent surrender.

'I don't want to . . .' she began, and Latisha actually half-choked on the breath she was holding, '. . . have to wait the night here and get on a plane tomorrow,' Catalina concluded, as Latisha burst into a fit of coughs. 'Are you okay?' Catalina asked, concerned.

Latisha nodded wordlessly. Reaching for her wine glass, she sank its contents in one go, washing down the last spasms of coughing. Then she put the empty glass back down on the table, inhaled deeply and stood up, shaking back her heavy braids, squaring her wide shoulders. Walking round the coffee table, she held out her hand to Catalina.

'I am now,' she said. 'Let's go, hon. You're a pro. You can totally nail this. The sooner you give the journos out there what they want, the sooner you can get on-board that LuxeLiner, settle into bed and get a good night's sleep.'

She flashed a smile as Catalina leaned forward and took her hand. Pulling her boss to her feet, however, Latisha had to conceal a wince at how frighteningly easy it was: if Catalina weighed the hundred pounds that was the standard for Los Angeles women, it was only because of the heaviness of her hair.

'And you should eat something,' Latisha continued. 'Grab a bite, settle into bed and go to sleep. I'm gonna take a Zopiclone and crash myself. You've got your Valium, right?'

Catalina nodded. She strongly disliked turbulence, and always took a Valium before take-off in case the flight got bumpy.

'Well, that should zonk you out,' Latisha said, 'and you can take a Zopi with it too. I checked your handbag to make sure you've got vials of both, just in case. We've got a majorly busy time ahead of us over the next week – we need to get all the beauty sleep we can.'

Standing up, even in the three-inch stacked heels of her Robert Clergerie ankle boots, Catalina barely came up to her assistant's shoulder: Latisha had gone to university on a hockey scholarship and had an athlete's build. Latisha took Catalina's hair in both hands, pulled it gently to the crown of her head, took a no-snag Maddyloo elastic out of her jeans pocket – Latisha was always fully stocked with these small but important necessities – and fastened it around the twist of hair, arranging it into a loose bun that revealed Catalina's features and gave her a little extra height.

Catalina stood, acquiescent, while her assistant prepped

her for the press call, dabbing her lips with tinted gloss and her cheeks with a touch of cream blusher to give her peaky face some much-needed colour. Latisha dropped the make-up back into her shoulder bag and surveyed her tiny boss, who resembled, at that moment, a depressed teenager rather than an international star. Her Latin colouring meant that her skin was naturally a pale golden shade, but her miserable state of mind made her look greyish and drawn, and there would have been pronounced dark shadows under her eyes without the reapplication of By Terry Touche Veloutée concealer (infinitely superior to the Yves Saint Laurent version, according to Catalina's make-up artist, which in his opinion was not only far too light but also had a brush that was too fine to give the even coverage that the By Terry one achieved).

Relieved as Latisha was to have her employer on her feet and ready for the waiting press, it was hard to see her in such a despondent, depressive state. It was as if her loss had hollowed her out inside. Latisha had worked for Catalina for nearly a decade; they had seen each other through personal ups and downs, celebrated Catalina's successes, grown together in many ways, shared hotel suites whenever they travelled, were indubitably each other's best friend. And in all that time, Latisha had never seen Catalina so heartsick. She had truly been in love, and she had lost not just her lover but her faith in her own ability to pick a trustworthy partner ever again.

Impulsively, Latisha pulled Catalina towards her and enfolded her in a hug into which the star almost completely disappeared.

'It'll be okay,' she said into Catalina's hair. 'Honestly, it'll be okay, I promise. I know it's a shitty cliché, but time really does heal everything. You'll meet someone, you'll see, the right one this time. Hey, who knows?' She dropped a quick kiss on the top of Catalina's head. 'Maybe it'll happen even sooner than you think!'

Above Catalina's head, Latisha saw her own reflection in the mirror over the sofa. But, unlike her voice, which was soft and consoling, the expression in her eyes was quite impossible to interpret.

Chapter Two

It was like the sun rising in a sudden burst of light, illumination flooding a pitch-dark room, a chandelier hung with a thousand blazing, faceted crystals: that was Catalina's effect every time she stepped onstage, thrilling a whole arena with the force of her charisma. And she treated every press call like a performance. From the moment she entered the main room of the Marlborough Suite, she was brilliant with energy, her eyes sparkling, her lips parted, looking as excited to see the ranks of waiting media as if it were her first press conference ever and she couldn't wait to meet the world. No matter the troubles of her personal life, professionally she was always able to flip the switch to the Dazzle setting.

Latisha, following in her wake, wore a satisfied smile. She had known that all she needed to do was to convince Catalina to take the Pure Air flight. After that, Catalina's nearly two decades of performing would ensure that she gave the press all the glamour and sparkle that they expected from her.

Every head turned as Catalina entered the lounge. Despite her small stature, she was effortlessly magnetic. The assembled gathering was too cool to exclaim out loud or mob her for autographs, but a low whisper of excitement and anticipation ran around the various groups, her name echoing again and again, as if she had deliberately postponed her arrival for maximum drama.

'I'm so sorry to be a little slow,' she said in her charmingly accented English as Vanessa bustled forward to greet her.

'Oh, not at all,' Vanessa reassured her; like Latisha, part of her job was to keep an unworried demeanour, no matter how much she'd been concerned about Catalina's failure to emerge for the scheduled interview. Wrapping her arm companionably through the singer's, she escorted her up onto the low dais in front of the eager massed ranks of journalists, cameras and TV crews. Latisha stationed herself by the side of the stage. Usually she would take this time to grab a few moments for herself, as Catalina was generally more than capable of handling the press by herself; but, despite Catalina's ability to turn up her wattage to full force, Latisha knew that her boss was not at her best and might need some help.

Sure enough, Latisha's protective instincts were proved correct five minutes in, when a journalist from *Style* asked, 'Catalina, who are you wearing?' and Catalina's pretty forehead contorted in confusion.

'*Who* am I wearing?' she repeated, baffled.

'She means which designer,' Latisha explained swiftly, leaning forward to flash a smile at the fashion journalist. 'Sorry, Cat's a little tired.'

'Ah, yes! I knew that! Who I am wearing! *Lo siento!*' Catalina smiled too, her pretty little white teeth flashing, her lips curving so sweetly that even the most hardened hacks in front of her found themselves smiling back. 'It's fashion language, and I love fashion! Okay, I am wearing Isabel Marant, I think . . .'

She pulled at the hem of her semi-transparent pale grey and white sweater, a cashmere-silk knit that looked gossamer-light.

'With a T-shirt from . . .' She glanced at Latisha, and sidled sideways across the stage to her, making a cute comic show of turning her back to her assistant, arching her shoulders so that Latisha could tug back her T-shirt to see the label.

'T by Alexander Wang,' Latisha announced.

'And J Brand jeans,' Catalina said, looking down at her matchstick legs, so thin now that even if she stood with them pressed together, there were several gaps between them. 'I like them because they have a high waist. I hate to have to keep pulling up my jeans so they don't fall down and show my ass.'

She winked at the *Elle* journalist, her lush eyelashes flickering down and up so charmingly that the writer actually went a little pink.

Vanessa, observing from the sidelines the way that Catalina was captivating the posse of journalists, nodded approvingly. Vanessa had been hell-bent on snagging Catalina to travel on this inaugural flight, and her sense of satisfaction now was at its peak; Vanessa had been working on this project for longer than she even cared to think about, bringing it to fruition, pulling together so many diverse strands that it had been like weaving a fiendishly complex tapestry. And there was its central decorative motif, Catalina, up onstage, now lifting up one leg to show off her boots, balancing like a gymnast on the other foot, joking that the shoes would come off as soon as she relaxed into Luxe Class, and that she had been promised that luxurious sheepskin slippers were awaiting her on-board. The journalists were laughing, utterly charmed by her. Even the hardened camera operators were smiling at her antics.

So many celebrities, given lavish freebies in exchange for publicity, fulfilled their end of the bargain by doing the absolute minimum in return. If Vanessa had not selected carefully, she might well have had to deal with spoilt rock stars turning up at the last minute, refusing to pose for the photographers, retiring to one of the private lounges of the Marlborough Suite to indulge in drugs, sex, or both. But word travelled fast in PR, and the VIPs who took but didn't give were swiftly and discreetly blacklisted in preference for ones like Catalina.

Or – Vanessa walked over to a cluster of female journalists eagerly surrounding another of the celebrities – Danny Zasio, the internationally famous chef. Danny had, as the press release described it, 'executive designed' the Luxe Class menu; he had a string of Michelin-star restaurants from Tokyo to Dubai, and was travelling back to LA, where he lived, to start filming a new series of his insanely popular Food Network series, *Eat Me!*.

Danny was holding court, the deep lines in his forehead furrowing, the equally deep creases at the sides of his mouth curving into ruggedly handsome brackets, which the journalists had plenty of time to admire, as questions to him were barely needed. They wouldn't have to work to prompt a shy interview subject here. Danny literally never stopped his patter, one of the reasons that his television career had experienced such a meteoric rise. The others were his genuine talent and his rough-and-ready good looks; he was the classic cheeky-chappie Essex boy who would have worked a market stall, sold second-hand cars or become a City trader if he hadn't had a natural gift for cooking.

There was definitely a pathological side to his charm. Unlike Catalina, Danny couldn't rest, be still, turn off the people-pleasing side of his character that was so crucial to his professional success. He had had sex with every single female journalist who had ever interviewed him; once he had started the process of seducing them into writing a hugely flattering profile of him, he simply couldn't stop. He was perfectly capable of talking about his wife and children, who formed a crucial part of his image as a family man, even when he was stripping off his clothes and jumping on his latest conquest.

Because Danny's ace in the hole was his complete lack of shame. It was very attractive, a purely animalistic appeal: men wanted to be him, or at least have a drink with him, while women wanted to let his lack of inhibition lure them into all sorts of naughtiness they wouldn't normally have dreamed of performing. Right then, having reduced the experienced, cynical female journalists into giggling, hair-twiddling, dewy-eyed fangirls, Danny was winding down his spiel, his bright eyes sliding across the room to find new people to charm.

Like a shark, he needed to keep moving or die. Once he had everyone in a room thoroughly under his spell, he got restless, and headed off to find new worlds to conquer. Danny's energy had once been entirely natural, but now that he was in his forties, with a work and travel schedule that would have been punishing for someone twenty years younger, he was fuelled by Adderall, aka prescription speed. It was usually prescribed for people with attention deficit disorder, from which Danny unquestionably suffered, but he was using it primarily for all the traditional benefits of amphetamines, and he was almost audibly buzzing as his gaze landed, with great appreciation, on Catalina's small frame as she stepped down from the dais.

'Oi oi! I know who *you* are, sexy! The "Chasing Midnight" girl!' he shouted cheerfully at her. 'I bloody loved that song! And your video – fucking *hot*! You'd make a fortune as a pole dancer, love!'

Catalina's eyes widened at this ribald comment. Latisha, used to having to run interference for Catalina, moved closer to her side as Danny started across the room towards them.

'Hah, Danny! Always joking!'

Vanessa swooped in to handle the awkward moment, expertly using her large frame to block Danny's trajectory. Linking her arm through the chef's, she said jovially, 'Tony's just about to introduce some of the cabin crew we've hand-picked to staff Luxe Class for the flight. Why don't you come over and say hi to them? They'll be the ones looking after you for the duration, so you can start working your magic on them now . . .'

It was perfectly done: Vanessa was making it clear that Catalina was off-limits to Danny, but the female flight attendants were fair game. As a waiter came over to refill Danny's champagne coupe, Vanessa indicated a blonde flight attendant in a distractingly short and tight cobalt blue skirt suit, and Danny, always distractable, turned very happily away from Catalina to leer approvingly at his new target.

Meanwhile, Pure Air's founder and CEO, Lord Tony Moore, was ascending the dais for the central presentation. Vanessa, who worked very closely with him, had familiarly called him by his first name, and certainly he made a point of cultivating a hail-fellow-well-met image. What he was really like in private very few people knew. His staff joked that he was actually a robot, powering down at the end of each working day, because though he was always cheerful and good-humoured, he had no actual, discernible personality. It was impossible to divine any specific preferences of his and proceed accordingly. He seemed to have no chinks, no weaknesses. It made him extremely boring as a dinner companion, but incredibly effective in business, and he had deliberately made himself the figurehead of Pure Air, branding the airline as one man's vision. Everyone in Britain would have instantly recognized his handsome face with its bright blue eyes, its white permasmile, and the mane of golden hair that curled magnificently back from his high forehead.

He beamed that permasmile around the room now. Behind him was a wraparound glossy backboard featuring three different images of the huge, sleek white LuxeLiner, pictured against a sky as gloriously blue as the cobalt drops of water painted onto its ergonomic sweep of tail fin. The drops had been strategically chosen to echo Lord Tony's first-ever brand, Pure Water, extended now to include the Pure Spa chain and, next year, Pure Hotels. A born showman, Lord Tony was, like Donald Trump, the frontman for the various Pure spin-offs rather than the finance behind them, but he had unerring instincts for marketing and salesmanship, and his physical presence, plus his ability to stay relaxed and fluent under the spotlight of press attention, made him the ideal company figurehead.

In addition, Lord Tony was prepared to do absolutely anything to promote his companies: appear on reality shows, get dunked in gunge on live TV, engage in all sorts of ridiculous stunts, always smiling, and always wearing at least one piece of clothing in the bright blue that symbolized the Pure brand. Today, it was a custom-made shirt, worn under a pale grey two-piece suit that had also been tailor-made for his big frame, a blue silk handkerchief tucked into the breast pocket.

'Well, *hello*, everyone! Isn't this just the most magnificent party?' he said happily.

Vanessa started clapping, sending a sharp look around at her staff and the selected members of the Pure Air 111 cabin crew, who had joined the launch after their flight briefing. They all promptly joined in, followed after a few seconds by the rest of the guests. There was absolutely nothing Lord Tony loved more in the world than applause. Tossing back his golden curls, he threw his arms wide to receive it, some of the champagne spilling from the coupe that he held; it was his first glass, and he had barely touched it. Lord Tony's drug of choice was not alcohol, but adulation.

'Bang on schedule! So much plotting and planning, and so many design decisions to make along the way, and here we are!' he said euphorically as the photographers snapped away, capturing him in relief against the LuxeLiner background. 'From the moment I first decided to commission these two amazing aircrafts as the flagships for my Pure fleet, it's been an incredible journey, the realization of my most ambitious dream yet! But that's what I always say: dream as high as the sky, and reach for the stars!'

Vanessa automatically lip-synched along to these last words: they were his signature theme, the slogan of the airline, and they were always accompanied by the dramatic gesture of arms stretched up to the ceiling. More champagne dribbled out from the coupe as Lord Tony duly thrust his outstretched arms aloft, his smile magnificent, his personal magnetism so powerful that it dwarfed even that of Danny Zasio, who was clapping and whooping by the side of the stage.

'Believe me,' Lord Tony said as the applause ebbed, 'more planning has gone into this than you can possibly imagine!'

Vanessa's nod of agreement was heartfelt. The behind-the-scenes work she had put in had been all-consuming, much more than Lord Tony could possibly imagine. She had been living, breathing and sleeping the launch of Pure Air 111 for the last six months, fine-tuning every detail, and even now she was running through what seemed like an endless, last-minute checklist to be completed before she could fully relax on-board and allow herself to bask in the triumph of every-thing coming together, just as she had so carefully strategized.

'You'll all be given press packs, of course,' Lord Tony said, indicating the table by the exit door stacked high with bright blue and silver folders, shiny and sleek. 'But right now I want to introduce some of the key members of the crew, the absolute best of the best of my brilliant Pure Air people, personally selected by me to give all my passengers the most perfect on-board service experience. You all know how hands-on I am!'

From another CEO, this could have sounded suspiciously like sexual harassment: if Danny Zasio, for instance, had been introducing a group of attractive staff members with those words, the journalists would have assumed that he had slept with all of the women, and introduced considerable innuendo into their coverage. But Lord Tony Moore's affect was as sexless as the robot to which his staff compared him. As he gestured to a woman to approach the dais, there was not a hint of anything off-colour, merely a cheerfully benevolent boss appreciating a particularly valued employee.

'First and foremost,' he was saying, 'our amazing cabin service director, who's been with us almost since the launch of Pure Air, but doesn't look a day older than when she started – Lucinda Waters, up you come!'

The woman duly ascending the stairs was doing so with the grace of a catwalk model in the tight-fitting pencil skirt of her uniform, hitching it up fractionally with a tiny movement invisible to the photographers. It was immediately obvious why she would be the first member of the cabin crew called up to be presented to the media. In her mid-thirties, she was tall, very slender, with her black hair straightened and pulled back into an immaculate bun at the nape of her neck, her pale brown skin matte-smooth with equally immaculately applied foundation, her almond eyes outlined neatly in black pencil, her full lips painted soft coral. She could have stepped right out of a television commercial for Pure Air.

As befitted the responsibility of her position, her demeanour was sober and poised; even her smile for the cameras was measured. She had just been running the crew briefing, delegating all the various on-board duties with absolute precision, ensuring that everyone knew their roles backwards and forwards. It was like being a director of a play, but with the extra weight of all the actors having potential life and death duties of care to their charges. Despite her comparatively young age, Lucinda was the most senior of all the cabin service directors in the Pure Air fleet, highly efficient, competent and meticulous. She knew absolutely every single member of the crew, their strengths and weaknesses: nothing escaped either her own notice or that of her grapevine of informants who kept her fully briefed about everything that happened both on flights and on layovers.

Lucinda was not liked, which was more than fine with her. Being liked, in her opinion, would have meant that she was weak. Instead, she was feared and respected, which she infinitely preferred: she led from the top and worked at least as hard as any member of her crew, although she used assignments of the most disliked tasks or rosters as a way of keeping them in line. And though Lord Tony had boasted of hand-selecting the crew for this very important flight, it had actually been Lucinda who had assembled the team, Lucinda who had picked out flight attendants who were attractive enough to be photographed for publicity purposes, competent enough to take on the responsibility of a maiden flight on a brand-new aircraft, and deferential enough to her to be rewarded with such a prime assignment.

'Lucinda's going to be running the Luxe cabin for us,' Lord Tony said, throwing an arm around her shoulders; he was famously physically affectionate with his staff members, and, again, his asexual demeanour meant that he could indulge himself in this without anyone raising an eyebrow. People would more easily believe that Lord Tony had been born without genitals than that he had groped a member of his staff.

He pointed at Danny Zasio, who was attempting to press a glass of champagne on the pretty blonde flight attendant, despite her blushing and insisting that she couldn't possibly drink on duty.

'See that man over there? Danny Zasio? Mr Hellraiser?' Lord Tony said jovially.

His audience turned as one. Danny raised his glass to Lord Tony with a shit-eating grin.

'All right, Tone!' he said, winking irrepressibly at his host. 'Just getting to know this *very* charming trolley dolly of yours – lovely girl!'

The flight attendant blushed even more, the red of her cheeks contrasting with the blue of her uniform.

'Believe me,' Lord Tony continued cheerfully, 'if there's one person that can handle even Mr Danny Zasio in party mode, it's Lucinda! I've seen her deal with a whole first-class cabin full of rampaging hedge-funders without getting a hair out of place!'

At this, Lucinda allowed herself a small smile of satisfaction. Lord Tony was quite right: she prided herself on being able to deal with absolutely anything. She glanced sideways, at the man who was being guided by Vanessa towards the dais. Karl Frost was her right-hand man, her chief lieutenant, who had come up through the ranks with her, though not quite as rapidly or to the same level. Lucinda was a born leader, able to give orders, even unpopular ones, and see them carried out, while Karl was the perfect sidekick, efficient, trustworthy, and loyal to a fault. She ruled through a blend of intimidation and discipline, and although Karl was the closest thing to a friend she had in Pure Air – or, in fact, anywhere – she was perfectly well aware that he, too, followed her primarily because of those two factors.

'And by Lucinda's side in the Luxe cabin, we have Karl Frost, our very able chief purser!' Lord Tony was announcing.

Lord Tony made a sweeping gesture of summons, and the chief purser came positively bounding up the stairs. Pale-skinned, his hair clipped very close to his well-formed skull, his eyes bright and his smile wide, Karl was not only dapper but the picture of energy. The Pure Air blue three-piece suit was so fitted to his trim, muscled figure that he looked almost dandy-like, his coral, blue and white silk tie knotted jauntily at his Adam's apple, his shoes and teeth gleaming. He tripped athletically over to Lord Tony's other side so that the peer could throw his other arm over Karl's shoulders and pose for the cameras bracketed by the two leaders of his crack Luxe cabin team.

'These two fantastic people are going to be looking after us all the way to LA in five-star style!' Lord Tony said happily. 'And joining them, here's a very special new recruit to Pure Air. Angela, will you come up here?'

The blonde flight attendant, who was still fending off the offer of champagne from Danny Zasio, looked up at the stage, clearly taken by surprise.

'Hah, Angela! You didn't expect me to be calling you up, did you?' Lord Tony beamed. 'Ladies and gentlemen, Angela's quite a celebrity in her own way. You all know that recently we merged with ReillyFly after the tragic death of poor Terry O'Reilly . . .'

This provoked sniggers among the gathered media. Terry O'Reilly, an extremely flamboyant Irishman famous for running an airline whose low fares were more than balanced out by eye-watering charges for anything from a glass of water on the plane to replacing a boarding pass, had dropped dead recently of a heart attack under very unfortunate circumstances. His latest wheeze had been to charge passengers for using an 'all frills' toilet on-board his planes, accessed by the swipe of a credit card. The only other toilet was a pod design, deliberately made too miniature for anyone over five feet tall to be able to sit down on the lavatory seat without bruising their knees painfully against the door. All sorts of special interests groups had duly taken the bait and campaigned vociferously against this two-tier system, which Terry O'Reilly had gleefully used as a way to promote his rock-bottom fares even further.

Disaster, however, had struck when, demonstrating to a group of journalists on-board a grounded ReillyFly plane how the credit card swipe worked, Terry had entered an 'all frills' toilet, shut the door behind him and then been unable to open it again. Attempts to swipe a card from outside to trigger the door's opening mechanism had been met with beeping and a panel lighting up with the information that the toilet was already in use.

Normally, all airplane lavatory doors were designed to be easily opened by a member of cabin crew using a coin in the plastic tab-release socket, in case a passenger were taken ill inside; but Terry O'Reilly had been the agent of his own downfall, insisting that the release socket was located at the base of the toilet door, so that cabin crew could spot someone on their knees fiddling with the lock, trying to sneak in without paying. That had required a special design, which, unfortunately, had proved to be much harder to operate in an emergency than anyone had anticipated.

Realizing that he was trapped, and beginning to feel claustrophobic in the small space, Terry O'Reilly had swiftly panicked and started banging on the door, shouting, in his familiar profanity-laced brogue, that some fucker needed to get him the fuck out of there right fucking now. And then had come the unmistakeable noise of a very overweight airline magnate falling heavily over the lavatory, with the wince-inducing crack of skull against sink on the way down. Unfortunately, by the time the only member of the cabin crew who hadn't succumbed to total panic had managed to wedge a fifty-pence coin into the very awkwardly placed lock release and swing the door open, the combination of a stress-induced heart attack and the blow to the head had meant that Terry O'Reilly was a goner, no matter how heroically the cabin attendant had tried to apply CPR.

Lord Tony, seeing an excellent business opportunity, had swept in, taken over ReillyFly, done a complete rebrand and relaunch, and cherry-picked selected ReillyFly employees to move to Pure Air routes. The young woman whom he had just named was one of that select group, and both Lucinda and Karl's lips were curling in disdain for her humble origins as a ReillyFly serf as Angela made her way shyly up onto the dais.

'. . . and Angela Stiven, bless her,' Lord Tony announced, 'is the very flight attendant who battled so heroically to save poor Terry!'

Lucinda had been opposed to Angela working this flight at all – let alone in Luxe Class! – but Lord Tony had overruled her, enjoying the extra fillip of publicity that her presence would bring. The world of air-travel professionals operated on a distinctly demarcated class system, and Pure Air crew were hugely proud of the fact that their airline had been rated one of the top ten in the world for three years running. They were up there with Etihad, British Airways, Emirates and Qantas, while ReillyFly, notorious for treating its passengers like cattle, shaking them awake to hard-sell them scratch cards on-board, was, compared to Pure Air, the scum of the earth, its staff right at the bottom of the pecking order. They didn't even fly long-haul.

Karl and Lucinda's short-haul flying days were far behind them. Long-haul was infinitely superior for all sorts of reasons: on those routes, you were put up in nice hotels for layovers, where you could mingle with the jet set, feel yourself to be part of the glamorous elite. You didn't have to live close to airports, as you had plenty of notice when your roster was drawn up, and might only be going into work once a week, as you would be away for so much longer, up to ten days at a stretch; you could live in another country and fly yourself in cheaply using the deep crew discounts available even for airlines for which you didn't work. You didn't have gruelling turnarounds on multiple flights, which so often meant helping to clean the aircraft, dealing with the knock-on effect of delays, plus the extra stress of repeated planeloads of passengers pushing and shoving to stow their over-large carry-on baggage and get to their seats.

Once you graduated to long-haul, working your way up

to business and then first class, you never had to deal with passengers pushing and shoving again. People travelling at that level might be entitled, spoilt even, but they weren't trying to cram a suitcase into an overhead storage compartment, threatening to punch you because it wouldn't fit, or kicking the seat in front of them because its occupant wanted to recline. At its best, you served champagne and caviar to elegant, grateful travellers rather than practically throwing stale rolls at belligerent people complaining about you refusing to serve them another drink because, frankly, they already looked several sheets to the wind.

As a result, cabin crew in first class looked down from a very dizzy height on their comrades working in the economy section, let alone ones from an airline that didn't offer a higher class at all. The first question one flight attendant on a layover would put to another in the hotel crew room was which airline they worked for. If the response named one that was considerably socially inferior, the questioner was considered very polite if they raised an eyebrow, replied, 'Oh, how nice for you', and walked away. Less well-mannered people would simply turn their back without even a word.

Lucinda and Karl, the crème de la crème of Pure Air, one of the top airlines in the world, had barely even acknowledged the existence of the cheap-as-chips ReillyFly. The fact that their boss had chosen to allow any staff from a bargain bucket airline to join them had shocked every employee of Pure Air to the core, and the handful of ReillyFly crew who had initially been over the moon at their new, exalted status were learning the hard way that they would need to prove themselves for years to their colleagues merely to be addressed civilly by them, let alone be considered their equals.

In mergers between airlines, the staff of the lower-status fleet were always treated appallingly by the employees of the higher-class one. Confined as they were to small spaces for most of their work day, flight attendants were not only obsessed with hierarchy between the cabin classes; the British Airways employees on old contracts, which gave them many more privileges, ruthlessly mocked their counterparts on the new ones, who were paid much less, had shorter turnarounds between flights, and – the worst humiliation at all – were required to wear their uniform hats and jackets at all times, even when they nipped to the loo. It was a visible sign of the two-tier system that the old-contract BA staff relished tremendously.

So the expressions that Lucinda and Karl were now wearing as they regarded Angela were identical: heads tilted back so that they could look down their noses more effectively, lips pursed, their nostrils flaring as if they had just smelt something extremely unpleasant, clearly revolted by the mere idea that an ex-ReillyFly employee could be considered their equal.

'Angela here was the one who got that toilet door open, pulled Terry out and spent fifteen minutes giving him CPR!' Lord Tony was saying, holding out both hands to Angela. 'The only one who kept her wits about her! I hear the ambulance crew said they couldn't have done a better job themselves. Sadly, poor Terry didn't make it . . .'

'So she's being rewarded for *not* saving his life?' the *Sunday Herald* diary writer whispered to her photographer colleague, who snorted out a laugh loud enough to encourage the diarist to note down her observation for use in her column.

'. . . but that's the kind of cabin crew we want on Pure Air!' Lord Tony finished. 'Calm, collected people who keep their heads and don't panic in a crisis! She's a very special crew member for a very special flight. Angela, my dear, welcome to Luxe Class on the LuxeLiner!'

Belying Lord Tony's introduction of her as calm and collected, Angela was visibly nervous and pink-cheeked. It was no surprise that Danny had paid such attention to her: she was only twenty-three, and with her wisp-fine blonde hair, round blue eyes and the sprinkling of freckles over her nose, she looked very sweet and innocent, just the kind of target a predatory older man would want to corrupt. Working on a bargain basement airline like ReillyFly had certainly not brought her into contact with anyone as famous as Danny Zasio, and as he flirted heavily with her it had been quite a struggle for her to maintain an appropriately professional manner, especially as she couldn't help finding him extremely attractive. He was worldly and sophisticated, teasing and seductive, which, coupled with his celebrity, was absolutely dazzling to a comparatively sheltered girl. Who would have imagined that Danny Zasio off the TV, looking even more gorgeous in real life, would have been paying her such lavish compliments, and actually listening to the pathetic little comments she managed to stammer out in return?

Her confidence was particularly low that evening, so she was especially vulnerable to being overwhelmed by Danny's fulsome flattery. The pre-flight briefing session had been a cripplingly humiliating endurance test for her. Lucinda had seemed to take exquisite pleasure in firing the most complicated and arcane questions at Angela, encouraging the rest of the crew to laugh sycophantically if Angela took more than a few seconds to respond, even making her stand up and bend over in front of everyone to ensure that there was no visible knicker line to be spotted through her uniform skirt. This was strictly against union rules, but Karl, Lucinda's loyal vassal, was the union rep, and it would be impossible for poor Angela to make a complaint; she knew perfectly well how detrimental that would be to her future on Pure Air. All she could do was take whatever Lucinda chose to dish out, keep her head down and survive as best she could.

So Angela was dreading not only the coming flight, on which Lucinda would clearly do her best to catch Angela out in every tiny mistake in procedure she made, but the layover, when Lucinda would doubtless forbid any other Pure Air crew to socialize with Angela. She had been so excited to travel to Los Angeles, but exploring it on her own would be lonely enough, let alone the prospect of being cut dead every time she tried to enter the crew room for a nice friendly chat with someone. And then there was the return flight with the same crew to be endured . . .

Lord Tony summoning her up onto the dais, calling even more attention to her, was the last thing she had expected or wanted. It was bound to make Lucinda and Karl even more hostile. She glanced briefly at their expressions and felt herself wilt at their matching sneers as she managed to stutter out a few words in a light Northern Irish accent about how proud she was to wear the Pure Air uniform and how much she hoped that she'd be able to live up to the trust Lord Tony was placing in her. She added, as cringingly as a dog exposing its vulnerable belly to show submission, that it would be very hard to live up to the very high standards of her fellow cabin crew, but that she'd work with everything she had not to let them down.

'Oh, Lucinda and Karl will look after you!' Lord Tony assured her, blithely unaware of the roiling tensions between his employees. 'We're one big happy family at Pure Air!'

He turned to beam at his cabin director and senior purser, who, sensing the eyes of the media once more upon them, promptly wiped the contempt off their faces, replacing it with polite smiles and little nods of assent. At a gesture from her boss, Angela went over to stand beside Lucinda and Tony, humbly positioning herself a little behind them, her hands clasped in front of her in perfect imitation of their stances.

'Right, you've met some of our lovely crew, and now it's boarding time for the lucky passengers on our maiden voyage!' Lord Tony said happily. 'As you all know, this is a really unique concept in luxury aviation. Our LuxeLiner is business class and Luxe Class only, premium all the way. We've triumphantly negotiated a very special slot here at Heathrow, taking off at 10 p.m. in London and flying through the night to land on the dot of midnight in LA, making it the ideal flight for high-flying business travellers – sleep through the night, get settled in LA and then wake up fresh for work the next morning. We're confidently expecting that a *very* exclusive clientele will travel with us on a regular basis. Look who we have aboard tonight! Catalina, Danny

Zasio, and Jane Browne, of course! Two Oscar nominees on this flight, and many more to come in the future!'

Vanessa tutted, looking at her watch: it was indeed boarding time, but Lord Tony found it very hard to stop giving a speech once he had begun. Now he was gesturing at Jane Browne, the actress, who was standing quietly to one side of the Marlborough Suite, doing her best to remain unobtrusive. This kind of flashy press junket was anathema to Jane, who preferred to fade into the background when she wasn't playing a part that required her to stand out: but her publicist had insisted that it would be an extra fillip for her profile precisely because her trip was being made for the Oscar ceremony.

Although she had been nominated for a Best Supporting Actress Oscar for her role as Charlotte Brontë in a British biopic of the Brontë sisters, it was not quite as thrilling as it sounded. Yes, having an Oscar nomination was a career-making achievement, but that was as far as it would go: everyone knew Jane was going to lose to either Carey Mulligan or Laura Linney. She smiled politely at Lord Tony. He was trying to beckon her up onstage, but Jane, choosing to interpret his gesture as a wave, gave a friendly wave back, declining the invitation. She had already talked extensively to various members of the press, something she never enjoyed, and felt that she had more than fulfilled the requirement to do publicity in return for her free flight.

Also, glancing at Vanessa, Jane could see that the publicity director was chafing at the bit to escort Pure Air 111's passengers on-board.

'Vanessa, I'm happy to say we've got clearance! Your take-off slot's confirmed.'

The Marlborough Suite director, arriving back by Vanessa's side, was over the moon at being able to announce the good news, and his voice was a little louder than it should have been. A couple of journalists looked back, interested that this information was being confirmed, when it should have been taken for granted. Vanessa, deeply irritated, smiled brightly at them while hissing under her breath at him, 'Shh! For heaven's sake! Are all the limos ready outside?'

'Absolutely! I just thought you'd want to know.'

Vanessa's crocodile smile deepened.

'I never doubted it for a moment,' she said, still *sotto voce*. 'No way was BAA going to fuck with me. Right! Time to get our VIPs to the plane!'

Lucinda, Karl and Angela were whisked away so that they would be on-board and ready to greet the first wave of passengers with ice-cold champagne and hot canapés; a last toast to the LuxeLiner voyage was made; the final shots were taken of Lord Tony and the gathered celebrities. And then the inner circle of VIPs – Lord Tony, Catalina, Danny Zasio, Jane Browne, Latisha and Vanessa – were formally ushered out of the Marlborough Suite and into the waiting limousines that would chauffeur them directly to the gate, where the white wide-bodied jet airliner was waiting and ready. The co-pilot had returned from her walk-around of the plane, and the pilots were running through their final checks and initializing their computers.

In Luxe Class, there were five dedicated cabin crew. The large front section of the airplane, with its flatbed suites, full-shower bathrooms and circular bar, would be, for the next ten hours, the home for twenty Luxe Class passengers, ready to be tenderly pampered, massaged, fed and watered. As tenderly, Lord Tony had once facetiously observed, as Japanese cows being fattened up to become Kobe beef, who were given beer to drink, had sake wine worked into their flanks and were played classical music to keep them in a state of blissful relaxation.

Behind the Japanese cows, three hundred and fifty business passengers would be looked after by ten more flight attendants, not quite as lavishly, but certainly to a very high standard of luxury. There were three pilots in the cockpit: the captain, the co-pilot, plus the third, known as an international relief officer, whose presence was mandatory under the US Federal Aviation Regulations.

The flight was fully booked. The Luxe Class bar shelves groaned with vintage champagne, premier cru Château Margaux and Saint-Émilion red wine, fresh sushi, even lobsters waiting to be steamed on demand. The business-class galley's champagne might not be vintage, the burgundies not premier cru, the lobster rolls pre-made, but the food and beverage director had exercised stringent quality control: for the first six months of the LuxeLiner's premium service, Lord Tony wanted the press and public alike to rave about the on-board amenities.

After that, small economies of scale could be introduced. The vintages would be slightly less highly rated, the canapés a little less lavish. No one would notice; the travel articles would already have been written, and the image of the Pure Air LuxeLiner would be established in the minds of business travellers and the PAs who made their bookings as equal to Singapore or Qatar Airlines, the *ne plus ultra* of the luxury travel world.

Lord Tony, of course, was first onto the plane. He wouldn't have dreamed of missing its maiden voyage, had a huge welcome reception planned at LAX to drum up publicity on both sides of the Atlantic. And though he had left the aircraft just a couple of hours ago, he was once again struck with satisfaction at the sight of his dream finally made real. The chrome of the Luxe Class bar gleamed cobalt blue under the subtle mood lighting, lounge music playing softly in the background. Karl was behind the bar, setting out the canapés and stacks of blue linen cocktail napkins, while Angela and Lucinda flanked the entrance, carrying silver trays loaded with champagne flutes – Bellinis, with champagne and peach juice also offered separately, to suit all tastes. Their smiles, their smooth hair, their regulation-coloured nails and lips were as shiny and immaculate as every surface on the brand-new aircraft.

Not a chip, not a smudge on anything at all, from the staff to the fittings. Not only was the LuxeLiner perfect, thought Lord Tony; this Pure Air inaugural flight would be perfect in every way. He heaved a deep sigh of utter happiness and stepped on-board, the mauve carpet luxuriant beneath his feet as he headed for the bar, swivelling around, propping his large frame against it to welcome his VIP guests. Danny Zasio, always the first when it came to free booze, was almost immediately behind him, snagging a glass from Angela with a lascivious wink that made her cheeks go pink once again, and drew a very appraising glance from Lucinda.

Catalina came next, Latisha by her side, Jane Browne behind them chatting in a soft voice to Vanessa. Journalists from the *Telegraph Ultratravel* supplement and *Condé Nast*

Traveller followed. In a few minutes, the rest of the Luxe Class passengers would be escorted from their airside lounge and onto the plane, with the business-class travellers boarding after them.

Three hundred and eighty-eight people in total, about to be launched into the foggy, turbulent night skies for a ten-hour flight. In those ten hours, alliances would be formed and broken. Power struggles would play out, scandals would erupt; a flight attendant would be summarily fired. Unlikely groupings of people would join the mile-high club – a fantasy for some, a nightmare for others – as Catalina's extremely determined stalker implemented the final stages of their long-held plan. And another LuxeLiner traveller, who had recently escalated his criminal activities from fraud to murder, would be targeting a new victim.

It was going to be a *very* bumpy ride.

Chapter Three

Eight months ago

They watch me prowl
You don't stand a chance, boy
You let me down
Now I wanna play with my toy

Feline eyes see right through you
Just wait till you see what I can do . . .

Behind the tiny figure of Catalina, gyrating onstage, the video of the song, shot in black and white, played on huge screens. Giant Catalinas, fifteen feet tall, writhed on the floor in black catsuits, shoving their little round bottoms high into the air, clawing their hands seductively; they snarled at the cameras, showing perfect, pointy little white teeth, a snarl that enlarged, took over the screen, morphed into something much bigger and scarier as the camera pulled back to show Catalina's transformation into a black panther, and the film burst into colour.

The song was her tribute to the first version of the film *Cat People*, the story of a mysterious young woman tormented by the fear that she would take the form of a panther when her sexuality was aroused. Catalina had seen the film years ago, loved it, and conceived the song and the video together as a tribute; the result had been so successful it had become not only the first single released from her album, but had provided the title for the album as well.

> *Midnight strikes*
> *I change*
> *We play a new game*
> *Not family or house*
> *More cat and mouse*

> *Some turn into wolves*
> *Others to chancers*
> *Some bark around*
> *Others are dancers*

> *Hear me purr but don't be fooled*
> *You will hear my roar real soon . . .*
> *I'm chasing midnight!*

The lithe black panther, prowling through the night streets of New York, hissing at the steam rising from the striped vent stacks, causing yellow cabs to veer around her and crash into night buses, was a superb feat of CGI – the video had cost a fortune to shoot. And yet Catalina, alone onstage, dancing like a wild thing as she ululated out the lyrics into her head mike, dressed in a skintight black PVC catsuit with strategic Lycra panels, was so compelling that every eye in the huge Mobile Power stadium was focused only on her. Her tiny hips swung in tight little circles, bumped and ground; her hands clawed the air in front of her so sexily that the standing audience in the pit had not stopped screaming since she stepped onstage.

Three near-naked male dancers, their modesty scarcely covered by strips of black fabric wound around their crotches and lower limbs, flew down from the stadium ceiling, landed on all fours, deftly unhooked themselves from their wires, and advanced on Catalina, the wires shooting back up again into the rigging. She turned and launched herself straight at them, sprinting from a standing start; as she jumped, she soared up into the air, and was caught by all three of them and held above their heads.

A dance sequence, created by one of the most avant-garde choreographers of the moment, followed during the instrumental break. Catalina was thrown from man to man, crouching, snarling, backbending, clawing their faces, ripping their bodies. By the time she leaped back down the catwalk to the B-stage, the secondary stage right in the centre of the stadium floor, almost completely surrounded by the audience, the three dancers lay in theatrical attitudes on the main stage, playing dead, limbs thrown out at odd angles, and Catalina was triumphant.

Midnight strikes
I change
We play a new game
Hear me purr but don't be fooled
You will hear my roar real soon . . .
I'm chasing midnight!

The entire audience sang along with her now. Her arms were thrown wide, her head back, her white teeth sparkling as she finished the song on a long snarl that was murder on her vocal chords. She only started it; the sound techs kicked in then, using her recorded vocals. She hated that, hated not singing completely live, but after a mere two shows doing the effect herself, her voice had been in serious trouble and her vocal coach had come down on her like a ton of bricks. Days of sucking disgusting, musty-tasting Vocalzone lozenges, which had myrrh in them, apparently, had barely helped; Catalina never remembered the baby Jesus being *fed* the myrrh the Wise Men brought him, and there was a reason for that. A baby would have spat that nasty stuff out right away.

Her jaw was still wide in a snarl as she held the pose, the amplified roar echoing round the stadium. Her right arm rose further in a final, huge, shoulder-turning, theatrically exaggerated claw at the air, every spotlight on her.

And then, snap – darkness fell. The audience burst into frantic, wailing applause. Catalina turned and ran offstage, tiny lights down the catwalk leading her way, the dancers now on their feet, ready to guide her into the wings where her dressers were waiting for her final costume change of the night. They stripped the catsuit off and wiped her entire body down with wet wipes as she stood there; sweat, mixed with the talcum powder that had eased her into the skintight outfit, was literally pouring off her.

'Remind me whose idea it was for me to dance like that in PVC,' she panted, as she did every single night, and Zoe, her lead dresser, laughed and answered:

'Bitch, please, like anyone makes you do *anything* you don't want to do!'

It was the reply Zoe gave every single night, a comforting call and response to help Catalina come back down to earth for a brief moment, as the audience in the stadium went wild, pounded their feet, screamed for her to return to the stage. Two dressers on their knees, one in front of Catalina, one behind, finished wet-wiping the sweat from her lower body and started to work golden-flecked oil into her legs and concave abdomen. Zoe, being the head dresser and utterly trusted by her employer, did the same for Catalina's bare torso, her miniature pointed breasts, as a hairdresser undid Catalina's hair from its tight bun and worked its curly waves loose and voluminous over her slender shoulders.

'CA – TA – LINA!' the crowd screamed, their feet now stamping in unison, beating out a drum tattoo. 'CA – TA – LINA!'

She had announced, before launching into 'Chasing Midnight', that this would be her last song for the night; but naturally, no one had believed her. Of course there would be an encore. There was always an encore. Hardcore fans had followed the Chasing Midnight tour avidly on the Internet; they knew the playlist backwards, knew which song would end the show. But they were the loudest of all in yelling for her to come back, even though they knew it was unnecessary, that Catalina would emerge onstage even without the hysterical volume of wails pleading with her to return. It was an essential part of the ritual: fans delighted to become supplicants, pleading and begging, abandoning themselves to their need; grown men and women screaming like toddlers wanting more ice cream, mouths wide, stamping the ground as if they were throwing a gigantic crowd tantrum. When the lights suddenly all snapped on, and the diminutive figure of Catalina, dressed now in a gold-fringed bandeau top and matching miniskirt that barely covered her bottom, her feet bare, appeared onstage, holding a microphone, their cries nearly took the roof off the stadium.

'*Hola a todos!*' she said, smiling at the cries of '*Hola Catalina!*' that crashed back at her in waves. '*Hola Berlin!* You've been a fantastic audience – we've had a magical time!'

'*Te amo*, Catalina!' yelled a fan from the front in German-accented Spanish. '*Te quiero!*'

'*Gracias!*' she said, smiling down at him. '*Gracias a todos!* I am so happy to be here! It's been a beautiful, beautiful night spent with all of you! And now, I am going to finish with an old song of mine that some of you may know . . .'

It was, of course, one of her first and biggest hits, a love song that started slowly but built into a full-on pop anthem: '*Corazón*' – 'Heart'. Catalina began so softly that the audience, singing along with her, knowing all the words both in Spanish and in English, were initially louder than her, loving the sound of their own voices belting out the sweet lyrics. The words were a little clumsy; Catalina had learnt English in fits and starts, but even in the early days, she had always been determined to only sing lyrics that she herself had written. So it made her wince a little now sometimes when she heard an entire stadium singing:

I wish that you were deep inside my bones
My ribcage yearns for you like an empty shell

It really sounded so much better in Spanish . . . And yet, the magic of the soaring tune, the irresistibly catchy chorus, carried the song, its cadences rising as her backing singers walked onstage from either side of the wings, wearing black bandeau fringed bras and slim fringed black trousers. It was an outfit that echoed Catalina's, while ensuring that the star stood out from the rest – an old stage trick. The two singers had been selected, too, not to dwarf the tiny star. Neither of them were over five foot five, in order to avoid making her look like a child between them. The process of casting backing singers involved a careful choice, where their voices were by no means the only factor: Madonna, white-skinned and blonde, had made a practice for years of hiring a pair of backing singers with more Latina complexions so she would stand out from them, and with slightly curvier figures than hers to make her seem slimmer by comparison.

As the pair of singers joined Catalina, the three of them moved as one, their choreography perfectly synchronized, heading down the catwalk to the central B-stage. Ten dancers, also barefoot, shimmering in gold and black costumes, glided on in pairs, one partner carried by the other; it was a series of love duets, men with men, women with women, men with women, many combinations of love playing out behind Catalina and her singers. The mingled voices rose in exquisite harmonies, the volume now drowning out the audience, who kept singing, their faces ecstatic, the song a story of travelling through love, loss and mourning to the gradual, tortuous process of learning to love all over again.

Catalina reached out for the hand of Luz, the closer singer. Frankie, the other one, moved a little behind the other two, one hand on Luz's shoulder. The women, on the B-stage now, meshed their bodies together in a close threesome as their voices twined around each other. Higher and higher they rose, up to the top note, and now Luz was subtly backing up the high F with which the song ended. Catalina was exhausted, her voice under stress, and another of the reasons Luz had been hired was because her own timbre blended in so well with Catalina's that, at moments like this, she could support Catalina's top notes without anyone being aware of it.

Corazónnnnnn . . .

The singers were holding their mikes in one hand, linking fingers with a partner; now the clasped hands were raised to their hearts, their heads turned to face each other, the last moment of the love song deeply intimate. Couples in the audience did the same, turning to each other, kissing and hugging as the dancing pairs onstage lowered their partners into a deep embrace and held the pose, the lights slowly beginning to dim.

'*Auf Wiedersehen, Berlin!*' Catalina called. 'I see you next time, okay? I love you all!'

Everyone onstage waved goodbye, the dancers exiting in couples, heads on each other's shoulders, arms wrapped around waists. As Catalina, Luz and Frankie walked back down the catwalk they all held hands, fingers entwined, Catalina in the centre, linked until they reached the main stage. And then Luz and Frankie slipped away, their dark outfits blending into the shadows, as Catalina stood under a single spotlight for a final beat, waving at her fans, the fringe of her golden outfit shimmering as brightly as her oiled limbs, her dark hair tumbling down her back, her lips wide in a glorious smile.

Every stage light snapped off at once. The arena was plunged into black night. And then the house lights came up, and she was gone.

There was a long moment of silence. Heaving breaths in and out from her quick dash into the wings, her ribcage rising and falling in great, yoga-trained efforts, Catalina revelled in every passing, soundless second: they were the proof that she had moved the audience to that ultimate tribute, a shared, emotional silence. It was as if everyone in the huge stadium were holding their breath. And then they let it out in a long sigh of happiness, mingled with regret that it was over, and broke into a thunderous ovation.

'Great show!' Zoe exulted, knowing to wait to speak until after the applause had started.

Catalina stood, arms wide, not saying a word, being lightly towelled down by her head dresser. Her vocal coach had advised against ending the set list with '*Corazón*': its seemingly effortless slow build was fiendishly demanding, and even with Luz's help, it took everything she had to nail the notes after all the dancing and stunts she had performed during the show. She loved to push herself, but this was always the moment when she asked herself what the hell she had been thinking. Next time, she'd end on a light little dance number that made her troupe do almost all of the work. Maybe they could even carry her on a litter while she sang.

But Pink would make the worst fun of me if I let the guys carry me around! she thought, grinning. *I'd never live it down with her!*

'Open wide!' Latisha appeared, and Catalina dutifully did as she was told so that her assistant could spray her throat with her vocal coach's special hydrating atomizer. It tasted a little better than the Vocalzone lozenges, but not much.

'How are you doing?' Latisha asked, and Catalina flipped one hand from side to side, indicating that she was okay, but no more than that.

'Fine, we'll whip through the meet-and-greets,' Latisha said efficiently. 'No probs. Take five here to catch your breath. Here's your birch water – try to drink the whole bottle. I have the competition winners all set up in the main guest room.'

Catalina nodded thanks, took the bottle of birch water into which Latisha had thoughtfully placed a straw, and started sipping it as Latisha spoke into her head mike, telling the staffer in the guest room that Catalina would be there in a few minutes. Coconut water was so last year: instead, everyone in the know was drinking water made from the sap of the birch tree, which was supposed to be just as hydrating but with fewer calories.

Behind Latisha, his back to one of the flats, loomed the enormous figure of Gerhart Zwölf, Catalina's new bodyguard. He had been hired here, on the German leg of the tour, when the previous bodyguard had apparently sneaked out from the hotel to visit Berghain, the notorious Berlin techno/sex club, and had such a good time there that he went AWOL, neither turning up for work the next day nor calling in. The fixer for the German leg of the tour had shrugged on receiving this information, commenting, 'Not the first time that's happened at Berghain; won't be the last', and hired a local guy as an emergency replacement.

So far, Gerhardt seemed very efficient. He said only the minimum required in any situation, and kept the ideal bodyguard distance, always there when Catalina looked around, but never so close that she felt oppressed by his presence. Tall, granite-faced, his close-cropped fair hair, which was prematurely silvering, echoing the winter-grey of his eyes, Gerhardt stood calmly to one side. He was tactfully positioned at an angle, which meant that Catalina was in his eyeline, but he was not looking directly at her during the intimate process of towelling her down. The only part of his body that moved was his gaze, constantly flickering back and forth, surveying the scene, processing any new entrants; the rest of him might have been carved out of the same granite as his face. He wore a black T-shirt and black jeans, his hands clasped loosely at his waist in classic bouncer stance, and not a muscle in his solidly built arms moved, not a corded vein twitching as he took in Latisha's words.

One of Zoe's assistants was wrapping another towel around Catalina's hair to soak up some of the sweat. Another handed Zoe a bottle of Jo Malone Lime, Basil and Mandarin cologne, which she sprayed liberally on Catalina's neck and upper body to freshen her up. She backed away to let Catalina's make-up artist approach; swiftly, Catalina's face was blotted with rice-paper tissues, smudges of make-up under her eyes were dabbed away with cotton buds pre-soaked in make-up remover, and her full lips were coated in Guerlain gold gloss.

'Okay, you're good,' the make-up artist said, stepping back as Catalina's hairdresser came in to unwind the towel from Catalina's hair, spray it quickly and fix the heavy, disordered locks into a photo-ready arrangement around her little heart-shaped face. Zoe knelt in front of her, and Catalina raised one foot and then the other, balancing with a light hand on Zoe's shoulder, as the dresser slipped ballerina flats, lined with comfort insoles, onto Catalina's size-four feet.

The hairdresser said, 'Done.' By this time, Catalina had finished the water, and she handed the empty bottle to Zoe with a smile of thanks, taking a step towards Latisha.

This was the signal for a phalanx to form around the star. Latisha took point, informing the guest room on her head mike that Catalina was on her way; Gerhardt was on Catalina's right side, while hair and make-up were following closely in case any touch-ups were needed. As they reached the concrete corridor, three security staff employed by the stadium fell in with them, boxing Catalina in completely, so that no member of the public would be able to reach out and touch her as she passed. She was so short that she was barely visible as the tightly packed posse moved through the backstage area, just a flicker of gold fringe showing between the large, black-clad bodies of the bodyguards.

The staffer in the main guest room had done a great job with the German fans and competition winners eagerly waiting for the meet-and-greet. Hopped up on fizzy drinks and cake, they broke into whoops of excitement as Catalina entered the room. TV screens played her videos in the background and the *Chasing Midnight* album was piped through the speaker system as Catalina was shepherded down the line, shaking hands, posing for photos, signing pictures of herself and taking selfies with the expertise of a star who has, by now, snapped selfies on every single variety of camera phone in the world, thousands and thousands of times over.

'You're so tiny!'

'I love you!'

'Wow, you are so small!'

'I'm your biggest-ever fan!'

'Oh, you're just like a *fairy*!'

This last was from a saucer-eyed ten-year-old girl who was both taller and wider than Catalina, and drew a particularly adorable smile from the singer. But by the time she reached the end of the line, half an hour later, she was exhausted, though her smile was still in place, her eyes as sparkling as ever; none of the fans would have realized how utterly drained she was. The phalanx re-formed before heading down the corridor to Catalina's suite of rooms, which comprised a private sitting room and bathroom. Catalina never issued many riders on her contracts: scented candles, white flowers, Jo Malone diffusers, tiger nuts and chicken breast slices were her limit of self-indulgence. She never entertained backstage, she didn't drink – she had no head for alcohol – and her philosophy was that if she had done her job properly onstage, she would have no energy left afterwards for anything but changing out of her stage clothes, showering, drinking some more birch water, snacking on the dietetically correct protein of tiger nuts and chicken, pulling the hood of her onesie down over her face and slipping back to her hotel to sleep.

So her dressing room was always an oasis of tranquillity, white and calm. She was craving it by now, just as she was craving stripping off the sweat-drenched costume, whose boning was digging into her, and stepping under the cool water in the shower to wash off her clammy skin. All through the meet-and-greets that followed her shows – which were mandatory, part of the contract with the venues – all through the smiles and the bright interest in the lines fans came out with, she was thinking of nothing else but her white, silent room, the running of water in her shower, Zoe taking her dripping stage clothes from her to hand-wash, Latisha handing her another bottle of birch water, both of them knowing not to say a word to her, as that would mean she'd have to use her voice in response . . .

They had reached the door with the gold star on it. Catalina's shoulders sagged in relief. Latisha opened the door, and Gerhardt stepped forward, about to conduct his standard sweep of the suite before nodding for Catalina to enter. Gerhardt had grasped instantly how essential it was to avoid requiring Catalina to say anything after a concert, and she was very grateful to him for never asking if she was okay, or if she needed anything; he assumed that she would let him know if she did. He cast one swift glance to make sure she was surrounded by the security staff, protected from any overeager fans who might try to ambush her, before he walked into the suite.

And then he stopped dead. His wide back blocked the doorway almost completely, and Catalina, tired as she was, immediately felt herself tense up. Something was wrong. Something was very badly wrong indeed. Gerhardt's shoulder muscles bunched as he reached for Latisha, swivelled, spinning her round, pushing her away, her eyes wide and her mouth in an O of shock. In the gap between their bodies, Catalina saw – not everything, but enough to make her gasp and cling to Latisha.

Her sanctuary was no longer completely white. On the back wall had been sprayed thick lines of red, a huge heart outline, placed so that it would be the first thing anyone saw upon opening the door. Inside were written three words. Latisha had recovered almost instantly, was spinning Catalina around just as Gerhardt had done to her, turning her away from the sight while Gerhardt summoned a security guard inside and slammed the door shut behind the two of them.

But the damage had been done. Catalina had read the words sprayed inside the heart.

CAT
IS
MINE

Chapter Four

On-board

'Well, hello, everyone! Welcome to the LuxeLiner!'

The cockpit door swung open, and Brian Levett, the captain of the plane, strode down the aisle and into the Luxe Class bar. Lord Tony, who had been leaning against the bar, chatting happily to the writer for *Condé Nast Traveller*, perked up at the sight of him. Brian and Lord Tony had a great deal in common: they were never happier than when flashing a bright smile and watching people's eyes light up, dazzled by their charm and charisma.

'Brian! We missed you at the launch!' his boss said, as Brian, resplendent in his fitted uniform and peaked cap, turned every head in the cabin. The uniform drew the eye, but the way Brian filled it out was what kept them staring.

'Sorry about that. Checks to run, m'lord,' Brian said lightly as Lord Tony slapped him in best manly fashion on the back. 'Business before pleasure.'

Vanessa, who didn't want the journalists questioning anything about the LuxeLiner – there had been a minor issue with the hydraulics, now resolved, but it was her job to make sure that no one picked up on that – sailed forward to stop Lord Tony from continuing to loudly express his regret that the highly photogenic pilot hadn't been able to leave his plane to attend the launch. Safety came first, but she was just as disappointed as her boss at the fact that Brian could not participate in the press photos. He was so good-looking that he looked more like an actor cast to play the part of a dashing airline captain than a trained professional with over fifteen years of experience: his curly dark locks were barely contained by the peaked cap, under whose brim his clear blue eyes sparkled charmingly. His shoulders were wide, his stomach flat, his hips lean, and the captain's uniform showed off every aspect of his enviable figure, fitting him like a glove.

'He took that uniform to his tailor to get it made to measure,' Karl muttered to Angela, who was at the bar replenishing the champagne glasses on her tray. 'That's why it looks like Armani on him. Honestly, he's as vain as a barrel of monkeys.'

'I've heard a lot about him,' Angela said under her breath. 'Isn't he supposed to be going out with . . .'

Careful to be discreet, she didn't name names; instead, she slid her eyes sideways across the bar lounge area to where Lucinda, tall and sleek, was proffering a tray of truffled quail's eggs to Catalina and Latisha.

'*Uh-huh*,' Karl confirmed. 'Plus he's married, of course. All pilots are. Doesn't stop him trying it on with every new hire, though. You've been warned, dear.'

Angela nodded fervently.

'I've got a very strict no-crew rule,' she said firmly. 'I don't think it's ever a good idea.'

'Well, isn't that virtuous of you!' Karl said, raising an eyebrow. 'How lovely to have that much self-control!'

Angela reddened and ducked her head.

'I didn't mean . . .' she started awkwardly.

'To be all judgy of those of us who might like to suck some crew cock every now and then when we're away from home?' Karl finished. 'It's called a layover for a reason, sweetie.'

'I *really* didn't mean to offend you,' Angela said bravely, lifting her chin up again. 'I just—'

'Of course you didn't, Sister-Angela-fresh-from-the-convent,' Karl said, tossing his head as he expertly scattered pre-cut chives over a plate of circular sandwiches; rye bread layered with smoked salmon and capers in a crème fraiche dressing. He was very aware that, as the chef who had conceived the on-board menu, Danny Zasio was keeping an eye on every single plate of food that came out of the galley, checking for quality control. Karl had trained with great concentration for this maiden flight. In the galley was a binder of photographs demonstrating how every single Luxe Class dish should be plated, but Karl, having memorized every detail, was confident he wouldn't need to consult it.

Garnishing the plate with a sprinkling of fried caper flowers, he handed it to Angela, who was biting her lip, pretending that the comparison to a nun hadn't upset her.

'Everyone's drinks are fine for now,' he instructed her. 'Take this round instead. You know how to describe it, right? Done your homework on all the menu deets?'

Angela nodded very seriously as she took the plate and turned to see Brian looming over her, tall and ridiculously handsome.

'Well, hello!' he said, doing a comic wiggle of his eyebrows in Groucho Marx style. 'How're *you* doing? You're the new girl, right? The little heroine who tried to save Terry O'Reilly?' He winked at Lord Tony. 'Phwoar, I wouldn't mind this pretty little thing doing mouth-to-mouth on *me*, eh?' he commented. 'Watch out if m'lord pretends to faint, young lady – you'll know just what he's after!'

The group gathered around Brian all laughed at this, none louder than Lord Tony himself. Lucinda, who was returning the empty serving plate to the bar, slipped behind it, muttering to Karl, 'As *if*.'

'Oh, I *know*,' Karl agreed in a whisper, glancing at their boss. 'You can't imagine Tony actually having sex with anyone, can you? He's all teeth and hair and plastic genitals, like Action Man.'

Lucinda's demeanour was so impeccable that she did not allow herself a single spontaneous facial expression in front of passengers; she turned away, therefore, to smirk briefly at the bottles arranged behind the bar, before rearranging her features into an expression of perfect composure once more.

'Plastic genitals,' she said under her breath. 'That's brilliant, Karl.'

'I know,' he said complacently. 'It just popped into my head.'

'How's Little Miss ReillyFly doing so far?' Lucinda asked, swiftly assembling a plate of yellowtail tartare with jalapeno garnish. She glanced over at Angela, who was circulating with the smoked salmon, and noticed that Brian's gaze was as glued to the young stewardess's bottom, tightly outlined in the bright blue skirt, as if he were doing another spot check to ensure that her knicker line were entirely invisible.

Lucinda's posture was so impeccable that her back couldn't stiffen any further, but her gaze hardened as Karl sniffed and said, 'Already told me she wouldn't dream of messing around with crew members as it's always a bad idea! *Beyond* holier than thou. I'm nicknaming her Sister Angela.'

Karl knew exactly what effect his words would have on Lucinda, who had been involved in an affair with Brian for the last six years. Lucinda was perfectly aware that Brian was married, and after all this time she only half-believed his glib assurances that he would leave his wife when the children were older and the time was right. But she was simply unable to resist him. Brian's easy charm and physical assurance were such a contrast to Lucinda's extremely disciplined self-control that she was addicted to the way he made her feel.

The only time Lucinda completely let down her guard was when she was alone with Brian. It wasn't a conscious decision; she couldn't help it. He melted her with one touch, made her feel like a sixteen-year-old again, giggly and silly and irresponsible, as light as champagne bubbles. For a woman whose job was to ensure that every cabin on an entire aircraft ran as smooth as silk, and who watched her own demeanour and weight like a hawk, Brian was her one indulgence, and she was as hooked on him as other people were on alcohol or cocaine.

And if Lucinda were being brutally honest with herself, she had to admit that she also relished the prestige of being the mistress of the highest-ranking flight captain in the Pure Air fleet. She had plenty of status, of course. As cabin service director, she wielded a great deal of power over her fellow employees. But when she and Brian flew a route together, on-board they were the ultimate power couple, and she relished that hugely. When they were part of the same crew it was taken for granted that they would share a room for their layovers, and those were Lucinda's days and nights of glory, when she could convince herself that she and Brian had so much in common that he would truly divorce his wife for her some day.

However, she and Brian weren't always rostered onto the same routes, as much as Lucinda juggled schedules to make it happen. Although she strove with all her might not to acknowledge it, she was perfectly well aware that Brian was pathologically incapable of being alone, and had a whole stable of crew and hotel staff rotating in and out of his hotel room when Lucinda wasn't there. After watching a historical documentary late one night on TV, struggling with jet lag, she had made a comparison of Brian to Louis XV of France, nicknamed Louis the Beloved, charm and power personified – after all, on-board the plane he captained, Brian *was* king, his word literally law. The part that really drove it home, however, was that even though the king had adored his main mistress, Madame de Pompadour, she had never been enough for him. He had always had a string of other women, and Pompadour, in the end, effectively became a pimp for him in order to keep him close, procuring younger and younger women to maintain some sort of control over his love life.

That Lucinda could never imagine doing. But she had learnt the hard way to ignore any gossip that reached her about what Brian got up to behind her back. There was no point confronting Brian with what she might have heard on the crew grapevine: she had tried it in the early stages, only for him to effortlessly counter her complaints by flashing her his very best smile, pulling her into an embrace, telling her she was the only one for him and not to listen to the envious, miserable bastards who had sad little lives of their own and wanted to ruin any happiness that others enjoyed.

It always worked, much to her chagrin. She would go weak, as she always did, at the scent of his skin and the feel of his arms around her, while Brian stroked her hair and told her not to listen to jealous rumours. Why spoil the time they had together with a scene, he'd say, when they always ended up in bed anyway? And then he would start to undress her, and she would forget anything but what he was doing to her with his clever hands and mouth . . .

There was a difference, however, between ignoring what went on behind her back and closing her eyes to what was happening right in front of her. The former she had taught herself to do: the latter was simply impossible. Brian went too far sometimes, convinced himself that he could get away with murder. And though he and she would be sleeping together in Los Angeles, she was damned if she was going to put up with watching him flirting with Little Miss ReillyFly all the way over the Atlantic as a kind of twisted foreplay for him.

'Oops! I'm actually feeling sorry for the poor little bitch now,' Karl commented, taking in the narrow, assessing look with which Lucinda was regarding the unsuspecting Angela.

'More fizz, please, lovely people!' Danny Zasio, champagne glass in hand, plonked himself down on a bright blue leather-upholstered bar stool, swivelled it around to face the bar, put his feet up on the chrome rail and flashed a cheeky grin at Karl and Lucinda. Karl reached for a chilled champagne bottle, apologizing for not having noticed that Danny needed a refill, but Danny waved Karl's polite contrition away in the friendliest of manners.

'Here, give me that plate,' he said, reaching for the platter over which Lucinda's hands had momentarily frozen as she concentrated on the way Brian was checking out Angela's rear end. 'The jalapeno slices should be at just a bit more of an angle on the yellowtail, like this. The green colour pops against the fish if you do it this way. See?'

His narrow, nimble fingers flashed over the platter, making a minimal adjustment to the positioning of every finely sliced jalapeno ring against the glowing mother-of-pearl slices of yellowtail, each one of which was twisted into a little curl and set on a crispy wonton base. Karl and Lucinda nodded as one.

'That looks *much* better,' Karl said appreciatively, sliding the full champagne glass back to Danny. 'Amazing what a difference a little thing like that can make.'

'Hey, that's why I make the big bucks!' Danny said in an execrable American accent. 'You're doing a great job, guys. Keep it up. Check with me if you're not sure about anything, okay?'

'Thank you, Mr Zasio,' Lucinda said politely, taking the plate from him. 'We'll be sure to do that. We want to get everything absolutely right.'

'Oh, any time!' Danny winked. 'Hey, any chance you two could put in a good word for me with Blondie over there? I'd love her to take me on a private tour of one of those luxury bathrooms you have on here, if you know what I mean.'

With perfect timing, Angela came up to the bar, saying, 'Sparkling water with lime for Catalina's assistant, please, Karl.'

'Hey, beautiful!' Danny swivelled to face her. 'Still being all shy and sweet with me? What do I need to do to get you to be friendly? I hear you give *great* mouth-to-mouth!'

Poor Angela was cursed with an overactive sympathetic nervous system, which meant that she blushed much easier than most people in any case, and especially when highly attractive men persisted in flirting with her. She was well aware of this tendency: it wasn't just that she felt her cheeks become heated with extra blood flow, but the men in question usually teasingly commented on the fact that her face had gone pink, which of course exacerbated it still further. She had invested in the entire Clinique Redness Solutions range, and applied a light layer of pale yellow colour-correcting primer to her cheeks beneath her foundation every morning, but she was seriously beginning to consider researching if there was some sort of medication she could take for the condition.

'I don't mean to be unfriendly, Mr Zasio,' she said, darting a quick glance over at Lord Tony. She was caught between a rock and a hard place: on the one hand, she couldn't be seen flirting with a passenger, but on the other, she was worried that Danny was being critical of her professional manner in front of the boss who'd handpicked her for this promotion.

'Danny, *please*. And that was shitty of me,' he said with a candour that was very attractive. 'You're doing a fantastic job, angel. Just perfect.'

He reached out and touched her hand to reassure her, just briefly. But it was the kind of contact that makes two people realize that they're physically attracted to each other, the goosebump moment that raises the hairs on the back of the arm, tugs a string that pulls right up between the legs, makes both of them very conscious of the precise distance between their bodies. Angela's round blue eyes widened involuntarily, her lips parted; the hand that reached out to take the water she had requested trembled slightly as she took it and slipped away, moving as fast as she could on her two-inch court heels.

And Danny, watching her go, wore an expression of arrested and intense concentration. He had been partly joking before about taking Angela into one of the bathrooms; now he was absolutely serious. Glancing down at his crotch, he grinned, swivelled back to face the bar, adjusting his jeans to hide the erection that had started to burgeon the second he had touched Angela.

Thoughtfully, he sipped his champagne, pondering his plan of attack. She was very prim and proper, not one of the flirtatious hussies who barely needed a nod and wink of encouragement to eagerly join him in a plane toilet. But he loved a challenge, and there was something very alluring about this buttoned-up little Irish girl with the freckles on her nose. He mulled over ways and means, drinking his champagne, while Lucinda, circulating now with the yellow-tail sashimi wontons, was scheming just as hard.

Lucinda hated to admit it, but there was something out

of the ordinary about Angela. Under considerable stress, Angela had nevertheless correctly answered every single question Lucinda had fired at her during the briefing, even the most obscure ones; she had memorized the entire wine list and pairing suggestions, and knew where the most random of items were stored on the plane, from sewing kits to the second emergency fire axe.

Reluctantly, Lucinda had been impressed. Angela had both brains and looks, and though she might not be experienced in luxury cabin service, she was clearly working so hard at absorbing the steep learning curve that it justified Lord Tony's decision to promote her so drastically from no-frills ReillyFly to the five-star Luxe Class cabin. If Angela decided to set her sights on Brian, she would be a real rival to Lucinda. And Lucinda, with the Louis XV and Madame de Pompadour comparison never far from her mind, was unhappily aware of how that monarch, like almost all men in the world, had preferred younger women . . .

Brian was being discreet, but Lucinda could tell that his eyes were still tracking Angela's movements round the cabin. *Fresh meat*, Lucinda thought bitterly. *Fresh, innocent-looking, butter-wouldn't-melt-in-her-mouth meat.*

If Lucinda could somehow convince Angela to sneak off with Danny, and then make sure that all the cabin crew knew about it, then Angela would have clearly chosen Danny over Brian. Surely Brian's pride wouldn't allow him, after that, to try to seduce Angela, let alone seriously. Maybe it would even help push Brian more into Lucinda's arms. It would emphasize that she was the one for him, that he wasn't getting any younger and that it was time for him, finally, to make the decision to leave his wife and settle down with Lucinda . . . as much as he could. Lucinda was too rational to believe that Brian would ever be entirely faithful to her. If you wanted faithful, you didn't date a pilot.

Brian was chatting to Lord Tony and the Condé Nast journalist, an arm now thrown familiarly around the woman's shoulders, charming the pants off her even as he regularly glanced across the cabin at Angela. The journalist was oblivious to the fact that she didn't have his full attention. Though she must have been in her fifties, she was giggling like a schoolgirl as she looked up at the pilot's handsome face. The photographer Vanessa had hired asked for a pose, and Brian pulled off his uniform cap with a dashing flourish and popped it on the journalist's head. Despite being a hardened hack of thirty years standing, her smile for the camera was positively giddy under the gold-braided peak of the hat.

The photographer gestured Lucinda forward to present the serving plate to the threesome. Vanessa nodded in approval of Lucinda's perfect appearance as she proffered the exquisitely arranged canapés.

'But Brian, you must have one too!' the journalist cooed, licking her fingers. 'They're simply delicious!'

'Can't, my lovely,' he said with a regretful grimace. 'I can't tell you how careful we pilots need to be with what we eat. Separate meals for me and Ginny, the first officer – on separate carts too, eh, Lucinda?'

Lucinda nodded in agreement.

'It's a very standard precaution,' Vanessa said smoothly to the journalist, always ready to divert conversation away from anything awkward, like the disastrous concept of a captain and first officer eating the same contaminated food, falling prey to the same food poisoning, and being simultaneously incapacitated to fly the plane. 'Didn't you *love* the sashimi? Danny's been an absolute genius thinking up lovely little nibbles for our Luxe Class guests.'

'Oh, it was delicious,' the journalist agreed eagerly, taking another.

'We'll have to share a bite of something when I'm not working,' Brian said to the journalist, winking at her; it was a cheerful bit of flirtation, nothing seriously meant by it, and even as the journalist said eagerly how lovely that would be, Brian's gaze was dancing past her, focusing again on Angela's neat figure, specifically her rounded bottom in the sleekly cut uniform skirt. It was discreetly done, and only the hyper-alert Lucinda, deftly handing a blue linen napkin to the journalist with one hand, the serving plate poised on her other palm, noticed the flicker of Brian's eyes that betrayed where his real interest lay.

'Napkin, madam?' Lucinda said, her voice as composed as always; it had been thoroughly drilled into every member of the Pure Air crew never to use a word as common as 'serviette'.

And as the journalist took it, smiling her thanks, Lucinda returned the smile with a perfectly professional one of her own. No one could have spotted a flicker in her own dark eyes as she waited politely to retrieve the soiled napkin from the journalist. No one could have realized that her antipathy to Angela had now reached crisis proportions. Lucinda had been standing right there when Brian flirted professionally with another woman, and he hadn't even bothered to favour his girlfriend with the swiftest of rueful smiles. Instead, he had looked away from her to check out Angela's rear end.

'Karl,' she said in a low voice as she returned to the bar to begin the process of clearing up for take-off. 'Do Kevin and Emma Louise have their usual stash on them?'

Karl made a comic face.

'We're off to LA!' he said. 'Of course they do!'

He paused and looked at Lucinda more carefully.

'Why're you asking?' he said. 'You *never* do anything like that.'

And then he noticed the set of Lucinda's lips.

'Oh,' she said lightly. 'Don't be silly, Karl. I'm not asking for *me*.'

Karl flinched.

'Lucinda—' he began.

'Just get it sorted, Karl,' she said, looking at her watch. 'It's time to get people to their seats. I'll start that. You talk to the Terrible Twins, okay?'

Karl, beginning to clear the canapé plates and take them to the galley to be locked away for take-off, found himself grimacing. The last time Lucinda had formed a grudge against a flight attendant who had attracted too much attention from Brian, she had organized the planting of a banana in the young woman's bag on a flight landing in Australia and tipped off a friend at customs to search her. The maximum penalty for not declaring foodstuffs brought into the country was ten thousand Australian dollars, and Lucinda's friend, a bio-security officer, had ensured that the poor woman had to pay every penny of that sum; at over five thousand sterling, it was a fortune on a flight attendant's salary.

Worse, Pure Air had an incredibly strict morals policy, as Lucinda knew very well. The customs violation meant automatic dismissal from the airline; the flight attendant had not only gone into debt and lost her job, but was blacklisted from her profession of choice. She had had to beg and plead with Pure Air just to fly her back to the UK again.

But that girl who got shafted in Aus was having a good old flirt with Brian, Karl thought, wincing as he stacked the plates onto his trolley. *I'm not saying the poor bitch deserved what she got, but she shouldn't have slutted around with Lucinda's man in front of her. That was just stupid.*

Angela, however, couldn't be accused of flirting with anyone. *Probably doesn't even know how,* Karl thought sarcastically. Angela was a complete innocent in this situation; nearly two decades of experience with cabin crew, gay bars, and cabin crew in gay bars had given Karl the ability to spot a slut at twenty paces as swiftly as he could pick up the lingering smell of poppers. Sister Angela, bless her, smelt like daisies after the rain, and, annoying though her po-faced stance on crew sex was, she didn't deserve one of Lucinda's scorched-earth revenge ploys.

Angela doesn't even fancy Brian! Karl thought, rolling his eyes as he manoeuvred the trolley out from behind the bar. *She went all googly over Danny Zasio, though she's much too stick-up-her-bum to actually let her hair down and do anything naughty with him . . .*

Oh. Karl paused for a second as he realized what Lucinda was planning, why she had told him to requisition Kevin and Emma Louise's stash.

Very clever, Lucinda. Very clever indeed.

You had to give her credit, he thought, pushing the trolley discreetly round the bar and down the aisle to the galley. Lucinda had seen Angela's reaction when Danny Zasio touched her and had come up with a cunning plan to discredit her rival in only a few minutes. Lucinda was terrifying. Karl would never dream of getting between her and what she wanted.

Which was why he was going to follow her commands to the letter, without warning Angela what lay in store for her. Karl knew exactly on which side his bread was buttered. When his boss told him to jump, all he asked was how high. It had been he who had procured the fatal banana and put it at the bottom of that poor bitch's crew bag on the Sydney flight.

No question, Angela was going down on this trip.

Maybe even literally! he thought, and couldn't repress a little smirk at his pun as he deftly swivelled his cargo into the galley.

Chapter Five

'Ladies, I'm so sorry but I'm going to have to break you up,' Vanessa said, coming up behind Catalina and Latisha and tapping them lightly on the shoulders. 'We're getting close to take-off. Latisha, can we get you anything before you're banished behind the curtain? Another water, maybe?'

'Oh, that would be lovely, thanks, Vanessa,' Latisha said gratefully.

'Not a problem! I'll be right back.' She smiled at Latisha. 'I'm *so* sorry we couldn't accommodate you in Luxe. Normally there'd be no problem, but obviously this is a very unique situation . . . the flight was in such demand, and we had so many requests from our Pure Blue premium members we had to run a lottery to assign the Luxe Class seats. There just wasn't one to spare. I did explain that when we started talking about having Catalina on the flight . . .'

'Oh, it's fine,' Latisha assured her. 'You told me at the time. No worries, I'm cool with it.'

Vanessa smiled gratefully.

'I've got you one of the best seats in business,' she assured her. 'A bulkhead, with a footrest – lots of legroom. Very comfy indeed.'

She bustled away to get Latisha her glass of water.

'*I'm* sorry there wasn't a place for you in Luxe Class,' Catalina said to her assistant. 'I'll miss you.' She looked suddenly very wistful. 'I'll be lonely without you, Tish. I know it sounds stupid, but I really will.' She caught herself. 'Ugh, how selfish of me to complain when I'm the one with the bed and you're not! Sorry!'

Latisha reached out to squeeze Catalina's hand. She was all too aware of how much Catalina had been depending on her for company ever since the break-up.

'Hon, even if I was up here, we'd be in separate pods,' she pointed out. 'Not sitting next to each other so we could chat, you know? And we shouldn't be chatting anyway – we should both be trying to sleep right through. Like I said before, I'm going to take a Zopiclone to make sure I get some zzz, and you should too. We've got tons of press meeting the plane in LA, and you'll want to look your best for that.'

'I'll try,' Catalina said obediently, though she still looked anxious about not having Latisha with her.

'You'll be okay, hon.' Latisha squeezed her hand again. 'Listen to some music, chill out, go to sleep in your lovely big bed, zonk out and wake up all nice and relaxed. And don't feel guilty that I don't get a bed!' she admonished, reading Catalina's expression. 'I was the one pushing for us to come over on this flight! Great publicity, plus it's a freebie. I don't care how much you make, I'm still all about the freebies! Oh, thanks, Vanessa.'

She took the fresh glass of sparkling water with lime that Vanessa had brought her.

'I'll walk you back to your seat,' Vanessa said. 'Make sure you're all settled in nicely. Our business class is really very luxurious. The seats are what we call the cradle kind – they recline to a one-hundred-and-sixty-degree angle, and the cradle means you can go back all the way without bothering the person behind you at all, as the frame behind the seat stays locked in place . . .' She looked at Catalina. 'She'll be *very* comfortable,' she assured Catalina, as Latisha dropped a kiss on her boss's cheek.

'Get some sleep,' Latisha told her firmly, pulling her cashmere throw around her shoulders and picking up her leather travel bag, a recent gift from Catalina to thank her for all the extra hand-holding Latisha had done for her boss since her bad break-up. It was by the Milanese company Valextra, which specialized in discreetly logo-free, exquisitely made items, recognizable only by fellow devotees of the brand who were able to spend thousands of dollars on a handbag, the opposite of a Birkin. Latisha stroked the side of the bag lovingly, smiling at Catalina.

'Best present *ever*, by the way,' she said to her boss as she turned away to follow Vanessa. 'I *love* it. Hey, I made sure all your devices are fully charged, as usual, but try to sleep, hon. We'll be in LA before you know it.'

'Miss Montes? Shall I show you to your pod? And can I get you a last drink before take-off?'

Angela appeared at Catalina's side. Catalina smiled at her.

'No, thank you, I'm fine,' she said politely. 'I'm very excited to see these new . . . pods?'

Angela's face lit up with pleasure.

'We're very excited about them,' she said with touching

pride in her new job at Pure Air. 'They're nicer than any other airline's, honestly. I really think you'll be very comfortable with us.'

Catalina's little exclamation of surprise on seeing the space that would be hers for the ten-hour flight was music to Angela's ears. A moulded area shaped like an extended comma held a wide leather seat in the ball of the comma, with various cleverly planned compartments and slide-out trays built ergonomically into the sides, all labelled with gold-embossed leather tags. On the seat was a folded cashmere blanket, cobalt blue and bordered in darker blue, tied with a wide satin ribbon, two generous square pillows and a silk eye mask. Arranged beside these were a pair of cobalt cashmere socks, tucked into a pair of dark blue suede, fleece-lined slippers, and a matching blue suede toiletry bag placed behind this grouping at precisely the angle prescribed by the inflight design team – the Luxe Class cabin crew had studied not only photographs of how to plate up the various meals, but of how to arrange all of the aesthetic elements of the new service.

'It looks lovely,' Catalina said sincerely. 'Like a really cosy, comfy nest.'

'I'm so pleased,' Angela said, beaming. 'I'll definitely pass that feedback on. Can I get you settled?'

'No, I'm fine. Thank you so much.' Catalina stifled a little yawn.

'We have a special area for your handbag here.' Angela unclipped a compartment and slid out a deep, leather-lined tray. 'It's designed to let you put everything in, and there are all sorts of little slots and nooks inside where you can store your various electronic devices and charge them while they're all tucked away . . .'

But she was well-trained and sensitive enough for her voice to trail off at this stage, perceiving clearly that Catalina wanted nothing more than to be left alone.

'Your seat belt's just here,' Angela finished up quickly, pointing out the pull tabs for the leather-covered belt. 'I'll let you get comfortable. There's a padded drawer right there to stow away your shoes. Once we're at cruising altitude I'll come back to make up your bed, but right now, please just relax.'

She slipped away as Catalina sank gratefully into the seat, her frame so tiny she hardly needed to push the assembled goodies from the wide leather cushion. Pulling off her heels, she dropped them into the drawer and eased on the soft knitted socks. She'd meant to change into a pair of silk and cashmere leggings that she had in her bag, but she was too exhausted; she'd just curl up in her jeans right now, tuck the pillows behind her head, bundle up in the blanket, slip on the silk eye mask and go to sleep. She didn't even need the Zopiclone Latisha had suggested; she was sure she would pass out straight away.

This was the true luxury of being rich. You were so absolutely cosseted while travelling. You had space around you to stretch out, no one behind you shoving their knees in your back if you tried to recline your seat. No risk of spilling your drink as you held it in one hand while precariously trying to put up your flimsy plastic seat tray with the other, so that you could reach the magazine you'd previously stowed in the stained fabric slot below. No apologizing to your neighbour for elbowing him or her as you tried to pull open the plastic packet containing your stale roll, or twist your plastic knife into the tiny packet of greasy spread to extract some of its contents. No having to get up every time someone in your row needed to go to the toilet, all of you unfastening your headphones, clambering awkwardly out of your mess of pillows and blankets, your magazines and bottles of water tumbling to the floor and getting stuck beneath the seats.

Catalina didn't even have a seat neighbour. Some first-class configurations meant you had to keep a privacy screen permanently raised to avoid making eye contact with someone sitting diagonally opposite you, but Latisha had been right: Catalina was perfectly isolated in her enveloping pod. Angela was escorting another Luxe Class traveller to the closest one, and she had a brief glimpse of him as he stepped inside: tall, with light brown hair and a pleasant tenor voice, thanking Angela as she ran through the list of amenities and demonstrated to him where to store his various gadgets, just like a personal butler showing someone to a luxury hotel suite.

The passenger took off his jacket, handing it to Angela to hang up as she showed him the built-in wardrobe, thanking her again, his manners impeccable. Then he moved around the curve of the comma and disappeared from view as he took his seat, Angela's smooth blonde head and bright blue suit shoulders whisking away past the wall of Catalina's pod.

And then quiet fell, barely anything to be heard but the soft music piped into the pod. Angela was escorting Jane Browne, the actress, into the pod behind Catalina, but the layout was designed so cleverly, the sound insulation so

effective, that even Angela's soft murmur was almost in-
audible to Catalina. This was another of the benefits of being
super-rich: you were protected from having to listen to other
people's conversations or from being forced to respond to
an over-chatty fellow traveller.

Latisha had loaded some magazines for her boss on her
iPad, just in case, but Catalina was unlikely to glance at them.
She might watch a film if she couldn't sleep, listen to some
music, maybe scroll through friends' Instagram and Tumblr
feeds. But she wasn't much of a reader. So it was extremely
unlikely that she would reach out to the perfectly arranged
stack of print magazines and newspapers in the purpose-
designed slot to her left and pull out the one on top, the
first-ever Pure Air Luxe Class inflight magazine, to spot her
own face on the cover. She was smiling sweetly at the camera,
blue skies behind her, with the caption: 'Chasing Midnight
. . . all the way to LA! Catalina headlines our maiden flight.'

Vanessa had already organized for Catalina to sign a stack
of these magazine covers in the Marlborough Suite, as well
as several glossy printouts of the image, which would be
framed for various Pure Air offices around the world.
However, Catalina had never seen this particular, customized
version before, and it would disappoint her stalker hugely
to realize that she probably never would.

Because the copy in her personal stack of magazines had
been graffitied as a special, extra treat for Catalina; a love
note from her stalker. Around her heart-shaped face was
drawn another, larger heart in red marker pen, just like the
heart that had been sprayed on the wall of the Berlin dressing
room. And inside it, echoing that image equally powerfully,

were written, with strong, confident strokes, those same three words:

CAT

IS

MINE

The great airliner began to push back from the gate, all its passengers now ensconced in their extremely comfortable seats. Flight attendants moved smoothly down the aisles, performing their last checks before belting themselves into their own jump seats for take-off. In the pod that paralleled Catalina's on the other side of the plane, Lord Tony Moore stretched out his long legs and drew in a slow breath of pure satisfaction. Brian Levett, his eyes bright with excitement, whistled softly beneath his breath as he deftly piloted the plane through a long slow turning arc and onto the runway. Catalina, happily unaware that her stalker's presence on-board the plane meant that she would need to be on high alert, swallowed her usual pre-flight Valium. Jane Browne reached for her copy of the inflight magazine with Catalina on the cover, this image clear of any heart drawn in red marker. Danny Zasio, who had cunningly stashed a glass of champagne by the side of his leather armchair, retrieved it and started sipping, unwilling to lose his buzz even for a few moments.

And the killer aboard slumped in relief. Right up until then, he had been bracing himself against the possibility of a last-minute arrest, police boarding the plane to take him off in handcuffs. Clearly, the new identity he had assumed had passed muster, arousing no suspicion with the passport authorities. He would land in LA, slip into the crowds and disappear, half a world away from London and the woman he had murdered three days ago, having left nothing behind that would link him to the crime.

Pure Air 111 was cleared for take-off. The wheels gathered speed. It might have been a huge animal, haunches tensing, running now, preparing to spring into the air, the lift-off so seamless that its passengers were quite unaware of the moment where the last set of wheels parted company with the tarmac. The huge airplane soared so powerfully up into the night sky it seemed effortless, the blunt nose piercing through the cloud cover as easily as if it weren't carrying heavy freight, with every seat occupied, the cargo hold crammed with suitcases and the wine storage lockers loaded with expensive bottles. The plane sliced through the heavy cloud cover, rocking a little from side to side, like an ocean liner cutting through the waves, as it started its steady climb on its trajectory up to the cruising altitude of thirty-five thousand feet.

Pure Air 111 had embarked on its maiden voyage across the Atlantic to Los Angeles. Ten hours in the air, five thousand, four hundred and forty miles to fly, pushing through headwinds all the way. Darkness on take-off; during the journey the sun would rise and set again, night would fall once more. And before the midnight landing, Catalina would discover, in the most terrifying way, not only the presence of her stalker on-board, but their identity and the precise, horrific details of exactly what they wanted from her . . .

The stalker settled back into their seat, closing their eyes in delicious anticipation. Nearly two years of planning were about to culminate in one glorious moment of triumph, and then they would be with Catalina forever. The stalker knew every word of Catalina's songs, of course, but the chorus of her most recent hit summed up so perfectly what they were feeling that they smiled to themselves as, through their earphones, her voice sang in her beautiful clear soprano:

Hear me purr but don't be fooled
You will hear my roar real soon . . .
I'm chasing midnight!

Chapter Six

Eight months ago: Berlin

The immediate aftermath of the incident in Berlin had been a whirl of barely controlled panic. Gerhardt and the head of arena security had conferred, locking down backstage to organize a search for any intruders. The credentials of every employee were checked, as was the background of every visitor, including the competition winners of the meet and greet. No one had been lurking in Catalina's dressing room, waiting to jump out and surprise her, but after having done a sweep of the suite, Gerhardt and Latisha, along with Catalina's manager, immediately agreed that the star should be taken straight back to the hotel, should not go inside the dressing room at all. Catalina must be kept as calm as possible: there were months of the Chasing Midnight tour still to go, and the star, as well as being protected, must also get the R&R that was so vital for her to be able to perform at her best.

So Latisha and Catalina's manager remained at the arena to go through the CCTV footage with the duty staff, hoping to spot the person who had entered the dressing room while Catalina was onstage, while Gerhardt was tasked with whisking his charge away unobtrusively. Latisha bundled a stunned Catalina into her onesie and pulled the hood down over her face, while Gerhardt arranged a taxi to pick them up by an inconspicuous side door rather than travelling in the pre-booked limousine waiting by the stage exit. He rang ahead to the hotel to ensure that its head of security was waiting to meet them in the parking garage, taking them up to the Royal Suite in an unmarked, extremely discreet lift that was used for VIPs requiring complete anonymity.

Catalina didn't usually require this level of secrecy about her movements. She had a hugely loyal fan base, was famous for being unstintingly generous and friendly with autograph hunters, willing to stop and take selfies with as many fans as she possibly could. That was how she had built her career, putting her all into every performance, no matter how few people showed, signing flyers after every tiny gig, doing any local radio show that would have her on, laughing charmingly at the host's inane jokes. The word had spread: Catalina was not just a great singer and dancer, she had a wonderful personality, was a great interview, up for anything, unspoilt, a truly hard worker. This was how you ensured longevity in the pop world, which famously ate up one-hit wonders and spat them out the other side of success, reducing them to lip-synching to their best-known song at conventions or doing reunion shows in small venues for the handful of people who remembered their moment of glory.

So it went against everything Catalina had worked for to skip her ritual pause-and-wave at the loyal devotees who were gathered behind the aluminium barriers outside the arena, lined up screaming her name and snapping photos to post online. It had become a game for them to see which onesie she was wearing that evening, and Latisha made sure that Catalina had a whole collection so that she never had to wear the same one twice in a row. The Twitter hashtag #catsonesies was familiar to all of her followers, who competed to be the first to post their pictures of her leaving a gig, dressed in her latest getup.

Tonight, however, Latisha had dragged out the plainest onesie she could find for her boss, a neutral slub grey. Catalina's diminutive frame looked like a child's next to the hulking Gerhardt as they stepped out of the lift and followed the manager down the corridor to the double doors of the Royal Suite. Two security supervisors were standing there, and even though they had already been instructed to sweep the suite for possible intruders, Gerhardt left the flagging Catalina securely with them while he conducted his own search. She was leaning against the wall in exhaustion by the time he emerged and beckoned her inside to the sitting room of the suite.

'Go wash,' he said to her, his use of words always efficiently minimal. 'It is safe. I will check your food while you clean up.'

She nodded and went through the enormous bedroom to the equally enormous bathroom, hugely relieved to unzip the onesie and strip off the tight gold-fringed costume beneath it. Well made as it was, the costume's boning always cut into her if she had worn it for an extended length of time, carving red gutters in her skin that ran with sweat, making the lining of the two-piece outfit clammy. Even the fringing was wet and sticky. As she peeled off the satin top and skirt, the trails of fringe clung to her like sticky, unpleasant cobwebs. It was a huge pleasure to drop the costume to the bathroom floor and step away from it without a second thought. Catalina was, while not exactly spoilt, completely unused to picking up after herself on tour.

The Royal Suite was one of the most luxurious sets of hotel rooms available in the whole of Berlin. Besides the standard underfloor heating, built-in music system and non-fogging mirrors, the bathroom boasted a fridge for temperature-sensitive face creams, towel-warming drawers and an Aquavision television screen. But Catalina barely noticed any of the six-star extras that graced the suites where she stayed on tour. Her entire priority was a gigantic shower in which she could blast her sore muscles with a rainfall effect overhead and six power jets at shoulder, waist and thigh level, pounding away the aches and strains of the night's show. Her foaming body wash was a specially made blend of eucalyptus, peppermint, lemon and bay oils, the scent designed to intensify with the heat of the water. Head ducked, Catalina breathed it in deeply to soothe her lungs and help her voice.

After her shower, Latisha always worked a second blend of essential oils into Catalina's skin: more eucalyptus and peppermint, now with black pepper and marjoram to help her muscles relax. It felt lonely to do it on her own, lonely to be in the huge bathroom without her assistant and friend, but the familiar scent helped to soothe Catalina, and even though she was still tense and afraid by the shock of having her dressing room invaded, when she looked at herself in the mirror, belting the hotel robe around her, her expression was fairly calm under the big white towel wrapped around her wet hair.

She slid her feet into the hotel's spa slippers and crossed the marble floor to the door, almost reluctant to leave this sanctuary. Inside, she was completely safe. There was only one door, and Gerhardt was outside; no one could get in to hurt her, and it smelt so divine in the bathroom. And yet, in here by herself, she still felt . . . her hand paused on the brass door handle as she tried to work out the exact sensation . . . yes, *lonely*.

Touring was a very isolated activity, of course. You were either frantically busy in a whirl of interviews, promotion and performance, yet with no real human contact, as you were always on show; or you were dumped back into your hotel suite, all the attention suddenly withdrawn, left to manage your spinning, disoriented mind and body in solitary confusion.

Catalina knew dozens of A-list pop stars who dealt with the roller-coaster ride of touring through self-medication, partying, or, most frequently, a combination of the two. They'd take over whole floors of hotels, get their roadies to audition the most attractive groupies for their sexual flexibility and general willingness to please, order in a stash of drugs and booze, and proposition the hottest room-service waiters till they overloaded their bodies enough to pass out in a happy haze.

You could handle this lifestyle for a while if you were young and had a strong constitution, but it took its toll. Even the young stars, waking up with drug and drink hangovers, prodded out of bed and into the shower by their minders, given Adderall and espressos by their assistants to wake them up, would begin to flag. Promotional appearances would be blown off, tour dates would be cancelled. The star would be hospitalized for 'exhaustion', 'dehydration', 'an allergic reaction' or a combination of all three, tweeting winsome pictures of themselves from their hospital beds, drips in their arm, water bottles in their hands, cutely written captions attached, apologizing for disappointing their fans, rows of hearts following the message.

And then, after the tour, there would, if at all possible, be a discreet stay in a drying-out centre. Somewhere in Arizona or Montana, ideally, far from the temptations of California, out in wide-open spaces where the star could recharge their batteries, breathe fresh air, detox thoroughly and emerge a month or so later, bright-eyed and bushy-tailed once again. Ready, hopefully, to be photographed in a series of staged paparazzi set-ups on holiday in Mexico or Hawaii, demonstrating their health and energy, hopefully putting to bed any lingering rumours about their pharmaceutical habits.

It was a very familiar circuit: Catalina had seen some of her peers go through the stages so many times she couldn't even count their rehab stays any longer. But it was one she herself had easily avoided. Partly it was her dance training: she had been in ballet and jazz dance classes since she was very small, and the discipline of eating healthily, getting plenty of sleep, maintaining her body in optimal form, had stayed with her into stardom. But also it was the luck of the draw. She didn't have an addictive personality; if she craved anything, it was performing, and she'd never enjoyed the disorienting effects of drink, let alone anything stronger. If she wasn't suffering from jet lag, she wouldn't even take a sleeping pill. Instead, she and Latisha would wind down together every night after a show, eating a light meal and drinking Sleepytime tea.

God, I'm so boring! Catalina thought ruefully as she turned the handle. And she was only realizing now that, although she might not be addicted to any substances stronger than Sleepytime tea, she was, however, very dependent on having Latisha there to curl up with on her gigantic king-sized bed, chatting as they both wound down from their ridiculously busy days. As Catalina's head began to nod in slumber, Latisha would tuck her into bed and slip off to her own room across the living room of the suite.

What am I going to do tonight? Catalina found herself consumed with anxiety. It was a double whammy: not only had a creepy stalker managed to get into her dressing room, but they had deprived her of Latisha's presence to help soothe her to sleep. Who knew how long Latisha would be at the arena, going through the CCTV footage?

Catalina's worry must have shown all too clearly on her face, because Gerhardt, waiting in the living room, standing there with the air of a man who could remain in that position all night if he had to, took one look at his client's expression and stepped towards her, frowning in concern.

'You are not happy,' he said simply. 'Do not worry, please. I am here. No one will come in to make problems for you any more.'

Quite without meaning to, Catalina drew in a deep breath and let it go again, very comforted, not just by his words but also his physical presence. All bodyguards were poised and physically competent, naturally, but there was something unusually centred about Gerhardt, as if an invisible lead plumb line had been dropped through his skull, down his perfectly straight spine, ending dead even between his spaced-apart feet. She felt that he was the ultimate immovable object, that she could push and push at him without shifting him even in the slightest, and for some reason she found that extremely relaxing.

'Sit down, please,' he said. 'You must eat something.'

He gestured to the table that had been wheeled in by room service while she was in the shower. It bore plates of chicken salad, warm rye bread wrapped in a napkin, steamed green beans and broccoli florets dressed in extra-virgin olive oil and lemon juice, sliced fresh fruit, birch water, and a big silver pot of steaming tea.

'You did not eat your tiger nuts at the arena,' he added. 'So I ordered some more. They are in that bowl.'

'Thank you!' Catalina said gratefully. 'I do really like them.'

'They are an excellent source of protein,' Gerhardt said gravely, his solidly carved features not moving into even the hint of a smile. 'Better even than almonds. Please, sit.'

He indicated the chair placed by the table at an angle that would allow Catalina to see beyond it to the fireplace, where a wrought-iron grate held a neat stack of logs that were burning gently.

She still hesitated.

'It's odd to sit while you're standing there,' she said awkwardly. 'Latisha always sits with me and we have a talk about how the day went . . . why don't you take a seat too?'

Gerhardt shook his head.

'I am sorry, but no,' he said firmly. 'I cannot sit when I

am on duty. I can go to stand in the hallway if I make you feel odd.'

'No! Please, stay!' Her voice had risen, and she felt embarrassed by this display of panic. 'I just . . .' she added feebly, sinking down in the chair. 'It's just that . . .'

'Tonight was a shock,' Gerhardt agreed.

In an attempt to make her feel less like he was looming over her, he backed away to stand next to the wide, ornately carved oak mantelpiece; despite the modern smartness of the bathroom accoutrements, the hotel was designed upon graciously old-fashioned lines. Beside Gerhardt's tall, imposing frame, however, even the bulk of the polished wooden mantelpiece looked dwarfed, as did the basket that held extra logs for the fire.

'I am very sorry that something like this happened to you,' he continued, as Catalina forced herself to spoon some chicken salad onto a piece of rye bread and take a bite. 'I will wait here in the sitting room with you until Latisha returns.'

Catalina's head jerked; she looked up at him, horrified.

'Oh – you won't go when she comes back, will you?' she said instinctively. 'I mean . . . I think I'd be scared . . .'

'I will stay here all night, of course,' Gerhardt assured her at once. 'Please do not worry. I wait here with you until Latisha returns, and then I remove myself to the foyer.'

'But you can't stay there until morning!' Catalina protested. 'You won't get any sleep! This is all so—'

'Catalina, please.'

Gerhardt raised one shovel-sized hand. He was so economical with his movements that any gesture of his immediately drew attention, and the deep baritone boom of his voice cut through any higher-pitched noise like the plucking of a double-bass string.

'This is my job,' he said. 'To do my job, I do not just protect you. I must also make you *feel* protected. I will organize a rota from now on, but tonight I will take an armchair into the foyer of the suite.' His composed features softened into the smallest of smiles, his straight mouth allowing itself to quirk fractionally at the corners. 'Do not worry. I will not stand up all night,' he added. 'Though I could if it was required.'

'I couldn't stand up all night,' Catalina admitted, taking a handful of tiger nuts and beginning to nibble at them. This unusual conversation was having the relaxing effect she required after a performance. She needed to be taken out of her own head, stop the analysis of how tonight's show had gone: she had a terrible tendency to pick holes in her own performance, remembering only the tiny mistakes she'd made. Latisha was very skilled at steering Catalina away from this mental scab-picking, distracting her from obsessing; apart from being exhausting, it was quite unnecessary, as the tour manager would give them notes tomorrow during their warm-up.

I should give Latisha a raise, Catalina thought. *It's only when someone isn't around that you realize how much work they do.* She made a mental note to get her manager to order Latisha the biggest gift box possible from Jo Malone, which was both her and Latisha's favourite perfumery. One of the big cream ones, tied with a black grosgrain ribbon, the kind you hated to throw away after you used the contents, because it was just so smart. *Plus a gift card, too, in case there's more stuff she wants and doesn't get in the box.*

Feeling better for having done something nice for her assistant – or at least having planned it – Catalina temporarily forgot about the stalker. She was now fascinated by the idea of being able to stand still for hours on end, a subject she had never considered before. She poured herself some birch water as she considered the physical challenge this would entail.

'I can *dance* for hours,' she said thoughtfully, eating some more tiger nuts, 'but I think standing still for that long would be much more exhausting.'

'It is the most tiring thing of all, to stand still,' Gerhardt agreed. 'I have practised Iyengar yoga for many years, and that is what Mr Iyengar says. The most tiring pose is tree, or standing pose. And the hardest is corpse pose, where you lie down. It is hardest because it seems the easiest, but it can still never be completely perfect.'

'Oh, *interesting*.' Catalina ate some more chicken salad on rye bread; her appetite was returning as she engaged in conversation. 'I mean, some people would think that was depressing, but I understand it. You can never get anything completely perfect. I look back at my songs and videos, and there's always something I'd change. But I still have to go on singing the songs as they are, and they'll always be imperfect, and I have to make my peace with that . . .'

She trailed off, staring ahead of her at the softly flickering fire.

'What is it?' Gerhardt's pale grey eyes looked directly at her now. Previously, they had been scanning back and forth between the door that led to the foyer and the table; out of respect for his client, he had avoided focusing on Catalina's pretty face, her small frame enveloped in the big white robe. But now, her attention distracted by the crackling flames in the grate, he took in her expression, the frown that was creasing her forehead, the way her lips were pinched together.

Slowly, she reached up and pulled off the towel that had been wrapped around her head. Bundling it in her hands, she twisted it into a ball, unconsciously cradling it against her stomach, as people pull pillows against them for bulk and protection.

'It's the video for "Chasing Midnight",' she said to the towel. Her voice was small now, but the years of vocal training projected it to Gerhardt despite that. 'I know everyone tells me not to, but I can't help googling myself sometimes and reading what people say about me, not just the reviews and the fan posts that Latisha and the team show me . . . I know a lot of women thought the video was sexist.'

Gerhardt said nothing, which was exactly the right response. His silence was, like his stance, entirely neutral, allowing Catalina to work out her thought process aloud without interruption. Latisha would have protested at this point, shut down Catalina's concerns with a torrent of reassurances, but that would have had the effect of leaving her doubts to fester.

'I've been looking at it myself,' she continued, sinking her fingers further into the towel, 'and I see what they mean. Have you watched it?' She corrected herself instantly. 'Well, of course you've seen the last two nights at the show! But you're so focused . . . you wouldn't be looking at the screens, because you'd be too busy checking that there isn't anyone acting oddly or trying to get onstage with me . . .'

Gerhardt nodded.

'I do not watch the screens at the show,' he agreed. 'You are correct. But I have seen this video many times when I am at the gym. You are very popular – they play your videos a lot.'

'And what did you think?'

Catalina raised her big dark eyes to his face, requiring him to look back at her as he answered. He paused for a moment, considering his response. She wondered for a moment whether she should urge him to be honest, not worry about her feelings, and then her every instinct told her that she didn't have to bother. Gerhardt would tell her the absolute truth as he saw it, bluntly but not rudely.

'I thought that you were a very pretty girl,' Gerhardt said, 'with a very nice voice. But I also thought that at the gym I do not want to see a girl wearing almost no clothes on her hands and knees in a cage. Or even when I am not at the gym. It makes me feel' – he considered his words – 'strange.'

'Strange how?'

'A woman should not be in a cage,' Gerhardt said frankly. 'I understand, of course, that you tell a story with the song, but still, I am lifting weights at the gym, and I look to the screen and what I see is a woman in a cage, like an animal. And I feel uncomfortable.'

'I was trying to say that we're all animals,' Catalina said, leaning forward, her well-defined dark brows pulling together. 'You know, deep down.'

'I understand,' Gerhardt repeated. 'And I agree. But

animals are not naked like humans, and that is a big differ-ence.' He actually grinned, which carved deep creases on either side of his mouth and softened his crow's feet into laughter lines for a brief second. 'Maybe if you wear a big fur suit, perhaps, I might feel better.'

At the start of the 'Chasing Midnight' video, Catalina had been, as Gerhardt said, on all fours inside a cage, dressed in a very exiguous black Etro bikini, writhing, clasping the bars, arching her back in cat stretches, the camera lingering over various crevices and curves of her body in a way that was unmistakeably lascivious.

This was, naturally, part of the message of the song: that women shouldn't repress their sexuality, lock it up like something bad or sinful. Catalina was often taken aback by how unbalanced the USA seemed. Janet Jackson had got in big trouble with the censors at the Super Bowl because Justin Timberlake had pulled away a piece of her bustier, revealing some of her breast. And yet driving down any highway in the country you could see huge billboards advertising strip clubs with very salacious images of women with big boobs spilling out of their sexy lingerie. Network TV was very strict, but you just had to tune into MTV or HBO to see endless images of half-naked video vixens or 'adult documentaries' of Nevada brothels. The States was a *very* confusing country.

Still, Catalina had fans as young as ten, and as the older sibling of four younger sisters back home in Córdoba she was horrified at the idea that she was promoting sexist images of women. Gerhardt was only confirming what she had read in comments on the blogs and her YouTube videos. And she hadn't just been upset by the women who thought the imagery was sexist. The male commenters who had perved all over the sight of Catalina nearly naked in a cage had been even worse.

'I meant for the story of the video to be liberating,' she said, wincing. 'You know, she starts off in a cage, but she's put herself there. She needs to escape, and in the end she does.'

Gerhardt considered this thoughtfully.

'I do not know what women think,' he commented after a little while, 'but as a man, I see you in the cage, and that does not seem right to me. And also, as a man, I see a lot – excuse me – of different parts of your body in the video. Not the whole body, which is, I think, healthier, but different parts in close-up. I remember that for a while all we see is your bottom. It is a nice bottom, of course, but I do not like the videos that show us women's bottoms so close up.'

His German accent every time he pronounced the word 'bottom' was so unintentionally amusing that Catalina had to stifle a giggle.

'I get something wrong?' he asked, seeing her face contort with the effort of not laughing.

'No! It's just funny when you say "bottom". "Bottom."' She made an attempt at copying his guttural accent. 'It sounds so . . . serious. Like the bottom's in trouble, because it did something wrong.'

Then she realized how sexual that sounded, and grabbed her glass of water, drinking to cover her embarrassment.

'I really tried to stay away from, you know, X-rated stuff,' she said, setting down the glass again and clearing her throat. 'No pole dancing or twerking while pointing big foam fingers at my . . . um, at my front bottom. I don't want to do that to sell my music, and I think it sets a bad example. I want to celebrate women's bodies and their sexuality, empower them to feel free to express themselves . . .'

She heaved a deep sigh.

'Ugh! That's the line the publicist practises with me for interviews! And I believe every word, but it sounds so fake when I come out with it. Journalists always ask me about the video when I'm doing press, whether I think it's sending the right message. I always say yes, it's empowering, freeing women to be sexual, showing we're all animals underneath. And I mean it, but . . .'

'But still, there is your bottom in the cage,' Gerhardt finished gently.

'Yes! Still there is my bottom in the cage!'

Catalina was laughing now, partly at the German pronunciation of 'bottom' again, and partly in relief that someone had finally been honest with her.

'The choreography seemed okay at the time,' she confessed to him. 'I was thinking, "I'm an animal, I'm trapped inside here, I need to get out and be free to be myself." But I agree, when I saw the rough cut, I did think, Oh, this is more like . . . um . . .'

She cleared her throat again. Gerhardt was so solemn and poised she was much too embarrassed to use the word 'sexy' in conversation with him, let alone 'porn', which was, frankly, the most accurate word to use in this context.

'I wasn't so happy with it,' she admitted. 'But everyone else loved it. And they kept saying it was showing the spirit of the song. So I thought I was the one who was wrong.'

'But it is *your* bottom in the close-up,' Gerhardt pointed out. 'Not theirs.'

'Yes.' She pulled a face. 'Yes, it is. And that's why . . .'

She was getting used to talking to someone who stood so still, barely moving a muscle. It had been disconcerting at first, but already she was taking it for granted, together with the fact that she could break off a sentence to collect and shape her muddled thoughts, and that he would wait quietly for her to finish.

This was the difference between talking to a woman and a man, she observed to herself. A woman would want to help the talker along, suggest alternative endings to her sentences, while a man – particularly a patient, strong and silent type – would be much more comfortable with a long pause in the conversation, seeing no need to hurry in to fill it.

'Okay, I'm scared that it's connected to this thing that happened tonight,' Catalina said in a sudden rush of words. 'The weird . . . stalker . . . whatever you'd call them. I saw what they wrote – *Cat Is Mine*. This didn't happen before I made that video in the cage, with my bottom sticking right into the camera. I'm frightened that watching that video set whoever it is off, made them crazy . . .'

Her voice trailed off, not because she was unconvinced by what she was saying, but because Gerhardt had started to shake his head firmly about halfway through with such conviction that it was hard to keep talking through it.

'What?' she said. 'Why are you doing that?'

'Because it is not true,' he said simply. 'Crazy people are crazy people. Believe me, I have seen many things. I was in the army for a long time, a military policeman. A person who is crazy like that will pick their target for their own crazy reasons. Because the victim is wearing blue, because they are short, because they are the first one they see when they turn round the corner. So you see, this is not a true reason at all.'

Gerhardt was fixing her with a very clear stare; Catalina felt as if those eyes, their irises the colour of steel, were drilling right into her brain to make sure that she took his words in.

'Also, to be honest, you do not know that this has not happened before,' he pointed out. 'Maybe not this exact intrusion, that someone goes into your dressing room and makes a drawing there for you. But trust me, Catalina, with a star like you, famous over the world, there will be many, many odd people who write to you, send you things, try to become close to you. My job is not just to be your bodyguard; it is also to tell the people around you what to look for in the behaviour of fans, the things that they send you, to check anything they think is not right. I am trained to see the warning signs. There will have been many times before your bottom was in the cage' – the creases on either side of his narrow mouth deepened – 'that people have done crazy things to try to obtain your attention.'

Quite unconsciously, Catalina drew in a long breath of relief at his words and let it out again. He hadn't lied to her, not at all, but what he had said was oddly reassuring. She had never intended to make a video that reduced her to a mash-up of her own sexual parts, and she never would again. Still, the confidence in Gerhardt's voice had convinced her that the video itself hadn't been the issue; had stopped her, at least, from blaming herself.

She glanced down at the bunched-up towel that had been pressed against her stomach all this time. Her fingers loosened their grip on it, and slowly she unfolded the tightly packed damp fabric.

'I should hang this up in the bathroom,' she said automatically, but she looked up at Gerhardt again instead of making any move to get up.

'Thank you,' she said softly.

'Don't thank me,' he said, his expression neutral. 'All I said was the truth.'

But although his voice and features were once more entirely professional, his eyes, meeting Catalina's dark ones, had a silvery glow to them that was much less impersonal. The silence that fell was different to the ones before. It was suspended, as if both parties were holding their breath, though their ribcages rose and fell in unison. Catalina's lips were slightly parted, the towel dangling from her fingers; when the doorbell of the suite rang, it startled her so much that she dropped the damp fabric to the floor.

'Stay here,' Gerhardt said automatically, turning and heading to the foyer. A moment later, Latisha burst into the sitting room, braids dancing behind her, not pausing even to take off her puffa coat in her concern to see how Catalina was doing.

'Oh good, you're eating dinner! Great! I was worried . . . well, awesome!' Latisha exclaimed. 'Keep going . . . you need to make sure you take in enough calories after the show . . . cool, you ordered tiger nuts! I was going to check, 'cause you didn't have time to eat them back at the arena . . .'

'Gerhardt ordered them for me,' Catalina said, smiling at the bodyguard, who had followed Latisha in and was opening both of the double doors that led to the foyer. 'He thought the same thing.'

'Wow, very thoughtful of you, Gerhardt!' Latisha said, taking off her coat and hanging it up in the hallway cupboard. 'You've, like, only been here ten minutes and you already know what Cat eats after a show. Nice.'

There was the faintest edge to her voice, and Catalina glanced at her assistant a little curiously, wondering what had caused this.

'Are you really tired, Tish?' she asked.

'Nah, I'm okay, hon.'

Latisha came over to stroke Catalina's hair briefly before taking off her coat, throwing it onto a sofa and sinking into the other chair at the table.

'God, your eating plan keeps me so healthy!' she said, looking at the food laid out before her. 'Sometimes I just want a damn burger, don't you?'

The energy in the suite had completely altered, a head of steam dissipating on Latisha's entrance. The women's friendship was so long-established that they settled immediately into a close, almost sisterly ease with each other.

'What happened at the arena?' Gerhardt asked politely as Latisha reached for her favourite white wine, Vermentino Aragosta, which was already uncorked and waiting in an ice bucket.

'Damn it, nothing,' she said, on a sigh, pouring herself a glass. 'I left the people there going through the footage all over again, but I swear we went back and forth over it already and there's nothing that pops out. There isn't a camera that directly shows the dressing-room door – that'd be too easy, right? – but there's one about ten feet down the corridor, and we checked that and the entrance surveillance. Nothing out of the ordinary after Cat left to go onstage. Me, you' – she looked at Gerhardt – 'arena staff, the caterers. No one who wasn't authorized to be there. Of course the cops are going to run everyone's background again and hope something pops out, but the random nutjob theory's out. Which is a shame.'

Gerhardt was already picking up one of the armchairs, a hefty chintz affair with wide padded arms; he hefted it as easily as if it were a slender dining chair as he carried it through the double doors and into the foyer.

'What, he's doing interior decoration now too?' Latisha said through a mouthful of chicken. 'The foyer isn't welcoming enough for him?'

'He's staying there overnight,' Catalina said hastily.

'*Really?*' Latisha's brows shot up.

'I'll feel safer,' Catalina said.

'I've got the whole of hotel security on this too, Cat,' Latisha said, leaning forward. 'Seriously, no one can get in. They have an extra guy just to watch this floor.'

Gerhardt had placed the chair in the foyer, its back to a wall, angled so that he could see both doors without turning his head; now he stood just inside the sitting room, hands clasped once again, waiting for instructions.

'Gerhardt, what do you think?' Catalina looked at him.

'I am happy to stay here,' he said, perfectly composed. 'Like I said, my job is not just to keep you safe, but to make you feel safe. But I am also happy to discuss the situation with hotel security and then go to my room if I feel it is under control.'

Catalina hesitated momentarily, but enough for both her employees to become fully aware of her wishes.

'Hey, Gerhardt can stay in here if you want.' Latisha gestured theatrically with her wine glass around the sitting room. 'You want me to crash with you in your room? Those beds are so huge we won't even know the other one's there.'

'I think I'll be okay by myself in my bedroom if Gerhardt doesn't mind staying in the foyer tonight,' Catalina said, smiling at her assistant and bodyguard. 'Thanks, both of you. I feel way better now you're here.'

'Hey, this is most likely just a one-off freak incident,' Latisha said. 'That's what the arena people said. And we've never had anything like this before. It'll be okay, Cat. Whoever this weirdo is, they've probably shot their bolt.'

Gerhardt was already backing away to close the double doors. Catalina followed him with her eyes until he disappeared from view, feeling oddly bereft to see him go.

'It's okay, Cat,' Latisha repeated, forking up some more chicken with one hand, the other still holding the wine glass. 'Sheesh, I'm *starving*,' she added in parentheses.

She drank a long swig of wine and set down the glass, smacking her lips.

'You'll see,' she predicted cheerfully. 'It's all over. We'll never hear from this creep again.'

Chapter Seven

On-board

'Miss Montes? Can I show you to the bar while we make up your bed? Or do you prefer to keep the seat configuration for now?'

Catalina, who had been dozing lightly in the leather armchair, started at the gentle tap on her arm. She reached up to pull off her eye mask, the illumination in the pod such a soft, glowing shade of deep blue that she barely found herself blinking as her irises adjusted to the gentle light.

'It's so cosy!' she said drowsily, smiling up at Lucinda, who was bent over her solicitously.

'I'm so glad to hear that,' Lucinda said politely. 'I'll be sure to let Lord Tony know. Would you like me just to leave you for the moment?'

'No, it would be great to have the bed made up. Thanks.' Catalina let out a yawn, just managing to cover her pretty pointed white teeth with a small hand in time. 'Sorry! I took a Valium when I sat down, and it's made me very . . . relaxed.'

'Not at all! I'll try to get your pod made up for you as soon as possible. Did Angela show you all the amenities?' Lucinda asked. 'We have a desk that doubles as a vanity table with adjustable lighting, your own personal minibar, designated storage areas, charging pods—'

'It's all lovely,' Catalina said diplomatically. 'I'll check it out later, I'm sure, but right now I think I'll have some tea at the bar and then try to sleep when my bed's ready.'

'Of course,' Lucinda purred, her smile unfaltering. 'Naturally. Let me escort you to the bar and make sure we have a seat for you . . .'

She reached down and unfastened Catalina's soft, padded leather seat belt as the latter began to swing her legs over the side of the chair.

'Excuse me,' Lucinda said apologetically. 'We found in trials that the seat belts are so comfortable that passengers simply aren't aware they have them on.'

Deliciously comfortable in her sheepskin-lined slippers, Catalina followed Lucinda as docilely as the lamb they were made of down the quiet, mauve-carpeted aisle between the pods. Another door slid open, and Angela emerged, followed by Jane Browne, the actress, who smiled at Catalina as she came out.

'Hi! I feel like I'm in a posh spa, don't you?' Jane observed. She disliked crowds, but was very happy to chat one-to-one. 'That bit where you're about to go in for your blissful massage and are all docile, you know? I've got the slippers, I just need the robe . . .'

'I'm sorry,' Angela said to her nervously. 'We don't actually provide robes—'

'No robes, I'm afraid!' Lucinda cut in swiftly. 'I'll be very happy to pass on that feedback.'

'Oh please, no, I was joking!' Jane said hurriedly. 'Honestly,

I'm not at all used to travelling like this. I feel incredibly spoilt already.' She smiled again at Catalina. 'This must be so normal to you,' she said frankly. 'For me it's the biggest treat.'

'It's a very big treat for me too,' Catalina said, returning the smile. She had been introduced to Jane at the launch in the Marlborough Suite, but was only barely aware of who she was. 'I think that's the most comfortable seat I've ever been in.'

'It's all been ergonomically designed by the very best designers and engineers,' Lucinda said proudly as they reached the bar. Lord Tony and Danny were already on bar stools, bantering cheerfully with Karl, and Catalina flinched a little at the noise.

'We have a window table here we could seat you at,' Angela suggested, picking up on this, and Lucinda's meticulously applied fake lashes fluttered in annoyance as Catalina gave a grateful smile to Angela. As the cabin service director, Lucinda should be ministering to the needs of the most VIP passenger. Angela, once again, had stepped on Lucinda's toes without even realizing it.

'Would you like to join me?' Catalina asked Jane hopefully. From the few words they had exchanged, the actress seemed unaffected and down to earth, and if Catalina had to wait while her bed was made up, she would much rather have company than be alone with her thoughts. Besides, the small white table, moulded in a curve flowing out from the airplane wall, was designed for a cosy tête-à-tête, and Jane was clearly also recoiling from the boisterous, champagne-fuelled atmosphere at the bar, tipsy male voices raised jovially over the noise of Karl rattling ice in a cocktail shaker.

'I'd love to,' Jane said with great sincerity, dropping onto one of the seats, a little moulded low-backed stool with a round cobalt blue suede cushion on top. 'How cute! It's like sitting on a mushroom.'

Catalina giggled at this as she sat down too.

'It is! And we're both so small. We're like little . . . what's the word?'

'Gnomes,' Jane said cheerfully. 'Or elves, if we're being a bit more flattering about ourselves.'

Angela smothered a smile at this, and Lucinda, disapproving of a crew member intruding, as she saw it, into a passenger conversation, jerked her sleek dark head sharply at her subordinate.

'The beds, Angela,' she said.

Angela disappeared as swiftly as if she had been fired from a cannon.

'What can I get you ladies to drink?' Lucinda trained her most winning smile on the two celebrities at the table, now that she had taken command of the situation and made it clear to Angela that she was not to be familiar with the VIPs.

'Mint tea, please,' Catalina said at the same time as Jane said:

'Green tea, please.'

The two girls giggled.

'Nearly snap!' Jane said. 'We're being very healthy.'

Catalina grimaced.

'It's okay for the men,' she said, rolling her eyes at the noisy, happy band of brothers at the bar. 'They can drink much more than us, and even if they get off the plane a bit funny' – she held out her hand and wobbled it – 'the photographers don't care, you know? But if *we* aren't perfect, the Internet will rip us apart, say that we don't look good in the pap photos at the airport. And I need to work the day after we arrive. I have big rehearsals. I don't drink anyway, but even if I did, I couldn't now.' She paused to consider what she had just said. 'Does that make sense in English?' Her pretty forehead corrugated. 'I'm so used to talking in English,' she explained, 'but no one ever corrects me any more. So sometimes I think I say nonsense and they all just smile and agree anyway.'

Jane grinned, her rubbery, mobile little features contorting charmingly. There would be no Botox or fillers in Jane's future; her career had established her not as a sex symbol, but as a serious actress, able to play a heroine in one film and a character part the next.

'Your English was fine,' she assured Catalina. 'Do you want me to let you know if you make a mistake?'

'Yes! Please, that would be great!' Catalina said enthusiastically. 'Latisha – she's my assistant, my best friend – she used to, but now she doesn't stop to do it any more.'

'Okay, it's a deal,' Jane said. 'I know what you mean – I'm learning Italian at the moment for a film. It's a historical epic and I really want not just to say the lines phonetically, but understand everything I say. It's brutal right now, but I'm getting there. Full immersion. It's just a shame I have to take a break for this trip.'

'The Oscars, though! You're nominated!' Catalina said. 'That's so exciting!'

'I don't have a chance of winning,' Jane said ruefully. 'But me and the screenwriter are the only ones nominated, and the producers would pretty much have blacklisted me if I didn't go.'

She pulled another face, this one making her look like a comic gremlin; somehow she managed to make her eyes bulge.

'I know I have to get better at all this promotion stuff,' she said. 'The thing with me is that I'm just an actress. I'm not a star, you know? I'm terrible at all the red-carpet events, all those interviewers asking me about my love life and who I'm wearing. I honestly don't care what I'm wearing, *ever*. They even have this thing at the Oscars called the "mani cam" – did you know that? You get your nails done and then you put your hand into this box on the red carpet with a camera at the end of it and wiggle your fingers up it, so everyone can see if you accidentally chipped a nail on your way to the ceremony.'

'Not *really*?' Catalina said in disbelief.

Jane clicked swiftly on her iPad and brought up a link.

'"*Girls*' Allison Williams showcased a pale nude mani on the cam. The actress offset her soft nail color with a bold Fred Leighton cocktail ring,"' she read in a perky parody American TV presenter accent, turning the screen so that Catalina could see the photo. '"Her fingers strut down the mani cam red carpet to show off her perfect crescent moon manicure!" There's a video of her strutting her fingers,' she added in her normal voice. 'Want to see?'

'Ugh!' Catalina exclaimed. 'It's like they're trying to catch us out for not being perfect, every single time! Oh, thank you . . .'

Lucinda brought the tea on a silver tray, a small bone-china teapot and cup and saucer for each woman. The china was banded with Pure Air blue and rimmed with gold, delicate scents of mint and green tea rising in the air from the narrow spouts. There was a little plate of round sugar-dusted short-bread, too; Catalina and Jane both waved it away politely as Lucinda was about to place it on the table, looked at each other, and laughed in recognition of their mutual need to perpetually watch their weight.

'Miss Browne?' a light male voice said from behind Lucinda, and Jane glanced up.

It was the passenger seated in the pod beside Catalina, a pleasant-faced man in his thirties, with light brown hair and hazel eyes. His features were average, but his jaw was firm and his lips well-shaped, and his tentative smile as he looked down at Jane was very charming.

'So sorry to interrupt!' he said. 'I just wanted to say how much I enjoyed your performance in *Tragic Sisters*. I honestly thought you were the standout of the film, and I'm not surprised the Oscars nomination committee agreed with me.'

'Oh, thank you!' Jane said. 'I thought Melody was brilliant as Emily, but I'm really happy about the nomination, of course.'

She held out her hand to him, Lucinda having discreetly removed herself.

'Michael Coggin-Carr,' he said, shaking it. 'Well, I won't bother you while you're talking to your friend. I'd be very honoured to buy you a drink later, perhaps, if you feel like one.'

With a smile and a nod at Catalina, he turned and went over to the bar, joining the lively group there.

'I love it when they say hi and then go straight away,' Jane said in an undertone to Catalina. 'Don't you? It means they're not pushy – you can chat to them later, if you want to, and they won't be all weird and creepy.'

'Yes, really nice manners,' Catalina agreed. 'But wait . . . you were in *Tragic Sisters*?'

She stared incredulously at Jane.

'Yes. Melody Dale was the star – she played Emily Brontë, which was the most fun. She got to roam the moors and throw herself on Bramwell's grave and have a really dramatic death,' Jane said. 'It was pretty dark, eh? All the Brontë siblings dying within seven years of each other. By the time I conked it, the audience must have been absolutely exhausted with it all.'

Catalina still looked completely baffled.

'Oh, I played Charlotte Brontë,' Jane said with a grin. She reached up, parted her shortish hair in the middle and plastered it back to her skull; simultaneously, she dropped her gaze, set her mouth firmly in an intellectual line, and stiffened her back into a proper Victorian stance, as if she were laced tightly into a corset beneath her clothes. 'See it now?'

'That's crazy!' Catalina's voice rose so high with her incredulity that Michael Coggin-Carr briefly glanced back from the bar. 'You're joking! I saw that film just a month ago and I never recognized you!'

'Yes, I get that all the time,' Jane said happily. 'I love it – it's the best compliment ever. Did you see *And When We Fall*?'

This had been the first big-budget film from Maitland Parks, a mumblecore writer/director who had stepped up to the big time with his latest. Set between Portland, Oregon, and London, it was a loosely plotted story of a love quartet between four very attractive young people who spent most of the film naked, having sex with each other, discussing the sex they'd had with each other, or starting to have sex with each other again.

'You were in that too?' Catalina's voice was almost squeaking with surprise.

'I was Lucy! The American hipster hippie who kept going on about natural body hair. Remember?'

Catalina shook her head in wonder.

'I feel really stupid!' she admitted. 'I mean, I saw you with all your clothes off for *two hours* of that film, and I never recognized you . . .'

Jane slumped her shoulders, tilted her head to one side, adopted the vacant expression of a naturally pretty girl who had never bothered to develop her brains, and bit her lip seductively.

'Wow!' Catalina clapped her hands. 'Okay, now I see it!'

Something else struck her. She bent forward to pour her tea, avoiding Jane's eyes as she asked, 'Did you . . . um, do you feel weird about going naked?'

'Not remotely,' Jane said simply as she poured out her own tea. 'It's not me, it's the character. But it's different for you,' she added. 'I mean, I'm the furthest thing from being an international sex symbol you could find. But you –' Her unabashed gaze took in Catalina's face and figure. 'You dance *amazingly*,' Jane commented appreciatively. 'I love watching you in your videos – you have so much energy! It's very sexy.'

Unfortunately, Jane's complimentary words summoned up for Catalina a sudden, vivid flash of the last time she'd had sex, a few months ago. It was simultaneously so powerful and so poignant that her teacup rattled on the saucer, her hands were shaking so much. Gerhardt's big hands around her waist, her fingers gripping the muscles in his shoulders, her back arched in such a deep curve that her damp hair tumbled right down to cover Gerhardt's wrists, his thighs bucking below her . . .

Oh no! she thought miserably, her entire body responding instantly to the memory. It was torture, this combination of the flashbacks to the shatteringly powerful sex, the loss of his companionship, the horror of his betrayal and the awful despairing pit she was trying so hard not to fall into: the pit where the sides looked too high and dark for her ever to scale them, the pit where she was scared she'd spend the rest of her life, single and alone, because obviously her instincts were so messed up that she'd fallen hopelessly in love with someone who had let her down so horribly . . .

Jane fell silent too, embarrassed that she had made a comment that had caused Catalina to react so oddly.

'The girls are having a nice little chat, eh?' Lord Tony said happily, glancing over at Catalina and Jane. 'We must get them over for a drink!'

He stuck out his hand in greeting to Michael Coggin-Carr, who was ordering a mojito from Karl.

'I saw you talking to them . . . are you a friend? I'm Lord Tony,' he added modestly, as if Michael might be unaware of his identity.

'Hi,' Michael said, returning the airline boss's smile and

handshake. 'Michael Coggin-Carr. No, I'm just a humble fan of Jane Browne's. I told her how much I admired her work and then I promptly buggered off so she doesn't think I'm some weirdo stalker trying to pick her up.' He grimaced. 'I'm sure she gets a lot of that.'

'Oh, I bet little Catalina gets *waaay* more!' Danny said, already a few sheets to the wind. 'She's a hot little number, isn't she? I usually go all out for the blondes' – he winked, long and suggestively, at Angela, who was bustling through the lounge – 'but I'd make an exception for that one. What a spinner! Did you see that video where she's in a cage? Hot stuff. Bloody hell, the *arse* on her!'

Lord Tony put his hand on Danny's arm.

'Steady on,' he muttered. 'You might make the girl a bit self-conscious.'

'That's Catalina? The pop star?' Michael, taking his mojito from Karl, looked genuinely surprised. 'God, I wouldn't have recognized her! I just thought she was a very pretty girl.'

'Did you not know she was on this flight?' Vanessa asked, annoyed by this implied failure of her publicity drive. 'It was all *over* the media.'

Michael shook his head apologetically.

'Know what a spinner is?' Danny had turned to the two businessmen next to him, who were clearly relishing this opportunity to hobnob so closely with major celebrities. They shook their heads in eager anticipation.

'It's a chick so small and skinny you can sit her on your dick and spin her round like a whirly toy,' Danny said, sitting back on his stool and miming this action, his eyebrows wiggling like Groucho Marx's. 'Wheee! Watch her go!'

The businessmen chortled at this, their faces going red as they sneaked furtive glances at Catalina's insubstantial frame. Michael, with a disgusted expression, pointedly turned his back on Danny, engaging Vanessa in polite conversation. And Lord Tony stood up and strolled leisurely around the curve of the bar, jerking his head at Karl as he went. The steward immediately set down the glass he was polishing and walked back to join his boss at the service entrance at the back.

'Lord Tony?' Karl said with suitable deference.

'Yes, Karl,' Lord Tony said, his expression more thoughtful than usual. He reached up to stroke his chin, looking rather like a bishop dealing with a delicate situation involving a wayward cleric. 'I'm just a *little* bit aware that Danny's becoming rather . . . cheerful.'

'I'll be careful with the drinks, sir,' Karl assured him. 'I've been noticing the, um, condition. In these circumstances, I tend to absent myself from the bar for a while, which slows the drinks service down. And I was planning to have Angela escort Mr Zasio to his pod – I think she's finished making it up. Usually, once a passenger settles into bed, they sleep it off for a while, which definitely helps.'

'Good thinking, Karl!'

Lord Tony slapped the air steward on the back. He tended, with his employees, to have the air of a hereditary peer talking to a member of staff who had served the family for the last forty years, and the Pure Air cabin crew all found themselves playing along with the act instinctively. Karl executed a little bow that was almost like a butler's as Lord Tony continued: 'He does seem to have taken a shine to Angela, doesn't he? I'm sure she'll settle him in nicely.'

'Oh, definitely, sir,' Karl agreed as Lord Tony strolled back to his bar stool, hands in his pockets, whistling lightly, as if he were surveying his lands on a stroll around his stately home.

'God, he thinks he's the Lord of Creation,' Karl muttered to Lucinda as she came up to the bar. 'I get so forelock-tugging with him, you know? Yes sir, no sir, two bags full sir.'

'It's because he thinks he's a proper lord,' Lucinda hissed back; she would never allow herself this *lèse-majesté* with anyone but Karl. 'Born one, instead of a barrow boy who worked his way up. You know we shouldn't actually be calling him Lord Tony? That's for sons of earls and dukes. It should just be Lord Moore of Wherever.'

'Ooh, I didn't know that,' Karl said.

Lucinda nodded significantly.

'Have you got things sorted out with Kevin and Emma Louise?' she asked pointedly.

'No, sorry,' Karl said, flustered. 'I've been rammed at the bar. Danny Zasio's getting totalled with those businessmen and they've been boozing non-stop. But Lord Tony just told me to pull a go-slow, so I can nip off and do the business for you now. Ooh, and you'll love this: Lord Tony wants Angela to take Danny Z back to his pod. Says he's taken a shine to her.'

'Well, that's one way of putting it!' Lucinda said. She smiled unpleasantly. 'Perfect. Couldn't have planned it better myself. Buzz off now and get the goodies from the Twins. Two of them. Chop chop.'

Typical of Lucinda to make me do her dirty work, Karl

thought resignedly as he headed off to find the two other members of the Luxe Class cabin crew. Lucinda could perfectly well have asked the Terrible Twins herself, but she wouldn't have dreamt of dirtying her hands. And this way she had deniability if anyone got caught with the stuff.

Even as he grumbled, however, he couldn't help admiring the cabin service director's Machiavellian manipulative skills. Admiration, mingled with that most crucial element recommended by the author of *The Prince*: fear. Karl might be Lucinda's closest ally, but he would never dream of crossing her or getting on her wrong side. Who knew what might prompt Lucinda to decide to plant a banana in his hand luggage, for instance?

Though of course, she'd never do it herself, he reflected ironically. *She'd order someone else to carry out her dirty work. Just in case.*

Muffled giggles were emanating from Michael Coggin-Carr's pod as Kevin and Emma Louise busied themselves making it up. The duty of making up the beds had been planned as a one-person job, but the two flight attendants always functioned best as a team, and Lucinda assigned them to joint tasks when she had them on crew together. They had been in training together, become fast friends then, and been near inseparable ever since, sharing a flat in Golders Green – a great area, and a swift drive to Heathrow down the North Circular and M4 – and indulging in wild and raucous partying on layovers. Emma Louise liked to say that they shared everything they possibly could. Kevin was gay, and she was straight, so they hunted the gay clubs for pretty, sexually ambiguous young men, stocking up on party drugs to help overcome any lingering doubts their targets might have had about the proposed threesome.

Which was exactly why Karl had been tasked with approaching them now.

'All right, you two,' he said, arriving at the pod door, and noticing with professional appreciation that though their whispered conversation was going strong, their hands were moving with swift efficiency through the routine of smoothing the blanket, folding down the top sheet, and plumping the pillows on the generously sized bed.

'Hi Karl! I *love* the night light, don't you? Look how gorge!' Kevin gushed enthusiastically, switching it on; the protocol was for the flight attendants, on this night flight, to make the pods up to full sleep mode. Passengers could, of course, decide to watch their TV or do some work at the built-in desk, but the whole Luxe Class concept was sold on offering one of the best night's sleep one could have in the air, which justified the sky-high prices. People paid vast sums of money not to sit up and watch films, but to lie down, stretch full-length, sleep in a proper bed, and that amenity was what the staff were trained to emphasize.

The light that suffused the pod was a deep purple-blue, so relaxing that Karl actually had to fight the impulse to yawn. He reached out to click on the reading light, checking the angle; yes, it was perfectly directed to form a gentle golden pool on the lower edge of the starched white pillows with their cobalt blue trim. He switched it off again, nodded and stood back, letting them finish. In a whisk of movement, a trio of blue-foiled chocolates were placed on the bed, a fluffy towel and hand towel, fastened with a satin ribbon, were pulled out from a drawer under the bed and arranged at the base of the mattress, and a freshening room scent – honey and lavender, which research had shown to be sleep-inducing but not too perfumed for male travellers – was sprayed in a swift arc over the pillow area.

'Done and dusted in record time,' Kevin said complacently.

Karl nodded approvingly and crooked the middle finger of his right hand, summoning the Twins to follow him to the back cabin wall, between the shower room and the toilet.

'I need a couple of X from you two,' he said, after a fast scan of the area to make sure they wouldn't be overheard. 'And no, they're not for me.'

'Don't tell me Lucinda wants 'em for a bit of mile-high action with Brian in the cockpit!' Emma Louise giggled. 'In front of Ginny and Harold! Or are they joining in too?'

The sheer unlikelihood of this made all three of them chortle. Ginny, the first officer, and Harold, the international relief officer, were both as starchy and tightly buttoned as Brian was charming and relaxed. It was quite unimaginable to picture them joining in a foursome orgy with Brian and Lucinda.

'As if Lucinda'd share Brian with anyone,' Kevin said *sotto voce*. 'Have you *seen* the way she's been glaring at Angela? If looks could kill! God, she's got on Lucinda's wrong side and no mistake!' He shuddered, theatrically and with great enjoyment. 'I'm *sooo* glad I'm not her,' he said. 'Honestly, if we were in *Flowers in the Attic*, Lucinda'd be locking Angela up in the attic and shoving arsenic into her quicker than you can say "younger and prettier".'

'Actually, Angela's better than I expected for someone

coming off ReillyFly,' Emma Louise said snobbishly. 'She knows her place, I'll give her that.'

'The trouble is that Brian thinks her place is on his d—' Kevin started salaciously, but Karl cut in firmly: they needed to get back to their respective tasks.

'I need two,' he said. 'Cough 'em up, pronto.'

'I'll have to nip to the loo,' Emma Louise said with a wink.

'She mules them on- and off-board,' Kevin explained, as Karl recoiled. 'Safest way.'

'Haven't had time to pop them out for the journey yet. Won't be a mo!' Emma Louise said with a sunny smile, disappearing into the toilet.

'Oh fucking *hell*,' Karl muttered in horror. 'Thank God I'm not taking them myself.'

'They're all wrapped up in loads of cling film, honestly,' Kevin said. 'You'd never know where they'd been.' He giggled again. 'Closest *I ever* get to a snatch, I can tell you!'

Christ, the things I do for Lucinda, Karl thought ruefully as he returned to the bar area, the two ecstasy pills tucked into his jacket pocket, wrapped in a tissue, leaving Kevin and Emma Louise to whisk through making up the other pods. *She totally owes me for this!* He reflected briefly and decided that this was a big enough favour for him to request in return not to be made to go near the lobsters for a whole month.

This would be a big concession, as the lobsters were already the bane of every single first-class flight attendant on Pure Air's existing routes. Serving the crustaceans freshly cooked on-board was a major marketing point, and Vanessa loved it: being able to publicize Pure Air as the lobster and champagne airline was an excellent way to emphasize how much the airline lavished five-star treats on their passengers.

In order to cook the lobsters on-board, however, they needed to be brought into the aircraft live, packed tightly in a polystyrene box; it was the cabin crew's job, after taking an order, to place the poor victims in a steamer, which gave them a slow and painful death. Boiling water, obviously, would have been a safety hazard, and an experiment in the test kitchens with a microwave had blown up the machine, so that was out too.

In consequence the lobsters, rather than perishing quickly in boiling water, suffered horribly, a sight that meant none of the crew could bear to eat any kind of shellfish. Serving them was almost as painful an experience. They needed to be presented whole, to make the point that they had just been cooked to order, but the big, slippery shells slid over the plates so extensively on a moving plane that the flight attendants were perpetually terrified of dropping them in passengers' laps or on the floor.

And ironically, after the white-knuckle stress that went into preparing and serving them, the passengers barely ended up eating the lobsters anyway. Even the most eager and greedy diner soon found that a large crustacean, even in the comparatively generous seating of first class, was much too messy to manage. After a few attempts at cracking open shell and claws, with the consequent shooting forth of steaming hot, fish-scented liquid, never completely caught by the bibs thoughtfully provided by the cabin crew, the Pure Air traveller would give up and buzz their call bell to order another option from the menu. The lobster would be carried back to the galley – slipping and sliding even more precariously around the plate now that it was in pieces – and dumped into the bin. After seeing their painful deaths, the crew couldn't face eating any, and flight attendants were strictly forbidden from taking any food off the plane with them for themselves or others – it was grounds for dismissal. So the whole lobster holocaust was almost entirely in vain, which was extremely distressing to the more sensitive members of the crew.

Ooh, I'll tell Angela to make sure Vanessa gets a lobster on-board, Karl thought, with a blinding flash of inspiration. *And Danny Zasio too. Maybe if they both tackle those bloody things, they'll realize what an incredibly stupid idea it is.*

He found Lucinda presiding behind the bar, and since she showed no signs of yielding her place to him, he slipped the miniature packet between two bottles on the glass-backed shelves, calling her attention to where he had concealed it with a discreet nod.

'Get Angela over here,' Lucinda instructed him out of the corner of her mouth, turning to retrieve the package. Her back to the bar to conceal what she was doing, she ground up the tablets in the pestle and mortar used for mashing mint leaves for mojitos. Karl summoned Angela, who came immediately, highly aware of the need to instantly respond to Lucinda's orders. She was surprised, but pleased, to find Lucinda in a much friendlier state of mind than previously, favouring Angela with a pleasant smile and a nod of greeting.

Danny also greeted Angela's arrival with open and unabashed delight.

'Isn't she lovely, with all those little freckles! Cor, just look at her! Yeah, I like blondes,' he slurred to Lucinda with faux confidentiality, his voice still carrying to Angela and the businessmen beside him, 'but not the flashy ones, you know? That other stewardess is okay, but she's all tits and teeth. And her hair's fried harder than KFC chicken nuggets. I like a nice natural girl. Silicone and bleach-free. Know what I mean?'

Lucinda did indeed know exactly what he meant. Emma Louise, to whom Danny was referring, had fallen subject to the classic transformation that came over young women who were assigned to the LAX route; it was known in crew lingo as getting 'Maliboobed', and Lucinda had seen it more times than she could count. This might be the inaugural flight of the midnight service to LA, but Pure Air had been flying there for a decade, and it had taken Emma Louise the standard two years to complete the full morphing.

The operation to take her breasts from a 32B to a 32D cup size, and the colour change from Light Natural Brown to Metallic Silver Blonde had been accomplished with comparative swiftness. What always took the time was the slow process of Invisalign braces, gradually nudging gappy British teeth into a formation as regular as soldiers on a parade ground, followed by the whitening treatments and veneers to even up the line. Twenty-four months later, Emma Louise was flashing the perfect Hollywood smile, bright as her meticulously maintained Metallic Silver Blonde hair.

'I don't like more than a handful,' Danny continued, staring pointedly at Angela's small-chested frame. 'Lovely little mouthfuls. Mmm, tasty.'

Angela, predictably, went bright red again, hugely grateful

that her blouse and jacket would conceal the stiffening of her nipples. Danny was just the kind of man she fancied, her guilty weakness. Prim and proper girls so often preferred bad boys whose stock-in-trade was breaking down their resistance, and Danny's cheeky Cockney charm, his brash good looks and sturdy frame were exactly what made Angela's legs go weak.

Danny had rolled his shirtsleeves up to his elbows, displaying his wide, muscly forearms, heavily dusted with golden hair. His shirt had one more button undone than was strictly appropriate, showing the beginning of the cleft between his pectorals, plus more thick golden chest hair. His trousers were stretched tightly over his thickset thighs as he sprawled on the stool, one arm propped on the bar. Angela didn't dare to look any lower than his chest. Even standing a few feet from him, she could smell his expensive aftershave and his own scent, soapy and clean but musky beneath. It was making her head whirl.

'Mr Zasio wanted you to have a quick toast with him,' Lucinda said, smiling so charmingly that Karl, on his way over to ask Catalina and Jane if they wanted to order anything more, shuddered at the sight. That smile never, ever boded well.

'I *did*?' Danny asked blankly.

But Lucinda, very experienced in managing passengers, rolled right over these words with, 'Angela, I poured you a bitter lemon – that's what you usually like, isn't it?'

This was the classic offer you couldn't refuse. Lucinda had set up the drinks, a shot of tequila with a champagne float for Danny, the glass of bitter lemon with a sprig of mint in it for Angela, paired together on the gleaming bar top. Another glass of bitter lemon was at Lucinda's slender elbow.

'We'll all raise a glass to the LuxeLiner maiden voyage!' she continued, and saw with satisfaction that Angela's body language had relaxed with the realization that Lucinda was joining in the toast. Angela stepped up to the bar, taking her glass. Lucinda noticed her give it a cautious sniff under the pretext of admiring the sprig of mint: *clever girl not to trust me completely*, Lucinda thought. *She's wondering if I might have put some alcohol in it.*

Reassured, Angela smiled at Lucinda and Danny, ducking her gaze with delightful modesty as she met the latter's hot blue stare.

'Fuck, she's adorable!' Danny announced to the world as he picked up his glass, clinked it with the ones the two stewardesses were holding, and, to Lucinda's considerable gratification, sank his doctored drink in one pull. No white residue could be seen at the bottom of the shot glass as far as she could tell, but she removed it swiftly just in case, especially because Lord Tony mustn't catch her serving a shot to Danny after he'd warned Karl to go slow with serving him any more alcohol.

The timing had been perfect: she'd waited till Lord Tony was on his way to the toilet before setting up the drinks, and now he was strolling back, beaming approval at the world. Angela set down her near-empty glass as Lucinda said, 'Angela, Mr Zasio's pod is made up for him, isn't it? Why don't you show him all its facilities?'

Danny was already jumping down from the stool, wobbling slightly but still reasonably steady on his feet, so close to

Angela that he was almost touching her. She saw a glint of gold chain around his wide neck, tangled in his body hair, and bit her lip, sure that she was the colour of a boiled lobster right now.

'Please follow me, Mr Zasio,' she said, happy to hear how steady her voice sounded. Her experience of keeping cool when faced with drunk, shouting ReillyFly passengers – angry at a charge for printing their boarding passes at the airport; or because their hand luggage was three hundred grams over the allotted ten-kilo cabin weight – had been the ultimate training in how to stay calm in a crisis.

'Oh, call me Danny, *please*,' he said intimately. To Angela's horror, as they turned into the little corridor between the pods, she felt him blow softly on the back of her neck. Every single faint hair that was too downy and short to be scraped and sprayed into her regulation bun lifted in delicious, erotic sensation. She pictured him licking her there, and it took a nerve-wracking effort in muscular control to keep her pace level; she knew perfectly well that he was staring at her bottom.

The plane lurched, throwing them sideways; it wasn't a big bump, but the flight had been so smooth up until then that crew and passengers alike had become accustomed to walking around easily, not having to hold on to anything. As a result, even the experienced Angela tipped on the heels of her court shoes, and Danny grabbed her round the waist, ostensibly to steady her. His square hands came close to spanning it, hot even through the fabric of her jacket and blouse, and her nipples went hard all over again.

'Careful there,' he said, and now his lips did touch the

back of her neck. 'If you're going to fall over, I want to be underneath.'

'Mr Zasio . . .' she said helplessly. She had meant to reproach him, but the words came out so feebly that she tailed off.

Angela was used, too, to fending off overenthusiastic male travellers with wandering hands; she had perfected an icy tone that was almost as effective as a dash of cold water at shrinking their equipment. But this wasn't at all like dealing with a grabby, tattooed drunk on the Marbella route stinking of cheap beer. This was Danny Zasio, who she'd had a crush on for years watching him on TV, who smelt of expensive aftershave, equally expensive tequila, and himself, which was the best smell of all. As soon as he'd touched her, she'd completely forgotten she was at work. And even now that she was standing again, one hand out to the wall to balance herself, he wasn't letting go, and her voice was so far from icy she could have warmed her hands on it.

'Your pod's just here!' she heard herself say in a squeak. 'Please, do go in.'

The protocol was to stand by the open door, one hand raised to gesture the passenger in. Once the bed was made up, the space became even more personal, so the customer must be the first to enter it, to feel that, on this busy, crowded flight, they had an oasis of repose that was all their own. The flight attendant would then ask politely if the passenger wanted them to point out the extra features, only entering once they had been invited.

This excellently planned etiquette, however, promptly went to hell in a handbasket. Angela paused just after the door, indicating the inside of the pod to Danny; he went in, but as he did so, he gave her a huge wink, took her extended hand and drew her inside with him, right around the curve of the comma-shaped pod, to the head of the bed where they couldn't be seen if they sat down. Which Danny promptly achieved by pulling her onto his lap.

'God, you're turning me on,' he muttered into her ear, licking and kissing it in a way that made Angela feel that her entire lower body was melting over his wide-spread thighs. 'You're feeling it too, aren't you? I'm so fucking hot for you right now.'

'Mr Zasio, *please* . . .' she hissed frantically; it was the sack if she got caught letting a passenger kiss her, and getting hired by Pure Air was the dream of a lifetime, let alone being catapulted into Luxe Class. 'Please, let me go . . .'

'Not until you call me Danny,' he whispered into her ear, closing his teeth momentarily on the lobe. Angela shuddered with pleasure from head to toe. 'Say my name, babe, and then maybe I'll let you go. For now.'

'Danny, *please* . . .'

He put one hand behind her neck, pulled her head around and shoved his tongue into her mouth, fast and furious, less a kiss than a stamp of possession, a marker he was putting down. When he let her go she was trembling, her lips a little bruised, and panicking that her thong underwear was so wet that it would start to drip. She thanked God that, at least, her skirt was fully lined.

'I know you've got stuff to do,' he said, leering at her as, red-faced, she climbed off his lap and frantically straightened her clothing, awkwardly ducking and bending so she wouldn't be seen above the wall of the pod. 'But we've got business to finish, you and I, eh?' He reached out to put one hand on the cheek of her bottom. 'You come and find me when the lights go down, babe,' he said softly. 'Or I'll come and find you, and that's a promise. I'll be counting the minutes.'

Angela, who had been trained to have a professional response in the face of disaster, to run across a smoke-filled cabin, wrestle open an airplane door, activate the emergency slide and marshal a planeload of panicking passengers down it, couldn't get a word out. Danny lolled back on the bed, grinning at how flustered she was, his eyes glinting with anticipation.

'*Oh* yeah,' he commented as she bent over to check her reflection in the vanity mirror, ensuring that her bun was as smooth as ever. She had to lick her fingers to plaster down the strays, unhappily aware that this would draw an extra groan of excitement from Danny; she scrambled out of his pod so discombobulated that she didn't trust herself to go straight back to the bar again and escort the next passenger to their pod. Instead, she nipped into the toilet at the far end of the cabin, horrified to see how red her cheeks were, how bright her eyes. Her pupils looked bigger, darker than usual, which she put down to her level of arousal, and her heart was pounding as hard as if it were trying to escape from her ribcage. She thought almost hysterically of the film *Alien*: it felt like an entity trying to force its way out of her body.

She stuck her hands under the cold tap, desperately telling herself to breathe slower, evenly, to calm herself down. All the while knowing that if Danny had followed her to the toilet and tapped on the door, she'd let him in, pull her skirt up for him, drag her thong to one side, let him do whatever he wanted to her . . .

I mustn't, I mustn't, I mustn't! she told herself frantically. This was her first LuxeLiner flight, her huge opportunity to show that she deserved this enormous promotion. Having sex with Danny would torpedo everything. You couldn't do anything on a plane without another member of the crew knowing about it; and what one knew, everyone else would in just a few minutes.

But as soon as she thought it, as soon as she told herself that she mustn't, couldn't, have sex with Danny, all she heard were those three words – *sex with Danny, sex with Danny, sex with Danny* – like the rhythm of her heart still drumming against the slatted bones that contained it.

He's a married man! she told herself viciously, clutching the tiny gold crucifix she wore, tucked away behind the sleek neckline of her white blouse. *He's a married man, Angela Stiven! Get a grip on yourself!*

She met her own eyes once more in the mirror as she dried her hands.

I am not going to have sex with him, she said to herself, absolutely resolved. *I am not.*

And then the ecstasy she had unknowingly taken started to kick in.

Chapter Eight

Seven months ago

Catalina's narrow chest heaved, her heart pumping madly, as the silence she had left behind her in the huge Tokyo Mobile Power stadium after her triumphant performance of '*Corazón*' finally exploded into a riot of applause, the audience screaming, howling, stamping their feet so loudly it felt as if the stadium were rocking.

'Fantastic show!' Zoe said happily as she towelled Catalina down. 'God, listen to them yelling!'

Catalina smiled, but as usual, after singing '*Corazón*', she stayed silent, her vocal chords throbbing with the demands she had just placed on them. She looked for Latisha, more than ready for the relief of her throat spray, nasty though it was. But instead of her personal assistant, it was Gerhardt who loomed up, the bottle of spray dwarfed by his big hand.

'Latisha has a stomach problem,' he said apologetically. 'She told me to make sure you have your spray as soon as you come offstage.'

Catalina opened her mouth wide, and Gerhardt bent almost double to make sure he was aiming the nozzle right to the back of her throat. She averted her eyes, embarrassed suddenly to have him so close to her, his fingers even grazing her cheek briefly. In the last few weeks, ever since the evening they had spent talking in her suite, Catalina had spent much too much time thinking about Gerhardt. Bizarrely, the red heart and the threatening words 'Cat Is Mine' sprayed on the dressing-room wall actually impinged much less on her awareness than Gerhardt himself.

She had told herself, firmly and often, that she had just imprinted on Gerhardt because of the shock of that night. It made complete sense: he was the bodyguard whisking her away from danger, keeping her safe, distracting her from worrying, even staying up overnight in the foyer of the suite to ensure she had a good night's sleep. No wonder that after that she would find herself relying on him, looking out for his calm presence in the background of a room, feeling jittery when he went off shift. She had even – so humiliating to admit, even to herself – found herself exaggerating her fears about the stalker popping up again specifically so that she could have more contact with Gerhardt.

Had Latisha noticed her boss's interest in her new body-guard? Catalina thought so. Latisha had taken, recently, to dropping Gerhardt's name into their evening chats to see if she could make Catalina blush or react. But if Latisha knew that every night, when Catalina retired to bed, it was Gerhardt she imagined as she reached for her vibrator, Gerhardt she pictured on top of her, underneath her – 'before, behind, between, above, below', to quote a poem she'd read recently in her perpetual quest to improve her English and get inspir-ation for her lyrics – well, what *would* Latisha say?

Probably *Don't fuck the hired help, honey*, Catalina thought, imagining Latisha saying those words in her drawling

American accent. And Latisha would, of course, be right. But it had been a year since Catalina finally, painfully, called time on her long-term relationship with the boyfriend she'd had since seventeen, an Argentinian rancher and polo player whom she had barely even seen for the last few years. She was just so busy all the time, touring and recording and rehearsing, building her career, and Fernando was equally absorbed back home with his horse breeding and the demands of the international polo circuit.

She was pretty sure he hadn't been completely faithful to her, and she couldn't blame him; how frustrating must it be to be in a relationship with one of the world's biggest sex symbols, but hardly ever get to have sex with her? The pressure on them when Catalina went back to Argentina, or their assistants managed to get their schedules to dovetail briefly, was immense. Catalina, of course, needed to see her large family too, so when she and Fernando did manage to claw out some time together, the pressures on them as a couple had been immense. You could only fuck each other's brains out for so long, and after that, as your breath slowly returned and the sweat dried on your bodies, as you lay side by side, looking up at the revolving blades of the ceiling fan, cooling down, the same old questions would return to torment you: where was this going? Were you going to get engaged, plan to have children? How much commitment did you want? Could you even call this a relationship when you only saw each other four times a year?

The last time, at Fernando's *estancia* in Córdoba, they hadn't even been able to enjoy the sex before the questions had started up again like dark thunderclouds filling the sky, the atmospheric pressure so heavy that they could barely breathe through it. The storm had broken when Catalina had heard herself blurting out the three crucial words: 'This isn't working.'

Significantly, Fernando hadn't uttered a word of protest in response; instead, he had, in the saddest of tones, agreed with her. They had both cried, engaged in grieving break-up sex that had been much better than the previous, rather frenzied bout, and said goodbye the next day with mutual affection but no regrets. No more tears, either: she had waved him farewell from the helicopter he had chartered to pick her up, and as she watched him and the *estancia* diminishing below her, fading away to tiny specks, she had known, with a fundamental calm, that it was not where she belonged.

And much as she had once cared about Fernando, she had barely thought of him since. She had heard on the family grapevine that he had almost immediately started seeing someone else, a Brazilian gemstone heiress; when her instinctive reaction was to be happy for him, without a whisper of jealousy, she had extra confirmation that the relationship had clearly been over long before its official termination.

Catalina hadn't even considered dating anyone else after the break-up. Musicians tended to put their personal life on hold during a tour as big as the one organized for Chasing Midnight. With four continents in eight months, fifty dates in total, it was a massive project, terminating in three dates in Buenos Aires. Then she'd go to her sprawling beach house in Punta del Este, the famously gorgeous millionaires' playground in Uruguay where the richest Argentinians hung out, and crash completely for a month, doing nothing but eating, swimming, hosting family and friends, and getting endless massages.

And *then*, maybe, she'd start thinking about the parlous state of her love life. Catalina and Fernando had lasted so long because they had wanted the same things: marriage, children, a stable home life, true love that would hopefully last the whole of their lives. But he had been ready years ago, and she simply hadn't; she was still building her career, couldn't even consider slowing down that momentum, had refused to even get engaged, because it would have been unfair to him to agree to that when marriage was not even on the horizon for her.

Now she was twenty-seven, at the height of her career. *Chasing Midnight* had gone multi-platinum, was even heading for diamond status, which meant a massive ten million copies sold. And she even had a song nominated for an Oscar! Ironically, after this crazy push to the top, she had been meaning to think seriously about marrying Fernando, committing to spending a good part of her time on the *estancia*, building a recording studio there, seeing all the dreams they'd had together finally coming true.

However, by the time she could honestly say that she was ready to settle down, the bond between herself and Fernando had worn much too thin and threadbare to repair. Love might have conquered all, but they weren't in love any more. They had just been living on the last fumes of the feelings they had once had for each other, and the acknowledgement of that fact had been a huge relief, setting them both free. No wonder Fernando had met someone else so soon.

No: Catalina had no regrets. But all her sexual feelings had to go *somewhere.* For years it had been Fernando's handsome Latin face that Catalina had seen when she turned on her vibrator late at night and closed her eyes; now it was Gerhardt's granite features and silver eyes that she pictured above her, his narrow lips hard on hers, his big powerful body weighing her down . . . and again, that line of poetry came into her mind: before, behind, between, above, below . . .

Don't fuck the hired help! she heard in Latisha's voice, like a self-invented mantra. And that brought her back to the here and now. As the make-up artist finished blotting the sweat off her face with rice paper, Catalina realized with dismay that she had been so lost in her own selfish thoughts that she hadn't even asked about her assistant's stomach problems.

'Latisha!' she blurted out, her lips moving just as the make-up artist was approaching them with the applicator loaded with gold gloss.

'Oops, sorry!' the make-up artist apologized, quickly wiping the smear off Catalina's cheek.

'No, it was my fault . . . Latisha! How is she?'

Zoe, who was reaching for Catalina's ballet flats, turned to stare at her boss, her eyebrows raised.

'We just told you, babe,' she said, kneeling down in front of her. 'Were you off in your head somewhere? Tish thinks she had some bad sushi. She threw up for a bit and then the nurse here gave her an anti-emetic and she made it back to the hotel. She looked awful, all grey.'

Catalina hadn't heard a word of this; she had been lost in memories of Fernando and fantasies about Gerhardt. She looked past Zoe, lifting her legs one by one so that Zoe could fit the flat shoes to her feet, and spotted Gerhardt beyond the group of dressers and make-up artists around her, his face impassive. Sensing her gaze on him, his eyes, which had been surveying the far side of the wings, swivelled to meet hers, and the brief contact sent a jolt through her; she stumbled, had to put weight on the hand leaning on Zoe's shoulder, felt the dresser shift in counterbalance.

'Sorry!' she mumbled, dragging her eyes from Gerhardt.

Zoe said, a little surprised, 'You're all over the place this evening! You okay, babe?'

'A little tired, I think,' Catalina said feebly.

'Hey, I hear you. It's a *looong* tour,' Zoe said ruefully, standing up. 'You're done. We're good to go.'

During the entire process of the meet-and-greet, Catalina made a huge and deliberate effort not to look at Gerhardt at all. In fact, every time she saw his black-clad bulk, or heard him rumble a word or two for crowd control as she smiled and signed copies of the CD and posed for photographs, she averted her head, much to the surprise of some of the Japanese fans, who had to contort their own bodies into odd angles to match her own.

It's not his fault – he's doing a great job, she thought rather desperately as she waved a final goodbye to the roomful of people and headed back to her dressing room. *But having him around the whole time is getting very distracting. And you never get over a crush when you see the person every day* . . . She smiled ruefully, remembering how obsessed she had been with Enrique, the guitarist in her backing band, when she had been thirteen; Enrique, at eighteen, hadn't even looked twice at a skinny little girl, thank goodness, so she had been free to indulge her infatuation with him to her heart's content. It had lasted until he left the band, and she had sobbed for weeks afterwards, absolutely convinced that she would never love again and that her life, in any meaningful way, was over . . .

Well, she wasn't that thirteen-year-old any more. She was by no means as dramatic. But she was just as passionate, and just as liable to crushes, and this one on Gerhardt was showing no signs of fading; in fact, it felt like it was getting more intense every day she spent with him at her side.

Taking a deep breath, telling herself that what she needed right then was a long, cold shower, she actually outstripped Latisha's assistant, reaching the dressing room before anyone else. Behind her, Gerhardt said something sharply – since Berlin, Catalina was never to be the first person into her dressing room, just in case.

But that was almost a month ago, it hasn't happened since . . . we're on a different continent, for God's sake, I'll be fine . . .

She turned the handle, pushed the door open and stopped dead in her tracks, staring in horror at the sight that met her eyes. It was Berlin again, but on steroids. The stalker had definitely escalated.

The red heart was much larger this time, covering almost the entire back wall, its shape sprayed over the white sofa, the big mirror, dominating everything. And over the white carpet were scattered big blown-up pictures of Catalina, the floor thick with them. Catalina looked down and realized that every one of them was daubed with red marker pen.

Over her face and body were drawn, again and again, the same boldly executed heart.

Staring closely at them, she noticed the worst thing of all. The bodies were all naked, and they were not hers. They must have belonged to porn stars, because they were splayed in every conceivable way, as if they were in competition to display as much of the insides of their bodies as they actually could without cutting themselves open. The poses were humiliating, obscene, and to see her head attached to each body, her smiling face, her fall of hair, was a truly profound shock. It had been done with Photoshop, so well that they looked horribly plausible, as if it really was her. Only the knowledge that she would never have posed for anything like that made her instantly sure of how they had been created.

And inside each heart were the same three words that filled up the back wall of the room.

CAT

IS

MINE

Catalina looked speechlessly from one photograph to the next, a seemingly endless series of naked images of her, touching herself, opening herself, inviting penetration everywhere. She retched, but it was a scream that rose inside her, and suddenly the red of the spray paint was all that she could see. Red was flooding her vision, blinding her. She turned, stumbling sightlessly away from those terrifying images, the menacing words, and her body hit a wall, a solid, warm, muscled, incredibly reassuring wall. Gerhardt's huge frame, so big it seemed to go on forever. She grabbed onto his

T-shirt with both hands, clinging to him, burying her head into his chest as she started to sob with quickly spiralling hysteria.

Her legs buckled under her. Instantly, Gerhardt bent at the knees, snatching her up before she could fall. Her body folded over on itself, contorting into a tight ball of gold fringe, glossy limbs and tumbling hair, her face completely concealed against his T-shirt, her tears soaking into the cotton fabric. She was wailing now, terrified and overwhelmed, her sobs so high-pitched that her vocal chords would be sore and bruised when she finally ran out of breath. She could hear nothing but her own weeping. Not the exclamations of shock and dismay from her entourage, not Gerhardt's curt bark at them all to get out of the way, not the stream of commands he snapped out to them as he strode from the room, his arms wrapped tightly around her, carrying her away as fast and as far as he could from the room the stalker had so completely filled with the evidence of their obsession.

Chapter Nine

On-board

'God, that chef guy looks just about ready to join the mile-high club with that stewardess!' Jane said to Catalina, craning her head to watch Danny and Angela as they disappeared around the corner of the bar. 'Did he just *lick her neck*?'

She shook her head.

'I must have seen it wrong. He can't be *that* drunk, can he?'

'He can, I think,' Catalina said. 'He was drinking champagne the whole time at the airport. And he just did a shot as well.'

'Probably pre-loaded on the way to the airport, come to think of it,' Jane said.

'Pre-loaded?' Catalina's forehead creased charmingly.

'When you drink before you get to a party,' Jane explained.

'Oh! I should remember that for a song,' Catalina said thoughtfully. 'I'm sure it would rhyme with lots of words. Loaded, folded, holded . . .'

Jane giggled.

'Sorry, that's not a word!' she said. 'It's "held".'

'Oh! Thanks. I use a rhyming dictionary a lot,' Catalina confessed. 'They're very helpful.'

'Ladies, can I offer you more tea? A snack? Would you like to see the à la carte menu, maybe?' Lucinda asked, and they both started a little; they had been so happily involved in conversation they hadn't noticed her approach. Independently, both Catalina and Jane thought how pleasant the other one was, how easily their chat had flowed. When they said simultaneously:

'No thanks, I'm a bit tired,' they looked back at each other and giggled.

'Separated at birth,' Jane murmured.

'Would you like to be shown to your pods?' Lucinda suggested, and they both nodded in reply, which made them giggle again.

'I just want to say hi to Latisha before I settle down,' Catalina said. 'Is it okay if I go back to see her for a moment?'

'Oh, of *course*!' Lucinda said, giving the impression that anything the most A-list guest on-board asked to do, short of actually flying the plane, would be smiled upon by its staff. 'You'll find your assistant seated on the far side of the right-hand aisle, by the window. Miss Browne, shall I show you to your pod first, in that case?'

'Thank you,' Jane said, glancing at Catalina as they both stood up. 'See you later?'

'Oh, for sure!' Catalina flashed her a very pretty smile. 'I would definitely like that.'

Lucinda gestured elegantly for Jane to follow her to the far side of the bar, and Catalina reached back for the elasticated band that was holding her hair back in a loose bun. Taking it out, she scraped her heavy mane of hair tightly to her scalp, running her fingers through it to get it as flat as possible, pulling her hair into a tight plait at the nape of her neck. She had found that people were much less likely to recognize her if she smoothed back the cascade of curls for which she was so well known. She still drew attention for being a very pretty girl, but without that instant snap of identification of her as Catalina, the pop star – at least for long enough for her to go about her business.

Pulling back the heavy sapphire curtain that separated Luxe Class from the business-class section of the plane, she slipped through, keeping her head ducked. There was a row of lavatories on one side of the aisle, so any business-class travellers who saw her emerge would assume that Catalina had visited one and was returning to her business-class seat, not that she was a Luxe Class passenger briefly slumming it by comparison.

Latisha, in her coveted bulkhead seat, was almost immediately behind the bank of toilets, and Catalina spotted her straight away; her assistant, clearly, had already taken her sleeping pill and crashed out. Her seat was cosily reclined inside its plastic shell, a modular curving lounger design that brought her lower limbs up, her ankles propped on a slide-out, padded footrest. Her eyes were covered in a mask, her head tilted to one side on the ergonomic pillow with which she always travelled, her body wrapped in a blue Pure Air blanket and her neck swathed in a cashmere scarf. Her lips were parted, and a series of bubbling snores was issuing from her nose.

Luckily, her seatmate was plugged into the entertainment console, a games device in his hands, busily firing and swiping away, his eyes too fixed on the screen to notice

Catalina standing beside him in the aisle, and his ears too filled with the soundtrack to be able to hear the rumbling of Latisha's breathing. He was in his mid-thirties, good-looking, with fashionably ruffled hair and a strong jaw, but he was as intent on his game as a ten-year-old boy. It would have taken much more than a snoring seatmate and a young woman hovering by his side to divert an iota of his attention from the job of jumping over the onscreen obstacles to reach his target.

Catalina, very familiar with the noises Latisha made when asleep, let alone knocked out on Zopiclone, couldn't help smiling affectionately at the familiar sound, even though she was disappointed not to be able to chat to her for a little while. The separation on the flight was making her realize how dependent she had become on Latisha. Previously, they had been joined at the hip during Catalina's tours, but saw much less of each other socially during the downtimes when Catalina was resting and writing new songs. But for the last few months, Catalina had leaned far too much on Latisha for company and support, and she was only now beginning to understand that.

She looked down at Latisha's sleeping face, and nodded to herself. It was good that she was cosily tucked up and asleep, good that Catalina would have to cope on her own for the duration of the flight. Maybe, after she'd slept, she would go and find that nice Jane and drink more tea with her. Perhaps she would arrange to meet up with Jane in LA during Oscars week, too. Catalina needed to start lifting some of the burden she had placed on her assistant's shoulders, make some new friendships, fill the void in other ways, not just by turning poor Latisha into a sort of surrogate spouse.

What had happened to Catalina had been awful, a profound betrayal of trust. But she needed to start the process of recovering, and that meant learning once again how to be on her own, start giving her assistant some much-needed space.

No wonder she kept talking about taking her sleeping pill, Catalina thought guiltily. *She must really have needed a break from me and all my misery. I'm sure I've been driving her crazy for the last few months, and she's been so sweet and patient with me, never complaining, letting me whine and cry as much as I wanted . . .*

Well, it was time for Catalina to stop crying, or at least doing it on Latisha's broad shoulders. Latisha could sleep all the way to LA. Catalina wouldn't bother her again; she should have left her alone in the first place. Turning away to return to Luxe Class, she resolved to tell Tish, when they were safely landed, that things were going to change: she was going to be less needy and clinging in future, behave as an employer should, keep some professional boundaries. It was the right thing to do.

I'll send Tish on an all-expenses-paid holiday to Cabo, after the Oscars are over, Catalina resolved nobly. Cabo San Lucas, in Mexico, was Latisha's favourite getaway destination, and Catalina would pay for her and a friend to go, not inflict her own company on Tish any more: that way it would be a proper holiday for her.

Catalina would miss Tish horribly, and that would be the right thing too. She'd move back into her house, restart her life. Begin going on dates arranged by her publicist – who was champing at the bit to set her up with Hollywood's most eligible bachelors – dip her toe back in the water. Put the painful memories of her ex-boyfriend's pernicious, untrustworthy behaviour firmly behind her once and for all.

Her first, fragile steps towards healing her wounds would have been utterly derailed, however, if she had realized how close she was to the source of that betrayal. A male passenger in an aisle bulkhead seat on the other side of the cabin had been expecting to see Catalina ever since the 'Fasten Seat Belt' sign had been switched off; very well aware of how close she was to her assistant, he had known that her sweet nature would mean that she would come in to check on the latter's comfort. His heart racing, he had watched Catalina as she stood looking down at Latisha, feeling a painful blow to his chest as he saw her smile so affectionately at someone who wasn't him. And when her slim figure turned and left the cabin, his silvery grey gaze lingered on her narrow hips, her tight round bottom, with a nostalgia that was equally painful.

She disappeared, and he closed his eyes, telling himself that the worst thing he could possibly do was to indulge himself in the kind of memories that would do nothing but mess with his mind, interfering with the self-control that he needed to perform his tasks on this flight. He mustered every ounce of professionalism left to him in the attempt to take charge of his mind and body.

But I could never be professional around her, he thought bitterly. *That was always the problem. I could never control myself when I was with her.*

Should I have done things differently? Did my pride fuck

up the best thing that ever happened to me? Could I have tried to fight harder for it, to make her see how wrong she was?

Gerhardt's eyes snapped open again. He had asked himself these questions a million times in the last few months without ever reaching any satisfactory answers. And all he could see with his eyes closed was Catalina, naked, her arms reaching out for him. He longed to turn on the TV screen to see something, anything that would help him blot out the images in his mind, but that was strictly forbidden.

Dammit. He looked down at his foot, which was tapping like a maniac's against his footrest. This flight was going to be sheer torture for him, knowing she was so close. He realized that he was grinding his teeth against the impulse to jump up, stride through to Luxe Class, find her and blurt out all the things his pride had prevented him from saying before in a doubtless crazy-sounding rant that would probably send her into utter panic.

His foot tapped even faster. Nine hours to go. How the hell was he going to cope?

Chapter Ten

Seven months ago

CAT
IS
MINE

The words seemed to be everywhere: not just looming, gigantic, on the back wall of the dressing room, but underfoot, all over the photographs of Catalina, now covered with red marker pen. With the woman in the pictures sobbing in his arms, Gerhardt swivelled to get her out of the room, barking at everyone to clear the way even as he grabbed for his overcoat, which was hanging by the door. It was a small piece of good luck in this crisis that it was chilly in Tokyo that time of year, necessitating the big coat; he snatched it off the hook and threw it with one hand over his charge, easily strong enough to support her entire body with his other arm. He tucked the folds of the coat around Catalina, whose face was still buried in his shoulder, her tears beginning to dampen his cotton T-shirt. The dark flood of her hair blended into the black coat, rendering her an anonymous bundle in his arms as he stalked down the long backstage corridor of the stadium, heading for the waiting limousine.

There was no time to set up a decoy exit as he had done

back in Berlin: Catalina was too hysterically upset for him to do anything but get her back to the hotel as soon as possible. As soon as Gerhardt emerged through the artists' entrance, the limo driver leapt to open the back door. Gerhardt strode so quickly towards the car that he had Catalina inside before the waiting fans could grasp that it was her in his arms; they only realized it as the limo started to pull away. The hardcore fans right at the front of the barriers started to call her name, yelling that she was sick. The arena security guards stationed to hold the hordes back were backing up, arms wide, making space for the long black car as the fans pressed forward, the news rapidly spreading among them that Catalina was leaving without her usual smiles and waves for her most devoted followers, that she hadn't even been able to walk under her own steam.

Sitting back into the deep leather seat, Gerhardt tried, quietly but desperately, to settle Catalina to his side. But she was still clinging onto his T-shirt, refusing to move, and he sighed and gave up, keeping his arms wrapped tightly around her and splaying his big legs as wide as he could. His entire focus was on keeping her bottom away from his burgeoning erection. If he balanced her on the left thigh, he could manage it, he thought, sweat beading on his forehead. He dressed to the right; she wouldn't feel it unless she moved over, unless her folded knees brushed against it . . .

Please God, let her not brush against it! The mere thought was making him even harder. Wanting to calm her down, he patted her between her narrow shoulders, very relieved to hear her sobs abate to some degree as he did so. He drew awkward circles on her back with his palm, telling himself that he was reassuring her the way he would do with a small child, comforting but clearly asexual. The sobs slowed down, turned to gulping, uneven breaths, and, encouraged, Gerhardt raised his hand, stroking her head now, amazed at how thick and dense her curls were.

As he touched her hair, his fingers, despite his best intentions, began to tangle in the ringlets, the gesture turning into a caress. Catalina looked up at him, her eyes wide, the make-up smudged all around them with her tears, making them look as huge as a panda's. The gold gloss on her lips had rubbed off on his T-shirt. He froze, staring down at her as nervously as if she were a wild animal that he had rescued but which might bite or scratch him now that it realized it was trapped with him in an enclosed space.

When Catalina's hands unclenched from his T-shirt and reached up, however, it wasn't to scratch him. They wrapped around his thick neck, pulling his head down to hers. No biting – not at first, anyway. Her mouth tasted of salt tears and a slightly bitter undercurrent of medicinal throat spray, but to Gerhardt it was as delicious as if she had just been eating ripe cherries. She was unstoppable, irresistible, her arms wound tightly around him; her wiry, strong dancer's body coiled up in his lap as she kissed him passionately, the feel of her small hands running over his buzz-cut hair utterly delicious.

He did try, briefly, to reach up and pull her away, but she moaned against his mouth in protest as she realized what he was attempting, and the sound was so heady, so sexual, so powerfully indicative of how much she wanted him that his hands found themselves sliding down her back instead, reaching to cup her tiny round bottom, hearing her moan again, this time in utter and complete encouragement as she shifted herself right up against him, and even the idea of keeping her away from his now huge and thrusting erection became completely impossible.

He felt dizzy, barely any blood left in his head at all; it had all rushed to his crotch. She wasn't letting him even catch his breath, was kissing him as if every single pent-up emotion, all the fear about her stalker having escalated, all the rush and excitement of performing to tens of thousands of people, had flooded up through her and into him, carrying him away with her on a fast-running river that had burst its banks so triumphantly that all of his professional detachment and reserve was totally forgotten.

It only gradually dawned on him that they were back at the Mandarin Oriental, that the limousine had come to a halt, because the driver was knocking on the panel that separated the compartments with what sounded like his mobile phone, a series of increasingly loud taps. He must have tried to talk over the intercom first, but that had gone completely unheeded by Gerhardt and Catalina. Gerhardt could only thank the Lord that the panel was dark glass.

'Catalina,' he said against her lips, his voice ragged and hoarse. 'We're here.'

He dragged his mouth away from hers, horrified at how loudly he was breathing; it sounded like he'd just benched five hundred pounds and then sprinted a mile. His panting reverberated around the inside of the limousine. He couldn't look down at her; that would set him off again. More roughly than he would have liked, he lifted her off him and placed her onto the seat, one big arm braced to hold her there while he not only caught his breath but got his penis under some sort of basic control.

'I need a minute,' he said between gritted teeth, hoping to God that she'd understand; he was scared that if she touched him again, he'd actually come in his trousers.

She shifted around beside him, and he sank his teeth into his lower lip, the pain stopping him from imagining what she looked like doing that. Then he realized that she was pulling on his overcoat, covering herself up, which sent a huge sigh of relief rushing out through his nostrils.

'Right!' he said, his voice sounding relatively more normal than it had before. 'We go!'

He glanced at her, just fractionally. 'I can't carry you,' he said, and was appalled at the naked panic he could hear in his own voice. His erection, which had subsided to some degree, perked up again at the image of Catalina once again in his arms.

'I can walk,' she said softly, and leaned forward to tap on the panel, signalling to the driver to come around and open the back door for them.

She was holding the long overcoat up in her fists, folds of the heavy material gathered like curtain, ruching so that she could walk without tripping over as she climbed neatly out of the limo and onto the concrete of the parking garage. Since the Berlin incident, her security protocol had become more strict: she now only entered and left hotels through the private channels that all five-star hotels maintained for their VIP clients. Catalina had resisted this at first. Having built her career by being hugely friendly and responsive to her fans, to sneak in and out of hotels like this, avoiding the waiting multitudes who wanted photo opportunities, went against everything she stood for.

But Gerhardt had been firm on the subject, and now she could not have been more grateful. She flitted across the garage to the lifts, a ridiculous-looking tiny creature in gold ballet shoes and an overcoat fifteen sizes too big for her, its shoulder seams alone reaching down to her elbows, its sleeves so long she looked like a child impersonating Charlie Chaplin in her father's coat. Gerhardt followed, pulling the key card out of his back trouser pocket, welcoming the effects of the chilly air on his overheated body, taking his time; she was tapping one foot impatiently by the time he reached her and slid the card through the slot to activate the command panel.

'Now, listen . . .' he began as they stepped into the lift, and then stopped, gulping, as she promptly shrugged the overcoat off, letting it fall to her feet, standing there, her body gilded by the body oil, the shining walls of the elevator cage reflecting off her gold-fringed costume, the fringe trembling as she breathed in and out. Luckily for Gerhardt's self-discipline, Catalina spotted her own reflection in the mirrored lift doors and gasped in shock at her smeared make-up, licking her fingertips and doing her best to wipe off as much of it as possible.

'I look like a crazy psycho clown!' she exclaimed, half-laughing at herself. 'Like a mad girl in a pop video!'

As long as he managed not to watch her putting her fingers in her mouth, he'd be okay. He'd talk to her but not look at her, absolutely not watch her licking her fingers . . .

'Listen, Catalina,' he said, mustering up his firmest, deepest voice, the one that had had recalcitrant soldiers jumping to obey him back in his days as an army sergeant. 'This is a very upsetting situation and I think, it is obvious, it has made you very . . .'

What was another word for 'upset'? He was even forgetting his English under the stress, dammit.

'Very confused,' he finally managed. 'Very upset and confused. So obviously it seems to me that what just happened is because you were very upset and confused.'

Jesus, he sounded ridiculous. But the tone, he told himself, was just as important as the words, and at least he was managing the first part.

'So I will obviously take you back to the suite,' he continued, 'and make sure that it is all safe. I will call hotel security from there . . .'

Goddammit, he should have done that from the car! He was totally fucking up his job. He was going to have to hire more bodyguards, a whole team: station two of them to ensure the security of Catalina's dressing room, probably two in her hotel suite as well. She would hate that, hate it all. Catalina had always been very opposed to having a big entourage, thinking it was pretentious and unnecessary. When she'd interviewed him, she'd explained that, in her many years of performing, without exception, all the big stars she'd known who surrounded themselves with squadrons of bodyguards did so purely for their own egos.

'I've seen them tell people they need to get out of elevators,' she'd explained very seriously, 'so the star they're with can be in there alone. Or male bodyguards going into women's toilets at a club or an awards ceremony, clearing out the place so, you know, the woman they're "protecting" can go in there and do drugs without anyone seeing. Or *their* bodyguards will start fights with someone else's body-guards, because the two of them are feuding. Just . . . stupid. It's showing off, to me, to have lots of people around you. It's not necessary and it makes you look bad. I don't like it.'

But now it was inevitable. She would have to accustom herself to being followed at all times, have a phalanx of guards with her for the rest of the tour, at least. He pulled his phone out of his pocket, texting Catalina's manager, making sure that the CCTV footage was being thoroughly checked, still averting his eyes from her slender golden shape. The lift pinged; she bent down to retrieve his overcoat as the doors slid open, bundling it up, walking swiftly to the big doors of the suite, waiting for him to open them.

'I need to ring security,' he said. 'They must wait with you while I and another of them sweep the suite—'

But Catalina had snatched the key card from his hand, was swiping it and pushing the door open triumphantly.

'No,' she said, walking in. 'No one else. I'll wait in the hall while you check. But I don't want to see anyone else.'

'Catalina—'

'*No one else!*' she almost screamed, stamping her tiny, gold-clad foot, the fringes on her outfit dancing with the movement. And Gerhardt, who already felt that he had almost totally lost control of the situation, didn't have the strength to contradict her when she was so worked up; he had never seen her like this. He looked around swiftly, assessing the foyer, which wasn't secure: it had connecting doors to both the bedroom and the living room sides of the suite. Off it, however, was a gleaming black and marble toilet, and after checking that no one was lurking there in ambush, he took her arm, guided her inside, and told her to lock the door and not come out until she heard his voice.

He swept the living room, the dining room, both with floor-to-ceiling windows with spectacular views over the Tokyo skyline, the dark shape of Mount Fuji looming behind them, just distinguishable behind the glittering lights of the skyscrapers; then the study, the pantry, and beyond them the door that connected to the adjoining suite in which Latisha, presumably, was recovering from food poisoning. Gerhardt locked that door, securing the perimeter for now, and returned through the hallway again, heading from the public to the private area of the Presidential Suite. Into the gigantic bedroom, the adjoining wardrobe room, the rather vulgarly lavish bathroom, with its floors, walls and built-in bath all made from grey-dappled white marble and its fittings of shiny black granite. Lots of cupboards, which meant many more places to search in this part of the suite, but Gerhardt took even longer than he needed to. In fact, he double-checked every built-in cupboard, every set of shelves, every empty suitcase, to the point that an onlooker would have assumed his theory was that Catalina was being stalked by a person of extremely restricted growth.

It was obvious that the twin cupboards bracketing the entrance doors were completely empty: their lights came on as soon as Gerhardt opened them, illuminating the entire interior, making it clear that the very expensive polished wooden hangers were the only occupants. But he still spent a couple of minutes staring inside each one before, reluctantly, closing the cupboards and turning to face the locked door of the toilet.

He drew a deep breath up from his groin, in through his nose, out through his mouth, centring himself. His feet were apart, his hands clasped at his waist, his stance that of a consummate professional. Whatever happened, he was determined to resume the role for which he was paid, and that meant resisting her this time if she made another advance, no matter how seductive she was, how much she insisted . . .

Clearing his throat, he said loudly, 'Catalina, it is safe. You can come out now.'

He heard the lock slide back, saw the handle turn. There was a huge lump in his throat that, despite his best efforts, was suddenly making breathing very difficult. And then she emerged, shaking her hair back from her shoulders, her eyes raised to his, looking straight at him.

God help him, however, he couldn't meet her stare. Because she was now stark naked, and he was made of flesh and bone, and there was no way he could help himself from looking her up and down with a mixture of incredulity and wonder – her tiny little breasts, her concave stomach, the little triangle of tight dark curls . . .

He opened his mouth to say something firm and reproachful, something that would make it clear that she needed to put some clothes on immediately, but not a single word of English came out. Forget English – he couldn't even manage his native German. And then she was right in front of him, her hands on his shoulders, her legs bending lithely, going up on her toes as she jumped up as easily as a ballerina, her thighs wrapping round his waist, as light as thistledown.

Her hair fell around their faces; her mouth found his unerringly.

'Fuck my brains out,' she said against his lips. 'That's what I want, and I'm your boss. I'm *ordering* you to take me to bed and fuck my brains out.'

Somehow she was reaching down, dragging his T-shirt out of his belted trousers, her hands eager on his naked back and stomach, her lips now on his neck, kissing and biting him so enticingly that he heard himself laugh and groan simultaneously. He was walking towards the bedroom, still telling himself that he was just going to drop her on the bed and leave. Passing the walk-in wardrobe, turning right, heading for the king-sized bed, Catalina entwined around him like a spider monkey. His knees bumped against the bed, and she leaned back, still with her legs locked around him, and pulled his T-shirt up and over his head, temporarily blinding him.

He stumbled, and the next thing he knew was that he was tumbling forward, still sightless, falling on top of her, the T-shirt coming off now, her warm, slick, naked, oiled body underneath him. He smelled the scent of that fresh lime perfume they sprayed on her, blended with her own light sweat, and he saw her face, her hair splayed out all around it, her lips swollen from kissing him and her eyes huge and dark, and he let out a long, hopeless sigh of defeat even as he felt her hands at his waist, tugging open his belt, unbuttoning his trousers, reaching for his cock.

'Do you have anything?' she was asking urgently.

'One, in my wallet . . . for emergencies . . .'

Now it was Catalina's turn to laugh.

'This is *definitely* an emergency!' she agreed, his cock now liberated. She was pushing down his trousers, his briefs, already positioning him where she wanted him, spreadeagled below him; he lurched to one side, grabbing his wallet from his trousers, dragging out the condom, his big fingers suddenly clumsy, tearing at the foil wrapper without much success, so that she snatched it from him, whipped off the packaging, and started to roll it onto him, the sensation of her fingertips on his swollen penis so extreme that for a second he saw nothing but blackness as his eyes swivelled right back into his skull.

'Fuck,' he heard himself say, 'fuck, *fuck* . . .'

'Yes, *exactly* . . .'

He managed to kick off his shoes, but not his socks. His trousers and briefs were around his knees, and he got them to his ankles, but no further, because that would have taken more time, too much time, and she was pulling him right onto her, into her, one hand around his cock, directing it inside her, her legs again tight round his waist, her entire body so hot and tight and wet that he heard himself make a crazy noise, almost like a yell of triumph, as he sank fully into her, held it for a glorious moment, pulled back and repeated the amazing, phenomenal, head-blowing sensation that had just overwhelmed him. He held onto the rhythm for dear life, sure that if he didn't stick to it, didn't fuck her with strokes as regular as if a metronome were ticking out the beats per minute, he would lose it completely, come there and then . . .

No, don't think about coming, don't, don't . . .

She was kissing him frantically, her lithe silky tongue in his mouth, her pelvis arching below him, bringing her up at an angle that allowed her to slide one hand to her crotch and start to make herself come.

'Don't stop! Don't stop!' she moaned at him as her hips started jerking, her tight curls rubbing against his; it was as if she were finding the friction, working it to bring her to an even higher climax. 'Oh, fuck, yes, *fuck* . . .'

He was looking down at her, cradling her face in his hands; he saw the exact moment when speech failed her, when the orgasm took over and she could no longer manage a coherent word. From then on, it was just gasps and moans and incoherent screams of pleasure. And it was exactly as he had imagined, secretly, all those times he had seen her videos, back in his hotel room remembering her dancing onstage, when he had finally let his guard down and taken his cock in his hand and closed his eyes and seen her, like this, his cock driving inside her, knowing that she was dripping wet for him and no one else, that when she sang about how wild she was, it was he who would reap the benefits, he who would fuck her so thoroughly that she wouldn't be able to say a word, would barely even remember her own name . . .

It was too much, the realization of this fantasy beyond anything that he had allowed himself to imagine. Catalina seducing him completely, stripping off and ordering him to fuck her, undressing him, dragging him down onto the bed, pulling out his cock and guiding him into her, already hot and wet for him – in all his craziest scenarios, *that* one had never even occurred to him. As he watched her come yet again, her head thrown back, thrashing from side to side, her mouth wide, a stream of wails issuing from her pretty lips, the full realization that it was his cock, him inside her that had caused this transformation, he couldn't hold it back any more, couldn't obey the metronome . . .

His hips rose and plunged faster and faster, a speed that made her positively shriek her head off. It was to an accompaniment of her screams that he let go, shot inside her, feeling as if his entire body were knotting up inexorably at the root of his cock and then, with a glorious rush of heat and fire, exploding in a release that was so extreme that a white light, almost painful in its intensity, shot across his vision.

He didn't remember anything directly after that. He was collapsed, done, as limp as a used condom, a sack of skin and bones. She had drained him completely. Dimly, he sensed her wriggling beneath his weight, and he managed, with his last flicker of energy, to reach down, pull out the condom, tie it up and drop it on the floor. Then he flopped back, feeling her curl into his arms, the mattress and pillows cool and soft and yielding, the sweat drying slowly on his skin.

'So I did a good job, boss?' he said eventually, drowsily, into her hair.

'What?' she mumbled, obviously half-asleep.

'You told me – *ordered* me – to take you to bed and fuck your brains out. Did I perform satisfactorily?'

'Mmm,' she murmured, reaching back and stroking his thigh. 'For now. But get your rest. I'm going to have more orders for you in a little while.'

She was asleep almost immediately, curled up in a ball, snuffling quietly to herself. He craved nothing more than to follow suit, but forced himself instead to clamber off the bed, cover her with a silk-smooth Egyptian cotton sheet and a soft satin-trimmed blanket, and go into the living room to ring Catalina's manager, back at the arena, who reported that, again, there had been no CCTV installed backstage that directly covered the dressing-room door. Gerhardt cursed at this reflexively, but he already knew the bad news: he'd checked out the area automatically as he had walked out of the dressing room, Catalina in his arms.

The good news was that there was a camera further down the corridor. The bad news, the manager promptly informed Gerhardt, was that camera had been manually turned – probably with a mop or broom handle – so that it faced in the opposite direction. And again, neither the staff nor the security cameras at the artists' entrance reported any unauthorized visitors, or even any attempts to access the backstage area.

It was looking, more and more certainly, like an inside job.

And with that thought, Gerhardt returned to the bedroom and retrieved his clothes, turning off the lights. In the hallway, he pulled on his trousers and T-shirt, grimacing at the realization that he was still wearing his socks: he knew that was the worst no-no, a man who kept his socks on during sex. He made a series of phone calls, to the hotel manager, to the agency that had supplied him to Catalina, sorting out the extra security staff he would need from now on. And then he padded through the rest of the suite, unlocking the connecting door with a whisper-quiet snick of metal, turning the handle equally silently, easing it ajar, hearing Latisha's famous snoring almost as soon as the door began to open.

He had a tiny torch on his key ring, and he used it to navigate around the bedroom and into the bathroom. No signs of recent activity, nothing to indicate that Latisha's stomach was still upset, apart from a box of Imodium prominently placed on the marble sink surround.

You can't prove a negative, he thought as he exited the bathroom and conducted a brief, careful sweep of Latisha's bedroom and living room, her regular bubbling snores providing assurance that he was not disturbing her. He wasn't expecting to find an empty red spray can, red marker pens, extra photographs of Catalina like the ones in the dressing room. He was just checking, because that was his job, to make sure, to explore every possibility.

He closed the connecting door once more, the snores still rumbling evenly behind him, and returned to the bedroom, standing there in the dark, looking down at Catalina's sleeping body, shaking his head in disbelief at the events of that evening. He had behaved in a totally unprofessional way. It had been her will against his, and this tiny little slip of a thing had turned out to be as much of a powerhouse offstage as she was on when she wanted to get her way.

'Come back to bed,' her voice said from the darkness.

'I should stay up,' he said, hearing that his voice was more feeble, less determined than hers. She was breaking him, and this was a terrible time for this to happen: the worst, when she was in crisis, when there was a stalker after her.

'I'm *ordering* you to come back to bed,' she said firmly. 'And I'm the boss.'

He *had* made sure that there would be two guards outside the doors of the suite, he told himself as he pulled off his T-shirt, unzipped his trousers and sat down on the edge of the wide mattress to, finally, take off his socks.

'Close the blinds,' she said drowsily, but on this one, at least, he was going to overrule her.

'No,' he said, sliding under the sheet and blanket, taking her in his arms. 'I need to wake with the dawn.'

'*Wake?*' she said, reaching down to touch him where he was already stiffening at being so close to her. 'You think you're going to get any sleep?'

'I don't have more condoms,' Gerhardt said, realizing again that his voice was sounding as weak as his cock was getting firm. No woman had ever had an effect like this on him before, God forbid one who he was working for; this had the potential to swiftly become the most disastrous mess, one that could completely derail the career that he had painstakingly built over more than a decade . . .

'Oh well,' she purred, coming to her knees and straddling him in one quick, lithe movement, bending to kiss him before slowly, tantalizingly, beginning to work her way from his mouth to his neck, his chest, her hands tracing the muscles of his pecs and abdomen. 'I'm sure we can think of *something* to do . . .'

Her hair was trailing over his torso, her tongue tracing wet circles on his skin. Gerhardt groaned and cupped his hands around her head and squeezed his eyes shut against the knowledge that what he was doing was completely wrong, a total dereliction of his professional duty. But right then, God help him, as her mouth closed around him, and he heard a noise come from the back of his throat that sounded dragged up from the centre of his body, deep and guttural, he would pay any price just to live through this moment of pleasure.

Because there would definitely be a price to pay. He wasn't deluded enough, sex-crazed enough, to think that there wouldn't be consequences for crossing the line like this.

But he could not, even then, imagine how high the cost would be.

Chapter Eleven

On-board

I have to go home, Catalina thought with great resolve as the curtain fell shut behind her and she crossed the threshold back into Luxe Class. *Back to my own house. It's time. I have to face it. And Tish shouldn't have to come with me. She's had enough to put up with looking after me like a nursemaid this last few months – she needs to be in her own place too. We'll cancel the hotel booking as soon as we land in LA, and we'll each go back to our own houses.*

Like grown women, not scared little girls hiding out in yet another hotel suite.

She bit her lip, looking very much like the scared little girl she was trying not to act like any more. Home was a mansion on Oriole Way, one of the 'Bird Streets' in the famous enclave in the Hollywood Hills, nicknamed that because all the roads had been given avian names: Blue Jay Way, Nightingale Drive, Bluebird Avenue, Skylark Lane. A short hop to the Sunset Strip, it was also very close to Beverly Hills and the studios, and thus hugely popular with film stars and producers. Catalina had paid more than eight million dollars for her house, with its spectacular views over

175

the city; she had fallen in love with it on sight. And right then, she was dreading the idea of having to return to it.

It was too full of memories, too much empty space, three thousand square feet of white walls and shining walnut floors. Too much floor-to-ceiling glass, through which she could sit in miserable solitude with her superb views of other spectacular, architecturally sleek houses where people were living together, in love, happily settled down, building a future. Too many places where she had once been kissed, been embraced, made love to; where she'd thought that she was finally half of one of those lucky couples who were together, in love, happily settled, with the future stretching out before them as glittering and bright as the lights of the Strip below . . .

But there was no point going back in time. Catalina had made a horrible mistake, but she'd been saved by Latisha's loyalty and smartness before the consequences became truly dire. She was single, but that was better than being with someone who had systematically lied to her and tricked her into falling in love with him. And she would eventually meet someone new, someone she would care about even more than him, impossible though that seemed to her right now. She could not imagine loving anyone more than she had loved Gerhardt. He had filled her heart completely, to brimming point; she had felt, those months they had spent together, as if she were literally spilling over with happiness, like a fountain perpetually bubbling with golden champagne.

She swallowed hard. Enough dwelling on the past. She'd wallowed in it long enough, and it was time for her to stop thinking about it, or at least make a resolution to try to put it behind her. The resolve made her feel marginally better, as if a weight had lifted, even slightly, from her shoulders.

There was a flash of blue uniform in a pod as she passed down the row, a steward talking to a passenger. She knew that one of the flight attendants would be eager to walk her back to her pod, ask her if there was anything she wanted, but all she craved right then was to be left alone. Spoilt as it might seem, one of the downsides of being an A-list celebrity was that service staff found it almost impossible to restrain themselves around you, were always trying to lavish you with attention and unnecessary help.

So Catalina ducked her head and slipped past unseen like a little grey ghost, moving as lightly as a feather down the aisle to her pod at the far end of the row. 1A, the seat number that meant you were the most important traveller on the plane, front and left, nothing ahead of you but a toilet, a shower and the cockpit door.

The bed was made up, the blue blankets pulled tight and smooth over the mattress, hospital corners pleated at a forty-five-degree angle, a fresh eye mask laid out for her on it beside a sealed packet of Pure Air-branded foam earplugs. The crisp white pillows were plumped enticingly; the top sheet, with its navy border, was turned back over the blankets, again at a protractor-sharp forty-five-degree angle. The pod was infused with a soft, glowing blue light and smelt deliciously of honey and lavender. It was such an oasis of calm and peace that it would have made even a raging meth addict pause, feel sleepy, and decide that it might be rather nice to lie down for a few minutes.

There was only one flaw in the near-perfect scene before Catalina: the two large, glossy photographs of her propped up on those plumped bed pillows, each one daubed with the design that she tried very hard not to see when she closed her eyes and went to sleep at night. The big heart, thickly and confidently drawn in red marker pen, framing each image of her, was appallingly familiar by now. And so were those terrifying words inside the heart, both a threat and a promise:

CAT

IS

MINE

However, shocking as the photographs were, they weren't the worst thing laid out on the bed. That was the A4 sheet of paper lying on the blanket, bearing, in the same red marker, a further message, one that might have been specifically calculated to chill every drop of blood in its recipient's body. Catalina took a couple of steps, her legs shaking, and bent over to read the two short sentences written neatly on the paper.

Are you ready to join the mile-high club? It's time.

It sounded as if there were a dog in the pod with her, an exhausted Labrador who had been out in the park for hours, chasing sticks, playing with other dogs, diving into ponds, and had finally collapsed back at home on the hearthrug, panting loudly, its tongue hanging out of its mouth. It took a good few seconds for Catalina to realize that the noise was coming from her. She was puffing like a grampus, her chest pounding frantically, her panic audible. Which meant that someone – her stalker – might be coming up behind her and she wouldn't even realize . . .

She spun around so fast her slippers skidded on the carpet. There was no one behind her.

Kicking off the slippers so she could move faster, she tore out of the pod and back down the aisle, dodging past Angela, who was coming towards her with a tray carrying a champagne glass. Racing back to business class again, jumping over the legs of the very surprised passenger seated next to Latisha, Catalina found a tiny patch of carpet to stand on in front of Latisha's seat, straddling the footrest, leaning down to shake her assistant's shoulders.

'Tish! Tish! It's happened again! He's here! He's on the plane! Tish, wake up!' she panted into Latisha's sleeping face.

'Excuse me, is everything okay?' Latisha's seatmate asked, taking off his headphones, putting down his games console. His words were politely couched, but his tone made it clear that what he was actually saying, in his English way, was, 'What the hell are you doing, crazy lady?'

Catalina was beyond hearing him. She was too desperately occupied in trying to rouse Latisha. Unfortunately, she knew how deeply Latisha went under on a Zopiclone. Taking Latisha's face in her hands, she hissed at her, 'Tish! Tish, *wake up*! Please, wake up! I need you!'

'Look, do you even *know* this lady?' the passenger beside Latisha was asking. 'What's happening? This is *not* okay!'

'She's my assistant,' Catalina managed to say. 'I need her, I need her to *wake up now* . . .'

Latisha's teeth were rattling in her head. Catalina was

practically banging it against the pillow, frantic with her insistence that Latisha return to consciousness. Latisha's snores had stopped: her eyelids were flickering, her full lips parted as she slurred out, 'Whaaa . . . Whaaa . . .'

'You really shouldn't be bashing her head like that!'

The passenger sitting beside Latisha was deeply concerned now. He reached for the great catch-all phrase that people use nowadays as a socially acceptable way to criticize another's behaviour.

'It's not appropriate,' he said firmly. 'I'm calling a flight attendant.'

He reached up to press the call bell above him. However, Catalina, hugely encouraged by seeing the whites of Latisha's eyes as her eyelids blinked, paid him no attention, redoubling her efforts to shake her assistant awake; it was no wonder that when the flight attendant arrived, he was very taken aback to see the person he immediately recognized as the flight's most prestigious celebrity passenger apparently assaulting a moaning, sleeping woman.

'Sir, could I ask you to stand up for a moment?' he asked the passenger, who was already unbuckling his seat belt and swinging himself out into the aisle, commenting with a roll of his eyes:

'Please, be my guest. If I wanted to be around crazy women I'd still be with my ex-girlfriend.'

The steward cast the passenger an approving sideways glance at this quip as he bent down to click back the footrest, the ceiling of the LuxeLiner so high that he could almost fully stand up as he edged towards Catalina.

'Miss, um, Catalina!' he whispered to her, careful to be

discreet about her identity. 'My name's Greg, and it's a pleasure to meet you. *Such* a fan. Can I help at all? What seems to be the problem? And could I *please* ask you to stop banging this lady's head against her pillow?'

'I need her to wake up!' Catalina practically sobbed. 'I'm so scared! I'm being stalked, he's *on the plane with me* and Latisha knows about it . . .'

Greg reached out, covered Catalina's hands with his own, and gently detached them from Latisha's scalp.

'Whaa?' Latisha was mumbling. 'Whaa . . . hooo?'

'Oh God, she's drooling. That's not good,' Greg said, recoiling as he looked down at her. 'You made her drool.'

'She's taken a sleeping pill,' Catalina explained hurriedly. 'But I need her to wake up—'

'Oh, what's she taken?' Greg asked, with the immediate interest of a travel professional.

'A Zopiclone. But I'm being st—'

'A Zopi? And she took it recently?' Greg sucked in his breath noisily between his teeth and shook his head. 'Trust me, from experience,' he said with great conviction, 'there's no way she'll come to for at *least* a couple more hours. That stuff is the *best*.'

He loosened one hand, gingerly lifted a corner of Latisha's scarf, and dabbed at her mouth.

'Can't leave her all dribbly,' he said in parentheses. By dint of twisting himself round like a contortionist in front of Latisha's sleeping body, he managed to get Catalina to look at him.

'Excuse me, um, Miss . . .'

He hesitated. Catalina's iconic, first-name-only status

meant that it was always difficult for people to know how to address her. Under normal circumstances, she would smile and say, 'Call me Catalina, please,' but she was far beyond normal now; was, in fact, shaking from head to toe with the frustration of not being able to rouse Latisha.

'Miss Catalina,' he managed *sotto voce*. 'I'm sure you don't want other passengers recognizing you, do you? Everyone's looking, but they might not know who you are yet, and it wouldn't be good publicity, would it? People might already have started taking pictures or videos. That happens all the time now. It's a total nightmare, frankly.'

He darted a look around him.

'I tell you what. Let's get you back to Luxe pronto, shall we? And once we've got you safely there . . .'

Holding both of Catalina's hands once again, Greg started to guide her out of the bulkhead area, picking his way back to the aisle over the dangling wires of the games console, deftly turning Catalina so that her face was averted from the rest of the cabin.

'. . . I'll keep a *keen* eye on her – Latisha, right? – and as *soon* as she comes to, I'll pop into Luxe and let you know. How's that? Honestly,' he said in a confidential tone, 'there's simply *no* point going *near* her if she took a Zopi less than two hours ago. She's like a zombie right now. Did she have any wine with it?'

'A glass of champagne, at the launch,' Catalina said, reluctantly following him, realizing that Latisha was beyond waking up then and there. 'And one on-board. Then she had some water, though . . . two big glasses . . .'

Greg sucked air between his teeth again.

'Ooh, champagne would explain the drooling,' he said knowledgeably. 'Yes, let's definitely give it at least an hour. I promise, just as *soon* as I see *any* signs of life, I'll pop right up to your super-comfy pod – gorge, aren't they? – and let you know, so you can come and have a word with her. Okay, let's get you back there right now, shall we?'

The passenger was standing in the aisle, and both Greg and Catalina had to manoeuvre past him; Greg let go of one of her hands, and as he did so, she turned to look back at Latisha. She was hoping against hope that Greg was wrong, and that after all Catalina's efforts to wake her, Latisha would be stirring. Greg, however, worried that Catalina was going to throw herself upon Latisha and start shaking her again, tugged harder on her hand, swivelling her back around. And as she did, she caught sight of the other side of the cabin.

What – *who* – Catalina saw there absolutely paralyzed her. She felt ice-cold sweat spring out over her entire body as she stopped dead, staring in horror along the row at the man sitting on the far side of the cabin, in front of the bulkhead, occupying the equivalent seat to Latisha's game-playing companion. But Greg, by now desperate to get his famous charge back to the Luxe cabin before she was recognized, was positively dragging on her hand. She weighed so little that he was able to physically jerk her off her feet, pulling her into a stumbling run behind him, safely back through the gap she had left in the cobalt curtains.

'Oh, thank goodness!' he muttered as he spotted Lucinda. Signalling the cabin service director over to a discreet area by the main airline door, he was careful to position his body so that he concealed Catalina's small frame as much as possible from any interested viewers in the bar area.

'Lucinda,' he started as she reached then, 'we have *quite* the situation with Miss . . . Catalina – what do I call her? *Anyhoo*, she's been in business class trying to wake up her assistant, positively whacking the poor girl's head against her pillow. It was *beyond* dramatic, frankly, everyone looking over – I don't think they recognized her though, I got her out of there as quickly as I could . . .'

Despite his stream of words, he was succeeding beautifully in the essential task of cabin crew: delivering disturbing news to a colleague in public while keeping a bright smile on his face and his voice hushed. Equally, Lucinda absorbed this information without her smoothly composed expression altering in any way.

'The assistant's taken a Zopi,' Greg explained, 'so she's completely zonked out, and she actually started to *dribble* when she' – he nodded at Catalina – 'was shaking her.' He rolled his eyes. 'I wiped it up,' he added.

'I needed her to wake up,' Catalina said, now in a dull zombie voice. 'I need Tish.'

Her back to the door, hemmed in by the two blue-uniformed flight attendants, smaller than both of them, all Catalina could see was the cobalt of their jackets, the pale blue and coral print of Lucinda's perfectly knotted silk scarf and Greg's jaunty tie. But before her eyes was dancing the image of Gerhardt, staring back at her from the far side of the business-class cabin.

It had taken her a split second to recognize him, because he was dressed so differently to how she was used to seeing him: no black clothes, no workout gear. Instead, he looked so conventionally American that she had done a double take before she realized that it was unquestionably Gerhardt, wearing what Americans called a sports jacket over a blue chambray shirt, striped tie and chinos. On first glance he looked like a business traveller, though the breadth of his shoulders, the swell of his well-defined chest and arms, made that category less likely; noticing his buzz-cut hair and strong jaw, an observer who had originally made the first assumption would have modified it to ex-athlete, possibly turned professional sports commenter for an American TV channel.

But it was definitely Gerhardt. Catalina would have known him anywhere. Her mouth had gaped open in shock. Even after the discovery of the photographs and note, even after having told Latisha that he was on-board, this confirmation of her worst fears was sickening. Gerhardt, who had let her down so badly, who had tricked her, pretending to be a stalker so that she would be terrified enough to fall into his arms. Or maybe he truly *had* been a stalker, one who had got what he wanted way more easily than he had planned. She had positively thrown herself at him; he hadn't even needed to lift a finger to try to seduce her.

And the worst part of all was that when she had found out what he had done, Catalina had not only resisted believing it, she had wondered, for the most shaming moment, whether it even mattered. She and Gerhardt were blissfully, over-whelmingly happy: he had moved into the Oriole Way house, they were madly in love, unable to keep their hands off each other, planning the rest of their lives. Everything you dreamed of when you were single and lonely – everything you pictured to comfort yourself before falling asleep, promising yourself that some day you too would have a lover, a happy home, a secure future – that was what she had found with Gerhardt.

Even knowing what he had done, how cruelly he had deceived her, there had been such entreaty and wistfulness and love in his silvery eyes as he gazed at her from his seat that her first impulse was not to run from, but towards him. To jump on his lap, as she had always loved to do, to curl up in his arms and kiss him over and over, pretend that nothing bad had ever happened between them. Tease him about the stupid jacket and tie he was, for some reason, wearing. Pretend that he had never stalked her, that he hadn't somehow got into Luxe Class and left that terrifying note for her in her pod – how had he *done* that? Had he bribed a flight attendant? But would one of them really have risked their job like that, even for a lot of money?

A few minutes ago, Catalina had been telling herself that she needed to move on, leave the past behind her. Get over him. But now she had seen him again, she knew that nothing had changed. And that was the most humiliating revelation of all. She knew that he had stalked her – was *still* stalking her! – and she was stupidly, masochistically insane enough to remain hopelessly in love with the man who had frightened her so badly, put her through such emotional hell.

I'm going mad, she thought, pressing her hands to the side of her head. *I'm going completely mad. I'm beyond fucked up!*

How can I still be in love with my stalker? How can I feel like this after everything he's done to hurt me?

What's wrong with me?

'Let's get her back to her pod,' Lucinda said, looking in concern at Catalina's hands clamped to her temples. 'Thanks, Greg. I won't forget this.'

'Oh please, not at *all*,' Greg said, breaking into a blissful smile: every cabin crew member on Pure Air dreamed of hearing these words from the famously strict cabin service director. 'I'll let you know the *instant* her assistant wakes up.'

Lucinda swivelled away from Catalina, saying very softly to Greg, 'Make sure you talk to her discreetly before you bring her up here. Tell her about the freak-out, so she can decide how to handle it. If *she* –' her head tilted infinitesimally towards Catalina – 'makes a habit of throwing this kind of wobbly, no one'll know better what to do than her assistant.'

Greg nodded, pivoted and walked swiftly back to his cabin, such a bounce in his step he might have had springs in the heels of his perfectly polished shoes.

'He's there. In business class,' Catalina said, looking at Lucinda, still in the zombie voice. 'He's there.'

'Of course, that's his cabin,' said Lucinda reassuringly, assuming that Catalina was referring to Greg.

She took Catalina's arm in the lightest and most subtle of grasps.

'Right, let's get you back to your pod,' she said, walking Catalina back through the bar, deftly positioning herself between her charge and the rest of the room.

Lucinda had had aeons of experience in dealing with passengers who acted out on-board. In air rage trials, expensive lawyers would explain it away as 'an adverse reaction to their prescription medications', or 'an anti-histamine allergy of which they had not previously been aware', but in practice it was almost always caused by vast amounts of alcohol in combination with other substances. The excuse Peter Buck, of the band REM, had given at his air rage trial for trying to open a door mid-air, announcing that he was 'going home', and then upending a trolley, sending crockery flying, was that a sleeping pill had reacted with the fifteen glasses of wine he had drunk on the Seattle to London flight. Ian Brown, of the Stone Roses, had been jailed for two months for threatening to cut off a flight attendant's hands, while Liam Gallagher was banned from life from Cathay Pacific after throwing food at fellow passengers.

Lucinda hadn't been on any of those flights, but she had dealt with her fair share of threats, abuse and drink-fuelled behaviour from passengers. Her training was to avoid escalation at all costs: the ideal result would be to get Catalina tucked into bed without anyone noticing and pretend that this entire, bizarre incident had never taken place.

Catalina was saying something about her pod. Lucinda pressed forward, smiling brightly, feeling Catalina's footsteps slow as they neared it.

'We'll get you settled and cosy,' she said, just as she would to a recalcitrant child. 'All tucked up nicely, maybe with some camomile tea, so you can get your rest . . .'

'You'll see!' Catalina said more loudly, an edge to her voice now that set Lucinda's warning bells ringing. 'You'll see . . . it's in there! What he left me! It's on my bed!'

It was with great relief that Lucinda got her charge into

the pod, guiding her to sit down on the mattress. The interior was pristine, she noticed. Catalina hadn't got into bed yet; it looked as if she hadn't even entered the pod since it had been made up.

'They're not here! The photos!' Catalina was staring at the pillows for some reason. 'The note!' She turned back to Lucinda, her dark eyes huge and liquid. 'There were photos here, of me! And a note about joining the mile-high club! They were here, and now they're not! Someone put them on my bed and then took them away again!'

Drunk and aggressive, Lucinda recognized. Incoherent on pills and booze, ditto. But she was actually beginning to think that this situation was neither one of those. Americans had a great phrase for this: 'beyond her pay grade'. Catalina didn't seem as if she was medicated at all, she hadn't drunk a drop of alcohol from the bar, and she certainly didn't seem the type to have brought her own alcohol on-board. The impression Lucinda was getting from her was pure, unadulterated crazy.

She seems so together in all her interviews, really nice and sensible and down to earth, Lucinda thought, the smile still plastered on her face. *God, you really never can tell with a famous person, can you? I always say to people they shouldn't believe a word they read in the papers. You really never know what a celeb's like till you've seen them up close and personal.*

'Well,' she said, choosing her words carefully, 'if there was anything here that upset you, it's gone now, which is a relief, isn't it? Shall I help get you into bed?'

'No! No, I don't want to lie down!'

Catalina gripped Lucinda's hand, her grasp so strong that Lucinda winced.

'You don't understand,' she panted. 'I have to explain . . . I had this stalker, and I was in a relationship with him, and then I broke up with him, but now he's on the plane! I saw him in business class just now when I went back . . . he's *on the plane*! He must have sneaked in and left me the photos and the note, then taken them away again – that's why they're not here any more. He must have come back here while I was trying to wake up Tish . . .'

Lucinda was shaking her head firmly.

'I can assure you, we run a very tight ship with our security,' she said to Catalina, trying not to pull a face at the pain of Catalina's tight clasp, plus the fact that her rings were sinking into Lucinda's fingers. 'Absolutely no business-class passenger could get through into Luxe Class without one of us spotting them and making sure that they went straight back where they belonged. The bar's staffed the whole time, and the attendant isn't just stationed there to mix drinks – they have a perfect view of both sides of the plane. It's simply not possible that anyone could have come in once, let alone twice – and managed to get all the way up this aisle to your pod! It's never happened in my entire experience of running a first-class cabin.'

The complete conviction of Lucinda's voice had a distinct impact on Catalina. To the cabin service director's great relief, Catalina loosened her grip, her hand falling back into her lap, where it met the other one, twisting convulsively around each other like snakes in a bowl. But her next words demonstrated that Lucinda's reassurance had not achieved its desired effect.

'He must have an accomplice,' she whispered, staring down at the snakes. 'He must have someone helping him in Luxe Class.'

'Is everything okay?' Jane Browne appeared just behind Lucinda, at the entrance to the pod. 'Well, I mean' – she cleared her throat – 'um, obviously it isn't. I saw Catalina shoot off before, and she sounded a bit funny in the aisle just now . . .'

She took in the sight of Catalina slumped on her bed with Lucinda standing over her.

'Is there anything I can do to help?' she asked, glancing at Lucinda. 'Do please tell me if I'm not wanted.'

But Catalina was lifting her head now, looking at Jane as if she were her saviour. Jane was an Oscar-nominated actress, travelling to Los Angeles for the awards ceremony: even Catalina's increasingly paranoid imaginings couldn't slot Jane Browne into some kind of conspiracy with Gerhardt. If there was anyone on the LuxeLiner who was surely trustworthy, it had to be Jane. She reached out to her, and Jane squeezed past Lucinda and sat down on the bed, taking Catalina's out-stretched hands.

'What's going on, darling?' she said, her British accent sounding very crisp and reassuring to Catalina. 'You look like you've had a really nasty shock. What on earth's been upsetting you?'

Catalina opened her mouth, staring at Jane's nice, normal face, now pulled, with Jane's extraordinary, rubbery facility for facial contortions, into a perfect expression of concern and sympathy. Catalina had no idea what she was going to say, but she was determined not to burst into tears, and she swallowed hard to get control over herself. The words that eventually came out were, 'Will you come back to business class with me?'

Jane furrowed her forehead.

'Of course I will if you need me to,' she said, glancing up at Lucinda, perplexed. 'But could you tell me why?'

'There's someone there . . .' Catalina drew a long breath. 'He used to be my bodyguard, but he stalked me, and I had to sack him. I just saw him on the plane.'

The few wisps of sanity remaining to Catalina were telling her not to mention the photographs and the note. Lucinda had been visibly incredulous at the idea that they had first been sneaked into the pod and then, equally surreptitiously, removed, and Catalina couldn't prove that they had ever been there. She should have stayed by the bed when she saw them, rung for the flight attendants immediately. But sheer panic had sent her fleeing to find Latisha, and now it was too late: whoever had been adroit enough to pull that vanishing act would have the photos and note well hidden somewhere.

However, Gerhardt's presence would be undeniable proof that something was very odd on this flight. Catalina could point him out and, at the very least, the cabin crew could make sure he was watched, that he couldn't get any closer to her than he was now. This conviction made her rise to her feet, still holding Jane's hand, pulling Jane insistently to follow suit.

'This sounds awful!' Jane was saying as she stood up, sounding genuinely disturbed by Catalina's revelation. 'But if he's been stalking you, are you sure you want to go back and see him? Wouldn't you rather stay here where you're nice and safe and he can't get to you?'

'No, no,' Catalina said, trying to sound calm. 'I need to show you – to show *everyone* – where he is. Please, will you come? You too?' she asked Lucinda. 'When Tish wakes up, she'll say it's him too . . . but in the meantime you'll know, so you won't let him near me . . .'

Catalina was pleading frantically, aware that she sounded more than a little unbalanced. But she had a very powerful reason for trying to convince the two women to come with her: she was fighting her instincts with every ounce of determination she had. Her desperation that Jane and Lucinda should see Gerhardt for themselves was so that she could set up an unbreakable barrier between him and her. Because the best way to prevent herself from running back to Gerhardt and telling him she still loved him was to indicate her stalker in front of witnesses, so that shame would block her from being weak and foolish enough to go near him again.

Lucinda thought quickly and came to a decision.

'If you think it'll settle you down,' she said to Catalina, 'I'm very happy to take a quick look at the gentleman in question. Which seat did you say he was in?'

'The first row after the toilets,' Catalina said, swallowing hard again. 'Opposite to where Tish is. I can't be too close to him, though – we have to walk in on Tish's side –'

'Well, off we go then!' Lucinda said briskly. 'I'll be with you, and Miss Browne is being so kind as to come too, so you'll know you're quite safe and secure with us. We definitely want to put your mind at rest.'

Michael Coggin-Carr, across the aisle from Catalina, was sitting on his bed, his iPad in his lap, but with an air of being more aware of the goings-on in Catalina's pod than what was happening on its screen. His head turned to follow the three women with understandable curiosity as they passed, obviously aware that something unusual was taking place. Jane caught his eye for a moment and found herself pulling a face that conveyed gratitude for his tact in not coming over to see what was wrong; he responded by shrugging and smiling, as if to say that he knew it was none of his business.

Goodness, he's nice, Jane thought thankfully. *Not pushy at all. Thank goodness for that – the last thing we'd need with Catalina all wound up like this would be some man coming in trying to tell us all what to do . . .*

Lucinda preceded them along the aisle and through the bar, holding back the curtain for Catalina and Jane. The man sitting next to Latisha looked up instantly: after Catalina's recent incursion, he was now sensitized to the movement of the curtain. On seeing Catalina, he resignedly put down his console and took out his headphones, assuming he would have to move again, but was taken aback when the group promptly turned their backs to him. The three women clustered in the aisle next to his seat, but they were looking over at the far side of the cabin.

'Which one is he?' Jane asked softly, but Catalina was already gasping and clutching Jane's arm.

'He's not there!' she wailed. 'He's not there any more!'

Lucinda, in front of Jane, let out a sigh that only Jane could hear.

'Where was he sitting?' she asked neutrally.

'That seat, there!'

Catalina was pointing to the aisle seat of the pair beside the far window, in which was sitting a solidly built black man in a businessman's garb: suit, shirt and tie. Her gesture caught his eye and, briefly, he glanced up at the group of women. Then, not seeming to recognize either Catalina or Jane, his gaze returned to the newspaper he was holding.

Drinks had already been served in business class, and now the dinner service was taking place. Latisha was still fast asleep, but the passenger beside her was now avidly watching the latest instalment of the drama, as were the people in the front two rows. Lucinda had corralled Catalina behind her, however, discreetly protecting her as much as possible from view, and the singer was barely visible.

'14E,' Lucinda observed neutrally.

'Yes! But it's not him anymore! He's tall and white! That guy's completely different – they must have changed places!'

Catalina's voice was rising, becoming hysterical again. Greg, serving from the food trolley further down the aisle, was alert enough to realize something unusual was going on behind him; he swivelled around, took in the sight and came bustling up to them swiftly.

'Can I help?' he started, keen as always to impress Lucinda. She cut through him, saying quickly:

'Greg, 14E – has he changed seats with anyone during the flight?'

Greg looked over swiftly, took a breath, his eyes flickering, and said, 'No. No, that's the passenger who's always been seated there.'

Catalina promptly collapsed, her legs crumpling underneath her. Jane, who was still holding her hand, managed, with impressively swift reflexes, to dart her other arm around Catalina's narrow back, catch her in mid-fall and haul her up to her feet, supporting her entire weight for a few moments. Then Lucinda's own reflexes kicked in, and she snaked her arm underneath Catalina's shoulders, balancing out Jane's efforts. As one, Lucinda and Jane turned away, heading back to Luxe Class without another word, pretty much carrying a slumped Catalina between them.

'I called it, eh?' said the passenger beside Latisha to Greg. 'Crazy lady!'

He raised his hand and twirled a finger at his right temple. Greg gave him a glance whose meaning was quite indecipherable, paused for a beat as if unsure about which direction to take, and eventually pivoted to rejoin the other flight attendant who was staffing the dinner trolley.

Waiting back in the Luxe Class bar was Vanessa, who had added a wrap cardigan over her chiffon blouse. Somehow, Lucinda thought, managing not to flinch, this made her ensemble look even worse. Previously, the blouse had at least hung loosely around her torso and hips, but the narrow knitted belt of the cardigan cut awkwardly into her waist, emphasizing the bulges above and below. The irony, Lucinda reflected, was that Vanessa, in the year since she had been publicity director of Pure Air, had spearheaded a huge push to have the airline sponsor up-and-coming fashion designers, fly the latest Instagram-famous models to resorts to promote

Pure Air Getaways, was always fussing at Lord Tony to commission suits from Richard James and Ozwald Boateng.

And yet the poor thing just can't take her own advice and dress herself properly! She always looks like a pudding in a flowery sack!

But not a flicker of this sartorial judgement passed across Lucinda's face as Vanessa bustled over to the small group.

'Lucinda! Karl's been telling me – what on *earth . . .*' she began, but then shook her head, clearly reproving herself for saying anything in public. She jerked her head, indicating that they should go back to Catalina's pod.

As Lucinda and Jane followed, Catalina wedged between them, Danny Zasio strolled into the bar, a man on a mission. His blue eyes were narrowed, he was ruffling his hair, and his shirt was half-unbuttoned, his gold chest hair visibly sweaty. He glanced only momentarily at the three women, focusing on Lucinda's blue uniform, checking out her face and clearly not finding what he wanted there; Lucinda noticed with satisfaction that the pill she had slipped Danny had clearly taken effect. He looked both half-drunk and high.

During the time that Catalina's pod had been unoccupied, the photographs and note had not been returned. The bed was pristine, the blanket smooth. Catalina was so thoroughly exhausted by this time that she allowed Jane and Lucinda to put her into bed, fully clothed, and pull up the bedclothes to tuck her in. She had not said a word since her collapse, and, as they settled her back against the pillows, she lay there in continued silence, staring ahead of her at the blank flat TV screen.

'Mmm, a nice pot of tea, I think, Lucinda,' Vanessa said,

surveying Catalina's near-comatose state. 'With milk and sugar. I'll sit with her for a while.'

She pulled down the folding leather seat beside the bed and settled in it comfortably.

'Actually, make that two pots of tea,' she corrected herself. 'I could do with some too. And shortbread. You can catch me up later on all the ins and outs, but let's see if she'll have a cup of tea and a biccie first.'

Lucinda nodded and glided away. Jane, feeling surplus to requirements, said tentatively, 'I suppose I'll go and get some rest myself, if you're going to sit with her . . .'

Vanessa smiled widely at her.

'Thanks for your help,' she said. 'Really, this wasn't what you signed up for at all, was it?'

'Oh, it's fine!' Jane said. 'She's such a nice person. I just hope she . . .' – she pulled an expressive face – 'gets help,' she finished.

Vanessa winced.

'Honestly!' she said, 'When I was sorting all this out with your publicist months ago, and we were talking about the nice Oscar tie-in, having you and her on this flight together, both of you nominated for the awards . . . well, who'd have thought you and I'd find ourselves having to look after her, eh?'

Jane, not knowing what to say, smiled politely and slipped back to her pod. Wound up, unable to think about sleeping, she nevertheless climbed into bed. Beside her on the desk was the Pure Air inflight magazine she had been reading with the lovely, smiling picture of Catalina on the cover; Jane stared down at it. Unusually, for an actress with such a vividly mobile face, no one observing her would have been able to read the expression that played across her features as she propped the magazine against her knees and looked thoughtfully down at the photograph.

Chapter Twelve

Fourteen months ago

'Pull! Pull! You have two chin-ups to go!'

'I can't!' Jane wailed, hanging from the wobbling bar. 'I *can't!*'

'Don't drop! Don't you dare!' her coach, below her, yelled menacingly. 'If you drop, I'll make you get right up again!'

'I'm slipping!'

'Oh, for fuck's sake!'

Her coach grabbed Jane firmly round her thighs, lifting her fractionally, just enough so that the hands tightly gripping the bar could close around it again more securely: the chalk Jane had rubbed into them some minutes ago to help her grip was now thoroughly sweated off.

'Right, no excuses now!' the inexorable voice commanded. 'Two chin-ups! I want to see that chin hit the bar both times!'

Jane breathed in deeply and, with a guttural grunt, managed to engage her back and shoulders, her biceps swelling as she hauled herself barely high enough to satisfy her coach. She didn't touch her chin to the bar, but her nose was level with it for a split second before she sank back again. To her great relief, she felt firm hands clasp around her ankles, giving her some desperately needed support. Breathing in again, she grunted even louder and managed one final heave of her exhausted body.

'And *drop!*' her coach said cheerfully as Jane's feet landed on the crash mat below, followed almost immediately afterwards by the rest of her. She lay there, panting, arms thrown wide, her chest heaving, her sweaty body sticking to the plastic mat.

'You are *so* not in shape!' Simone, her coach, observed, looking down at her with a mixture of amusement and disbelief in her big brown eyes. 'Honestly, I had no idea what I was getting into. I mean, people I coach usually have *some* basic level of fitness.'

Simone was from New Zealand, which meant these last words came out as 'livil of fitnuss'. Jane, always working on her pronunciations for possible future jobs, couldn't help mouthing them back to herself.

'Are you copying my accent again?' Simone said menacingly.

'No, I'm not copying your iccent,' Jane said, and was rewarded with a kick to her shin from Simone's bare foot.

'Come on, get up, you lazy bitch!' Simone said severely. 'I'm being paid double my normal rate to train you and if you turn up on set as pathetic as a limp noodle, I'll have to give the money back.'

'I *feel* as pathetic as a limp noodle,' Jane said, managing, painfully, to get her legs under her. Slowly she hauled herself to standing again.

'I thought all actresses worked out,' Simone said. 'You always see them in magazines going to Pilates or yoga classes.'

'Yeah, those are the ones in LA who call the paparazzi to

show off that they're working out,' Jane said ironically. 'Most of us just don't eat much.'

'That's terrible,' Simone said, shaking her head in extreme disapproval.

Simone had masses of thick dark hair from her mixed Italian and Greek origins, but even with a vigorous head-shake, her heavy locks didn't move at all: they were wound and pinned into what she called 'trapeze horns', two tight little buns on the top of her skull, where they couldn't get caught on anything. Everything about Simone was stream-lined. She had the classic performer's body, fine-boned, the muscles very defined but long and lean, trained to minimize bulk. When you climbed ropes or fabric, or balanced on a trapeze every day of your life, you needed your body to be as aerodynamic and sleek as possible. Every extra pound counted when you were supporting your entire body weight on one arm, high in the air.

'But you work out so much, Simone,' Jane said, admiring her coach's muscle tone. 'You can eat whatever you want, right?'

'Wrong,' Simone said firmly. 'I stick to protein and vege-tables, mostly. Tofu, chicken, stir-fries. But lots of it – I don't believe in starving yourself.'

'I know a girl in LA on Adderall who doesn't actually eat at all,' Jane said, cunningly engaging Simone on a subject about which she knew her coach was passionate. That way Jane could avoid, for as long as possible, having to get back on the trapeze bar. 'It's amazing how people can survive on literally nothing and still do two hours of spin a day. Well, not *quite* nothing, to be fair. She'd have a boiled egg in the morning and one in the evening, plus lots of Diet Red Bull. Mind you, she did faint on set quite regularly.'

Simone shook her head again.

'Ridiculous,' she said.

'It's just part of being an actress,' Jane shrugged. 'If you're not naturally thin like me, it's hell on earth. I'm lucky, but I still have to be very careful what I eat. You honestly can't be too thin for some producers.'

'Ugh!' Simone levelled a firm gaze on her student. 'Well, you'll have to forget about that for now. I'm being paid stupid amounts of money to get you muscly and strong, not just skinny. Your arms are going to have to look like mine in a month.'

Grinning evilly, she flexed her right arm; every muscle was perfectly, elegantly defined. Jane stuck out her own arm and stared at it gloomily; it was positively soggy by comparison.

'I should just have stuck to period films,' she said dispiritedly. 'You actually can't have visible muscle for those. Unless you're playing a cook. Cooks had really big arms back then. All the kneading.'

'Whatever,' Simone said. 'Come on, rope climbing. Three times, and I want to hear you hit the ceiling each time. And if you whinge, I'll make you do it with a weights jacket on.'

Jane's expression of unmitigated horror was so extreme that Simone burst out laughing even as she waved Jane over to the rope. They were in a trapeze studio behind Old Street, a warehouse-heavy part of London that had recently become very fashionable: the area around the Tube station was known as Silicon Roundabout because of all the tech start-ups based there. Circus Space, the training school for amateur and professional performers, had been situated just along the road from the station for over a decade, but it was by no means the only studio that had chosen this location because the high ceilings were perfect for rigging trapeze bars and fabric hangs. It was a typical rehearsal space – white paint peeling off the walls, the high windows dirty and smeared with pigeon droppings – but Jane could only be grateful for the latter, as it meant that the trendy Millennials in what was probably yet another tech start-up across the street couldn't peer in and see how hopeless she was at all these physical challenges.

Groaning, she walked over to the rope, bending down to rub her palms in the chalk box on the way. She actually didn't mind the rope that much: once you knew the trick, climbing it was quite satisfying. But she had the theory that if she grumped about everything, she would wear down Simone, who would go easier on her. So far it didn't seem to be working, but Jane was optimistic by nature.

She took the rope in her right hand and wrapped it around her right ankle, as Simone had taught her, in a loop that passed under the arch of the foot. Finishing the twist, she reached up and tugged hard, lifting herself up. Effectively she was now standing on the rope beneath her foot, pulled taut. Then, her arms taking her weight, she kicked out her right leg, shook the rope loose, and wound her foot around it again, making a higher step that she could stand on once more. It was that simple: you just kept repeating those two steps, pulling up with your arms, rewrapping and stepping up with your foot. The ceiling wasn't that high, maybe twelve feet, and, as instructed, Jane slapped it with her palm before she started back down again.

'Yeah, baby!' Simone whooped happily. 'Spank that ceiling! Show it who's boss!'

Giggling, Jane started down again, careful not to descend too fast and give herself rope burn. The first ascent was deceptively easy, the second manageable, and the third was when the pain kicked in. Every upwards pull burnt down her biceps to her trapezius muscles and her lats; her back ached, and her palms felt as raw and slippery as if they were bleeding.

She reached the ceiling, slapping it so weakly that Simone yelled: 'Come on, bitch, call that a spank? Doesn't count if I can't hear it!'

'Aaah! I can't!'

Jane honestly thought that if she took her hand off the rope again, she'd never get back down. And getting back down was always harder than climbing up for some reason. You were more tired, yes, but it was also that lowering yourself seemed to strain the body harder; require more muscle control to hold yourself in that moment of suspension as you felt frantically for the swinging rope below you, tried desperately to hook your ankle round it and get the loop tight around your foot so it would mercifully take your weight once more and stop your arms feeling as if they were being wrenched out of the sockets.

The temptation to slide down, letting the rope run through her palms, taking the pain of rope burn as a return for feeling solid ground beneath her feet again, was huge. Rope burn was awful, but it meant that there would be literally no aerial training for Jane for maybe a couple of days until her hands recovered, which would almost be worth it . . .

Jane wavered. She had a sudden memory of Robin the Frog from *The Muppet Show*, singing about being halfway down the stairs.

'*I'm not at the bottom, I'm not at the top, so this is the stair where I always stop*,' she heard herself sing, her voice, trained from drama school, thin but in tune.

'What are you *doing*?' Simone put her hands on her hips, her head tilted back, looking up at Jane. 'Are you *singing*? Now I've really seen it all. Just sitting there on the rope, *singing*. You're a fucking loony tune.'

Jane started giggling.

'*Halfway down the stairs is a stair where I sit – There isn't any other stair quite like it*,' she warbled.

The rope around her instep was cutting off her circulation; she couldn't feel that foot any more. The blisters on her palms felt like they were growing blisters of their own. Sweat was dripping down the small of her back. She was clammy, and she had the strong feeling that her Green People Natural Aloe Vera deodorant had stopped being efficacious at least half an hour ago. And yet, the sight of Simone's incredulous face, the insults tripping so easily off her tongue in her New Zealand accent (or, as Simone would put it, New Zillind iccint), just made her want to smile.

'I'm stuck,' she said feebly. 'I really am stuck this time.'

She thought Simone would let loose with another stream of insults, tell her to get down on her own or die trying. But instead she nodded.

'Your legs are trembling,' Simone observed, walking right

up to the rope. 'And we don't want to skin your palms. Okay, here's what you do – let go with one hand at a time and reach down to my shoulders.'

Jane let go of the left first, gripping Simone's narrow, bony shoulder; this threw her so off balance that the right hand landed awkwardly, Jane's body twisting as her leg, still wrapped in the rope, swung out behind her. Simone had to grip her tightly under the arms, her strong hands biting into Jane's upper ribs, saying, 'Unwrap your foot! Quick now!'

Jane thrashed around like a fish with a hook in its mouth, flailing her right leg through the air. By the time it came free, Simone had lowered her client to the ground, taking Jane's weight seemingly effortlessly. Jane hopped around idiotically as the last coil of rope fell from her ankle, still supported by her hands on Simone's shoulders.

'You shouldn't be playing a flyer,' Simone said, unable to repress a smile at Jane's clumsy antics. 'Fuck knows what they were thinking! They should have cast you as a circus clown!'

Simone's skin was smooth and light golden brown from her Mediterranean heritage, as if she had a permanent tan. Her big dark eyes were outlined with black liner that flicked up at the outer corners, her brows dark and defined, her lips rose-red.

Jane's face had never been so close to Simone's before. She blurted out: 'Your make-up's so good! How do you keep it on when you work out? I'm dripping! I mean, I don't wear much anyway, but your eyeliner looks *perfect*.'

Simone loosened her hold on Jane, stepping back.

'It's semi-permanent. I got it done in Chinatown. Sydney,

not London,' she clarified. 'Lots of aerialists I know have it done. It saves a shitload of time and it never smudges.'

'You got your *eyelids* tattooed!' Jane marvelled. 'It must have hurt *so* much.'

'Hey,' Simone said, going over to the water dispenser and filling two plastic glasses. 'Aerialists have high pain thresholds. I always say I can teach anyone trapeze if they like being upside down and have a high pain threshold. Everything else you can learn, but those two things're crucial.'

'I *do* like being upside down,' Jane said, taking the water gratefully. 'One out of two.'

'I can't believe they'd cast someone in a film as a star flyer in a circus when she can't even climb a rope,' Simone observed.

'Oh, it happens all the time,' Jane said blithely. 'Actors are such liars. We'll say at auditions that we can ride horses or fence or climb ropes just to get the part, and cross our fingers it won't be too hard to learn in a hurry.'

Simone snorted.

'Well, you fucked that one up, didn't you?' she said. 'I've got my work cut out for me!'

Jane was playing the main female role in a film called *Angel Rising*, a trapeze artist cast in a groundbreaking cabaret act choreographed by a male ex-ballet dancer, whose performing career had come to an abrupt halt after a catastrophic fall. The story was a tightly plotted psychological erotic thriller in which the two leads circled each other warily, becoming lovers but never fully trusting each other. Mind games the choreographer played with the performer while training began to extend into their sexual relationship, leading the viewer to wonder whether the ex-dancer was setting his lover up for a fall as bad as his own. Meanwhile, flashbacks featuring Jane's character revealed that she might not be as innocent as she seemed, but instead have a secret revenge agenda of her own . . .

It wasn't high art, but it was great money, with a famous director and cinematographer attached to the project, while the actor cast opposite Jane was an international sex symbol. Jane had known she'd be able to handle the erotic scenes: after the near-orgy of *And When We Fall*, nothing else could ever be as demanding. But she had assumed she'd have a stunt double for most of the trapeze work, not realizing quite how many stunts the director would require her to perform herself.

'I'm lucky I've got you,' she said to Simone, smiling at her.

'Oh yeah? You won't be saying that in half an hour. You've only finished your conditioning now, sweetie.' The evil grin was back. 'Now you've got to get back on that trapeze and practise your cross-to-ankle hang drop.'

'I meant as my body double,' Jane said. 'You can do all the tough bits I'll never be able to manage.'

The faces of the two young women weren't physically alike, but their bodies were the same height, same whip-slim lean build. Simone had been flown over from Sydney, where she lived, specifically for this job. She had spent years in Cirque du Soleil's Middle East touring companies, travelling all around the region, from Hong Kong to Qatar and Dubai. Afterwards – the shelf life of a circus performer was brutally short – Simone had started choreographing and performing in music videos, which had caught the attention of *Angel Rising*'s producers: it was obviously very efficient to have a coach for their star who would also work as a body double on the film, training Jane up in precisely her own style.

'Yeah, but you're missing something,' Simone pointed out, grinning. 'The better you get, the less I have to do. So' – she nodded over to the static trapeze – 'march yourself over there and I'll spot you up. No rest for the wicked!'

It wasn't anything particular, no single, magic, transformative moment. Just the angle of Simone's cheek as she turned away, the line of her jaw, the strength and humour of her words, the arches of her bare feet with their orange-varnished toenails bright against the tatty, slightly ripped blue landing mat, the tremendous ease and trust that Jane had felt a short while ago with her hands on Simone's shoulders, their faces level with each other's, Simone's grip on her ribcage painfully tight yet reassuring, her fingers digging into the swell of Jane's tiny breasts . . .

'What was that song you were singing?' Simone asked as Jane followed her to the hanging trapeze.

'"Halfway Down the Stairs",' Jane said automatically. 'It's from an old Muppet movie.'

'It's funny,' Simone said. 'I'll remember it when I'm coaching someone who gets stuck.'

'Yeah, you should,' Jane said, with something odd enough in her voice that Simone glanced at her.

'What's up?' she said. 'You! Hah. Aerialist humour.'

Jane, standing just in front of the trapeze, brought her hands together in front of her, and in an action Simone called 'throwing the ball', bent her knees and jumped, hands coming low and then shooting up high, touching the bar and then, as Simone expertly grabbed her waist and hoisted it an extra inch, her fingers wrapping round it.

'Three beats up to sit, slide down to cross,' Simone instructed, behind and below her.

Jane started to swing back and forth.

'Great!' Simone called. 'Really high and clean! Feet closer together – nice! Those are your best beats ever!'

And that, Jane knew, was because her body had just taken over and was, for the first time in her aerial training, performing entirely on its own without any interference from her brain. The latter was entirely occupied with processing the realization that had just hit her.

She was falling in love with Simone.

Chapter Thirteen

On-board

'So *here* you are! I've been searching for you!'

Angela was in the galley, sliding a bright red lobster out of the steamer. She looked up to see Danny Zasio, arms propped on either side of the entryway, grinning at her. His eyes were bright, his blond hair ruffled, his shirt half-open: to her he was the embodiment of sex.

Oddly, though she would normally have been struck dumb with embarrassment at such a blatant approach from a man she found incredibly attractive, for the last half hour or so, she had been feeling strangely buzzy, uncharacteristically light-headed – *in the clouds, literally,* she thought, suppressing a giggle. It meant that she was able to smile back at him without even blushing.

'Jesus,' he added in parentheses, looking at the lobster. 'Whose fucking stupid idea was it to cook whole lobsters on a plane?'

'Yours, Mr Zasio,' Angela said pertly. 'And we all hate it.'

'Yeah, I see why! That shit's going to leak everywhere as soon as the stupid sod who orders it tries to crack it open! Here, I'll plate it for you.'

Before she could protest, he shouldered her aside, expertly

preparing the lobster, twisting off the claws and tail, unhinging the top shell to expose the meat. Breaking off the legs, he picked up the silver cracker and used it on them and the claws, his stubby fingers moving so fast that Angela could barely see everything he was doing.

'There you go,' he announced, arranging the pieces on the plate in perfect symmetry.

'Wow, it looks just like in a restaurant,' Angela said with great admiration.

'You like lobster?' Danny asked, turning to her.

'Yes, but—'

She had been going to say that, like every other member of the cabin crew, she couldn't bear to eat it any more after seeing the poor things cooked so slowly in the steamer. However, before she knew what he was planning, he slid two fingers still dripping with lobster juice into her open mouth.

'Yeah, suck them hard, babe,' he whispered. 'Lick it off.'

Angela obeyed instinctively, her eyes wide. And when she'd sucked the liquid from his fingers, Danny drew them out slowly and replaced them with his thumb, corkscrewing it between her lips in a very self-consciously pornographic way, drowning out her protests.

'Fuck,' he muttered, crowding her against the counter with his outthrust hips. 'I could do you right now, right here. This is so fucking hot.'

Angela was panicking, torn between huge physical excitement and an almost equally huge need to keep her job. She shook her head frantically, managing to dislodge Danny's thumb, and hissed urgently, 'Not here!'

Then she wanted to kick herself: she should have said, *No*, or *Not on-board*, or even *No, you're married*. And yet her stupid, treacherous brain had blurted out what she'd actually wanted to say. Danny was so hot, literally. The hips pressed insistently into hers, the thick, lightly sweaty chest hair visible at the open neck of his shirt . . . she shivered, imagining them both naked, his hair rubbing against her breasts. The picture was so powerful that she couldn't manage another word.

He pulled back, and the front of her body felt bare, bereft; she whimpered like an abandoned puppy. And this was insane, because she was at work, on the first day aboard the LuxeLiner, her dream job, and if anyone had walked into the galley during these last few minutes, she would have been summarily sacked.

Thank God they knew I had a lobster order, she thought with relief. *Everyone steers clear when those are being cooked.*

Oh my God, the lobster!

She swivelled round, grabbing for the plate, which needed to go to Mr Stevens in 6B before it went cold, but Danny was already holding it, smiling like the Cheshire Cat.

'I'm going to take this to the lucky punter,' he said, winking at her. 'I plated it up, didn't I? You bring the tray. Lead the way, darling.'

Wordlessly, Angela grabbed the tray, which was already arranged with a folded bib, linen napkins, halved lemons sheathed in muslin so they could be squeezed without the pips coming out, a bowl of mayonnaise sprinkled with cracked pepper, and some wet wipes, packaged in sleek blue sachets with the Pure Air logo. The only positive aspect to the whole miserable lobster-cooking situation was that, after a series of trials in the flight simulator that had all ended very messily, the catering manager had regretfully abandoned the idea of using fingerbowls.

Angela brushed past Danny, moving swiftly, so anxious to get the lobster to Mr Stevens as fast as possible that she didn't notice Karl and Lucinda at the bar, intently watching her head down the far aisle with Danny close on her heels.

'Very exciting, Mr Stevens,' Angela said smoothly as she entered his pod; again, the brutal experience of her time at ReillyFly was invaluable for helping her muster a professional expression and tone of voice, even with Danny Zasio literally breathing down her neck. 'Mr Zasio himself has prepared and brought you the lobster you ordered!'

Mr Stevens, a thirty-something hipster wearing heavy black-framed glasses, the latest in ironic facial hair and a T-shirt with a picture of The Tick on it, was watching an obscure comic series on his iPad; closing it, he dropped it in the leather-lined electronica slot.

'Oh, cool, man,' he drawled, seeing Danny. Angela placed the tray on the desk table and removed the bib, expertly clipping it around Mr Stevens' neck to protect what was probably a very expensive vintage T-shirt.

'Enjoy!'

Danny flourished the lobster plate with such a dramatic whirl that Angela had to duck away as the tail came sliding towards her face.

'And seriously,' he said as he managed to deliver the plate to its appointed place on the tray without spilling anything, which Angela considered a minor miracle, 'make the most of it, because if I have anything to do with it, this is coming off the menu. It's sodding crazy to do a whole lobster on a plane! I must have been tripping. We'll switch it to a nice thermidor instead. Maybe with artichokes! Have a bit of fun with it. Mix things up.'

'Yeah, lobster thermidor would be cool,' Mr Stevens agreed, adjusting his glasses. 'Like, so retro it's come full circle, right?'

Danny beamed at him, sensibly deciding not to engage with this hipster lingo.

'Happy dining!' he said, whisking himself out of the pod.

'Can I get you anything else, Mr Stevens? A pairing from the wine list?' Angela began to ask, but she was interrupted by Danny, who popped back in like a jack-in-the-box, saying, 'Excuse me, will you? Just need to consult with the stewardess on something technical . . .'

Grabbing Angela by her sleeve, he tugged her out of the pod, pulling her down the aisle. She tried to protest, but Danny was inexorable and she was scared to draw attention to the two of them. Already things had gone much too far for her to feel secure in her job. Danny impulsively plating and taking the lobster to a passenger was something over which Angela could not be expected to exert control, but Danny physically dragging her away while she was occupied in taking an order was inexcusable. She baulked as they neared the toilet and shower rooms, realizing what he had in mind, digging in her heels like a mule in court shoes.

She had come to a halt in front of the last pod. It was 1D, the mirror image of Catalina's on the other side of the plane, occupied by Lord Tony himself. He must have been watching a film, because they could hear him laughing at something funny on screen. Angela flinched at the sound of her employ-er's voice.

'Ho ho ho!' Danny imitated. 'Fuck me, he laughs like Father Christmas. Come on, love. He won't hear a thing with headphones on.'

He pretty much picked Angela up by her waist and carried her bodily into the shower room. Karl and Lucinda, who had positioned themselves further down the aisle, watched in great gratification as the door closed behind them.

'I'd say mission well and truly accomplished,' Karl commented quietly.

'Let's give them a few minutes to get going,' Lucinda said, allowing herself a rare evil smile.

But if they could have seen inside the shower compart-ment, they would have realized, to their surprise, that matters were already very much underway. Danny had clearly decided that the finger-sucking in the galley were all the preliminaries necessary; as soon as he had locked the door, he flipped Angela over the moulded sink surround in front of the large mirror. The sink was plastic made to resemble grey marble, veined with black, so effectively that as Angela's upper body smacked into it, she was taken aback to feel the warm surface rather than the expected chill of stone under the palms she had put out to support herself; she knew perfectly well, of course, that it wasn't stone, but in her dazed, ecstasy-fuelled state her perceptions were all askew.

There were actually two mirrors above the sink, a second round one, lit up with its own golden halo, angled to the side, and Angela could see her reflection in both, her face expressing disbelief at how swiftly this was all happening.

Danny was dragging up her skirt, ripping its slippery lining, pulling down her 10-denier Sunkissed Beige tights to her knees. He slid his fingers up her thighs, twanging her thong on his fingers lustfully.

'Dripping wet, you dirty girl!' he said, leering at her reflection. 'Don't worry, I've got just what you need, and I'm going to give it to you right now –'

His hands went to his crotch. Angela rested her head on the sink surround, her nose inches away from a neat stack of rolled white, blue-bordered hand towels and a faux-marble and chrome rack in which were stacked gleaming glass bottles of pale blue toiletries especially made for Pure Air. She could smell the scent, which was meant to echo fresh, sweet air, but which right then was making her head spin even more. Bending over had made her very dizzy for some reason.

She moaned, 'I feel really out of it . . .'

'Me too! I'm fucking tripping! Pissed off my face and high on you, love!'

A buckle unfastened, a zip went down. Danny's jeans dropped to the floor. Any objections Angela had were obliterated in a surge of lust stronger than anything she had felt before – the combination of Danny Zasio about to fuck her, the ecstasy she had been given, the sheer forbidden thrill of it all building to an inexorable demand between her legs.

I'll feel better once I've had sex, she told herself. *I'll get a good seeing-to and that'll sort me out.*

She spread her legs further, as much as she could with the tights around her knees – she couldn't afford to rip those, not without instant access to her spare pair – and braced herself, hands gripping the shelf, waiting for the fuck of a lifetime, all scruples gone. Red splotches of colour pooled on her cheeks as she watched herself in the mirror, her pupils weirdly enlarged.

'Do you have a condom?' she managed to ask. Danny, after a second's pause, mumbled curtly, 'Yeah, babe, sure, got it on.'

And then his hips rammed into her. His hips, but nothing else. That was all she could feel, the bones of his pelvis thudding against her bare buttocks again and again. She was wet and open and incredibly turned on, and this lack of consummation was torture; after a more few cock-free slams against her, she started to wriggle and writhe, indicating that she was, frankly, more than ready for him to put it in.

Still nothing. Was it like some sort of dry-humping foreplay? She glanced up in the main mirror, seeing Danny's face engorged and crimson, sweat beading on his forehead: he looked like a man engaged in serious, full-on sex.

And yet . . .

His hands were clamped on her waist, holding her steady, his hips still pounding hers. She was completely confused now. What was he *doing*? She reached back with one hand as he came in for another hump, and found herself cupping his balls, which were as hairy as expected, considering the rest of his body. But she couldn't find his cock . . .

He was barely pulling back between humps. She couldn't get any more of her fingers back there, could hardly manage to walk them down even a little bit to the root of his cock, but she tried, and just as she did he groaned, 'Yeah, you fucking dirty bitch, tickle my balls while I'm fucking you senseless!' and she realized with genuine amazement that Danny Zasio, celebrity chef, major sex symbol, who had convinced her so effectively and so fast to bend over for him, was actually, currently, having penetrative sex with her. Almost certainly without a condom, as she hadn't felt that telltale fine rubber ring. But definitely with a cock so small that she literally could not feel anything inside her at all.

'You're loving it, aren't you?' he practically caroled as her hand fell away and he pumped his hips even harder. 'You're loving getting fucked by me, yes you are . . .'

Her head swimming, completely disoriented now, Angela closed her eyes and concentrated. Could she truly not sense *anything*? She shifted position, bending over even further. She had a flash of Danny just a few minutes ago, cracking the lobster, his fingers clasping the shell, the little one thinner and less stubby than the rest, and she found herself visualizing that little finger plunging inside her over and over again – now she pictured it like that, she thought she might be able to feel it . . .

'I'm gonna come!' Danny yelled. 'Oh yeah, I'm gonna come in your face . . .'

Angela's eyes snapped open. He was stepping back, pushing her down with a palm between her shoulder blades, so that she was on her knees on the silky pile of the shower mat before she knew it. Danny was scrabbling at her hair, trying to tilt her face back, tugging grips out of the padded doughnut over which she had so carefully smoothed her hair that morning, fixing it into a satin-smooth bun.

'No! My *hair*!' she wailed, her hands shooting up to protect it. If he messed that up, she would never be able to get it back to its pristine state again without half a can of hairspray.

'I'm gonna shoot in your face!'

'*No!*' she wailed even louder. 'My *make-up*!'

Desperate to protect her appearance, Angela managed to get one hand over her eyes as the other slapped Danny away from her hair. Then two things happened simultaneously. She felt a hot, wet trickle on the back of the hand covering her face, a slug-like trail dripping down to her wrist. And Lucinda, outside in the aisle, adeptly slipped a fifty pence coin into the security slot on the front of the door, unfastening the lock and dodging across into the toilet opposite almost in the same movement.

Neither Danny nor Angela realized that the door was unlatched, not at first. Danny was groaning in release, rocking back on his heels in satisfaction and repeating, '*Oh* yeah, *oh* yeah, *oh* yeah,' like a meditation mantra while Angela, on her knees, was now panting in shock, literally unable to believe what had just happened. She didn't dare take her hands away from her face and hair, not at first. One weird and unpleasant thing after the other had happened to her so fast that she couldn't be sure that Danny didn't have another trick up his sleeve.

Eventually, still puffing like a steam train from panic, she gingerly lowered her hands. She wanted to cry, but knew that she couldn't; she might well have already smeared her eye make-up, and her bag with her emergency touch-up kit was back in the crew cupboard next to the galley. She'd have to walk back down that aisle without any extra cosmetic help, and she couldn't risk shedding a single tear.

'Top fuck!' Danny said behind her, heaving a long sigh of sheer pleasure. 'You loved it, right? Hey, you ever pegged a guy? Want to try? I've got a little bachelor pad in LA with all the gear. You should swing by and give it a go. Lots of girls really get into it. You'd be surprised.'

The plane yawed to the right. Not by much, a tilt off the vertical axis that was only a small course correction. Not enough for Angela and Danny, both experienced flyers, to pay it any attention. But the shower door was hinged on the right, and the slight angle meant that it started to swing open. Lucinda, in the toilet opposite, eased open her own door a crack and snapped a series of damning photos. Danny reaching around Angela's kneeling body to grab one of the hand towels and wipe off his cock; Angela staring up at him, shoulders hunched, mouth gaping open in incredulity at his last words, skirt hiked up around her waist, Sunkissed Beige tights just visible at her knees.

They're done already? Lucinda thought. She prided herself on never showing surprise, let alone incredulity, in front of anyone, so it was a real pleasure to allow herself, unobserved, to gape as much as she wanted to. *That poor bitch*, she reflected in a fleeting moment of empathy. *She's totally screwed in both senses of the word, and she didn't even enjoy one of them.*

Danny took a second hand towel and chucked it in Angela's direction.

'Here,' he said. 'You'll need to wipe yourself off.' He smirked. 'That was a *lot* of good stuff I just laid on you there.'

The towel landed on her head. Wordlessly, she reached up and took it off, dabbing at the not precisely copious volume of semen on the back of her hand. This was clearly Danny's limit as far as chivalrous gestures went. She had to climb to her feet again with the aid of the sink surround: Danny failed to extend her a gentlemanly hand, being too busy expanding on his previous invitation.

'I've got different sizes for the harness,' he was continuing, winking at her. 'You can get double ones, know what I mean? With those ones, you do yourself while you're doing me – it's like a two-for-one deal . . .'

'Please, *stop*!' Angela blurted out, sharper than she'd meant, certainly sharper than was indicated for the respectful tone required for conversation with a passenger. She turned her head away to avoid the sight of Danny ogling her in the mirror.

That was when she realized the door was open.

'Oh my *God*!'

Blood rushed to her face. She lunged for the door, but with her tights still around her knees her range of motion was limited, and even as her hand stretched out frantically to grab the handle, the last person in the world she wanted to see under these circumstances appeared in the aisle, a vision in head-to-toe blue.

Lord Tony had changed into lounging gear for the duration of the flight. Like Mary Tudor, who had reportedly said that when she died, 'Calais' would be found written on her heart, Lord Tony had his 'Pure' brand running so thoroughly through his blood that he joked that doctors were always amazed to realize it was red. His choice of loungewear, therefore, was cobalt, a T-shirt bearing the Pure Air logo above the cashmere drawstring-waisted bottoms that were a giveaway for loyalty-card-holding passengers who racked up over twenty thousand miles in twelve months with the airline.

His blond curls were tangled from being pressed against the back of his seat. Vanessa's fingers would have been itching, maternally, to reach up and smooth down her boss's messy hair: Angela's only piece of luck in this whole horrendous mishap was that Lord Tony's publicity director was not by his side.

Instead, he was accompanied by Karl, who, ostensibly concerned by strange noises emanating from the shower compartment, had duly fetched Lord Tony to 'see what was going on'. Karl, like Lucinda, had assumed that Danny and Angela would be caught mid-coitus, not so obviously post-. Karl's manscaped eyebrows shot up to the roots of his hair; his lips moved in a silent 'No *way*!' as he realized that Danny had taken barely three minutes to shoot his load. He was dying to exchange glances with Lucinda, but she had closed her toilet door again.

'Good God!' Lord Tony exclaimed, staring at the scene in front of him. Angela was trying to drag her tights up and her skirt down simultaneously. Her bun was messy, her face bright red, and tears, despite her best efforts, were starting to well up. Her tights ripped audibly under her fingernails, and that was the last straw: wailing in misery, she slumped back against the sink.

Danny was tucked in and zipped up by now. One of the very few benefits of having a micropenis was that it could be put away with lightning speed. He threw the semen-damp towel towards the built-in bin, missing it by a foot, and, leaving it on the floor for someone else to dispose of, strode manfully towards Lord Tony.

'Angela! I can't express how disappointed I am in you!' Lord Tony was saying to Angela, shaking his head, his face a picture of grief. 'I hand-selected you, put you in Luxe Class – I thought you could be trusted, despite your coming from ReillyFly. This is simply outrageous behaviour. You're fired!'

Tears were pouring down poor Angela's face by now.

'I should have known,' he said, sighing deeply. 'People often tell me I lead with my heart too much. But that's the kind of man I am. I want to have faith in humanity . . .'

Angela emitted a long, heaving sob. Danny, now in the aisle, took Lord Tony's arm and turned him away, walking back to his pod, cutting off the airline boss's peroration in mid-flow.

'Come on, Tone,' he said placatingly. 'It's not her fault. I'm just irresistible.' He glanced back at Karl. 'Bring us a bottle, will you, mate? Fizz,' he said, as the two men went into Lord Tony's pod.

'Yes, sir,' Karl said automatically. He looked at Angela, reduced to a hysterical, sodden mess; she would have slid to the floor if she weren't propped against the sink.

'Wash your face love,' he said sympathetically. The poor girl had paid a very high price for attracting Lucinda's boyfriend. 'I'll get your bag. You can freshen up as much as you want before you come out again.'

Angela's face was smeared with mascara and eye make-up, tears carving channels through her foundation. She managed a wordless 'Thank you' at Karl as he swung the door closed again.

That was the cue for Lucinda to emerge from the toilet opposite, her eyes sparkling in delight. She swept down the aisle in front of Karl as regally as a queen going to her coronation, only faster.

'I'm a bit sorry for her,' Karl said heroically to Lucinda.

'I know! She didn't even get a good shag!' she hissed back. 'Did you *see* the size of his cock?'

'No! Damn it, he was behind the door! Lord Tony got an eyeful, though.'

'Smaller than a cocktail sausage. I'm not joking,' Lucinda whispered, a smile plastered on her face. 'I bet she didn't even feel it.'

'You need to put those up your bum,' Karl said wisely. 'It's tighter, you know? I'm not saying it's going to be great, but you're going to get more traction there than the other place.'

'Some of us do our Kegels every day, Karl,' Lucinda snapped as they reached the bar area.

While Angela washed her face in cold water mingled with salt tears, Danny was doing his best to plead her case to her boss.

'Seriously, mate,' he said to a frowning Lord Tony, 'it's my bad, as they say in the States. I totally swept her off her feet.' He pulled down the leather-covered built-in seat and lowered himself onto it, feet propped on the edge of the bed. 'I can't help it,' he continued, throwing open his hands. 'You know me – see blonde, do blonde! Poor girl didn't stand a chance. She did try to tell me that it wasn't the time and place, but I knew she wanted it.' The leer stretched practically from ear to ear. 'And she really did, know what I mean? She was practically gagging—'

'Danny, please!' Lord Tony held up a hand. 'Save it for your poker nights!'

Thwarted, Danny slumped back in the seat.

'I'm just saying, it was a one-off,' he said. 'The Zasio magic. She's a nice girl. I only like the nice girls. She's not going to drop her knickers for a new guy on every flight.'

'She's not going to do it on *any* flight!' Lord Tony exclaimed, but Danny was already continuing:

'Seriously, Tone, I pulled out the big guns.' He chortled. 'She didn't stand a chance. So go on and give her another one, eh?'

Karl entered with a bottle of champagne and two chilled glasses. Conversation was suspended as he set down the tray and popped the cork, filling the glasses and setting the champagne bottle into the built-in cooler.

'Karl, what do you think of Angela?' Lord Tony asked the steward unexpectedly.

Karl hesitated. Lucinda wanted Angela fired, he knew – that had, after all, been the goal. But that poor girl, fucked over first by him and Lucinda slipping her the ecstasy, then by Danny with his cocktail sausage . . . At that image, Karl's memory snapped back to a hugely disappointing recent sexual encounter with someone on Grindr who had the profile photo of a male model. Well, the guy *had* been a male model, but the dick pics he had subsequently sent Karl had turned out not to belong to him, and as Karl had said tartly to him on seeing the goods, gay guys were always going to choose an ugly mug with a big cock over a pretty face with a micropenis.

Ugh, that micropenis! You couldn't find it in broad daylight with a magnifying glass!

And it was that vivid recollection that made Karl finally say, 'She's a nice girl, and a very hard worker, sir.'

'Everyone's a hard worker,' Lord Tony said, shrugging, as Karl retreated from the pod. 'No, I'm sorry, Danny. I can't possibly keep her on.'

The door of the shower swung open and Angela emerged. To her great credit, her appearance was as impeccable as it had been an hour earlier: hair smooth, bun perfectly centred, make-up fresh, a new pair of tights donned. Her eyes were still red, but her demeanour was perfect. A cloud of perfume was swirling around her, which Karl, a scent maven, immediately recognized as Elizabeth Arden's Pretty.

Very girlie, but then she is a right girlie, he thought. *Too sweet for me, though. It actually smells pink.*

'Chin up, love,' he said to her, and saw her swallow hard. 'You've got the rest of the flight to get through. Stiff upper lip it.'

She nodded, clearly not trusting herself to speak yet.

'Here.' Karl pulled out a little vial of Visine from his trouser pocket. 'Pop some eye drops in. You really ought to have your own. It's basic crew issue. And have you got a shot of something?'

Angela shook her head, her eyes conveying lack of understanding.

'Oh, fuck me with a broom, what do they *teach* you on the cattle-class airlines?' Sighing, Karl produced a miniature of Three Barrels brandy from his other pocket. 'You know nothing, Jon Snow,' he muttered, as Angela took both little bottles with a thankful glance and disappeared into the shower again. Karl nipped swiftly back down the aisle: Lucinda mustn't know that he had helped Angela in any way. He'd tucked her handbag beneath his jacket so Lucinda didn't see it. Karl was a past master at smuggling items around an aircraft without being noticed.

Well, I've done what I could, he thought, shrugging. Poor little bitch is on her own now. But if she wants to go on being cabin crew anywhere – even if the only airline that'll take her is Ryanair – she'd better keep her legs together in future for the rest of her career.

Because everyone who flew for a living would have seen those photos in the space of twenty-four hours from then. Lucinda was fully intending to spread them through her grapevine, which would then pass them on until there wouldn't be a single flight attendant in the world who hadn't had a good look at Angela, Danny Zasio and his cocktail sausage.

Karl shuddered at the thought. It was like that old joke, 'you shag one sheep . . .'. Even if Angela behaved impeccably for the rest of her career as cabin crew, she would never live this scandal down. Karl grimaced. It truly was a cruel and unusual punishment.

Chapter Fourteen

In his aisle seat in the back row of the plane, Gerhardt shifted, yet again unable to settle. He didn't expect to be comfortable: that wasn't part of his remit. But he did at least need to be able to sit in relative quiet so he could observe the cabin, and ever since seeing Catalina, he had been as jittery as if invisible fire ants were crawling all over him, torturing him with thousands of tiny bites. Luckily, the passenger in the window seat beside him was fast asleep, eye mask and ear plugs in, deaf and blind to the world. If he had been awake, he would already have been intensely irritated by Gerhardt's constant fidgeting, and Gerhardt had barely been there for fifteen minutes.

Gerhardt had been forced to switch seats. He knew, from bitter experience, how closely bonded Catalina was to Latisha. She was bound to come back again, see if her assistant had woken up yet, and the risk of her spotting him was simply too great for him to run. Catalina was clearly in great distress and the knowledge not only that she was extremely upset, but that there was nothing Gerhardt could do to help and comfort her, was eating away at him. He pictured her in Luxe Class, alone and crying, and that image forced him to his feet, pacing restlessly back and forth between the toilets, into the crew area and out again.

'God, he's *so* gorgeous!' sighed Lydia, one of the business-class cabin crew, to Greg as she unlatched the duty-free trolley. 'I love a silver fox, don't you?'

'Mmm, I like them younger,' Greg said, 'but he's got a *hard* body. I definitely wouldn't kick him out of bed.'

'He's so gloomy, like he's in torment!' Lydia, an avid reader of Gothic romances, continued, shivering deliciously. 'I bet there's something eating away at his soul . . . some terrible dark secret . . .'

'And only tying you up and giving you a good spanking'll make him feel better, I suppose,' Greg said, rolling his eyes. 'And eventually that'll turn him into a great husband. God, those porn books you read've made total idiots of grown women.'

'I *wish* he wanted to spank me! He doesn't even *look* at me!' Lydia complained. 'Which makes him even hotter, by the way.'

She shuddered in pleasure again as she pulled out the trolley.

'Honestly, what do you expect?' Greg said, backing away to let her turn the trolley in the tight space. 'You keep wiggling over to him, shaking your booty, bending over and sticking your Maliboobed tits in his face, lisping "Can I get you anything, sir? Anything at *all*?" in your special babydoll fuck-me-up-the bum voice. No wonder he's ignoring you! The poor sod's probably terrified if he asks for a glass of water, the next thing he knows you'll drop to your knees and try to blow him.'

'I *would*,' Lydia said immediately. 'I *so* would.'

'Whore.'

'You say that like it's a *bad* thing.'

Greg sniggered.

'Did I tell you what happened to my trolley dolly friend who works for Virgin last week?' he said, going over to the tannoy handset. 'She was on a long-haul to Singapore and she needed to wake up the cabin crew. So she punched in the number for the rest area and said loudly over the intercom, "Wake up, whores! The pigs are stirring and those twats need feeding!"'

Lydia was unsurprised: she had heard far worse than this.

'*But*,' Greg said gleefully, 'she'd only bloody punched in the wrong number – everyone in economy heard it! Nightmare! As soon as she hung up, she heard a lot of passengers starting to kick off, so she realized what had happened, grabbed the tannoy again and announced, "Will the passenger who just tampered with our information system please desist from doing so again".'

'Oh, "desist",' Lydia said, impressed. 'That's *very* professional-sounding.'

Greg clicked the safety switch off the tannoy and said suavely into it, 'Ladies and gentlemen – (*Pig twats*),' he mouthed for Lydia's benefit – 'we are now coming through the cabin with our superb range of duty-free goods, includ-ing our signature perfume, Pure Air, a fresh ozonic scent with aquatic notes and a hint of cucumber and watermelon, a perfect opportunity to treat yourself or purchase a gift for any friends you happen to be visiting . . .'

Gerhardt had heard flight announcements so often in the

last few months that they rolled right over him like Lydia's come-hither smiles. Shifting, he felt the heavy weight of the Sig Sauer P229 holster strapped to his right ankle, and decided, like a junkie needing distraction, that he might as well go into the toilet and check it yet again. Locking the door behind him, he reached down, pulled up his trouser leg and unholstered the semi-automatic in one fast movement, the reinforced thumb-break retention strap working as smoothly as it had the last three times he'd performed this action on-board the flight.

He placed the gun on the sink surround. He preferred the P226, with its ergonomic extended beavertail and custom wood grips, but the P229 was more compact, ideally suited to concealed carry. The 'loaded chamber' indicator on the top of the slide always made him scowl, however: it was a ridiculous precaution, a cave-in to greedy, lawsuit-chasing American lawyers. If you didn't know that your gun was loaded, you weren't fit to be handling one in the first place. And the damn lettering wouldn't even come off: Gerhardt had tried to scratch it off with the blade of his Swiss army knife, but it was laser-etched on.

He returned the Sig Sauer to the holster, careful to slide his trouser leg fully down to cover it. That was a classic giveaway with the ankle holster: the gun sat right at the top of the foot, the barrel nudging into the shoe. It gave you excellent, speedy access to your weapon, but you had to make sure that your trousers were not only cut right, of a light enough material to pull up swiftly – in Gerhardt's opinion, jeans were too heavy to be suitable, hence his choice of lightweight chinos – and fractionally too long, to afford that crucial extra bit of coverage to hide any sign of the gun.

He pulled the handcuffs out of his inside jacket pocket. Still there, still with the key in them. All in order. He dropped them back into the pocket. That was it; nothing else to check. Nothing to do. He would have loved to have paced the full length of the aisle, but he couldn't. No matter how much airline information sheets told you to take regular strolls up and down the plane, perform stretching exercises to avoid blood clots forming because of lack of circulation, cabin crew looked very dimly upon passengers actually doing anything of the sort.

Gerhardt stared at himself in the mirror. It was still incredible to him that Catalina had fallen in love with this craggy, expressionless face. His army nickname had been 'Easter Island', his troop joking that, with his big nose and jutting chin, he looked like one of those statues. They'd even pinned up postcards of the statues in their rec room, adding comments in marker pen.

Gerhardt had reacted to the nickname as impassively as always, but secretly it had amused him. It wasn't unflattering: the statues were big, strong, dominating, authoritative, exactly the image that he was required to project, both in the army and in civilian life as a bodyguard. And that image also appealed to women, which was no bad thing. He had no false modesty, was perfectly aware that the flight attendant with the shiny teeth and implausible breasts had been positively throwing herself at him ever since he'd boarded the plane.

However, the idea that *Catalina*, beautiful, talented Catalina, who was leagues ahead of the plastic-surgeried, faux-blonde stewardess in every respect, had found him so attractive that she'd literally jumped into his arms . . . *that* he had never truly let himself believe. Maybe that had been part of the problem. Maybe she had realized that Gerhardt was holding back, unable to trust the relationship with the same ardour that she did; she had teased him about his restraint, the emotional self-control that he brought to bear so strongly when they weren't in bed together.

But then, he thought with a pain as vivid as if someone had just punched him in the solar plexus, *especially after the tour finished, we were in bed almost all the time.*

The memories of that honeymoon period were as horrendous now as they had been beautiful to live through. The sense of loss was like a gaping hole in his chest, raw and bloody-edged, as if that punch had gone right through the skin, his attacker's fist burying itself into the red meat of his internal organs. Somehow the sheer unlikeliness of him having a relationship with Catalina made the agony even worse.

She had always been his celebrity crush. If he had been asked who his ideal woman was, he would instantly have named her. She was so talented, such a wonderful personality, so beautiful, with such a warm, open smile . . . such a wonderful dancer, sexual but not vulgar, a free spirit . . . he could have listed her attractions for hours. He had been on the phone to the Berlin branch of his agency instantly after the news had circulated through the closely linked bodyguard network that Catalina's previous bodyguard had gone AWOL after a visit to Berghain, the techno/sex club. Ironically, the grapevine of personal protection officers probably passed on information even faster than the cabin crew grapevine did – knowledge was power, after all.

Gerhardt, who had been resting up after a tough assignment as local advisor to a visiting Saudi minister – always exhausting, as it usually required overriding the wishes of a jealously protective Arab security team – had immediately rung in and begged for the job. His boss had laughed her head off, said that at least she knew Gerhardt was too straight-laced to get too fucked up in a club to make it into work, teased him about having crappy taste in pop music, and then agreed.

It had been overwhelming news. To be close to her almost all the time, to have her safety entrusted to him . . . he'd wanted to slap himself the instant he hung up the phone, tell himself to wake up, because this was literally a dream come true for him.

And in person, she had been even more than he could have imagined. From that first moment of meeting her in her hotel it had taken every ounce of his extremely impressive self-control, which years in the army had polished to a shiny shield, to maintain the impeccable professional demeanour that was essential to his job. She was so sweet, so friendly, not at all the spoilt diva he had been bracing himself to find out that she was, underneath her charming facade: ironically, in the long run, that would have made his life so much easier.

But that lovely smile she had given him as she shook his hand for the first time, the glance up from under her thick lashes, which was probably just how she greeted everyone, but which had made his entire body stiffen in an attempt to conceal his physical reaction to her . . . her manner, so un-affected despite her fame; the easy polite way she talked to anyone, exactly the same with a cleaner who stopped her in a hotel corridor to ask for an autograph as she was with fellow celebrities or the owner of the huge arena at which she was performing . . . the discovery that she was as beautiful on the inside as she was on the outside had been what had tipped him from lust into love.

Gerhardt had seen all kinds of appalling behaviour from celebrities. Tantrums, meltdowns, epic sulks. He had worked for famous people who either spoke with incredible rudeness to service staff or simply refused to talk directly to them at all: they would whisper their orders to their PA, making their employee do all the direct interacting with people they considered their social inferiors.

But Catalina was exquisite. Perfect. Unspoilt by fame, though happily enjoying all its advantages. Generous to a fault with everyone she cared about – her family, Latisha, Gerhardt himself . . . Memories of her sexual generosity flooded back, an instant rush of blood to his groin that gripped at his balls and stiffened his cock. It happened every damn time he thought about her. But now he was so close; close enough to walk up into Luxe Class, to find her and put his arms around her, snuggle her onto his lap in the way she had always loved, kiss her, feel her wrap her arms around his neck as she kissed him back with the sweet eagerness that had always melted his heart . . .

Oh, Christ damn it! He would never get over her, never! How could he be with any other woman after having been Catalina's lover? How could anyone else possibly match up to her? Even in her upset state just now, her face taut and white with distress, her actions crazy, she had blazed out to him like a shining star. There wasn't a woman in the world who could hold a candle to her.

He hadn't been able to look anywhere but at her. But had she even noticed his presence across the cabin? Did she realize he was on the plane? His lips drew into a tight line.

His past was in tatters. And if Catalina had seen him, that could ruin his future as well.

Chapter Fifteen

Five months ago

'Do you like it? I thought you would . . . well, I *hoped* you would! Oh God!' Catalina caught her breath. 'You don't, do you? Do you just not like it or do you really hate it?'

Her initial delight at finally being safe home again was fading as she nervously observed Gerhardt's reaction to her house. She stood in the centre of the hallway, beside a waist-high beaten silver vase filled with white blossom and delicate green leaves: the florist had visited that morning, and the house was perfumed with the scent of the blossom and the bowls of white roses placed in every room. The driver had dropped the couple off at the main entrance and was bringing in their luggage. As he disappeared from view into the lift, a Vuitton suitcase in either hand, Catalina realized that Gerhardt was turning his head from side to side, checking out the entrances and exits like a professional bodyguard.

But she had a security team in place now in LA, organized by Latisha and Gerhardt. They had swept the house before the arrival of its owner and stationed a guard at the gate who would be making regular patrols of the perimeter fence. The house and grounds were near impregnable, designed specifically to appeal to the kind of buyer who was famous enough to need to ward off any incursions by intruders. Which meant that Gerhardt was supposed to be off the clock.

'It's called Contemporary Architectural,' Catalina was now babbling, seeing Gerhardt's forehead contract into a frown. 'The style of the house. I mean, of course it's contemporary, and architectural, because it's a new house and someone had to design it, but that's what the realtors call it here . . . stupid, really! Do you not like it? Is it too boxy? It's what they're all like here, the houses. They're *big* boxes, though . . .'

Catalina's Oriole Way house was indeed a series of glass-walled boxes, stacked cleverly on top of each other so that their projecting terraces and balconies were angled to take best advantage of the house's position up in the Hollywood Hills, looking down on the escarpments plunging dramatically to the basin below, which contained the sprawl of the city. The occupants of the master bedroom's wraparound terrace, high above the notorious LA smog, could watch both the sunrise and the sunset, seeing the soft golden light reflected in the L-shaped pool below, which echoed the shape of the house itself. In the distance rose the skyscrapers of downtown, a surprisingly small cluster of silvery peaks: LA was not a high-rise town, and from far away, the brightly lit buildings looked like the Emerald City in Oz, the spires of a magical castle.

But even from the top floor of one of those downtown skyscrapers, you had to look up to the Bird Streets of the Hollywood Hills. They were the true Emerald City, the ultimate goal of so many who would never have the millions needed to buy here, let alone maintain their property immaculately. High up overlooking a city was always where the rich people chose to live: the air was fresher, the views more dramatic, the privacy easier to maintain. From the jagged corniches of the south of France to the green slopes reaching up from Florence to Fiesole, real estate in those areas commanded some of the highest prices in the whole of Europe.

And like the peaks above Cap Ferrat and Menton, or the pretty hillsides of Fiesole, this enclave north of Sunset Boulevard, between Hillcrest Road in Beverly Hills and Sunset Plaza in the Hollywood Hills, was small but perfectly formed. Leonardo di Caprio, Jennifer Aniston, Jodie Foster, Keanu Reeves, and many of the biggest LA TV and film producers all lived in this comparatively small area. It wasn't a place for wannabes, up-and-comers, or even B-listers. The Bird Streets were A-list all the way.

'Gerhardt? What's wrong?'

Catalina was panicking now. He still hadn't said a word. She had been standing back so he could take in the central hallway, which was double-height to allow for the turn of the cantilevered glass staircase, the treads pale green and glowing from the lights set discreetly into the base of each one. To the right was the cinema room, furnished with pale suede sofas and matching footstools on what seemed like acres of white carpet, a wet bar set into the side wall, a built-in fireplace running below the whole length of the enormous screen. To the left was the dining room, with its ten-seater glass table and grey leather woven chairs, which led into the enormous chef's kitchen shining with Viking and Miele appliances, which led out onto the pool and landscaped spa area, the water dropping away over the infinity edge to draw the eye to the blue skies beyond and the extraordinary view of the city . . .

Slowly, the truth dawned on Catalina. He didn't dislike her house. The problem was quite the reverse.

'Is it too much?' she asked, coming over, taking hold of the neck of his T-shirt with both hands and tugging on it, a gesture she had come to use when she wanted him to look down at her. Even in her wedges, her head barely came up to his collarbone.

Wordlessly, Gerhardt nodded, his big head rising and falling as heavily as the stone of the Easter Island statues after which he had been nicknamed.

'But we've stayed in so many amazing hotel suites!' she protested. 'That one in Melbourne was unbelievable – three full bathrooms! Here's much simpler than that! We have to cook our own meals and look after ourselves – I have a maid service, of course, but we don't need to get them in if you don't want . . . well, not every day . . .'

Her voice trailed off as she stared up at him, really nervous now. She was beginning to understand. The five-star hotel suites on tour had been fine with him because they had come as part of his job; paid to look after Catalina, morphing into her lover while still working as her bodyguard, he had naturally stayed with her in the luxury that befitted her status. But now, in her home, his skills infinitely less necessary unless they left its confines – which she was planning to do as little as possible – his male pride was kicking in. He was no longer working. His status here was merely her lover, her companion, and for a tough, alpha, army-trained male like Gerhardt, that was an uncomfortably passive role.

'I don't belong here, Catalina,' Gerhardt said gently. His hands covered hers but not, as she had feared, to detach her from her grip on his T-shirt. Instead he held them, looking down at her gravely, and though his words were ominous, the fact that he was still making physical contact went some way to reassuring her. She knew that he found it impossible to resist her physically, and was honest enough to admit to herself that she used that appeal mercilessly when she was trying to convince him to do something at which he was baulking. Sometimes she thought of herself as a tiny jockey perched high up on a big, stubborn horse that needed tugs on the reins, little kicks to the ribs to make it go where she needed.

And after my stallion takes a big jump, she would think naughtily on those occasions, *he needs a special treat as a reward – a nice juicy apple . . .*

'You do belong here! Because I need you. I don't feel safe without you,' she insisted, looking up at him with her eyes as wide as they would stretch, feeling some of his tense, nervous energy dissipate, his taut muscles relaxing slightly at the words that men always loved to hear.

Greatly encouraged by this reaction, she continued, ladling it on even thicker: 'You *have* to stay! I couldn't be here without you, not for even a little while! I'd be so frightened!'

'There is the guard at the gate,' Gerhardt said seriously. 'And the perimeter is secure. I am very impressed with the arrangements here.'

'It's not enough! I need you here with me! Please, Gerhardt!'

She tugged him down enough to kiss him, a sweet, unsexual press of her lips on his.

'You can't leave me!' she said firmly. 'I won't let you! Imagine me all by myself in this big house, scared of a stalker somehow getting in. It does happen, you know it does! Sandra Bullock had a guy break into her home in Beverly Hills' – for extra emphasis, she loosened one hand from his and pointed over in that direction – 'just last year! At one in the morning she heard a noise, opened her bedroom door and saw him standing there! She had to lock herself in her bedroom and call the cops – can you *imagine*? *Imagine* if that happened to me and you weren't here! What if they had a gun?'

The straight line of Gerhardt's mouth softened visibly, the muscles of his jaw unclenching: these were clear signs that he was coming round to her way of thinking. Catalina was too sensible to push for a verbal agreement from him then and there, however.

'Come and see outside,' she said, pulling on his hand, towing him behind her as she headed through the glass-walled dining room. In the bright rayon zigzag Missoni top and white jeans she had changed into for the benefits of the LAX paparazzi, she actually did resemble a tiny rider in silks, leading a large, slow-stepping horse.

'It's such a lovely day,' she added, deliberately changing the subject, 'and we need to get some Vitamin D after that flight! Ugh, the air gets so stale on planes, doesn't it?'

'Sometimes I have met VIP clients directly from the plane, on the air bridge, to escort them to their lounge,' Gerhardt said, nodding in agreement. 'The first time, I see that the officials who are experienced in this, they stand very far back as the crew opens the door, after a long flight. So I stand back too. Because many people all together in a small tube like that make a *lot* of bad smells, and the air is terrible when it first comes out. Even if you do not stand right by the door.'

He pulled a face. Catalina laughed.

'I bet! Everyone squashed into coach, and then fewer people in business and first, but eating much richer food . . . eew, that cheese soufflé; why did Tish think it was a good idea to eat that on a *plane*?' She wiggled her little nose. 'Pongy!'

Gerhardt, who had sat beside Catalina, with Latisha directly behind them, broke into a reluctant grin. Latisha's issues with digesting dairy products were a running joke between the two girls, one into which Gerhardt, travelling so closely with them, had been co-opted.

'Not just cheese,' he pointed out, his voice now tinged with amusement. 'It was Gorgonzola. Very strong.'

'Strong going in, strong coming out! I tell you, if she'd been sitting next to me I'd have banned her from ordering that soufflé! But she was behind me, so she got sneaky . . .'

Catalina was hugely relieved that she had, literally and metaphorically, managed to steer Gerhardt away from the subject of his not belonging here. It hadn't been difficult, in the rarefied, artificial atmosphere of a sold-out world tour, moving from one luxurious hotel suite to another, surrounded by a phalanx of bodyguards, to curl up in bed with him and persuade him to come to LA with her. Every night they had fallen asleep with the dream of being in a bed of their own, a house of their own, somewhere they could live for months on end. Somewhere, as Catalina had said, where you could get out of bed in the night to use the toilet and not bump into things, because you had got used to the last hotel room and forgotten you were in the new one, and that there was a dressing room between you and the toilet with a travertine-topped storage island right in the middle of it . . . and no matter how expensive that marble was, it still hurt like hell when you stumbled into it and bruised your thigh . . .

So the prospect of having a whole month here in LA together had been sheer bliss for both of them. Catalina's managing team was too sensible to work their prized asset into the ground. These four weeks in Los Angeles had been scheduled partially as recovery after the gruelling demands of the tour. Of course, she wasn't completely at leisure: she had rehearsals and then three nights in concert at the Staples Center, plus a big publicity push for the soon-to-be released Disney film for which she had written and recorded the theme song.

But by the standards of the last few months, the amount of space and peace she would have between these engage-ments was the equivalent of a rest cure at the famous Mayr Clinic in Switzerland. And then would come the last leg of the tour, Latin America, followed by Catalina's yearned-for retreat to her beach house in Punta del Este: months of sea, sun, sand, with nothing to do but lie in Gerhardt's arms, happily put back on the pounds she always lost on tour by eating fresh pasta in the exquisite beachside restaurants, and contemplate how perfect her life had so suddenly and unex-pectedly become.

With the gigantic clampdown in her security, there had been no more stalking incidents. A guard had been stationed permanently outside Catalina's dressing room at the venues during her shows, two more outside the hotel suite, while local teams in each city had encircled her on every public appearance. Normally, this would have made Catalina feel claustrophobic, maybe even paranoid, living and travelling in such tightly confined conditions, especially when, inevitably, all the private security officers were much taller than her; often, moving around, almost all she saw were black- or grey-covered shoulders and neatly shaved skulls.

However, it made all the difference in the world to have Gerhardt almost constantly by her side. It was something Catalina had never dreamed of: a performer never imagined that they would have the luxury of a lover travelling with them on tour. No one would put up with being uprooted from home for eight months, the boredom of kicking their heels during endless soundchecks, rehearsals and concerts, the fact that their partner was either exhausted, sleeping, or at someone else's disposal during their waking hours for a non-stop round of interviews and personal appearances. If a partner did make the mistake of joining a tour, bickering, feelings of neglect, fights, and eventually stormings-out would be the inevitable consequence.

Typically, a musician's partner or family would fly in now and then; often, the drop-ins would be unexpected, as the girlfriend or wife (it was always the girlfriend or wife in this case) was trying to catch their man out, see if he really was behaving as faithfully as he had promised when he went on tour. The trick was never to hire a private plane when making a surprise appearance, because the charter companies were always paid with the star's money, and hence they were predictably loyal to the star, not the girlfriend or wife. As soon as the latter made a booking, the airline charter would alert the former's PA or manager to make sure that no awkwardness would ensue. The hookers and groupies would be banished, the star would greet the lady in their life with perfectly feigned astonishment and delight, and the charter company would not only be ensured of the business for all the star's future private travel, but very juicy thank-you bonuses.

And, as the managers and PAs often observed to each other, it made the wife or girlfriend happy too, so in the end, everyone was a winner, weren't they?

The kind of closeness while travelling that Catalina and Gerhardt were enjoying, therefore, was almost unheard of. Stars did, occasionally, date their minders: Heidi Klum, the model and TV presenter, had rebounded from her break-up with Seal into with an affair with her long-term personal protection officer, and there were persistent rumours about one of the most A-list of current singers, who was married to a music mogul who was reputedly very jealous of her closeness to her bodyguard, despite his own notoriously wandering eye.

But rebounds or affairs with the person who happened to always be physically next to you were very different from what Catalina and Gerhardt shared. She had absolutely no doubt that she was in love with him, nor that he was in love with her, though the words had not yet been spoken. Catalina had never been bedevilled by any lack of self-confidence. Not only did she possess the innate assurance in her sexuality that was so bred into Latin Americans, but she had been a star from her youth onwards, though one who had had to work hard for everything she achieved. She had a very healthy and balanced ego: she had been quite happy to take her clothes off and throw herself, literally, into Gerhardt's arms, sure that he would catch her.

Well, now she had him, she was determined to keep him. Fear of her stalker had receded very far into the background. Her spiking anxiety now was that Gerhardt needed just the right kind of careful handling to prevent him from baulking at this crucial fence. Safely ensconced in her LA house, with its high security walls, guarded entrance gate and totally private pool area, she was completely protected from long-range paparazzi lenses or any stalker incursion. No threat could come from outside. It was the menace inside these walls that needed to be defused, the potential bomb that could explode if Gerhardt, even now, decided that after all he wasn't comfortable basking in the lap of luxury with, frankly, minimal professional duties to perform to make him feel as if he were earning his keep . . .

Grabbing a bottle of sugar-free green tea water from a built-in ice-filled granite cooler, she led Gerhardt out onto the terrace. Before them, the water of the L-shaped pool glistened, the tiles a shade of pale green that had been especially commissioned by the Contemporary Architectural architect from an Italian firm and shipped over at great expense. It had been worth every penny. The swimming pool looked vastly more enticing than a blue-tiled one, an oasis of delicious cool water on a hot sunny day, a refreshing contrast to the bright blue sky and the glittering buildings sprawling out in the valley below.

Around the pool, in elegantly organized conversational

groups, loungers and outdoor armchairs were arranged around heavy grey granite tables. But Catalina was leading Gerhardt over to a large daybed shaped like an open shell, a high pale grey rattan frame curving into an encircling roof above it to shelter its occupants from the California sun. The circular white mattress was piled high with beige and grey cushions; it was enticingly cosy and inviting, and it wasn't hard for Catalina to push Gerhardt down into its embrace, the pale grey wings seeming to enfold him on either side. He smiled up at her, half-unwillingly, not quite ready to relax into the lap of luxury.

'This is very nice,' he admitted grudgingly. 'Very comfortable.'

Catalina uncapped the bottle, sipped some of the green tea water and then climbed on top of him, straddling his wide-splayed thighs.

'*You're* very comfortable,' she said saucily.

His hands rose, despite himself, to cradle her narrow hips.

'Catalina, we need to discuss this seriously. Talk about if things can work,' he said.

'They *will* work,' she said passionately. '*How* they can work, not *if*! They *will* work!'

She bent down to kiss him, her mouth wet and cool from the water, her tongue sliding between his lips, a definite statement of possession.

'Is it about your place in Berlin?' she asked, sitting back up. 'Do you mind leaving that for so long?'

Gerhardt shook his head.

'It is all organized for that,' he said. 'Often a bodyguard must go away for long amounts of time, without that being

250

planned. So everything is kept simple. I text the cleaner to go in and clear out the fridge if I am away for longer than a week, and then to come in before I return. It is just a small apartment. Very basic. Not like this.'

'Have a drink!' Catalina said swiftly, distracting Gerhardt by handing him the water bottle before he could start surveying the luxury of his surroundings with Teutonic gloom all over again. 'It's so hot, you must be really thirsty . . .'

Gerhardt drank deeply.

'That was very strange,' he said, handing it back to her and grimacing. 'I thought it might be your lipstick that was odd to taste when you kissed me, but no, it is the water. What is it?'

'Green tea. Really healthy. My nutritionist says it's the latest thing,' Catalina said, arching back to set the bottle down on the terrace, her knees gripping his outer thighs for balance.

'But does your nutritionist drink it?' Gerhardt asked quizzically.

'I have no idea!' Catalina smiled down at him, noticing that her kiss, or possibly her backbend, had stirred something in Gerhardt's trousers; she reached down to help it on its way, tickling her little fingers up and down the growing ridge.

'Catalina—' he began, but she cut in.

'This is perfect,' she purred happily. 'We can have sex, sleep for a bit, jump in the pool, then do all of that all over again . . . it's the best cure for jet lag. We don't need to leave the house for days – I got them to stock the fridge with all sorts of food. I can book a chef to cook for us if we want, or we can order in. I just want to hole up here with you.

Barely any Internet or phone, I promise. I gave Tish a whole week off, so she won't come by – I don't have a single appointment for a good ten days.'

She beamed adorably, tossing back her hair.

'It's a holiday for both of us! Think of it like that, okay? We've both been working *sooo* hard – now we get to chill out for a bit. Honestly, we totally deserve this. I want to sleep for twelve hours straight tonight, don't you? And spend hours in the pool, and walk around the house totally naked . . . oh, and I have a whirlpool bath upstairs with the most amazing views of the city. Wait till you see it . . .'

But Gerhardt's thoughts were elsewhere, far from the incipient pleasures of the whirlpool bath with spectacular views.

'You will not be seeing Latisha for a week?' Gerhardt said doubtfully. 'Will she not miss you and be angry with me that I am here instead? Because before, certainly, you would have seen each other much more.'

Catalina's fingers paused in their clever stimulating caresses; she sat back on her heels.

'I suppose so,' she said, her brows drawing together. 'I mean, yes, she'd have been over here more if you weren't staying with me. But why's that a problem?'

'Maybe she will think that I have . . . taken her place, perhaps,' Gerhardt said carefully; this was a subject he had been wanting to broach for a while now, but had put off for fear of distressing Catalina while she was on tour. Now, however, was clearly the right time.

'You and Latisha are so close,' he continued. 'Will she not miss you?'

'*Miss* me? I don't know. I haven't thought about it.' She

considered the question briefly. 'Really, I think she'll be over the moon to have a proper holiday for once!' she finally said. 'I told my manager to get in touch with me directly if he needs to so Tish can really get a break. I thought it was perfect – you're here, so Tish doesn't need to worry about me at all.'

Catalina was genuinely baffled. She had been nervous that Gerhardt was about to criticize Latisha, and no one was allowed to do that but Catalina herself; this tack, however, had taken her completely aback.

'You are like sisters,' Gerhardt observed. 'I see how close you are.'

'Well, yeah, but even sisters need time off from each other! I have sisters, and I love them, but I don't want them round all the time,' she said firmly.

Back at the house, the door buzzer sounded twice, the signal that her driver had finished unloading the extensive luggage, closed the front door behind him, and was about to get back into the limousine and leave the property.

'We're all alone!' she said blissfully, her hands returning to Gerhardt's trouser ridge.

'Catalina . . .' He caught her hands to hold them for a moment, not wanting to talk about another woman while his cock was being unveiled. 'You don't think that Latisha is maybe not happy that I am now' – he searched for the word, looking embarrassed – 'close to you? Closer in a way than she is?'

'In a *way*! Yeah, like a friend! She's my best friend, so of course that's really special.' Catalina deftly slid her small hands free from his grip and started to unzip his trousers. 'But I promise you, I've never been close to Latisha like this!

She's totally straight, if that's what you're wondering. And so am I. There's nothing like that going on at all.' She glanced up at him briefly. 'Can we stop talking about Tish now? Seriously, it's all fine! I bet you Tish's pouring herself a huge drink right now, doing laundry – she loves doing laundry – and catching up on her shows, and feeling really glad that she doesn't even need to *hear* my name for a week unless there's some huge emergency . . .'

Gerhardt looked as if he were about to say something, and then decided against it. Catalina missed the expressions flitting across his face, being much too busy pulling down his briefs over the tentpole of his cock.

'There's a silly joke in Spanish about small hands making a small cock look bigger,' she said with a very satisfied smile. 'But mine make yours look *enormous*.'

'Hmm, I think my penis is perhaps a little larger than average,' Gerhardt said, trying to be dispassionately objective about his assessment.

'*Perhaps!*'

She giggled, and looked into his face, her hands working away busily, twisting and stroking with her thumbs up the big vein. To her delight, she saw his eyes go misty, his jaw slacken: these were the telltale signs that he was tipping over into full sex mode, bodyguard discretion forgotten.

Not quite, though.

'We are outside,' he said feebly; his head had been tipped back onto the pillows, but now he made a heroic effort to sit up again. 'We should go in – someone might come . . .'

'Yes, me and then you,' Catalina said, lowering to kiss the tip of his cock, trailing her tongue around the head. 'Then me again. There's no one else here and the guard on the gate won't let anyone in unless I say so. We can fuck stark naked on the grass if we want. Or in the pool. Oh God, let's do that next!'

She reached up, undid the gold chain holding up her silky Missoni halter top, and pulled it off, dropping it to the sofa beside her; she never needed to wear a bra, and the sight of her tiny breasts, dark nipples on shallow swells of golden skin, made Gerhardt's hips tilt up insistently towards the mouth that she was already fitting around him. His head flopped back on the pillows again; his hands reached up to cup her breasts. When she was in this kind of mood he had learned exactly how things would go: he needed to do nothing but to lie here in near bliss and stay hard for a good fifteen minutes, long enough for her to suck him as thoroughly as she wanted, then mount him and ride him to her heart's content. At that point he'd reach up and prop his thumb as extra stimulation where she wanted it, letting her rub and thrust against him, her tangled curls scratching deliciously against his.

He dragged more pillows behind his head and shoulders, tilting his upper body so he could watch everything, eat up with his eyes the sight of her fucking him so thoroughly, using him like her own personal jungle gym, climbing on and over him as lithely as the dancer she was. Even as she sucked him, her hands were hard at work on her own jeans, unfastening them, starting to drag them off; in a minute or so she would be astride him, he would be deep inside her, and the thought dragged a long, deep, groan of utter satisfaction right up from the root of his cock to the roof of his mouth.

All he had to do was stay hard until she was ready for him to let go. That was his entire job. Just hold off while watching the sight that millions of men around the world pictured when they closed their eyes and handled their cocks: Catalina, jumping lithely down now to kick off her jeans and thong, dropping to hands and knees on the daybed and crawling up his body like the panther she played in the 'Chasing Midnight' video. When she'd asked him what he thought of it, he'd been honest when he told her he didn't like the sight of her in a cage. But he had lied – by omission only, but still a lie. He hadn't added that every time he saw that video in the gym, his balls got so tight, his cock so hard that he had to stop whatever he was doing, walk swiftly to the men's toilets and shoot his load in a cubicle, biting his lips so he didn't moan in release and give himself away as he came hard into the bowl.

She was holding his dick now, fitting him between her legs, leaning down to kiss him; as he sank inside her, her lips met his, her tongue in his mouth, his cock inside her, like a circle of energy flooding evenly between them, linking them together above and below. His eyes rolled back in his skull; his arms were stretched wide. He might have been dropped from a great height onto the daybed, flung there, supine, for Catalina to fuck from today into the middle of next week.

Gerhardt hadn't managed to articulate his doubts. He'd have to find the right moment later, when they were fully clothed, too exhausted to consider fucking again for several hours. Okay, so that would be a while, but he could wait. He was clearly going to need to raise this issue carefully, to choose his words well in advance. To avoid putting up

Catalina's resistance to the idea Gerhardt had formed through observation over the last few weeks, and of which he was now convinced. He was quite sure by now that Latisha, for some reason, did not like Gerhardt, did not approve of her boss's new relationship, and was, in Gerhardt's professional opinion, becoming distinctly hostile to him.

Time to stop thinking about Latisha, though it had served its purpose. The concerns about her dislike of him had managed to diminish, for a minute or so, the build-up of pressure in his balls, regifting him a little control. Enough for him, now, to thrust his hips strategically just as she sank onto him, sending his cock even higher, butting almost too hard against her cervix, making her scream and gasp and tangle her hands in her hair and speed up even more. She was barely lifting herself off his cock now; instead she was stirring her hips in tight little circles in a way that she knew wouldn't allow him to keep control for much longer, which was specifically designed to drive him out of his mind.

He was going to come, faster than he'd meant to, but it was her fault: she knew what this did to him. Partly because the movement itself was so powerful, whipping his cock around with her superb muscle control; but partly, also, because this was how she moved onstage, whipping the fringe of her costume out horizontally as her hands held the mike and her hips traced circles and figures of eight in a way that made the blood rush to the crotches of many, many spectators who had all-too-vivid imaginings of what it would be like to have Catalina dance for them like that, an audience of one, up close and personal . . .

'Ah, fuck!' he blurted out, losing it at that thought, Catalina onstage and Catalina on top of him merging and blurring into one, his cock shooting in tribute to both of them, the star and the real woman. She knew at once that he was coming. Her circles became even more frenzied. She tilted and ground herself almost painfully against him, grabbing for one of his hands, pushing it into her crotch, working herself against his fingers, finding the angle and driving down, starting to scream, higher and higher until her voice was ragged and wailing.

His cock throbbed out the last drops of come. His body was limp as a rag below her, his cock the last part of him to stay taut. Her thighs tensed like wire, her pelvis jerked and she let go too, collapsing on top of him in a shower of limbs and hair, so light it was almost distressing for him, almost too light for a grown woman. Sometimes he had to remind himself that she was into her twenties, with hips and breasts, small as they were, not the child that she could feel like when she was in his arms and he took her tiny weight.

They had both solemnly got tested in Australia so that they could stop using condoms, and, great as the sex had been for him before, now it was mind-blowing. The sensation of nothing between them, not even the finest rubber money could buy; the knowledge that he had shot directly inside her, that he didn't need to stir himself and pull out, but could simply lie here, starfished, reaching up slowly to wrap his arms around his sweaty lover as the light breeze wafted around them, was the greatest joy he could imagine.

'Okay, we can walk around naked, like you want,' he said

drowsily into her mass of hair. 'I will enjoy that. We will be like Germans. You know how much we like to be naked in Germany?'

'I didn't,' she managed to mumble into his chest.

'Oh yes, it is very normal in my country. We call it FKK. Freikörperkultur. Free Body Culture. It is being together with nature, very relaxed and easy.'

'FKK! It sounds like the name of a gun! How funny . . .' She yawned heavily.

'No clothes for a whole week,' she said sleepily. 'Not unless we really, really want. No clothes and lots of sex in the pool . . .'

She was falling asleep, her voice trailing away, and he wrapped his arms around her tighter, settling her into a cosy curled-up ball on his chest. It had become a custom with them: after they had had sex with her on top, she would curl up like this, her body almost entirely on his, and snooze for at least an hour. And he loved it. He would doze lightly himself, but never quite let himself go. The sensation of watching over her, protecting her as she slept on him, was too profound for him to want to miss a moment of it.

This was his job, after all, what he had been doing all his adult life: successfully protecting people. So when he watched over the woman he loved as she slept on his broad chest, it felt like all the strings of his existence, professional and personal, were meshing together in a way he could never have imagined possible. It gave him a sense of satisfaction so profound it was like a warmth radiating through every bone and muscle, a physical sensation of utter relaxation and delight.

She was too young for him. Too famous for him. Too short for him: they looked positively comical together. But he could not resist a smile at the image he had seen many times, in mirrored lobbies and lifts, of them standing beside each other, Catalina so tiny and fragile that it was almost as if he could have balanced her on one palm, like a character in a cartoon talking to a fairy. He did not belong in her life. She was much too successful and rich for them to be any kind of a balanced couple.

And yet he had to admit that her willpower and her determination were more than a match for his. He had longed to be with her, craved it with all his heart and soul, but she had been the one to make it happen. He would never have dared to attempt to touch her in any kind of romantic way; it had been she who was the brave one, who had stripped off her clothes and forced his hand, who had broken down all of his defences with her courage and confidence.

With absolute certainly, Gerhardt knew that he would never be the one to call time on what was between them.

She has me for as long as she wants me, he said to himself as she began to make the little snuffling noises against his bare chest that were her form of post-coital snoring. Perhaps one day they would irritate him, though right now he couldn't imagine it; but sometimes those habits that one found charming in the beginning could turn annoying down the line.

Down the line. How long would it be? Weeks? Months? Years? He couldn't allow himself to think far into the future. He couldn't imagine that one day Catalina wouldn't tell him that this had all been a crazy fantasy of hers, fucking her bodyguard, and now that she'd fulfilled it, would he mind packing up his stuff and here was a one-way ticket back to Berlin; don't forget to text the cleaner and tell them you're coming so they can dust the place and get some milk in for you . . .

She has me as long as she wants me, he repeated to himself, feeling her chest rise and fall in his arms. *I will give her everything I have. It doesn't even matter if she doesn't love me back. I love her and I want to be by her side for the rest of my life.*

In Gerhardt's worst imaginings, he pictured Catalina breaking up with him because she was bored with him. Because the torrid affair with her bodyguard had burned itself out, and she had come to realize that a man like him could never be an equal to her in any way. That, surely, was how it was bound to end. But while it lasted, he would make the most of every moment, storing up memories that he would live off for the rest of his life.

Oddly, in one way, Gerhardt was right. Catalina would indeed have him as long as she chose. He would never be able to leave her; it would be she who would make the decision when the relationship would end. However, he could never have predicted the bizarre circumstances under which it would happen. Catalina was already in love with him, just as much as he loved her. She wanted to spend the rest of her life with him, just like he did with her.

And despite loving him with all her heart, she would break up with him anyway.

Chapter Sixteen

On-board

Angela felt as if she had been hit with a brick in the small of her back. No blood, no visible wound, but huge internal damage, a kidney punch that makes you want to curl up in a ball and rock yourself and sob with pain. Dropping the empty miniature of brandy in the toilet bin, the alcohol burning its way down the back of her throat, she thought bitterly back to the time when she had been a waitress, desperate to become a flight attendant, spending all her spare time working on her German with podcast lessons or Googling 'tips for airline cabin crew interviews'. At least when you were a waitress, if something this horrific happened to you at work – if, halfway through your first day, you shagged a customer, got caught and were summarily fired – you could run through the kitchen sobbing, exit through the back door and weep your heart out in decent solitude by the bins until, eventually, you pulled yourself together enough to stumble home and cry some more.

But on a plane there was nowhere to hide. She was trapped in here with her ex-colleagues, her ex-boss, the man who'd just totally taken advantage of her, been the most selfish lover she'd ever had – if you could even *call* it that . . .

She took a faltering breath. *Chin up*, Karl had said. *Stiff upper lip.* Clichés so true there was a reason they'd lasted this long. Angela pegged her chin higher, and it did help, a tiny bit. She felt fractionally more in control, fractionally more like the competent, groomed working professional she would have to be as soon as she left the toilet. The Visine – *thank God for Karl, and he's right, I have to start carrying that* – had cleared the whites of her eyes so she looked much less like an albino rabbit. She absolutely couldn't start crying again.

Time to get out there.

She knew she no longer had a job with Pure Air: there was no hope for a reprieve, no way she could redeem herself after the humiliation she had just endured. Her boss had seen her on her knees with her skirt around her waist, her tights pulled down, and drops of Danny Zasio's semen still trickling over her hand . . .

Chin up! Stiff upper lip! Angela reminded herself desperately. Her body still ached, and every time she thought of that mortifying image, nails screeched down a blackboard inside her head. It took all the courage she had to hold her head high, unlock the toilet door and step back out to face the consequences of her actions.

She hastened by Lord Tony's pod, in which Danny and the airline boss were still ensconced. Danny was chatting away amiably, his voice light and relaxed: she heard him say something about 'stupid bloody lobster' as she passed. How could he be so casual just after having done what he did to her? How could he have seduced her so fast while giving her nothing, nothing at all in return but trying to shoot in her face without even asking her first if that was okay, and then offering her the treat of pegging him on a future occasion?

Angela wasn't entirely sure what pegging was, but she could hazard a pretty good guess from the context, and for a terrible moment she pictured Danny holding out the harness he'd mentioned to her with a leer of encouragement. For some reason she imagined a pale pink studded one, like the ones the owners of female Staffies bought for their dogs. . . Oh God, she *really* had to stop thinking about this, had to avoid Danny as much as she possibly could . . .

She couldn't work his aisle. She just couldn't. She rounded the bar, turning her head away to avoid Lucinda's penetrating gaze, and headed for the other side of Luxe Class, looking for any call buttons that were lit up so she could throw herself into work again. At that point she'd have even welcomed an order for another lobster: it was impossible to think of anything else when you were cooking it but the poor crustacean steaming away, dying a slow and painful death . . .

She went right up to the far end of the aisle so that she could walk back slowly, linger there in comparative safety as much as possible. Vanessa, oddly, was sitting on the pull-down seat in Catalina's pod, sipping tea and reading a magazine, while Catalina seemed to be sleeping, her face turned to the wall. Vanessa gave Angela a swift smile, which meant both that she didn't need anything, and also that nobody had told her yet that Angela had been caught with Danny Zasio in the toilet and been sacked as a result. Angela returned Vanessa's smile as best she could and moved on, glancing into Michael Coggin-Carr's pod; he was asleep, or at least tucked up in bed, the lights dimmed to sleep mode.

'Excuse me?' came a quiet voice, and Angela swivelled obediently, entering Jane Browne's pod to see its occupant sitting in full lotus pose on her bed, feet laced through the opposite legs and over the knees in a way that looked extraordinarily uncomfortable. Jane's neat little unmemorable features, however, were perfectly serene as she looked up at Angela.

'Oh,' she said. 'I was going to ask for some camomile tea. Things got a bit crazy just now and I'm trying to calm down. But you look' – she tilted her head, considering Angela's expression with the analytical skills of a trained actress – '*completely* frazzled,' she finished. 'And you weren't even dealing with Catalina's big seeing-someone-who-wasn't-there meltdown.'

Angela had no idea what Jane was talking about. She paused, gulped, gulped again, tried to speak and couldn't. Standing in the doorway to the pod, her balance on the two-inch heels of her shoes felt unexpectedly precarious; she was afraid to move in case she tripped. The pain in her back was now overwhelming as she struggled with the vain attempt to reply in a normal tone of voice. Jane's eyes widened as she took in the sight of Angela wobbling slightly with her mouth open but no words coming forth.

'Take a breath right up from the pit of your stomach,' she said firmly. 'In through your mouth, pull it all the way up your back – feel it as it comes past your shoulder blades, feel them widening out as that happens – and then let the breath trickle out through your nose, nice and slow.'

Angela's cheeks were reddening dangerously, but she obeyed, an unexpected calm sweeping through her as her lungs emptied out.

'And again!' Jane said, but Angela was already drawing in her second breath.

After three cycles, Angela managed to meet Jane's eyes and say, 'Thank you,' in a relatively moderated tone.

'No problem. It's a yoga trick. I use it when I need to get centred on set,' Jane said easily. 'Do you feel a bit better now?'

'Yes, thank you. Can I get you anything, Ms Browne?' Angela said formally. 'Oh, sorry! You asked for tea!'

She pinched the bridge of her nose furiously to stop the tears that were forming yet again at the realization that she had forgotten Jane's initial request.

'It's fine, it's fine!' Jane said hurriedly. 'Honestly, I don't need it! Why don't you take a moment . . . sit down . . .'

'No! No, I'll get the tea now! Camomile! I remember, I really do!'

Angela hurried out of the pod.

Honestly, Jane thought, following the stewardess's head, her blonde doughnut bun flashing brightly over the top of the moulded wall as she went back to the bar. *This flight's just crazy! It's as if they're pumping hallucinogens or something through the air feed . . .*

She closed her eyes and rested the backs of her palms onto her knees, completing the traditional meditation yoga pose. She definitely needed some calm: Angela was unlikely to be in any better state when she returned. And Jane would be unable to resist the pull to ask her what was wrong and try to make it better. That was her curse: the oldest of a large family, she was always the shoulder that people cried on.

But I'm changing. Things will be different from now on. I'm going to look after people less and take care of myself more.

266

Because Jane had made a New Year's resolution, taken a good hard look at her life in January and decided that its focus needed a drastic alteration. She had been so focused on her career for so long that she hadn't taken time – or, maybe, been brave enough – to reach out for what she truly wanted. But when she had agreed to take this flight to Los Angeles, Jane had come to the resolution that it would be life-changing. She was literally counting the hours until she could put her plan into action.

Not that many, she thought. *Not that many at all. I just need to get up the courage and make that final push . . . risk it all to get my heart's desire . . .*

And the image of her heart's desire sent a delicious shiver of anticipation all the way down from the nape of Jane's neck to the base of her perfectly straight spine.

Chapter Seventeen

Los Angeles International Airport

'Nice-looking guy, eh? But not what you'd call a ladykiller!'

Special Agent Herrera of the Federal Bureau of Investigation nodded at the face of the man on the screen behind him.

'He's no Bradley Cooper,' she continued ironically. 'Or Idris Elba.'

'Mmm-*mmm*,' muttered one of the female airport security guards in the briefing room. 'My man Idris is *fine*.'

'Well, this guy does have nice regular features,' commented Special Agent Smithee, a fellow squad member of Herrera's who was partnering her on this arrest. 'Ladies like that, apparently.'

'When we're ovulating,' Herrera said. 'Did you see that study? Women go for guys with pretty, even features when they're fertile.' She grinned at Smithee, a squat, chunky guy with a face only a mother could love. 'Rest of the time, we prefer guys with more masculine, rugged features. Fact.'

'So women want the nice guys to father their kids, and then they cheat on them with the hunks?' Smithee summarized.

'Got it in one,' Herrera said. 'I'd say you're shit out of luck on both counts, Smithee.'

'*He's* no Idris Elba, that's for sure!' observed the security guard to general amusement.

'Well, damn lucky this guy isn't either,' Herrera said. 'He's done enough damage with his "nice regular features".' She tipped an imaginary cap to Smithee. 'Just imagine if he'd been a heart-throb,' she finished. 'We'd have *triple* the amount of vics to deal with!'

'We have a warrant here for his arrest for aggravated fraud, multiple targets,' Smithee said, wrapping up the banter portion of the security briefing and segueing into the serious part as he turned to look once more at the face of the man on the screen. 'Here's his MO: he poses as a banker who runs a real successful hedge fund. He gets to know rich, prominent women at social events, courts them, dates them, convinces them to invest with him, reels them in with initially good returns and then proceeds to clean them out. He relies on them being too embarrassed to prosecute – the publicity would be pretty rough. Plus, for shits and giggles, he's taken all sorts of photos of them together. Sexy stuff – you know, the kind of thing that'd be majorly embarrassing for them if they came out.' He coughed. 'Role play. Naughty stuff. Costumes. What there is of them.'

Someone at the back of the room let out a long, slow whistle, which Smithee responded to with an appreciative eyebrow raise.

'Oh yeah, and he likes to video the two of 'em bumping uglies, too,' Herrera added. 'He's apparently real persuasive. So once the money's gone, he pretty much blackmails them into keeping quiet with the shit he has on them. Nothing overt, you know? More "I'm so happy to have such great memories of our time together, sweetie, let's not fight over money". Very smooth.'

She grimaced.

'And until recently, that was how it worked. The vics just crawled away to lick their wounds in private and didn't say a word to anyone. But it looks like the guy's escalated drastically. We just heard he's wanted over there for murder.'

'No kidding,' Smithee said dourly. 'Up till now he's just been scamming his victims. But the latest wasn't just ready to press charges – she was ballsy enough to do some investigating to back up her case. All these rich ladies are just a few degrees of separation from each other, with their charity events and socializing. This one did some digging, asked around, managed to gee up a couple other women to go on the record about how he ripped them off. Our friends at Scotland Yard figure that she made the mistake of telling him what she was going to do, trying to convince him to give the three of them at least some of their money back.'

It was his turn to pull a face.

'That was a real big mistake,' he said grimly. 'Our guy drugged her and staged a fake overdose to stop her going to the cops. Played the grieving ex-boyfriend – his story was that he'd just broken up with her and she popped a few too many sleeping pills.'

Evan Jennings, the head of LAX security, frowned at this.

'So he's fleeing the jurisdiction?' he asked. 'How the hell did he make it onto the plane? And there's no way he booked this flight at the last minute. It was sold out months ago.'

'He's travelling under an alias,' Herrera clarified. 'He's had this flight booked for a while now under a false name. They think he bribed someone in the passport office and intercepted another guy's passport being delivered. The Brits are having a major crisis with passport couriers, apparently – tons of 'em going missing. Clever of him, 'cause it wouldn't be spotted in all the confusion. The Brits are unpicking it at their end, but it seems like he realized he chose the wrong woman this time and started laying down an escape route in advance. This flight's the last place in the world you'd look for a fugitive. No one would imagine he'd be on a plane with this much hoo-ha going on around it.'

'Pretty slick of him to figure that out,' Jennings commented with grudging respect. He glanced at his watch. 'Okay, we have to get this done and dusted,' he said. 'Some essential questions. First, is he violent?'

'He's not known to be,' Herrera said. 'It's been strictly white-collar crime up till now. But hey, the escalation, remember? This is all new territory for him.'

'I want everyone to keep in mind that this is a delicate, delicate situation,' Jennings said emphatically. 'We have a plane packed full of celebrities and VIPs and a big press conference scheduled for when it lands. That means that we're going to have to be extra discreet about the arrest. Normally, procedure would mandate going on-board before anyone deplanes and taking him off in cuffs, but no way can we do that in this case. It's an inaugural flight, we have the owner of the damn *airline* on-board, and if we try that we'll all get the sack. I've consulted with the airport commissioners and they're tearing their hair out at the idea. Can you imagine the headlines?'

'Sir, could we pull him out at passport control?' asked one of the security officers.

'Uh, can I make a request here? Ideally, we wanna see who his next target is,' Smithee said. 'That's the way this guy works – he always lines up the next lady well before he finishes with the one before. The Brits haven't been able to locate her, but this guy's so sneaky that means nothing. He could easily be using a different email account and cellphone to contact her. And if we can ID her, and prove that he was whispering sweet nothings to her while he was playing the grieving boyfriend back home, that'd help out the murder case against him a whole lot.'

'We're thinking he might try to call her when he lands,' Herrera chimed in. 'But if we get lucky, she might even be meeting him.'

'So you want to do it landside?' Jennings asked, perking up tremendously.

This was excellent news for the head of airport security. Once the target had cleared security and customs, making a detention in the crowded terminal was a considerably higher risk, as the subject would have many more possibilities for evading arrest. But it meant that the inaugural flight of Pure Air 111 would be only tangentially associated with the detention of the target, and for Jennings, very aware of the negative publicity implications that could put his own job on the line, that would definitely be worth the extra time and trouble.

The two special agents nodded as one.

'Nobody should approach him but us and our team,' Herrera cautioned. 'We'll do the hard part. But we'll absolutely require—'

'No problem. I'll have my guys stationed around the terminal as back-up,' Jennings assured them instantly.

The Idris Elba lover cleared her throat pointedly.

'People,' Jennings said. 'My people.'

Herrera winked at the female security officer.

'Final question: what if he exits with a fellow passenger?' Jennings asked.

Smithee frowned.

'He's travelling alone,' he said. 'Just a single ticket booked. There's no indication he's got a companion with him.'

'Yeah, but look at his MO,' Jennings pointed out astutely. 'He goes after high-profile women, dates them, defrauds them, and they're too embarrassed – or he has enough dirt on them – to press charges. So, this flight's just the kind of place to pick up another woman who fits that profile! There are shitloads of rich celebrities aboard, and not just up front. Plenty of bigwigs in business too. Those seats go for thousands of dollars a pop. What are you gonna do if he walks out landside arm in arm with' – he threw his arms wide to show that he was exaggerating for dramatic effect – 'Catalina?' he finished.

'She *did* break up with a boyfriend a while ago,' the security guard volunteered. 'The big white guy who looks like he belongs on Mount Rushmore.'

'Oh yeah, that's right,' Herrera said. She huffed out a laugh. 'Maybe our guy's trying to catch her on the rebound.'

She exchanged glances with Smithee.

'He isn't gonna try for Catalina,' she said confidently. 'She's way too high profile for him to risk that kind of publicity, especially not with him travelling under a false name. But you're right,' she said, nodding at Jennings. 'He could easily have found a fresh target on-board, some businesswoman or minor celeb. He could be starting to court this one, soften her up, while he's already got some woman over here all ready to start clearing out her savings accounts for him. That'd fit right in with his MO, wouldn't it? Line them up one after the other and clean them out.'

She bit her lip.

'Yeah, if he walks off the plane with someone, we're going to have to think on our feet,' she agreed. 'Especially depending on who it is. Talk about a whole new wrinkle to deal with . . .'

Chapter Eighteen

One year ago

'She looks *amazing*,' Laura Miller, the director of *Angel Rising*, enthused, reaching out to palpate Jane's newly defined bicep. 'Simone, honestly, you've done a fantastic job. This is even better that I hoped. I wanted real, lean muscle and you've totally delivered.'

Jane stood patiently while her director and coach talked about her as if she were a piece of meat: as an actress, she was more than used to it.

'Great!' Simone beamed at Laura. 'I've got to say, she worked her arse off. When she wasn't training, she was eating lean meat, or drinking high-protein shakes. Don't get too close to her unless she's been sucking a mint!'

She winked at Jane, who stuck her tongue out in reply.

'You know what a protein-based diet does to your breath?' she asked, seeing Laura frown in confusion. 'Poor Janey's Little Miss Stinky Mouth at the moment.'

'Shut *up*,' Jane said, elbowing her coach in her narrow ribcage.

'Eew! Don't breathe on me, stink-face!'

Simone made a big play of turning her head away from Jane's.

'You hear that, Olivier?'

Laura, grinning now, looked over at the stunningly handsome co-star of *Angel Rising*, Olivier Lautrec, a French actor in his early forties who had been a heart-throb for twenty years and was only becoming more attractive with age. A swift entry of the words 'tall, dark and handsome' into any online image search engine would swiftly produce a picture of Olivier wearing a loose shirt unbuttoned halfway down his lean chest, staring broodingly at the camera, his dark hair romantically tousled, incarnating Gallic masculinity. In French films, Olivier was an A-list star, who played tortured, intellectual heroes; in American ones, he was inevitably cast as the sexy Latin lover whose raw sexuality, as unfiltered as his Gauloises, derailed the previously happily married heroine into a torrid affair riddled with all sorts of exotic, un-American perversions.

The story would, inevitably, end badly. In American movies, infidelity committed by women with hot French men was always harshly punished. Male directors and producers didn't want their wives getting any ideas.

So Olivier had been perfect casting for the male lead of *Angel Rising*, the tortured yet compelling choreographer with a troubled past and a predilection for twisted sex games. Just one dark, ambiguous stare from beneath those drooping lids, one half-smile from those full lips, and pretty much any woman on the planet would drop her partner, children and underwear in swift succession to follow him wherever he was beckoning.

The irony was that Olivier had absolutely no sexual interest in females at all. Leaning against the mirrored wall of the rehearsal room – Olivier never merely stood when he could lounge – he was now looking down his haughty nose at the prospect of shooting sex scenes not only with a woman, but one who had halitosis from her low-carb diet.

'You must brush your teeth many times,' he informed Jane coldly. 'I refuse to kiss you otherwise, which is of course essential for the story we tell in this film.'

'I definitely will,' Jane said with great humility, despite the fact that in her brief acquaintance with Olivier, she had already noticed his own breath was far from minty-fresh.

She had heard from other previous co-stars of Olivier's that he could be hell to work with, as he had an ego the size of the Eiffel Tower and needed to dominate every set he was on, but that worked perfectly for the dynamic of *Angel Rising*. Jane's character was supposed to be subservient to Olivier's for most of the story, until the tables slowly started to turn. Jane had very little ego, in the negative sense of that expression, and like Elizabeth Bennet, she possessed a lively sense of the ridiculous. As long as it didn't affect her own work, there was nothing she enjoyed more than the absurd exaggerations and diva-esque behaviour of her fellow actors.

She glanced at Laura, immediately perceiving from the director's complacent expression that this was exactly the dynamic for which she had hoped in casting her actors: Olivier bossy, Jane meek. Laura gave Jane the swiftest, most fleeting of nods, a silent communication which indicated that deference was exactly the correct tack to take with Olivier.

'So, we're blocking out the later rehearsal scene today,' Laura said.

Everyone knew this perfectly well, but it was the cue for

the small group gathered in the dance studio to look serious and fall back into a loose semi-circle around the director, symbolically acknowledging that she had now taken control of the room. There were only four of them besides Laura and her assistant: the two actors, plus Simone and another choreographer, Lacey, who, like Olivier's character, was an ex-ballet dancer. Simone was tasked with the aerial part of the cabaret routine that Jane's character would perform, Lacey with the floor work, and the two of them had already started collaborating.

The scene they were working on today was the one in which Jane's attraction to Olivier would spill over into the physical. It was a turning point, the moment it became clear – both to Jane and to the audience – that it was her submission that stirred Olivier's desire. Although it would be revealed later on in *Angel Rising* that Jane's character had been playing a game of her own all along, allowing Olivier to seduce her in order to trap him into an admission that, years ago, he had hired someone to throw acid into the face of a rival male dancer at the Paris Opera Ballet, these scenes had to be absolutely believable, with Jane seeming dazzled by Olivier's louche charm and compelling physicality.

'He's going to be wrapping her, right?' Laura said, looking from Simone to Lacey. 'I have such a strong visual image of this. She's standing still, wearing just her leotard, and all that moves is her chest, breathing faster and faster, rising and falling' – she pressed her hand to her own collarbone – 'as he poses her almost like a serial killer with his latest victim's body. It's creepy, but really sexy. But I can't picture her stance . . .'

'Arabesque,' Lacey said instantly. 'I've worked this out already. He's making her hold the balance for a really long time, right? Till she's nearly crying? It's like he's saying, "*This is the price of working with me. You need to endure pain and suffering to create my art*".'

'*Exactly*,' Laura said in great satisfaction. 'And she's so thin – her bones will look so tiny beside him. Look . . .'

She reached out to run her fingers over Jane's protruding collarbone, the top slats of her ribcage bared by the spaghetti-strap leotard she was wearing.

'She's going to look so vulnerable! I want us to be genuinely frightened for her,' she commented. 'It's a real statement about the kind of performance art that has women commercializing their masochism.'

Simone rolled her eyes, but out of Laura's visual range – only Jane noticed it. And for a moment their gazes met, Simone's dark brown eyes smiling into Jane's lighter ones, sharing identical amusement. It wasn't just the ponderous significance with which Laura delivered these words, it was the hypocrisy. Laura, after all, had co-written a script that for its first eighty minutes was doing exactly what she was criticizing: commercializing female masochism. Jane's character was required to submit to every whim Olivier's one expressed, both professionally and personally, and almost always either in a skimpy leotard or naked.

It wasn't the kind of part Jane intended to make a practice of playing, but if the film were successful, it would establish her as a leading lady, not just an excellent ensemble actor. It was a gamble, of course, on many levels, as it always was when you accepted a role: she had been especially nervous of the performance side of *Falling Angel* even before she realized how much hard work it would entail. But then she had met Simone, and, much as Jane detested training, she'd have spent all day and all night training if it meant being with her coach.

It wasn't just that Jane was hugely attracted to Simone. Jane worked in a profession jam-packed with insanely attractive people, in front of and behind the cameras, and she had learnt years ago to distinguish crushes, even lust, from deeper feelings. Any professional actor knew that film sets in particular were, in gardening terminology, forcing houses for affairs, and that the emotions engendered by being thrown together in such proximity tended to be ephemeral. Mostly, they faded as soon as the shoot was over, which often led to considerable awkwardness when the participants had to reunite for the promotional tour.

Jane's training regime with Simone could easily have been just another one of those crushes. Working so closely for hours a day in very few clothes, sweating, laughing, Simone's hands constantly on Jane to adjust her, spot her, sometimes taking her whole weight if her arms gave out . . . it was a recipe for building intimacy. Jane could have resisted the physical attraction easily enough, however. There had been plenty of hot bodies shooting *And When We Fall*, but Jane had been perfectly able to keep her legs together when not engaging in the many and varied sex scenes. Unlike Milly Gamble, one of her co-stars, Jane only had sex when she liked the person's brain as much as their body.

That was exactly the trouble with Simone: she was not only sharp and clever, but her intelligence was so closely attuned to Jane's that Jane had never understood the expression 'being on someone's wavelength' so perfectly before. Almost from the first, the two women had clicked, teasing each other, finding exactly the same things funny or witty or meaningful. They could talk for hours about everything under the sun when they were alone, while, surrounded by other people at *Angel Rising* production meetings, exchanging looks of mutual understanding about a comment someone had made, Jane would feel as if she and Simone were the only ones in the room.

And the physical side of things grew more intense every day. Simone kneeling behind Jane as she sat on a padded mat, pushing Jane's back down till her nose touched her knees, forcing her legs straight; Simone's breath and hands warm on Jane's sweaty skin, her voice encouraging, her breasts pressing into Jane's shoulder blades; the smell of Simone's own sweat, mingled with her tea tree deodorant . . . Jane had actually gone to Holland and Barrett to buy tea tree deodorant a few weeks after starting to train with Simone, so that she could smell that scent even without Simone present. It wasn't the same without her, but it was still *something* . . .

'Simone, can you help me demonstrate?' Lacey was saying eagerly. 'You'll be Jane, of course.'

Simone grinned at Jane as she walked over to the two wide strips of fabric that hung from ceiling to floor, bright red, pooling theatrically on the wood below, the colour reflected in the huge mirrored walls, another burst of drama.

'I won't be doubling for you when they shoot this scene, Janey,' she said teasingly. 'You're going to have to do it all yourself. And it'll *hurt*.'

'Really?' Jane said feebly.

Simone's grin deepened as she took up a ballet arabesque, balancing on her right leg, the left lifting to an angle above ninety degrees, one arm extended high in front of her, the other trailing beautifully away behind.

'Standing still in balance is the *worst*,' she said cheerfully, even as she made the pose look effortless.

Almost as lean as a Giacometti statue, clad in the usual performer's gear of leotard, rolled-waist leggings, and a shrug wrapped snugly over her torso and tied at the waist, all faded to various shades of grey by wear and washing, Simone's raised and pointed foot traced one tight, perfect line to the fingers of the outstretched hand. Her feet were terribly calloused and knotted, not as damaged as a ballerina's by pointe work, but still seeming years older than the rest of her body. Almost since the first time she had met Simone, Jane had wanted to sit with those feet in her lap, work rich massage cream into every dry line, every snagged cuticle, wrap them in warm towels to let the cream sink in still further, buff off the ridges from her toenails, file them each into perfect symmetry, rub almond oil into their rough surfaces, kiss each shining nail in turn . . . glance up to see Simone smiling at her . . .

But Simone had a boyfriend called Rangi back home in New Zealand, a Maori guy to whom she barely ever referred, but whose existence hung over every moment of Jane's inter-actions with Simone. And Simone showed no hint of being attracted to Jane; she was hugely friendly, hugely fun and physically affectionate, just as if Jane were her younger sister, her favourite pupil. No signs of bisexuality, no references to a previous girlfriend; Jane had repeatedly mentioned women she had dated and seen not the remotest flicker of revulsion in her coach's eyes, but neither any responsive glimmer of interest.

I love her. And she'll never know. Or maybe she does know, and she's handling things perfectly, showing me in the nicest possible way that she isn't interested . . .

'Okay, I'm Olivier,' Lacey said intently, stepping up behind Simone, taking one of the two swathes of fabric and beginning to wind it high around Simone's raised thigh, tight into the intersection of Simone's legs, so intimately close that Jane could barely watch for raging jealousy. This was certainly not where the fabric would normally go for silks work: that was not between the buttocks, but beneath them, just above the big swell of muscle in the front thigh. No matter how lean a performer was, that muscle was always highly defined, providing a perfect ridge below which a tightly wrapped coil of fabric would not slip.

But for the purposes of this scene, Olivier was not teaching his pupil correct aerial silks practice. He was making it clear that he controlled her body, could wrap and bind and fasten it into place not just in the bedroom, but in the rehearsal room too. That Jane's character, Corinne, effectively belonged to him, in private and in public. The script required another cabaret performer to walk in halfway through this scene, and their reaction would reinforce for the audience the extremely unusual nature of Olivier's behaviour. He wouldn't miss a beat, would continue to wind the red silky fabric around Jane's limbs, binding her even more tightly and erotically, exposing her submission to the gaze of the very embarrassed onlooker.

Just as Lacey was currently doing to Simone, whose upraised leg was now twined in tight loops, her torso being crossed in explicit bindings of shockingly erotic bright red.

'I *love* that colour against the grey she's wearing,' Laura observed, and her assistant, who was taking photographs, nodded and muttered that he agreed. 'What if you took a loop around her neck?'

Simone let her head fall to one side, eyes bugging out in a comic 'they just hanged me' expression as Lacey answered: 'You know, we tried that, and it just looks weird. See?'

Simone straightened her neck again and Lacey took a turn around it with the silk. The material was much too thick: it cut Simone's neck off completely, making her head seem as if it were floating oddly above her body.

'*Not* sexy,' Lacey said.

'Yup, weird. Not sexy at *all*,' Laura nodded.

Whipping the fabric away, Lacey started to bind Simone's outstretched arm. The concept was for the scarlet colour to blaze diagonally across Simone's body, turning her into a living sculpture, as if her body were being written across by a huge red marker pen. Laura actually sighed in pleasure, but her emotion was entirely professional. Jane didn't dare to make any kind of noise at all: she was far too nervous that it might come out with such erotic fervour that she would utterly betray herself.

The palms of her hands were damp; her mouth was dry; moisture was distributing itself around her body in all sorts of betraying places. Between her legs, electricity was sparking and fizzing like a jet in a whirlpool bath sending bubbles insistently up inside her. She wanted desperately to shift, to rub herself, even momentarily, to try to relieve some of the pressure: but there was no way she could put a hand down there.

'But funny you should mention the neck thing – here's what we thought . . .'

Lacey finished wrapping the second red swathe of fabric around Simone's wrist; it fell, trailing, to the floor, as its counterpart did from Simone's raised ankle, like blood dripping down from severed veins. Stepping back, Lacey placed her hands loosely around Simone's neck, splaying her fingers down over Simone's collarbone. It was the final touch, extreme possessiveness exemplified in a perfectly symbolic gesture.

'*Wow*,' Laura said, and her assistant murmured his own approval.

'Let's see Olivier do that for a sec,' Lacey suggested, and Olivier pushed his shoulders off the wall. Moving lightly in his scuffed desert boots, his dark jeans hanging from his rangy hips in a faux-casual style, he took Lacey's place behind Simone.

'You okay to hold the arabesque a bit longer, Sim?' Lacey said to her. 'Not cutting off your circulation?'

'Oh yeah, no worries,' Simone said cheerfully. 'The silks are actually holding me up now. It's just the stretch, and that's no biggie.'

She glanced evilly at Jane.

'You're going to want to wrap them a bit tighter for Janey there,' she added. 'Get some nice shots of the silks really biting into her. That's just what a bastard guy like his character would do – tie her up too tight.'

'We can't bruise her,' Laura said thoughtfully, 'but, hmm, I love the idea of it digging in . . .'

'Oh, she'll get banged up a bit when you're shooting,' Simone pointed out. 'She's got rope burns on her ankles already, clumsy cow.'

Her dark eyes flickered to Jane's, teasingly challenging her, and Jane knew she would have to respond or raise some suspicions about her silence.

'Still here!' she managed. 'Haven't left the room! I can hear you talking about me!'

It was hard to get the words out; her mouth was so dry by now it felt gluey. She looked around rather frantically, and saw that Laura's assistant had brought in a small stack of bottles of water; she walked swiftly over to get one. Uncapping the bottle, she took a long swig, and then froze in place as, lowering it again, she saw the tableau being enacted behind her, reflected in the floor-to-ceiling mirror.

Olivier towered over Simone's small frame, his expression positively satanic, a dark lock of hair falling over his forehead, his lips twisted in his signature sneering expression. He clasped his hands around Simone's neck, imbuing the gesture with such a palpable eroticism that Laura sighed again in sheer professional delight. The tips of his long fingers reached to Simone's ribcage, and he did not splay them theatrically, as Lacey had done, but rested them there almost casually, as if he were merely showing off one of his many possessions.

And all this time, Simone was standing perfectly still, the line of her arabesque exquisite. She had been transformed by Lacey's fabric bindings into a beautiful object, only the flickers of her thick dark eyelashes, the bright expression in her big brown eyes humanizing her, reminding the viewer that she was real, not just a life-size doll.

Seeing Olivier's nicotine-stained hands on Simone sparked such powerfully confused reactions in Jane that she felt buffeted by them. She hated seeing a man's hands on Simone, felt a rush of resentment even against Simone's poor innocent boyfriend; she wanted to turn, run across the room, drag Olivier off Simone, forbid him from ever touching her again, start the complicated process of unbinding the woman she loved.

But also, she wanted to push Olivier away so that she could take his place. To stand there, her own hands encircling Simone's neck, sliding down to cover the peaks of Simone's small breasts, resting there to circle her nipples with her thumbs, kissing Simone's bare shoulders, licking the sweat from her skin, tracing Simone's arms, her waist, reaching down between her legs where the wide strip of red fabric bisected her equally small, tight buttocks, covering her mound. Run her fingers along the edge of the fabric, still kissing Simone's neck, hoping to hear the sweet little moans and writhes that would tell her that Simone was responding just as Jane wanted her to do, was encouraging Jane to slide her fingers beneath the silk, touch Simone's crotch, feel the dampness there that was not just sweat from the exertion of holding this pose, but Simone's physical reaction to Jane's kisses and caresses.

One hand would be still on Simone's breast, feeling the nipple as hard as if it had been sculpted, hearing Simone's breathing deepen as Jane pressed herself against Simone's back, letting Simone feel her own erect nipples, her own heat and sweat and arousal, as Jane painstakingly worked the tips of her fingers under the edge of the leotard, found the stretch lace of Simone's thong, heard Simone groan in anticipation as Jane slid her fingers under that too, found Simone's hot wet centre, parted her swollen lips, eased in and up and started to bring Simone to a pounding climax, her body still tethered in place by the strips of fabric, her hips beating against her restraints and Jane's swiftly working hand . . .

'I need to go to the loo,' she said frantically. 'Back in a sec!'

She was so discombobulated that it actually took her a few seconds to locate the door, though it was painted white and should have been easy to spot in the sea of mirrors boxing them in. But, having seen it reflected, when she turned around it wasn't where she expected to find it, and by the time she found the real door, not the reflected one, everyone, even Olivier, who was notoriously self-absorbed, was staring at her oddly.

'I have a bit of a urinary tract infection,' she heard herself babble as she reached the door. 'Sorry, too much inform-ation . . . sorry, everyone. Especially Olivier – you definitely don't need to hear that!'

Oh my God, I just made the biggest idiot of myself back there! I even told the woman I'm sexually obsessed with that I have a UTI, which I don't . . . oh, fuck it all . . .

It was a mercy that the toilets were just outside the rehearsal room. In a few seconds Jane had dived into a toilet stall, locked the door, dragged down her leggings and under-pants and, her buttocks dropped to the cold toilet seat, plunged her hand between her legs to bring herself to a climax that was almost as powerful as the one she'd imagined giving Simone.

Just one wasn't enough. The second followed almost instantaneously after the first, with just a few extra flicks of her fingertips – Jane's quirky sense of humour meant that she always thought of this as a 'buy one, get one free' deal. She gave herself a twenty-second recovery period before she allowed herself a final orgasm, fast and pounding, the old toilet seat rattling beneath her as her bottom banged against it again and again, her fingers working herself frantically, moisture flowing thick and rich, lubricating her so slickly that she came in a long rush of absolute physical delight, losing herself completely.

Her panting was crazy, her heart pounding against her ribcage; it was all she could do not to moan aloud. The other cubicle doors had been open, so that she knew she was alone in here, but if she allowed herself to make any sounds, she was scared she wouldn't be able to control the volume . . .

Done. That was all she could permit herself right now. They'd be wondering where she was if she stayed any longer. What *were* the symptoms of a UTI? Did you pee a lot or just a little? If it was the latter, they'd be expecting her back any moment.

She leaned her hot forehead against the concrete wall of the cubicle. Contact with the cold wall was a much-needed shock back to reality; she closed her eyes, her entire body still throbbing, wishing that she could press her exposed crotch against the wall too, cool that down as well, and the idea made her smile, picturing what an idiot she would look if anyone saw her trying it.

'Janey? Janey, you all right? You in here?'

It was Simone's voice. Jane jumped in shock, rattling

the toilet seat once more, and sat up, reaching down for the waistband of her leggings.

'Yes!' she called, her voice high and squeaky. 'Yes, coming!'

The irony that this was precisely what she had just been doing wasn't lost on her. Fumbling clumsily for her underpants as well, she heaved herself to her feet, reaching out en route for a wodge of toilet paper to blot her crotch as well as she could. Chucking it into the loo bowl, she pulled the wooden-handled chain to flush it away.

'You okay?' Simone was asking.

Simone was just on the other side of the door. If they were lovers, Jane would be unlatching it, pulling Simone in, kissing her frantically, their hands reaching down for each other, ready for a fast and furious mutual finger-fuck, tongues in each other's mouths, racing to make the other one come first. If they were lovers, they would have planned this, would have silently signalled to each other that Simone was to follow Jane into the toilets, unable to wait until rehearsal was over, burning up in the heat that blazed at the start of an affair.

But they weren't. Jane actually banged her forehead briefly against the concrete wall to remind herself of that crucial fact before, wincing from the impact, she unlocked the door of the toilet stall and braced herself for the sight of Simone, standing there with her hands on her hips, frowning in concern, her pretty red mouth pursed.

'What's up? You don't have a urinary tract infection!' she said accusingly. 'There's no *way* you could have something like that and not have told me about it! You'd've been nipping to the dunny and scratching yourself like a monkey all the time!'

Jane couldn't help giggling at this. God, how she loved Simone's way of expressing herself.

'I don't,' she said, thinking quickly. 'I just had a freak-out about not being able to hold that pose like you do. I'm never going to be that good.'

At least the last sentence was true. Simone's expression softened into reassurance.

'Aw, sweetie, have a hug,' she said, stepping forward to wrap her arms around Jane. She ran one calloused palm in circles over Jane's narrow shoulders, down to the centre of her back. Try as she might, Jane could not interpret these caresses as anything more than a friend comforting another friend.

'You're gonna be fine,' Simone said against the side of Jane's head. They were almost exactly the same height, Simone's breath warm on Jane's ear. 'You're really good. You're a quick learner and you're nice and flexible. And you honestly don't need to be that strong. I can do all the hardcore stunts.'

Her crotch was pressed against Jane's, both girls so thin that they had practically no breasts, let alone stomachs, to form a padded layer between them. Ribcage to ribcage, breast to breast, thigh to thigh: Jane was reminded of a Swinburne poem she had had to recite in drama school, about a young man and woman who were murdered during the French Revolution, tied together and thrown into the Loire river to drown. The point of the poem was that the young man was madly in love with the young woman, and, as they tied them up, he made a beautiful speech about it being a gift from God to die like this, bound tightly against her.

I shall drown with her, laughing for love; and she / Mix with me, touching me, lips and eyes . . . The lines came back to her as if she had learnt them yesterday. *And I should have held you, and you held me / As flesh holds flesh, and the soul the soul . . .*

'There you go!' Simone said cheerfully, administering a last pat to Jane's shoulder blades and pulling back. She peered at Jane's face. 'Did you bang your forehead? You're a bit red.'

She crossed to the sink, pulled out some green paper towels from the dispenser, ran them under the cold tap and pressed them against Jane's forehead.

'Here, you hold them there for a minute or so till it goes away,' she instructed. 'I'll pop back and tell them that you're fine. And you know I was just joking about tying you up tight, don't you?'

Jane nodded, taking the paper towels and holding them in place. Simone whisked herself out of the bathroom, leaving Jane staring after her and wishing with all her heart that Simone had been entirely serious about tying her up tight. She had never had any particular bondage or S&M fantasies before. She had played around with handcuffs occasionally, but then who didn't nowadays? That was just par for the course, considered almost obligatory as part of a well-balanced modern sex life.

But seeing Simone posed like that with the red fabric fastened so tightly between her legs . . . imagining herself in that same position, with Simone being the one to wrap her into place with the swathes of fabric, trapping Jane's limbs into immobility before proceeding to perform all manner of erotic perversions on her, with Jane barely able to move a muscle . . . the thought made her shiver so deeply that her whole thin frame rippled with it.

'Fuck!' she said loudly. 'Fuck, *stop* this! You have to get a grip!'

And, balling up the soggy towels with unnecessary force, she threw them so hard at the waste bin that they bounced off the side. Turning, she stomped towards the toilet door, dragging it open and practically slamming it behind her, which relieved her frustration enough for her to be able to plaster a smile onto her face as she re-entered the rehearsal room.

'Sorry about that!' she said brightly. 'All good now! Let's get going! Does someone want to tie me up?'

Chapter Nineteen

On-board

Catalina's eyes flickered open. The light enveloping her, diffuse sapphire blue, was both soothing and vaguely reminiscent of an expensive hospital. She turned her head to one side, disoriented, to see Vanessa, sitting on the leather seat reading a magazine. Then the huge body of the airplane moved beneath her like a ship breasting a gentle wave, and Vanessa looked over at the bed, her expression instantly softening into an appropriate nurturing one as she saw Catalina was awake.

'How are you doing, sweetie?' she asked. 'Ooh, that was a nasty time you had back there! Did you manage to sleep a bit?'

'I think so,' Catalina said slowly.

'It looked like you were,' Vanessa said comfortably. 'But I couldn't be sure. Oh good. Feeling better now?'

'Tish . . . is she awake?' Catalina asked, her speech still a little heavy with sleep.

Vanessa pursed her narrow lips.

'I doubt it, to be honest,' she said. 'She was out like a light and drooling into the bargain.'

Catalina shifted restlessly under the blanket, her hands

reaching up to the satin-trimmed border and starting to pull it down, her legs trying to kick it free.

'Need the loo?' Vanessa asked solicitously. 'I can give you a hand there if you're still feeling wobbly.'

'No – well yes, but right now I want to go and see if Tish is awake . . .'

Catalina was sitting up, her heavy mass of hair tumbling over her face, turning her into a miniature version of Cousin It from the Addams Family. Vanessa blanched at the idea of a second scene involving Catalina returning to business class on order to repeatedly bang her assistant's head on the back of her seat once more. Very swiftly for a large woman, she rose to her feet, smiling widely now in the characteristic crocodile expression that had cast terror, earlier on that day, into the breast of the manager of the Marlborough Suite.

It was rather intimidating to Catalina too, but since it was accompanied by the words 'I'll go check on her, shall I? You wait here, all cosy in bed. I'll get you a nice cup of tea sent in too – this lot's gone cold,' Catalina nodded, reassured, as Vanessa left the pod. As she walked down the aisle, the cockpit door opened behind her and Brian, the captain, emerged in a cloud of Chanel Allure Homme aftershave.

Faint sounds of coughing from the first officer and international relief officer were briefly audible before the door shut again behind Brian, who was superbly dapper in his three-button, single-breasted deep navy jacket, tailored closely to his excellent figure, the gold wings pinned above his left breast shining as if he had just buffed them up, the gold braid of his uniform cap equally gleaming. The bright blue Pure Air tie echoed perfectly the blue of Brian's eyes, and a couple of dark curls of hair emerged coquettishly from under the brim of his cap, curvetting around Brian's ears, signifying that, neatly buttoned up as he was, there was an unbridled, naughty side to him that would never be fully tamed.

It was a deliberately planned effect: after spraying himself with enough aftershave to nearly asphyxiate his fellow pilots, Brian had carefully pulled out a single twist of thick dark hair from above each ear and bitten his lips briefly to enhance their natural redness. He had the classic Irish colouring, eyes that, as the old expression ran, had been put in with a smutty finger, which meant they were framed with thick dark lashes that emphasized their azure colour.

'Well *hello* again!' he said, stopping at Catalina's pod, the first one on his royal progression down the aisle. 'How's the journey going for you, Miss Catalina?'

Catalina looked up at Brian looming over her, his broad shoulders and narrow waist very obvious in his tight-fitting uniform, the bright braid on cuffs and cap quite outshone by his resplendent white smile. Brian might not be a candidate for getting Maliboobed, but he had certainly succumbed to the cosmetic dentistry procedures so tempting to crews who did frequent flight runs to the US: his teeth were so perfect that each one looked as if it had been individually crafted from mother-of-pearl. Even Catalina, who was very accustomed to male beauty, blinked at the sight of him.

'I'm Brian, your pilot,' he said, extending a big warm hand for her to shake. 'And such a pleasure it is to fly a beautiful young lady like yourself! I saw you briefly earlier, but we weren't formally introduced, as you might say, and I wouldn't be a gentleman if I didn't greet our most VIP guest, would I?'

Brian's exaggeratedly Irish charm offensive was even more dazzling than his smile. Catalina, still disoriented, was unusually tongue-tied as she shook his hand. Brian did not let go afterwards.

'Wouldn't you like a little VIP tour of my cockpit?' he asked, leaning forward with an intimate smile, his fingers lacing through hers. 'It's a spanking new plane, everything tip-top – and a lovely view of the night sky. Very romantic. What d'you say?'

'I didn't think that was allowed any more,' Catalina said, confused.

'Oh, when it's a celebrity such as yourself, and I have the owner of the airline on-board' – Brian winked – 'there's not the least need to worry your pretty head about that! Shall we be off, then?'

He was pressing the centre of her palm with his thumb suggestively, his fingers almost entirely enclosing her hand. Catalina's eyes were fixed on him almost as if he were a snake charmer and she a particularly vulnerable python.

'I'm not sure,' she said, rather dazed. 'Maybe later? I'm a bit dizzy at the moment. I just woke up, and before that I had a shock – a nasty shock. I thought I was seeing things . . .'

'Well, then, the best thing to do is to take your mind off it!' Brian's other hand wrapped around Catalina's in a comforting gesture. 'Sure, now, when you step inside that cockpit, you'll forget about anything else,' he assured her. 'Why, I might even let you take a turn at the controls if you ask me nicely.' He beamed at her. 'You'd like that, wouldn't you?'

He secured her hand companionably under his arm in a way that looked very avuncular but meant that she couldn't extract it without making a big scene. And, dimly, she was aware that making a scene was something she should avoid at all costs. After trying to shake Latisha awake, then having hallucinated not only the sight of Gerhardt in business class but also the photos scattered over her bed, if she started to struggle with the captain of the plane, that would mean that by the time they landed in LAX, he would have radioed ahead to call the men and women in white coats to take her off to a secure facility.

She was feeling hugely pressured, however. Brian was escorting her out of the pod now, and she patted his arm with her other hand feebly. It was about as effective as a small child trying to calm down a silverback gorilla.

'Actually, I would like to take a rain check,' she said, an American expression whose origins she had never understood, but which she knew meant 'not now, later'. 'Is that okay?'

'Ah, come on now – no time like the present!' Brian said with great geniality, walking as swiftly with her down the aisle of the plane as a father who had sold his daughter into marriage but would only collect payment in full when he delivered her to the waiting groom.

'Um, excuse me? Captain?'

It was a light male voice from behind them, the words not imperative, but the tone somehow firm enough that Brian stopped and turned his head to see who was addressing him. It was Michael Coggin-Carr, standing by the entrance to his own pod opposite Catalina's, his good-looking features drawn up into a slight frown of concern.

'Miss, um, Catalina's had a pretty rough time of it recently,' Michael said. 'She was resting, and I think she might need a little bit more peace and quiet?'

Again, though the words were a query rather than a statement, there was something steady about Michael's gaze and stance that gave Brian pause.

'Ah, she's fine, aren't you?' he said bluffly, his Irish brogue intensifying. 'She'll love seeing the cockpit, so she will!'

'I don't really want—' Catalina started, but Brian rode rough-shod over this.

'Thanks for your concern,' he said to Michael dismissively, turning away again in the direction of the cockpit, 'but there's no need to get your head in a pickle.'

It was to his great surprise that he felt a touch on his arm, and, looking down, saw that Michael had grasped him lightly but firmly around the upper bicep.

'Captain, with all due respect,' Michael said, 'I think you may not realize that Miss, um, Catalina has been quite upset and may not be physically up to much. I couldn't help hearing that she collapsed a short while ago and had to be helped back to her seat . . .'

'Are you trying to *restrain* me?'

Brian swung fully round to confront Michael, whose hand dropped away from its grip; Catalina was able to slip from Brian's grasp as the captain focused on his new target. Very relieved, she ducked back into the entrance to her sitting area as Brian pushed his head towards Michael's like an angry bull's, his brows tightly knitted.

'I'm the captain of this plane!' he barked angrily. 'I have utter and total authority over its passengers!'

'I didn't mean to question your authority, sir,' Michael said with polite deference. 'Merely point out that you might not realize that Miss, um, Catalina may not be in a fit enough state to let you know how she's feeling.'

Michael's stance was as neutral and non-confrontational as Brian's was aggressive. His calm expression only angered the pilot further, however.

'If you think that you can—' Brian began, his face flushing red.

'What's going on here?'

Lucinda bustled up the aisle as fast as her tight pencil skirt would allow her, coming to a halt beside Michael Coggin-Carr.

'Gentlemen, I can hear you from the bar! Is everything all right? The passengers are trying to get some rest!'

She was addressing both of them, but her dark gaze was fixed squarely on Brian. It was Brian's voice that was audible in the bar, Brian's anger that needed to be defused.

'I was just seeing if Catalina, as our most VIP passenger, would like a tour of the cockpit,' Brian said sulkily. 'And this meddling chap—'

'Oh, how thoughtful of you!' Lucinda said, with such veiled hostility in her voice that Michael looked at her in surprise. 'It's not strictly allowed, of course, but you *are* in command . . .'

'Exactly!'

'Only, I think Miss Catalina's a little tired at the moment,' Michael ventured.

Lucinda glanced at Catalina, who was propping herself against the smooth white wall of her pod, looking like nothing so much as a limp rag draped there by the cleaners. Catalina managed a nod of agreement.

'Yes, Captain Levett,' Lucinda said, her words dripping with disdain, 'Miss Montes does look exhausted. It's the middle of the night for her, and she's had an upsetting flight experience so far. Best to leave her to rest, don't you think? Mr Coggin-Carr, thanks *so* much for your concern for her. Everything's *quite* under control now . . . do please feel free to go on with whatever you were doing. We wouldn't dream of disturbing you any longer . . .'

Michael Coggin-Carr nodded and went gratefully back to his pod without glancing again at the red-faced captain. Lucinda, smiling at Catalina, gestured at her to re-enter her pod, following her in.

'Can I get you anything, Miss Montes?' she asked. 'On behalf of Pure Air, I do want to apologize if Captain Levett overstepped his boundaries there a touch. He's famously enthusiastic, which is part of his charm, but it seems that he misread the situation here, doesn't it?'

She was plumping up the pillows as she spoke, shaking out and repositioning the sheets and blanket with the deftness and speed of long experience, working so fast she might have been a Disney princess surrounded by cute enchanted birds and mice, invisible to mere humans, helping her tug and untwist and smooth at the speed of light.

'Would you like to lie down again?' she asked, indicating the now immaculate bed with the professionalism of a product demonstrator on a shopping channel.

Catalina did, but she hesitated.

'Vanessa was going to see if Latisha – that's my assistant—'

But just then Vanessa herself bustled back to the pod, her body filling the entrance, the smell of her talc and perfume not quite managing to camouflage the scent of her own large body in motion.

'Your assistant's still fast asleep!' she announced cheerfully. 'And still snoring! Lucky that young man next to her has those big noise-cancelling headphones on. I think Greg was right – she'll be out for a good few hours still. Lucinda, so glad you're taking care of our guest.' She beamed at Catalina. 'I'll let Lucinda look after you now,' she said. 'I'll pop back in a wee while to see how you're doing, shall I?'

Meekly Catalina nodded and slid back between the sheets. There was something very maternally efficient about Vanessa: you naturally did what she told you. Lucinda exited the pod, biting her lip in fury as, passing Jane's cubicle, she saw Brian's peaked cap inside, heard his smooth Irish accent lilting away as he offered Jane a 'visit to his cockpit'.

Sometimes I think he only became a pilot so he could say 'my cockpit' all the time, Lucinda thought viciously. *And sometimes I also think that he isn't even Irish at all, he just puts on the accent to get off with women . . .*

Angela was in the bar, waiting for Jane's camomile tea. To relieve her pent-up fury, not only at Brian's perpetual flirting but the embarrassing scene he had just made, Lucinda hissed at Angela, 'We have pictures of you and Danny going at it, you slut. Karl took them on his phone. Everyone you work with'll have seen them by this time tomorrow.'

Angela visibly flinched, her body going limp, rosacea

bumps standing out on her cheeks under her reapplied make-up. Satisfied, Lucinda whisked past. She was doing a routine check of the galley when Karl appeared in the opposite entrance, pushing past the kitchen, his expression troubled.

'Hey,' he said, his voice lowered. 'I don't know what you just said to Angela, but she's actually sort of collapsed on the bar. She's got to make it through this flight, you know. We need every single pair of hands in Luxe. None of our passengers wants to sleep through – they're too hyped up by all the excitement and they're running us ragged. I've got to do another bloody lobster now for that tosspot in 6B with the stupid facial hair, believe it or not.'

Lucinda shrugged.

'I told Angela we had photos of her and Danny at it,' she said aggressively. 'So what?'

'Honestly, hasn't the poor bitch suffered enough?' Karl asked. 'And you know me, I never say that! I can watch *They Shoot Horses, Don't They?* back-to-back with *Steel Magnolias*.'

'She flirted with Brian,' Lucinda snapped.

'You know actually yeah not so much,' Karl said very fast, eliding all the words together. 'She really honestly didn't. It was all him flirting with her. And she's got the sack already – there's no need to tip her right over the edge! We've had one hysterical woman on the flight already! We don't need Angela having a complete nervous breakdown when it's all hands on deck, do we?'

He cleared his throat.

'I was thinking maybe I should delete those pics,' he suggested bravely.

'Don't you *dare!*'

Lucinda narrowed her eyes menacingly.

'Give me your phone,' she commanded, staring Karl down. He hesitated, but he didn't have the nerve to withstand a direct order from her: she was not only his boss; her powerful force of will also gave her psychological dominance over him. Lucinda had systematically broken every one of her fellow staffers, to the point that she merely had to stare at them to make it perfectly clear that a failure to comply with her latest demand would mean being condemned to the shittiest rosters on the worst routes with the slackest crew for the foreseeable future.

Reluctantly, he reached into his jacket pocket and produced the slim phone that carried the damning photographs of Angela on her knees in front of Danny. Lucinda took it from him without even a thank you, slid it into her own jacket pocket and, with the elegance of a dancer, swung in a tight circle on one heel in the narrow galley space. Her deportment as perfect as if she were a teacher at a finishing school, balancing a hardback book on her head, she swept out of the galley without a further word. Karl looked at her departing back and heaved a sigh, wishing he'd been on the ball enough to wipe those photos before he mentioned Angela's state of mind . . . or to blur the lens strategically with some lip balm before he'd taken them at all . . .

But, as always, he had done what Lucinda said. His not to reason why; his but to help her as she took down the latest hapless, naive, pretty bitch who had had the misfortune to catch the eye of Lucinda's married boyfriend.

Sometimes I really dislike myself, he thought bitterly. *I honestly thought planting that banana in that other poor cow's bag was my lowest point, but this is worse. Poor Angela's getting the shit ripped out of her while she's on-board with nowhere to hide. It's slow torture.*

Gloomily, he unfastened a storage door, pulled out a large Styrofoam box and extracted a live lobster, its claws strategically fastened together. Holding it as much at arm's length as he could, he popped it in the steamer and switched it on. It was impossible to avoid the parallels between the slow painful death of the crustacean and the agonizing way in which Lucinda was twisting the knife into her latest victim. He'd read somewhere that you could kill lobsters with one swift strategic stab in the right place where the head joined the neck – *just like people, really.* But Lucinda was too cruel to end things quickly. Like a cat playing with a mouse, she seemed determined to make Angela suffer as much as possible.

And it wasn't even as if Angela flirted back with Brian! he thought, roused still further by the injustice of it all. Though come to think of it, why shouldn't Angela have a flirt with a pilot if she wanted to? God knew, it was one of the perks of the job! Lucinda might consider Brian her own private property, fenced round and gated off with her as the perpetual security guard, but frankly, Karl thought that Brian's wife might beg to differ on that score . . . and circulating the photos of poor Angela in that humiliating situation would have been a completely unfair punishment even if Angela *had* flirted with Brian.

The pictures would never become public, of course. Lucinda and Karl would get the sack for bringing the airline into disrepute in two seconds flat. But it would be more than enough of a nightmare for Angela, if she did manage to get another job in cabin crew, to know that everyone she would be working with had already had a look at her on her knees in front of Danny Zasio, his sperm dripping down her hand as she desperately tried to keep it away from her make-up . . .

'Hi!'

The lobster was still steaming. Karl looked up from the timer to see Jane Browne standing at the entrance to the galley.

'Miss Browne!' he said gushingly. 'What can I do for you? I *loved* you in *Tragic Sisters*, by the way. You were so . . .'

'Depressing?' Jane suggested with a flicker of a smile.

'Oh *no*,' Karl hurried to reassure her. 'So moving! It was terribly sad but, you know, beautiful too. All those Brontë girls writing their wonderful books and then dying one by one because of the water getting poisoned by running through all the corpses piled up in the graveyard.' He shivered. '*So* dark.'

'We laughed all the time on set,' Jane assured him. 'It's often like that with films. I did one called *And When We Fall* which was full of shagging, and honestly, when you spend days naked in bed with people doing all sorts of freaky stuff, all you want to do after that is put all your clothes on and drink a nice cup of tea.' She grinned. 'People are very serious on comedies, but they play practical jokes on each other on tragedies. Melody Dale and I kept making each other crack up in her death scene.'

'Every one of the sisters died!' Karl said, his eyes wide. 'I didn't see *that* coming! I thought at least one of them would survive!'

'I know, right? Worse than a horror film,' Jane said cheerfully. 'It *was* a bit knackering – all those long walks in the mud, and not being able to see anything in the interior scenes because of barely having any candles . . .'

'*Very* atmospheric,' Karl said fervently. 'But look at me going on when you came to ask me for something! I'm so sorry – what *was* I thinking?'

'Oh, not at all.' Jane smiled very sweetly. 'I'm so glad you liked the film. But I *did* come to ask you for something – you in particular. You're Karl, right?'

Karl flushed at such a talented actress – Oscar-nominated, no less! – bothering to remember what he was called: she hadn't even glanced at the name-badge on his chest. Unfortunately, when he heard Jane's request, the flattered smile slid instantly from his face.

'I'm so sorry, Miss Browne,' he apologized, lowering his voice. 'But I can't. Not won't,' he hurried to say, 'but can't.' Swiftly, he explained that Lucinda had confiscated his phone. 'Oh, what a shame!' he said regretfully. 'If you'd only asked me five minutes ago, it would have been the perfect excuse! I couldn't have said no to you! Even *she* couldn't have got too cross with me. But now she's made me give her my mobile – she doesn't trust me, and I can't say she's wrong there, frankly – and there's no way I can get her to give it back.'

The timer beeped on the steamer. Murmuring that she would leave him to get on with the task he had in hand, Jane slipped from the galley entrance, leaving Karl, staring down at the deceased, now livid red lobster, feeling horribly guilty on multiple fronts.

To think I was so excited to be picked for the inaugural LuxeLiner flight to LA! he thought miserably. *God, if I'd only known! Non-stop drama, and none of it the fun kind!*

Not even the prospect of a fifty-hour layover, which he planned to spend almost entirely watching the muscle guys work out on Malibu Beach, could ease Karl's bruised and guilty spirits.

Chapter Twenty

'All going smoothly, Karl?'

Karl, still staring at the bright red lobster corpse, jumped at the sound of Vanessa's voice. It was the kind of bright, cheerful question that, like a grammatical structure he vaguely remembered from an English lesson at school, demanded the answer yes: not really a question at all, in other words, but a statement that he was required to confirm.

'Oh *yes*, Vanessa,' he said, in the sycophantic tone that he had found the PR director preferred. She hadn't been with Pure Air for long, but like Lucinda, she was extremely efficient at making her preferences known. You didn't bring Vanessa problems, you brought her solutions, and it was apparently impossible to be over-deferential while doing so. Many had tried, but none had yet succeeded in being so fawningly obsequious that they roused Vanessa's contempt for their blatant sucking-up.

It was all she had wanted to ask him, apparently, a quick check in. With that rather unnerving smile of hers, she drifted away, her large body moving with impressive ease down the aisle, away from the galley in which Karl was now plating up the lobster and crossing his fingers for no sudden bursts of turbulence that would bounce it off the plate as he carried it to 6B.

Meanwhile, Vanessa was on a mission: she was off to stroll the length of the plane, keeping a beady eye on how the carefully planned inaugural flight of Pure Air 111 was proceeding. Beyond the curtain in business class, the atmosphere was much less charged and rowdy than in Luxe, as there was no bar there to allow passengers to socialize over drinks with the tantalizing prospect of meeting a fellow traveller with whom to flirt heavily. One had been proposed by the designer, but it simply hadn't made sense in terms of the revenue that would be lost with the extra seats, even considering the tendency of passengers sitting at a bar while flying thirty thousand miles over the Atlantic to spend extravagantly in an attempt to impress other travellers and the airline crew.

Besides, most business-class passengers were actually travelling for work, the four-figure return flight paid for by their companies, which meant that they couldn't allow themselves to get drunk on the flight. They were either strategically napping so that they'd be fresh for morning meetings, or had their heads bent over their laptops or tablets, fingers tapping away.

As Vanessa entered business class, passing the toilets, she paused for a moment, glancing over at Latisha, on the far side of the cabin: she was still fast asleep, bundled up in her blankets. Vanessa had stopped just in front of 14E, the aisle bulkhead seat, which was occupied by one of the two air marshals on-board. It was standard procedure: one agent was stationed at the front of the cabin, one at the back. The air marshal was a squarely built black man who seemed absorbed in the magazine he was holding. He glanced up at Vanessa briefly, having noticed that she had just come through from Luxe Class, and thus checking that there was nothing suspicious about her appearance in the business cabin.

It took only a split second for him to register her as a high-level Pure Air employee who had passed security clearance. Vanessa's appearance, in her generously cut cherry-red trouser suit, was certainly distinctive: she had put her suit jacket back on, and the full effect was rather like a walking post box.

Reassured, the marshal's eyes dropped once more to the magazine he was pretending to read, and Vanessa, hips tilted at a sideways angle to avoid bumping them on the seat rests, continued her measured procession down one side of the plane. She noticed with pleasure how comfortable the travellers looked in their ergonomic seats. As she had explained to Catalina and Latisha, these were contained within fixed plastic shells, so that the passenger could recline as much as they wanted without affecting the person behind them.

No need for the Knee Defender here, that device which clipped onto the mechanism of the seat in front of the passenger, preventing it from being reclined. It was beleaguering airlines, had already caused problems on multiple flights. People had thrown glasses of water over each other, come to blows over the top of the seat that had been blocked, caused serious delays as airplanes were forced to make emergency landings and arrest the fighting passengers.

One of the plusses for flight attendants lucky enough to be assigned to the LuxeLiner was that they would never have to adjudicate between competing demands for minimal amounts of space. Working in economy was a waystation to the giddy heights of business and then first class for the truly ambitious flight attendant, who would shudder at even having to help out with a food service in cattle class. Karl's long-term goal was to work on private jets. It was where the real money, and the real perks, lay: the tips were lavish, the layovers equally generous, and no one ever made you cook lobster on-board, as private plane crew were responsible for the inflight catering and wouldn't have dreamt of choosing something so messy and fiddly.

It wasn't an easy jump to make, however. Private jet jobs were highly prized and hard to get. Successful candidates were required to speak multiple languages, be expert in choosing menus that would appeal to the fussiest of travellers, and possess wine sommelier skills versatile enough to suggest a pairing for anything from smoked swordfish and fried caper flower canapés to gluten-free brownies. The only exception to this rule was if they were extremely attractive, female, under size ten and under thirty; when a female candidate had model looks, the charter companies were happy to overlook the fact that she might not have all the above requirements.

But that meant that the other cabin crew needed to be extra-qualified to compensate for the girls who had been hired primarily as eye candy. Karl not only had to ensure his knowledge of food and wine was impeccable but serve at least five years in first (or Luxe) class before it would even be worth applying.

Vanessa was halfway down the aisle now, passing the centre galley. At the far side of the galley was a small disturbance, someone being encouraged to drink coffee by a flight attendant, the slurred voice of the reluctant coffee drinker bearing witness to the presumably drunken state of the passenger. Vanessa rolled her eyes. This was all too common; she would check later whether the passenger had been over-served, as the idiom went, by cabin crew who had been too generous with the free alcohol, or whether the passenger had been already tipsy when boarding, which should have been spotted by the gate staff.

Moving on towards the back of the plane, Vanessa's eyebrows raised as she noticed an anomaly in a centre row. It was a full flight, but the row was empty, the three passengers who were seated there all absent at once. This was unusual enough for her to speed up her step as she passed the toilets and approached the back galley, in which Greg and Lydia were chatting as they set out glasses of water and orange juice on trays.

As Vanessa hove into view, the flight attendants straightened up, instinctively reaching to smooth down their jackets and hair. It was unnecessary, however: they were already both as picture-perfect as befitted cabin crew specially selected for this maiden voyage. They had been lined up and photographed by the LuxeLiner in its hangar at Heathrow, and there would be another photo opportunity at LAX; great care had been taken by Pure Air staff to select not just the most attractive staff members, but the ones who were especially meticulous about their appearance.

Both Greg and Lydia, being younger members of staff than Karl and Lucinda, for instance, were on new contracts, which meant that Lydia was required to wear the regulation blue toque pinned at a sharp angle to her head at all times, while Greg had to have all three buttons of his jacket fastened over his waistcoat, ditto. They were both sharp as pins. Lydia's make-up was bright and perfect, while Greg's concealer was so discreetly applied and fixed with powder that, even in the bright lights of the galley, it was impossible to spot.

Vanessa nodded with approval of their high level of grooming even as she inquired pleasantly, 'Now, people, is there anyone in the rest area who isn't authorized to be there?'

A dead silence fell. Greg and Lydia's eyes slid sideways in unison to the far end of the galley, where beyond the ranks of metal-fronted storage compartments was located a nondescript grey door with a security lock, barely noticeable unless you were looking for it. The LuxeLiner had been designed for even longer-haul flights than the London–LAX route and thus had a large crew rest area as sleekly designed as the rest of the plane, its access door discreetly positioned so that no passenger could discover it by accident.

'Only,' Vanessa continued, 'I couldn't help noticing that we've got a middle back row all empty, which is very unusual on a full flight. I don't see any queues for the loos, so I ask myself where those three people can possibly have got to. And really, I've got only one answer.'

She looked from face to face. Reluctantly, Lydia and Greg gazed back at her. Their identical petrified expressions told Vanessa, as surely as a full confession, that her guess had been absolutely correct. It was Lydia, after a desperate glance at Greg, who bravely said, 'We're so sorry. We know we shouldn't have done it. But they'd been so nice, and it was the maiden flight, and they said it was their dream . . .'

'All *three* of them had the same dream?' Vanessa asked incredulously.

'It's a honeymooning couple,' Greg chimed in, 'and a lady they met because she was sitting next to them. They all had quite a lot to drink, and they started to get frisky under their blankets . . .'

'So I went over to ask them to please keep it down, as they were starting to draw attention from other passengers, and then the wife asked us if there was anywhere they could go,' Lydia said.

'And we talked about it and thought that maybe the best thing to do was to let them get it out of their systems,' Greg said, looking abashed. 'Because, ahem, it didn't look like they were going to stop.'

'They *definitely* weren't going to stop,' Lydia agreed.

'Honestly, we didn't over-serve them with drinks,' Greg added swiftly. 'It's not that. We're very careful.'

'We're *so* sorry,' Lydia chimed in.

Vanessa had kept a perfectly straight face during this confession, intimidating the two of them as much as possible. But now they had spilled the beans, she allowed her features to relax into a small, but perceptible, smirk.

'At least you didn't try lying to me and saying they'd all somehow sneaked in there when your backs were turned,' she commented. '*That* would really have pissed me off.'

Lydia had briefly considered trying to get that excuse past Vanessa; now she could have cried with relief that she hadn't made the attempt.

'You're the ones that'll suffer the most. Aren't you due for a bunk-up around now?' Vanessa continued. Cabin crew on the LHR–LAX route were contractually allowed two hours' rest per flight. 'So you'll have to have a lie-down in there after those three have been doing God knows what over all the soft furnishings! Rather you than me! You'd better be prepared to wipe everything down, eh?'

The attendants looked distinctly taken aback at this observation; they were both grimacing as Vanessa strode down the galley and cranked open the heavy metal handle of the door. There was a security lock, but with people inside it had not been engaged, so Vanessa could simply unlatch the door and throw it wide, letting the light from the galley flood into the scene in front of her.

It was quite a tableau. The rest area was cleverly laid out with a seating section at the front, and small tables for eating crew meals built in at the sides, while at the back three bunks lay side by side. Each was separated from the next at the head, a moulded plastic section wrapping around so that one crew member could sit and read by the built-in light, while their counterpart next to them could try to get some sleep, shielded from the light by their own curving headboard. Thick curtains on rails around each bunk, hospital bed-style, provided a degree of privacy.

It was a design much favoured by the crew, as bunks stacked one above the other were generally considered the worst solution: no one liked to have to clamber up a narrow ladder in a tight skirt, or be disturbed by someone clunking past them and settling in overhead. Much nicer to slide in beside a sleeping person, with plenty of space to ensure you didn't bump into each other unless you wanted to: crew weight requirements ensured that no one would be so large that they would overspill the allotted space.

The gold standard for crew accommodation, to many flight attendants, was still the Boeing 777, which had actual individual built-in bunks in curtained-off compartments, like ones on old-fashioned trains in films. But in those, of course, three passengers who had been overcome with desire for each other would not have been able to enact the kind of elaborate threesome that was currently underway in the LuxeLiner rest area.

Even Vanessa, who had seen a great deal of louche behaviour in her long career in publicity – from Formula One events to concert arenas and film premieres before her move to Pure Air – was taken aback by the sight before her. Rarely did orgies involve this level of . . . well, she could only describe it as professionalism. The first woman was lying in the central bunk, the second one kneeling between her legs: the man was squatting at the headboard, delivering a rapid series of thrusts into the first woman's mouth. It was all so well choreographed that Vanessa, turning to Greg beside her, asked dryly, 'Which one's supposed to be the wife again?'

'I can't see their faces!' Greg said. 'Um, from this angle both of them look alike to me . . .'

Both women were bleached blonde, with expensively done hair extensions. Then there were the large, round breasts, the completely waxed genitalia, the long fingernails. They might all have been flight attendants at the very final stages of being Maliboobed. Or, even more likely—

'They're porn stars, you idiots!' Vanessa said to Greg and

Lydia. 'Couldn't you *tell*? Where's the sense you were born with?'

And just as she said that, the man climaxed in a very showy fountain on the breasts the first woman was now holding together to receive it. Vanessa, who had grasped the whole situation, looked around the rest area and strode up to the iPhone, propped on a small black rubber tripod on one of the side tables, which had been recording the entire scene.

'Nice try,' she said, picking up the phone.

'They *truly* didn't look like that when they asked if they could go somewhere private!' Lydia assured Vanessa in a frantic tone. 'I promise, Vanessa! They were very nicely spoken – both the ladies had their hair pulled back, and they were all covered up – no cleavage or anything . . .'

'It's true,' Greg confirmed. 'They were in sweaters and jeans. One of the ladies actually had a *cardi* on!' he added as if that were the acme of respectability, glancing at the light cardigan Vanessa was wearing under the jacket. 'They *really* didn't look at all porno-ish! We'd have spotted that, we truly would.'

'So your defence is that you're idiots but not stupid,' Vanessa said, rolling her eyes. 'Good to know.'

The porn stars were sitting up now, the first woman looking around for something to wipe herself with, seeming unfazed by the unexpected audience.

'Hi,' she said to them in a friendly tone. 'Thanks so much for letting us, uh, live our dream.'

'Well, get her some tissues, for goodness' sake!' Vanessa said impatiently to the crew. 'You don't want that getting everywhere, do you? *So* unhygienic!'

318

Since Greg was clearly reluctant to go anywhere near the woman's breasts, Lydia elected to hurry over to one of the side tables and retrieve a handful of Kleenex from a dispenser.

'Where the hell's my phone?' exclaimed the male porn star. Climbing off the bunk to retrieve his phone and, presumably, check the footage, he had realized that it was no longer on its stand.

'Hey, give that back!' he said, spotting the iPhone held firmly in Vanessa's plump hands. 'That's mine! It's private property!'

'And you'll have it back just as soon as' – Vanessa clicked on the touchscreen – 'I delete this video, plus the automatic back-up . . . there we go. All yours, sir.'

Without batting an eye, she handed it back to the man, who was advancing towards her, his still-engorged cock swinging before him. Greg, safely to one side of Vanessa and thus not subject to her scrutiny, dropped his gaze appreciatively to take in the full endowment; Lydia, handing the tissues to the first woman, couldn't help but glance sideways as she did so, her eyes widening at the sight.

'Thank you,' the woman said cordially to Lydia.

'Um, you're welcome, madam,' Lydia managed, somewhat hypnotized by the scale of the male passenger's penis.

'All right, all right, show's over,' Vanessa said, trying very hard not to let any amusement leak into her voice: she needed to keep full authority over the scene.

'You two –' she nodded at the cabin crew – 'out you go. And actually, on second thoughts' – she reached forward and grabbed the iPhone back from the naked man, swiftly passing it to Greg – 'you and Lydia confiscate their phones from their seats, and any other gadgets they've got. I don't want them trying to shoot anything else en route, as it were.'

She fixed the porn stars with a firm stare.

'Your devices are off-limits while you're on-board,' she continued. 'You can watch our state-of-the-art inflight entertainment, or have a snooze, or read something, if you know how to read. Got it? You'll have all your belongings returned to you as you deplane.'

Exchanging glances of defeat, they started to retrieve their clothes from where they had been thrown. Guerilla porn-making: whether it was a current trend, or this small group had intended to start it off with a bang, as it were, Vanessa had no idea, but she could see how successful it would be. In this era of Photoshopping and filters, the public was keener than ever to think they were seeing the real thing, hence the popularity of selfies of stars without make-up, asleep, snaps that of course weren't true selfies at all. A poorly lit, grainy porn video shot indie-style on an iPhone during the inaugural flight of Pure Air 111, which could have been up online within hours of landing at LAX, would have been a tremendous Internet success.

Vanessa shooed Lydia and Greg out of the rest area to retrieve all the electronic devices from the three porn stars' seats. Glancing at the size of the male porn star's penis, Vanessa couldn't help having a moment of pity for the woman who had been servicing him orally; the muscles of her jaw must be absolutely exhausted. Still, every job had its downside, she supposed.

'I'll wait here,' she said, comfortably settling into one of the seats and giving the filmmakers a wide smile. 'Just to make sure you don't get up to anything else.'

The women were donning bright lace thong underwear and matching peekaboo bras that fastened at the front with ribbon, flimsy scraps of near-transparent material which were in complete contrast to the layers that covered them. Jeans for the women, chinos for the man, and then the turtleneck sweaters and cardigan adduced in self-defence by the flight attendants. There was even a faux-intellectual, sexy-librarian tortoiseshell-framed pair of glasses to go with the cardigan.

'I can't blame the crew too much,' Vanessa observed quite companionably as the women pulled their hair back with clips and elastic bands, the bleached blonde shade much less glaring when it was smoothed to the scalp rather than hanging loose around their faces. 'You *do* all look very respectable. And you two even have wedding rings!' she added, impressed, to the man and the cardigan-wearing woman. 'Very thorough!'

'We're married,' the woman said sullenly. 'That wasn't acting.'

'Oh, how nice,' Vanessa said cordially. 'Belated congratulations.'

There were some mutters of 'Bitch' under their breath as the three adult performers filed out of the rest area, but Vanessa sensibly ignored them. She glanced around her, the crocodile smile at full beam. Everything was going very satisfactorily. She had identified and dealt with this potential scandal with great expertise: there would be no porn films circulating on the Internet whose setting was the maiden flight of Pure Air 111, no sexy selfies shot under blankets.

She allowed herself a long moment to bask in her triumph before she heaved herself upright again, and, after finishing off what she needed to do in the cabin, she exited it, one hand holding down her jacket so it wouldn't fly open, to find Greg and Lydia waiting for her in the galley, mobile phones, MP3 players and tablets laid out on its metal surface like evidence garnered at a crime scene.

'We got everything, Vanessa. We checked and double-checked. And we're *so* sorry—' Lydia started again, but Vanessa raised her other hand in a papal gesture of dismissal, if not forgiveness.

'I don't want apologies,' she said firmly. 'But this absolutely can't happen again. They won't be the last to try this kind of thing, I bet. Spread the word among your colleagues: no letting anyone into the rest areas. Now that people can film themselves at it so easily, the stakes are much higher. You can busy yourselves going through all that lot –' she gestured at the collection of electronica – 'to make sure they didn't snap anything they shouldn't have before they started filming the main entertainment. And if you miss anything, and photos make it onto the Internet from this flight, I'll sack both of you and make sure you never set foot on a plane again as crew. Got it?'

Greg and Lydia nodded in unison like naughty children being reprimanded by their teacher, eyes wide, lips clamped shut to avoid saying anything else and annoying Vanessa still further. Making her way back down the far aisle, Vanessa was brimming over with satisfaction. Brian had assured her that the weather conditions coming into LA were excellent, which meant that the flight would be sure to arrive on time;

they would make their midnight landing slot, meet the waiting press, nail the superb publicity bonanza on both sides of the Atlantic. Everything was going perfectly to plan, and that little crisis at the back of the plane had allowed her to resolve things even better than she could have imagined.

She almost glided back to Luxe Class, barely bothering to survey the business passengers on this side of the aisle: her task was completed. Like God, Vanessa looked on her work and saw that it was good.

Chapter Twenty-One

Four months ago

'Cat, this is the deal, okay? I'm really freaked out,' Latisha said intently. 'There's been nothing at all from the stalker for the last three months or so. Do you see how weird that is?'

Catalina stared at her, taken aback. When Latisha had said she needed to talk to her urgently, she had expected it to be about – well, *something*. She had no idea how to respond to this; she shrugged, as Latisha seemed to expect a response, and waited for her to explain further.

'Okay, I know you're in this major love haze, but seriously, it's *very* weird!' Latisha answered her own question impatiently. 'We haven't had any letters or photos at *all*. I mean, none of the kind we're worried about, the "Cat Is Mine" ones. After Tokyo, there weren't any dressing-room invasions or any graffiti, nothing for the whole last leg of the tour, and now you've done three gigs here at the Staples Center and nothing out of the ordinary's happened either. No one's even made an *attempt* to sneak into your dressing room and go crazy with a can of spray paint. In the last twelve weeks or so – well, it's like the stalker dropped off a cliff. Literally.'

Even Catalina, sweet-natured as she was, couldn't find it in her heart to be gloomy at this thought. Dropping off a cliff would be painful, of course, and she wouldn't wish that on them – unless, perhaps, they'd had a heart attack at the top, so that they were dead before they even knew what was happening. In the glorious happiness of loving and being loved by Gerhardt, Catalina could even find it in her heart to wish a comparatively pleasant death on the stalker who had tormented her.

After all, if it weren't for the stalker, she was very well aware, she and Gerhardt wouldn't have been pushed into each other's company so quickly and so intensely. It might have taken them ages to get together; in the worst case scenario, it would never have happened at all. It had taken Catalina's absolute panic in Tokyo to make her refuse to take no for an answer when seducing him, and who knew if she would have been that brave and insistent under less extreme circumstances? Gerhardt had done his best to hold her off; he would never have been the one to make the first move on his boss.

I owe it all to Cat Is Mine! she reflected. *How they'd hate to know that they brought me true love and made me the happiest woman in the world!*

This thought brought a dazzling smile to her lips. And that smile caused Latisha, sitting opposite her in one of the big outdoor armchairs of the Oriole Way mansion, sheltered by a huge fabric umbrella from the harsh white glare of the Los Angeles sunshine, to put down her glass of Pellegrino on the glass-topped table and lean forward to fix a concerned stare at her employer.

'Cat, you're totally not getting what I'm saying at *all*,' she said very seriously. 'Think about it. For the last three months you haven't had a moment's trouble. This, from a stalker who was clearly escalating. When your dressing room got graffitied in Tokyo, it was way worse. Those gross photos! And then suddenly, overnight, the stalker just disappears? It's not that we've been hiding things from you or clearing up the spray paint so you don't see it. It just *hasn't happened*. I mean –' she gestured around her – 'this house is on the Star Maps route. Anyone could find out where you live, and you've been here for a whole month. We've really upped the security, but there hasn't been a single incident.'

'But that's good, right? Great!' Catalina was still beaming. 'I mean, maybe they *did* drop off a cliff!' She crossed herself quickly, her pious Catholic upbringing meaning that she couldn't say something like that without apologizing instantly to the baby Jesus. 'Not really,' she added hastily. 'But . . . maybe. Painlessly.'

'Yeah, that'd be the *only* positive explanation,' Latisha said, now looking distinctly apprehensive.

Catalina had no idea why her assistant was acting like this, or why Latisha had brought up the stalker issue apparently out of nowhere; they had miraculously vanished, which was wonderful, so why even mention it at all? It was an unpleasant memory from months ago which surely never needed to come up again.

'I consulted with Simon van Puren,' Latisha said, naming the top security expert in the US, whose name was very widely known because of the television appearances and books in which he advised on threat assessment and violence prevention. 'He was very concerned about the stalker just . . . stopping like that. He says it literally never happens unless, yeah, they got hit by a car. Which obviously isn't a good thing to assume, in case you're wrong. Hope for the best, plan for the worst, he says.'

'Oh Tish! You're scaring me!' Catalina tucked her legs under her, curling protectively into a little ball. 'Stop it!'

'I'm sorry, hon, but I think I have to scare you. Also, it's my job to keep you safe.'

'Not really. It's Gerhardt and his team's job,' Catalina corrected. 'And obviously, they're doing a great one, because I *am* safe!'

Catalina was frowning now. Latisha had rung earlier and insisted on coming round, even though Catalina had wanted a totally quiet day to recover after the exhaustion of three back-to-back concerts at the Staples Center. And now Latisha was stressing out her boss for apparently no reason at all. It felt as if Tish was making a fuss about nothing, seeing problems where none existed. And since Tish never, ever did that, a nasty little worm of worry and fear was beginning to twist inside Catalina's stomach.

Latisha pushed back her heavy braids.

'Simon van Puren said that if a stalker stops their tactics all of a sudden, it's because they figured out they're not working and they switch to another avenue of exploration,' she said. 'His words, not mine.'

Catalina was frowning even more deeply.

'But they didn't,' she pointed out. 'The stalker. They didn't switch to something else.'

'Maybe they did,' Latisha said, a weight of meaning behind those three words that baffled Catalina even further.

'Well, if they did, we haven't even noticed it!' she said,

frustrated and angry now at her failure to understand Latisha's point.

'I didn't talk about this with Simon van Puren,' Latisha said slowly. 'Because . . . well, it's none of his business. And people who work in the same field talk to each other, so if I'm wrong – which I'd really, really like to be – it could do a lot of harm to an innocent person. But the timeline is so suspicious. When you start looking at the facts, everything points one way.'

'Tish, I can't stand this! What are you talking about?' Catalina exclaimed impatiently. 'You're really scaring me now, and I don't even understand why! What do you *mean*?'

'Cat, I'm worried about Gerhardt,' Latisha said quietly.

Catalina's big dark eyes widened in fear. She swivelled around and sighed with relief when she spotted her boyfriend through the glass windows of the gym room, just visible as he lay on the weights bench, heaving an impossibly loaded set of dumbbells up and down above his powerful chest in a series of jerks.

'God, you freaked me out!' she said with relief. 'I thought you meant he was in danger.' She froze. '*Is* he in danger because he and I are together? Is that what you mean? Because the stalker stopped with me after Tokyo – do you think they've turned on Gerhardt instead? But he hasn't noticed anything – nothing's happened, or at least nothing he's told me . . .'

She unfurled her limbs and jumped to her feet, entirely preoccupied by fear for the man she loved.

'That's it!' she said. 'That's what you mean, right? Gerhardt's been getting threats, and he hasn't told me because he didn't want to worry me – oh God, why didn't he *tell* me? We're supposed to share things! He must have been so worried, and keeping it from me too – that's so much extra stress . . .'

Hurrying round the corner of the table to run to Gerhardt and make him tell her everything that had been going on behind her back, Catalina was very taken aback when Latisha's hand reached out and grabbed her wrist, stopping her in her tracks.

'Cat, *no*,' Latisha said strongly. 'You're misunderstanding me. I'm sorry, I'm truly sorry. I don't think Gerhardt's being targeted by the stalker.'

She drew a deep breath, looking up to meet Catalina's eyes.

'I think he *is* the stalker,' she finished.

Catalina actually laughed. That was the part, in retrospect, that made her feel sickest of all. She burst out laughing. It wasn't because she actually found Latisha's words funny – not at all – but because it was so ridiculous that she couldn't take it seriously, which meant Latisha *had* to be joking. It might be the worst, most tasteless joke in history, but it was clearly meant as humour. There was no way it was remotely, conceivably possible that *Gerhardt*, who loved her so passionately, could be the person who had terrorized her . . .

Latisha was gently guiding her boss back to her armchair. Catalina obeyed her assistant's familiar touch, sinking down to sit once more as Latisha began to explain. From her full lips poured out a steady, considered stream of words that she had clearly practised over and over before bringing this to her boss, an explanation of how she had reached her outlandish conclusion about the stalker's identity.

'The first-ever incident happened just days after he got hired,' Latisha was saying. 'And that whole thing about the previous guy going to that famous techno club and just disappearing? I mean, isn't that weird? Oh, Berghain's real – I've read about it,' she hastened to add, to show that she had done her research. 'People *do* go in and stay there for days. There was a big article about it in the *New York Times*. But the timing was just so convenient! Look, Gerhardt was based in Berlin. He'd just come off another job. He could have bribed that guy to drop out and asked the agency if he could take over when we rang to tell them the first guy hadn't shown up to work.'

'Gerhardt *did* ring the agency,' Catalina said, staring at Latisha, disbelieving that her assistant's accusation could actually have some basis in fact. 'He told me he did. He was a big fan of mine and he asked them for the job.'

'Yes, I know. I checked with the Berlin branch of the agency. Clever of him to admit it to you,' Latisha observed. 'That way, if people found out, he'd be covered, because he'd told you already. And asking for the job as your bodyguard could be perfectly innocent. I mean, if you're a fan of someone's, you'd be keen to work for them, wouldn't you? But Cat, the first incident in your dressing room happened almost straight after he came on-board! We never heard a peep out of Cat Is Mine before then, did we? And suddenly here they are, scaring the shit out of you, building up the pressure, making you freak out . . . which would make you *way* more likely to be vulnerable to a bodyguard who was hitting on you, because obviously you'd trust him more than anyone to keep you safe—'

'But it was me who did all the work!' Catalina protested. 'I threw myself at him, literally! *I* had to convince *him* to . . . well, to . . .'

Her voice died away as she saw Latisha's pitying expression.

'No, Tish, I promise . . . I swear . . .' she managed, after clearing her throat. 'You weren't there – I was. He was really torn about whether it was right or not. I had to work so hard to make him break down and admit he wanted to be with me. He didn't do anything himself, he didn't lift a finger. I mean, if he'd really been . . . doing what you said –' she couldn't bring herself to say the words 'spray painting my dressing room', or 'Photoshopping horrible photographs of me' – 'wouldn't he have tried to make me think that he was the only one who could save me?'

Even to her own ears, she was sounding horribly plaintive now.

'But he didn't do that at all! He was totally professional! He even suggested we get extra guards – I was the one that didn't want them!' she finished desperately.

'He'd have to do that, though, wouldn't he?' Latisha pointed out. 'It would have been so suspicious if he hadn't insisted on upping your security! But look at the timing of everything, Cat. It feels like way too much of a coincidence, doesn't it?'

She leaned forward to take Catalina's hands.

'Look, I can see how happy you are. I was happy for you too. He seems like a nice guy. I honestly don't have more of a sense of him than that, because, y'know, he doesn't talk that much! And since we got to LA you guys have been pretty much holed up together.'

'I thought you'd like a rest!' Catalina said hopelessly. 'That was *me* thinking I'd give you some time off, not Gerhardt! He isn't isolating me, honestly he isn't. I did my whole rehearsal schedule and all the Disney press and the gigs just fine—'

'Yeah, I know! I agree! This is *exactly* what's been eating at me!' Latisha said intensely. 'It's like one of those weird mirrors when you can see everything in two different ways. On one side, he's a good guy. You two fell for each other, the stalking shit just miraculously faded away for some reason no one can explain. But hey, that's a good thing, maybe the stalker did fall under a bus, and the reason you barely leave the house for anything but work is because you two are crazy about each other and just want to spend the whole time staring into each other's eyes and fucking each other's brains out. I mean, we've all been there.'

She took a breath.

'But the *other* side,' she continued, 'is that he set this whole thing up. Bribed the other guy to drop out very conveniently in Berlin, i.e. where Gerhardt lives. He took over and immediately started pulling nasty shit to scare the fuck out of you, which kept *me* busy with the arena people, trying to work out who'd done it, which meant he had access to you alone, without me – which hardly ever happens on tour. We're pretty much joined at the hip in private. And you're so used to having me with you all the time that he might very well assume you'd get freaked out at being by yourself and be easy pickings for a strong, silent type who was going to keep you safe by any means necessary.'

'It wasn't like that,' Catalina mumbled.

'And *now*,' Latisha concluded, the last piece of the case for the prosecution falling into place, 'he's making sure he's got you by keeping you to himself the whole damn time that you're not working, so by the time the tour's finished you two'll be joined at the hip and you won't know what to do without him.'

'I love him,' Catalina said in the tiniest of voices. 'And he loves me.'

'But if he's your stalker, of *course* he loves you!' Latisha said, her strong features contorted into a grimace of awkwardness. 'Look, Cat, this is the hardest thing in the world for me to say! You're my friend *and* my boss! You could turn around and sack me for this right now! Do you think I *want* to think this when you're so loved up and blissed out? I've never seen you so happy before! But I wouldn't be doing my job as a friend or your assistant if I didn't say it!'

She took another breath.

'Cat,' she repeated, 'if he's your stalker, he *does* love you. That's sort of the point. Okay, it would be in a totally weird, pervy kind of way, but still, he does love you. It's not like I think he's after your money, or a fame-whore wanting to date you as a springboard for his own career – trying to get a reality show or a slot on the next season of *Dancing with the Stars*. That would be way easier – it happens all the time. The lawyers'd sort out a prenup with tons of confidentiality clauses and make him sign it. But *this* . . .'

Catalina was crying now, slow, steady tears, and Latisha stared hopelessly at her boss's misery.

'It can't be true,' Catalina sobbed. 'It can't be true.'

Visions of those two dressing rooms, sprayed with blood-red paint meant to terrify and intimidate her, flooded through her mind. The pictures of her, scattered over the floor, obscene fake images of a body like hers contorted into pornographic poses, those daubed with red too: how could Gerhardt, who loved her, have done anything so awful, so revolting? How could she possibly imagine that he had sat down for hours, taking her face and twisting it, fixing it onto that kind of explicit, naked image, legs splayed, everything on view? To . . . what? Scare her into being so terrified that she would turn to him for comfort? How could anyone think that you could build a future on a foundation of fear and panic?

She couldn't believe it. None of this chimed in any way with the calm, self-contained man whom she thought she knew so well.

It's the quiet ones that are the worst, she remembered her mother saying years ago, and even then Catalina hadn't understood it. Wasn't it better to be poised than to scream and shout and scare people around you with your temper? But what Maria Montes had meant, her daughter knew, was that at least you knew where you were with a loud temperament. They didn't leave you in any doubt of what they were feeling. While a quiet man, who never used three words where one would do, might be much more likely to be nursing all sorts of secret plans and schemes . . .

'It can't be true,' she repeated through her tears. 'I won't believe it.'

'I'm not saying things couldn't have an innocent explanation,' Latisha assured her. 'But I wouldn't be doing my job if I didn't say something. Did anything make you look back and wonder? Did you notice anything that seemed odd at the time, that you didn't have an explanation for?'

Catalina shook her head dumbly. There was nothing. Everything had been perfect. Too perfect to be remotely possible? She had had to convince *him* to stay here in LA with her; Gerhardt had been worried that he wouldn't fit into the luxury of her daily life. Or had that been an incredibly clever act? God, now she was beginning to doubt everything, absolutely everything . . .

'Okay, you didn't. Great,' Latisha said soothingly. 'So here's an idea I have. Will you promise to listen to it?'

Now Catalina nodded her head. Gestures seemed all she could manage; words were beyond her. Latisha glanced swiftly at the gym room of the house, in which Gerhardt could now be seen performing an impressive series of chin-ups in a weights jacket.

'Let me try to clear him,' she said. 'Or at least . . . it's very hard to prove that someone's innocent, but I could at least get some negative proof, if you see what I mean.'

Catalina didn't, not at all, as her blank expression clearly demonstrated.

'Gerhardt's a bodyguard,' Latisha explained, 'not a computer expert. They're hired to protect you from physical threats, not cyberattacks. I mean, they're not that computer-savvy. If he were Photoshopping all those pictures of you, for instance, he'd probably have done it on his laptop, and even if he deleted it, he wouldn't have known how to wipe them off the hard drive permanently. If you're okay with that, I could take the laptop now and get someone I know to have a look at it. Does he go on it often?'

Catalina shook her head again, but this time managed to get out: 'Hardly at all. He used to watch sport on it sometimes, but I have the cinema screen here with surround sound, so . . .'

'Well, at least we know he's straight!' Latisha said, trying to bring some humour to the situation. However, seeing Catalina's pale, drawn face, she muttered an apology and moved on quickly.

'Okay, I can take it now,' she said, 'and get it looked at. I was talking to someone I know about the previous stalker threats and how to handle security. No one to do with our guys,' she hastened to add. 'She has someone she uses who's apparently totally discreet. He's a big geek, lives in the Valley, total agoraphobe, does this kind of thing to fund his own deep web stuff, couldn't give a shit about anyone else's . . . you know, the usual spotty tech head. I could drive the laptop over to him now.'

She squeezed Catalina's hands.

'If there's nothing on the laptop, he never needs to know, Cat,' she said. 'I promise you, this isn't a trawl to make him look bad. I *like* the guy, okay? I don't really know him, but he seems nice and steady and good for you. He isn't driving a Lamborghini or wearing a Patek Philippe that he got you to buy him. You look really happy. I'm not *looking* for trouble. It's just . . . why don't we try this? If he's innocent, there's no harm in it. No one gives a shit about the odd bit of porn, or whatever. This guy would be specifically looking for pictures of you. That's it.'

'His laptop's in the bedroom next to ours,' Catalina said in a dull monotone. 'I don't think he's even opened it since we got here. He charts all his exercise on his Fitbit and an app he's got on his phone.'

Latisha nodded and stood up.

'Tish?' Catalina looked at her, eyes wide and pleading. 'When you looked at all that security footage in the stadiums . . . did Gerhardt go into my dressing room at all?'

Latisha bit her full lip.

'Here's the thing, Cat,' she said. 'The whole CCTV situation in the stadiums wasn't any use. Not just in Tokyo, Berlin too. Some of the cameras just weren't working, and some of them were at the wrong angle to cover your dressing-room door. The trouble is, that's a hundred per cent normal. This kind of thing is really rare. Way more often what they're looking for on the cameras is an employee stealing some souvenir to sell on eBay, or backstage fights between members of the same band, or, y'know, Solange versus Jay-Z in an elevator. The cameras are there, sure, but those arenas don't spend money on them. Yes, the stalker could have moved a camera, made sure that it was hard to actually get consistent footage of the door of the room. But it's impossible to prove. These things break all the time, and the guys supposed to monitor them aren't paid shit, you know? They're a really unreliable tool. It's not like in the movies where they can track people all over town just switching from one to the next.'

Catalina waited, knowing there was more to come.

'That's why we ended up putting a guard outside your dressing-room door. After Berlin, remember, for the rest of the European leg?' Latisha continued. 'And as soon as we did that, everything stopped. Not a peep. Moscow, Dubai, Mumbai, Singapore – nothing. So we assumed all the shit was down to some crazy Euro nutcase who'd shot their bolt.

Gerhardt and I discussed it with the rest of the crew, and we took the guard off your door after Mumbai – we thought it wasn't necessary any more, plus it was reminding you of what'd happened. You got a lot more relaxed after we pulled him off duty.'

Latisha still hadn't answered the question, Catalina noticed.

'But Tish . . .' she began, her voice quavering.

'Okay, yes,' Latisha said honestly. 'Gerhardt went into your dressing room once, on camera. In Tokyo, the second time it happened. But Cat, so did I. So did Zoe, so did a couple of execs from Mobile Power management checking that all your riders were in place. That's the thing. We just couldn't get consistent footage that showed one person going in there both times with a can of spray paint and those photos.'

'Gerhardt wears a T-shirt and trousers when he's working,' Catalina said. 'No jacket or bag. He couldn't have had a spray can and photos on him. It would have been obvious.'

Latisha refrained from pointing out that Gerhardt could have brought those things in earlier, during one of his many visits to the dressing room, could have shoved them at the back of a cupboard or underneath a sofa cushion and retrieved them later on to use when he was sure of being unobserved. She simply nodded.

'So it's okay?' she asked.

Catalina nodded. 'He won't even notice, I'm sure,' she said.

'The guy says he can do it by tomorrow,' Latisha said, standing up. 'If I come back around this time . . .'

'He always works out from nine thirty to eleven,' Catalina said, her voice a mere vapour trail on the LA breeze. Latisha was tactful enough to say not another word: there was no reassurance that she could give which would make her boss feel any better. The glass walls of the house, wrapping like open arms around the pool area, meant that Catalina could track Latisha's progress across the patio, inside the open doors that led to the huge kitchen, through the study, then disappearing inside to reappear as she went up the central staircase, her body streaked briefly by flashes of green from the glass panels set into the atrium wall. She watched Latisha move through the hallway into the second bedroom, pass by the window, and bend over the desk there to retrieve the laptop.

Catalina was as sure as anyone could be that Latisha would find nothing on Gerhardt's laptop that would reveal that he was her stalker. That wasn't what was tormenting her now, making her ball up her body once again in her chair. Her misery was caused by the fact that Latisha, who was so close to Catalina, could not only suspect that Gerhardt could be Catalina's stalker, but think that Catalina's judgement might be so messed up that she could actually fall in love with someone who was mentally disturbed. Because to drive someone you loved, or thought you loved, to extremes of misery in order to make them fall in love with you was the height of psychotic manipulation.

Logically, Catalina could see how a bodyguard who had swiftly become the lover of his charge under these circumstances would be suspect, especially since now the stalker seemed to have completely dropped off the radar. If that were the case, having achieved what he wanted, Cat Is Mine could be retired forever as Gerhardt settled down happily into his relationship with Catalina . . .

Of course, Catalina was sure that Gerhardt hadn't been her stalker. But a question was nagging at her obsessively: if he *had* been, would she truly want to know? This love affair was so wonderful, so perfect – would it even matter if Gerhardt had done something crazy to drive her into his arms? The answer had to be yes, naturally – and yet part of her was wishing she could just let sleeping dogs lie.

After all, it was done now. They were in love; she was in seventh heaven; they couldn't look at each other without exchanging goofy, idiotic smiles, couldn't pass each other without touching, even briefly, a quick stroke of the finger-tips along the other one's arm, a kiss on the forehead. It was very sensible of them to have decided to effectively hole up here while in LA, city of the paparazzi, who would have sniffed out this new romance and given them no peace. Catalina and Gerhardt would have found it quite impossible to go out to dinner, a movie, even a walk in the canyons, without hugging, kissing, holding hands at the least, and, after her break-up with Fernando the press would particu-larly relish stolen paparazzi photos of her with that classic celebrity rebound, the bodyguard: dating the 'hired help', as the singer Seal had put it when his ex-wife Heidi Klum had an affair with her minder.

Catalina was almost as sure as she could be that Gerhardt hadn't staged the stalking incidents in order to get close to her. Why, in that case, was she so desperate to jump up, run into the house, grab Latisha as she came back down the stairs, take the laptop from her, tell her to cancel the appointment with the tech geek, and close the door once and for all on any investigation into her wonderful, miraculous boyfriend? Why was that impulse so strong that Catalina felt beads of sweat springing out on her forehead, the palms of her hands, the small of her back? All the years of hardcore rehearsing, performing, the relentless activity for which she had been trained since she was a small child, were nothing compared to the sheer effort of forcing herself to sit still now and watch the last traces of green reflected light fade along Latisha's back, see the brief flash of sunshine turn to dark again as the heavy front door opened and closed.

I could still call Tish. I could still call her and tell her to turn around, bring back the laptop, call off her taking it to the Valley . . .

If Catalina was so sure Gerhardt was innocent, why was her every instinct telling her to stop Latisha? Why wouldn't she want some proof, even negative, that there was nothing linking Gerhardt's laptop to Cat Is Mine? Catalina had always trusted her instincts in every aspect of *her* career: which songs to choose, whom to work with, whom to hire to protect her interests, whose advice to listen to and when. They had never led her astray, not until now. This was the first time she could remember that her brain and her instincts had been in such violent conflict, and the internal struggle was physically painful.

By this time tomorrow it will all be over, she told herself firmly, forcing herself to stand, to stretch her arms above her head, to start walking over to Gerhardt in the gym to begin her own workout. But she knew the next twenty-four hours would be agonizing. And curiously, not because she had any real doubts about her boyfriend. No, it was because a persistent voice inside her head was telling her that she had just made the worst mistake of her life.

And since she trusted Latisha unreservedly, she had no idea why.

Chapter Twenty-Two

Two months ago

'Jane! Jane, over here!'

'Love the dress, Jane. Give us a twirl!'

'Still got those muscles, Jane? Want to flex an arm for us?'

Jane was almost tempted: her biceps were not quite what they had been while filming *Angel Rising*, but she was still in what had to be the best shape of her life. After this, she thought ruefully, it would all be downhill. *Angel Rising* had been edited swiftly for a quick release, and Jane's body, worked so hard during training and shooting, still maintained most of its recently acquired muscle tone. Jane would never again climb a rope if she could possibly help it – no parts as cabin girls in *Pirates of the Caribbean 9: It Pays the Bills* for her – but she had hired a Pilates teacher a couple of times a week, reluctantly admitting to herself that she needed to make at least a minimal effort to keep fit. She was now a perfect sample size 6, which was very fortunate for borrowing designer dresses, as *Angel Rising* looked set to become a huge international success. Its *Black Swan*-like mix of art film, thriller and exquisitely shot transgressive sex was making it, as the writer and director had hoped, the guilty pleasure film of the year, the one you chose to see on a hot date to ensure your own personal steamy sex scene shortly thereafter.

So, after this London premiere in Leicester Square, Jane was booked for a solid three weeks of being flown around Europe, Asia and Australia to do press interviews and walk the red carpet in multiple cities in a dazzling variety of dresses. The publicists were delighted with her, as she fit into absolutely everything designers sent over. Her shoulders had widened during training, as was inevitable: all the upper body work gave one, as Simone put it, a back like a wardrobe. But, several months later, with no more compulsory chin-ups, Jane's torso had narrowed enough to slip perfectly into a Mary Katrantzou digitally patterned, optical illusion dress that would have made anyone above a size 8 look like a walking sofa.

Her lips had been painted bright fuchsia, her hair slicked back like a dancer's, her eyes heavily outlined in black. She looked Parisian-chic, Eva Green meets Vanessa Paradis on the red carpet, her arm entwined through Olivier Lautrec's, enthusiastically answering the same old questions as if she were hearing them for the first time, smiling up at Olivier, looking absolutely enchanted to be reunited with him months after the shoot had ended.

No one could possibly have guessed that she was angling her face as best she could to ignore his stinky Gauloise breath as, slouching with careless Gallic grace, he grunted a few husky, nonchalant words about what a pleasure it had been to work with her. That was the real job of actors, more often than not, pretending that the co-star with whom you smoul-dered so successfully onscreen hadn't annoyed you so much that, by the time the film wrapped, you'd had to use all of your training simply to avoid punching him in the face when you reunited for the publicity tour.

It turned out that Jane's ketosis breath from her strict protein diet had been nothing to Olivier's. He had not only smoked nearly constantly, which meant that he reeked of tobacco during the entire film shoot, but when he wasn't dragging on a Gauloise, he had been scarfing down garlicky pork rillettes on toast, his favourite food. As a result, his breath had stunk so badly that even the make-up artists, who were hardened by profession to early morning mouth, had flinched back from him on the first day's shooting and reached for the extra-strong Altoids, breathing through their parted lips as best they could.

Attempts to display a wide and tempting variety of mints and chewing gum in attractive bowls strewn around the make-up trailer had not borne fruit. From eleven o'clock, Olivier started on his tipple of choice, a Belgian golden ale, and though he never showed any signs of being affected by it, the stale beer odour on his stubble did nothing to settle Jane's already queasy stomach during the sexually charged scenes that comprised a large part of the film.

Laura, the director, did her best to convince Olivier to use the mints, but she had been rebuffed with a great deal of hand gesturing, shrugging, lower-lip thrusting and con-temptuous mutterings of '*Boh*' at the repressed English and their inability to appreciate the delicious tastes and smells of authentic French peasant cuisines. The make-up artists kept Jane stocked with Altoids and were very helpful about presenting her with a tissue to spit hers out into just before every scene; in desperation, she even took to applying a little Vicks Vaporub under her nostrils, as she had read in a crime novel that this was a procedure adopted by forensic examiners before slicing into an odoriferous corpse. It did help to some degree, but then it started visibly chafing her upper lip and she was banned from using it any more.

Which seemed highly unfair, as Olivier absolutely refused to moisturize his stubble in any way, and that meant that the various bits of her – quite a wide variety of bits – that had to come into contact with his mouth over the course of the shoot got rubbed raw. Baby oil, Vaseline, the most expensive men's grooming products available to humanity, Crème de la Mer, were all proposed to Olivier and all roundly rejected. A true Frenchman would die, apparently, rather than moisturize his chin for his partner's pleasure.

'Lucky for him he's a top,' said one of the make-up artists sourly. 'He could *not* get away with that otherwise.'

'You should know, Wayne,' commented one of the grips. 'You blow him every lunchtime, regular as clockwork.'

'I do *not*,' Wayne said unconvincingly, going bright red. 'Not *every* lunchtime.'

The only positive aspect to Olivier, in fact, was his homosexuality. Other actors cast in this kind of role might well have taken advantage: Jane was tied up in some way or other, with Olivier's hands running over her, for what felt like half the film. Olivier, however, was much more likely to grope a beer bottle than his co-star. When the cameras were rolling, he was all professionalism, effortlessly slipping into the role of a lustful, predatory choreographer treating his latest muse as merely another variation on an endless theme of female bodies to be used and cast aside. Seconds after Laura said, 'Cut!', however, Olivier was lighting up another cigarette and looking around him to confirm which of the crew would be chosen that day to follow him back to his trailer and get down on their knees on the uncomfortable scratchy carpet for the honour of servicing him.

Jane reminded herself now, with the all-too-familiar stink of unfiltered Gauloises, beer, and pork fat in her nostrils, that at least Olivier hadn't given her a moment's trouble in the groping department. It was definitely a consolation. The director of *And Then We Fall* had wanted her to have sex with his girlfriend in front of him in a hotel bedroom to get the part. She had refused, even though the girlfriend came into the room totally nude and bent over in front of her, which had actually been quite tempting, as she was utterly gorgeous; but the situation had been much too creepy and odd for Jane to acquiesce. Jane had taken her clothes off and writhed around a bit on the bed, which was standard practice on an audition for a film where the actors were mostly naked and having sex in various configurations ninety per cent of the time, but that was as far as she had been happy to go, and she had been cast anyway.

Her co-star on the film, Milly Gamble, had taken up the offer, as had one of the male actors, and it was true that the two of them had more screen time, but Jane knew she had stolen the film from under their noses. If she were brutally honest with herself, she wouldn't rule out the possibility that one day she might lie down on a casting couch. For the right part in the right film . . . for the one that everyone wanted, the one with Oscar nomination written all over it . . . for a female producer or director that she didn't find utterly repulsive . . . yes, it might happen. It was infinitely more common in Hollywood than people thought. The stakes there were so high: having the right to describe yourself as 'Academy Award nominee' in the opening credits to a film meant not only higher fees, but, much more importantly in Jane's perspective, a much better pick of the few good roles out there for women, the ten per cent that weren't just wives or girlfriends or mistresses.

But thank God she had had no serious casting couch dilemmas yet. Thank God she hadn't had a co-star on *Angel Rising* who had, as so often occurred, done more than the director wanted or needed, gone further, put his fingers where they weren't supposed to go during filming and dared her to break character and tell him to stop, or actually pulled aside her modesty thong and slipped his dick inside her during a sex scene, which had happened to a friend of Jane's. After a long horrified moment, she'd stopped the scene by pushing him away and yelling at him to get out, but he'd just apologized and pretended it had been an accident, and after a five-minute break he'd been on top of her again, filming had restarted, and his dick had been pushing against her thong once more, a very smug smile on his face.

Jane shuddered at the mere idea. Inside. Externally, however, her smile deepened and her eyes glowed even more appreciatively up at Olivier. Seeing this, the MTV interviewer to whom they were currently talking cooed eagerly, 'Ooh, I've got to say, Olivier and Jane, you two look absolutely *gorge* together! We've heard some saucy rumours – did any sparks fly on set?'

Gay Olivier looked down at lesbian Jane, and they exchanged a smile full of sex and heat and eroticism, a smile that had all the cameras snapping away, a smile that said they shared a secret that they would never tell, but oh, what delicious, naughty fun it had been making that secret together. . . The interviewer sighed in delight and commented that their chemistry was off the charts. Jane held her breath the entire time, as she was now staring directly up at Olivier's open lips and the reek of his breath was almost palpable. Like a total pro, she kept the pose going until she was sure all the cameras had captured what would be described as a spontaneous moment of pure sensuality between the two leads of the film; then she ducked her head, as if carried away by embarrassment, and placed one hand on the breast of Olivier's open-necked white shirt for a long moment.

This hadn't been planned. The publicists, of course, wanted them to flirt on the red carpet, were busy planting seeds of a story that their onscreen chemistry had spilled over into a torrid, secret, offscreen affair. Jane had gone further than she'd intended, and she hoped it hadn't come off as cheesy. When she pulled away, though, she caught sight of Laura, the director, standing to one side of the interview area with the film's publicist, both of their expressions so deeply appreciative that Jane relaxed in the certainty of a job well done.

She couldn't feel guilty for not coming out now. Neither she nor Olivier would have been cast in this film if they were known to be gay. The public wanted the fantasy of imagining themselves slipping into the roles she and Olivier played, inserting themselves into the film, believing that those sex scenes had truly happened; the knowledge that neither of the parties were even attracted to the other one's gender would be too difficult for that fantasy to work.

Would things change? Jane didn't think so. Film stars were sex objects, and the audience was predominantly straight. Her plan was to come out later, when she was forty-ish, way beyond being considered sexually desirable by Hollywood standards. Pull a Jodie Foster, acknowledge what had always been known but never quite said; live quietly till then, hopefully with a girlfriend who understood her situation, fake some affairs with her gay co-stars, maybe have a baby and coyly refuse to say who the father was. She would be fine with that compromise.

And then, just as she had firmly established her and Olivier's heterosexual credentials, she saw the small, slim figure of the woman with whom she was in love coming up the red carpet, and her interesting, rubbery, quirky features broke into her first genuinely spontaneous smile of the evening. For a moment, Jane Browne truly looked beautiful.

'Simone!' she exclaimed, almost running towards her coach. 'You came! I wasn't sure if you'd make it!'

'Me neither!' Simone said happily, her dark eyes sparkling at seeing Jane. 'I was working really hard putting a video together, but they insisted on flying me over, and finally I went, Oh, go on then, it's a freebie and I get to see Janey! Oh, it's great to see you! Wow, don't you look smart, just like a model!'

The two young women hugged, Jane leading Simone enthusiastically over to the waiting interviewers, the publicist trailing them closely.

'This is Simone DiGiovanni,' she began, 'my amazing coach and the choreographer on the film, and also my—'

'Simone's done a superb job of choreographing *Angel Rising*,' the publicist said smoothly, coming up behind Jane and Simone. 'Her work on Jane's cabaret routines is really groundbreaking. I know you've seen a short screener of some of the more spectacular parts – the hoop work is so amazing and sexy, isn't it? Jane trained *so* hard with Simone to get fit enough to pull off those scenes!'

Jane opened her mouth, looked at the publicist, and paused. As far as she was aware, it was no secret that Simone had been her body double for the more extreme stunts on the film. Simone had specifically choreographed these for herself to perform. There was no possibility that a novice could have done some of the trapeze drops, the silk hangs, or even held many poses for long enough for the camera to have captured them. Simone's contract specified that she get a body double credit on the film, as well as for her work as a coach and choreographer.

But clearly – Jane glanced at Laura, who was nodding significantly at her – a last-minute decision had been made: the production wanted to pretend that Jane had done much more of the physical work than she truly had. Which didn't sit well with Jane at all.

'Actually . . .' she began, but at that moment Simone, who was still holding her hand, squeezed it tightly. Her fingers bit so deeply into Jane's that Jane could feel every single one of Simone's callouses. Simone could hang from a bar by one hand, a brutally hard feat for a woman; she wasn't even using half her strength, but still Jane had to bite her lower lip to avoid gasping in pain.

'It's been an amazing experience working on *Angel Rising*

and training up Janey here for the aerial scenes,' Simone said cheerfully. 'I'm so excited to see her in action! I know she'll be just brilliant.'

Her dark eyes, looking into Jane's, conveyed the message that she was aware of the new set-up, was okay with it, or had at least made her peace with the situation. She and the publicist, flanking Jane, carried her along between them through the final wave of interviews, Simone talking about how hard Jane had worked, how she was a natural gymnast, could have competed seriously if she'd started younger – *well, at least the first one's true*, Jane thought ironically. She was merely required to smile modestly as Simone sang her praises, which was easy enough, but as they filed into the huge auditorium Jane was burning up with frustration, urgently wanting to talk to Simone.

Stars of the film were always seated at the back at premieres, as many actors could not bear to see themselves onscreen and would want to slip away as soon as the film started. Jane made Simone sit beside her on the end of a row. The lights dimmed, the music swelled, a single cello playing the slow, sexually suggestive theme of the film, and onscreen a shadowed female body that was definitely not Jane's began to twist and writhe slowly down a bright red strip of silk. Instantly, Jane was on her feet again, pulling Simone with her, making her way to the back doors. An usher held one open for them, looking star-struck at the sight of Jane dolled up to film-star perfection, and Jane, smiling thanks, shot through and dragged Simone into the loos, where they could be sure of not being overheard.

'It's fine, Janey,' Simone said instantly. 'Really, I'm okay. That was the deal.'

'It *wasn't* the deal! Not at all! Have they taken you off the credits?'

Jane's eyes were glowing with anger and frustration. She stalked over to the cubicles, pushing at all the doors to make sure no one was inside, especially no journalists. This would be a very juicy story that would unquestionably tank the film if it ever came out.

'They've called me a stunt double,' Simone said, shrugging. 'To make it sound like I only did a few of the really difficult bits no one'd believe you could pull off.'

'Oh, come *on*!' Jane burst out. 'You did at least *half* of it! I'm not remotely good enough to hold the poses like you did, let alone a lot of the drops!'

'Ah, hey, they gave me a big bonus to keep my mouth shut. Or actually, open it and say the right things,' Simone said easily. 'I'm not fussed, Janey, honestly. It's par for the course in video and TV – we're there to make the star look good, y'know?'

Jane actually stamped her foot, nearly dislocating the high heel of the Giuseppe Zanotti sandal chosen by the film's stylist to complement the dress.

'It's such bullshit!' she exclaimed, a word she never normally used. Simone's dark eyebrows shot up.

'Come on, Janey—' she started, but Jane, also very uncharacteristically, interrupted her. On set or onstage Jane could be whatever the role demanded; when not in character, she was mild-mannered, easy-going, even placid. She usually saved her emotional energy to channel into whichever demanding character she would be playing next, whether that was Charlotte Brontë watching her siblings die one by one

353

or a trapeze artist with a secret revenge scheme. So this sort of outburst was extremely unlike her, and she felt a heady rush as it poured out: for once, the words were her own; the passion she was expressing was from her own heart.

'It *is bullshit*!' she insisted, stamping her foot again. 'You did so much of the work, and you're getting shafted! I mean, yes, a bonus is good, but it's hush money. I bet they made you sign something to say you'd take it on condition of never being able to say when it's you onscreen rather than me, right?'

Simone tilted her head to one side, raised her shoulders, pantomiming, *What do you want me to say? Of course they did!* without actually having to speak the words and wind Jane up still further.

'Ugh!' Jane said furiously. 'But it's even worse for me, because I have to take credit for something I didn't do, which I *absolutely bloody hate*! How dare they put me in this position! It isn't about the acting at all, it doesn't have anything to do with the actual character, it doesn't take anything away from *my* work to say *you* were the one hanging upside down from a hoop by the back of your foot! As if I could *ever* learn to do that!'

'Yeah, but—'

'And now I'm going to have to do this whole fucking promotional tour smiling coyly when people tell me how amazing it is that I learned to do all of that so fast and what a genius I am! I hate this! And they couldn't even have *warned* me?'

Hectic colour was standing out on Jane's cheeks under the carefully applied make-up; her eyes were like torches, so bright that Simone could hardly look at her directly. Jane was burning up with anger.

'They just dumped it on me at the very last minute on the red carpet, a total *fait accompli*,' she continued, 'because they *knew* I'd kick off if they talked to me about it in advance and say I wasn't okay with it! They *knew that*! Bastards! Well, *I* haven't signed anything and been bought off. *I* haven't agreed to keep my mouth shut. I can just walk into the next interview I do and say, actually, there's been a bit of a misunderstanding – I couldn't hang upside down from a hoop by one foot if I lived to be a hundred . . .'

Her voice trailed off. She stared at herself in the big mirror over the nearest sink, surprised to see how high her colour was, how fervent her expression. It was an actor's fatal flaw always to catch a glimpse of themselves, or hear how their voice sounded at a certain moment, and then file it away for future use, but Jane was so incensed that, possibly for the first time in her adult life, the thought did not occur to her.

'You know you can't do that,' Simone said gently.

'I know I can't,' Jane echoed through gritted teeth. 'Fuck it, fuck it, *fuck it*!'

She let out a long sigh. Anger was ebbing from her, and what was replacing it she wasn't yet sure. Her ambition would not allow her to publicly contradict the publicity put out by a film production that was pushing hard to sell its movie to the world; that would be, quite simply, career suicide.

'It's just . . . how dare they ambush me like this?' she said more quietly. 'This shoot was such an amazing experience. Good script, great director, a fantastic part for me, a real breakout opportunity. And working with you was so . . . it was . . .'

She couldn't say it.

'Ah, come on now,' Simone said, trying for a lighter note. 'You hated every minute.'

'I loved it,' Jane said simply. 'I loved it. I loved being with you. I love you.'

She hadn't planned this in any way. The words just flew out of her. Having been kept inside for so long, they seized their opportunity, making their escape into the open air as easily as Jane might have yawned or sneezed, a physical release over which it felt that she had had no control at all. Simone's eyes were as wide as saucers, the irises almost black with shock.

It was fight or flight, and Jane's adrenalin was still pumping through her so furiously that it would not allow her to run away. Bridging the distance between them so quickly that Simone didn't realize what was happening, she took Simone's face between her hands and brought their mouths together. Breast to breast, as she'd dreamed of, their ribcages pressed together, their narrow waists and hips, their pelvic bones jutting against each other's through the fabric of their dresses. Jane's eyes were closed, her heart pounding in utter shock at her own bravery as her tongue found Simone's and her hands slid back to tangle in Simone's hair, wrapping around the back of her strong neck, feeling the lean muscles there, marvelling at how much strength Simone possessed in such a small, compact frame.

Simone moved, but not to push Jane away. Her hands closed around Jane's thin waist, the grip of each finger as distinct to Jane as if they were being branded onto her skin forever. Simone's hands, those wonderfully powerful, calloused hands . . . Jane shuddered from head to toe as Simone responded, kissing her back, her tongue deliciously moist as it traced Jane's lips. In her high heels, Jane was a few inches taller. Simone came up slightly on the balls of her feet, just enough to bring her face level with Jane's, so that they fit together perfectly, two matching halves of a whole.

Jane would have cried with happiness, but that would have meant breaking short this miraculous kiss, and not for the world would she have done that. The scent of Simone's body, so familiar to Jane from those months of training and filming so closely together, was an instant aphrodisiac, both sweet and salty. And oh, that tea tree deodorant! How well she remembered it from all those long days when she had been able to inhale the sweat on Simone's skin, but barely touch her as she longed to! It had been Simone who had touched Jane, spotting her, making adjustments, her hands so strong and firm and sure, but always professional; not like this, not like these caresses up and down her back, pulling Jane even closer, their mouths so welded together with endless wet, drugging kisses that they were barely able to breathe . . .

Simone pulled her head back, gasping as if she had been underwater and just resurfaced. Jane realized that she too was panting, catching air, her chest heaving. She leaned forward, resting her forehead against Simone's in perfect equilibrium; they were like two dolls of the same brand, the same size and shape, propped against one another by their small owner. She felt Simone's breath against her mouth, inhaled it, exhaled against Simone's lips, felt Simone doing the same. This was perfection, complete perfection. Her idea of heaven: to stay like this forever, their arms wrapped around each other's waists, their bodies entwined, breathing as one . . .

And then Simone lifted her head, so suddenly that Jane's jerked forward for a moment, the balance lost. Simone's eyes fluttered open, but she looked blind, as if she could not see Jane in front of her, could see nothing but what was inside her own head. She unwrapped her hands from around Jane's waist and stood up straight, her arms falling to her side, still looking like a doll, eyes wide, mouth slightly open.

Her lips moved. She said, 'I'm straight.'

This was not the first time Jane had heard these words, and she knew from experience that they were by no means insuperable.

'It's okay,' she said carefully. 'We don't have to classify anything as—'

'I have a boyfriend,' Simone said. 'I love him.'

Again, these words were not entirely unfamiliar to Jane. She wasn't what some of her gay friends called a 'flipper', a lesbian who made a practice of trying to seduce previously straight girls; she infinitely preferred someone who was already out, who wouldn't tumble into her arms trailing long complicated messy strands of drama and confusion. When you were young, it was practically inevitable that not everyone you dated would be openly gay. Young girls, as Jane vividly remembered, were nervous of being honest with themselves. They flirted with girls, some trying lesbianism on like an outfit they weren't sure suited them, some desperate to touch and kiss another woman in private but ready to deny it as soon as they were no longer alone with their lover. Even when they had been the one to make the move, they might well retreat afterwards, scared of their own nature, running back to their boyfriend for a while before they made another foray into getting tipsy with a girlfriend they secretly fancied.

But they had never looked shell-shocked afterwards. They had never had this blind stare or this zombie-doll appearance. Jane had no idea how to handle this and she was panicking desperately.

'I'm so sorry,' she said, near tears. 'Simone, I'm so sorry. It was too much . . . too fast . . . I got carried away . . .'

'I need to go,' Simone said. Despite her Mediterranean colouring, she had gone as white as the tiles on the bathroom wall behind her.

'Shall I come with—'

'No!' Simone said violently. She almost pushed Jane out of the way to get to the bathroom door; Jane stepped back just in time, tears springing to her eyes as Simone brushed past her. The sound of the door swinging shut behind Simone was like a lid closing down on Jane, boxing her into a small lonely space. She could barely draw breath. Stumbling over to the sink, she leaned both hands on the surround for support, staring at her reflection almost as blindly as Simone. She couldn't believe she had been such a fool.

How could she have been so completely unable to control her own emotions? She had ruined everything. How on earth was Simone supposed to react when Jane declared her love and then kissed her, all in the space of thirty seconds? How would *anyone* react? They would freak out and run away, of course, even if the kiss was wonderful – maybe even more so if the kiss was wonderful. It was way too much for anybody to be able to handle so unexpectedly.

Clearly! Jane thought grimly. *She couldn't have run away any faster!* She raised her head to look at herself fully in the mirror. Her fuchsia lip gloss had smeared; her narrow lips were temporarily swollen into how they would look if she had had collagen injections. Her black eyeliner was so smudged around her eyes she might have just staggered out of a club at two in the morning after having had wild sex with someone in a back room. She looked more sexually charged than she had ever done in her life.

And it was all for nothing. She had taken a huge risk and she had struck out completely.

'*Fuck*,' she said to her reflection furiously, tears starting to flow again. 'What the fuck is *wrong* with me! Why did I have to tell her I loved her? Why did I have to be such a fucking *girl*?'

Chapter Twenty-Three

On-board

David Webber, the air marshal who was posted at the front of the business-class cabin, shifted nervously in his seat. For some time he had been observing a passenger behaving in a way that was becoming of increasing concern to him, but it was such an unprecedented situation that he was engaged in a painful internal debate with himself about how to handle it. In any other circumstance, he would by now have been on high alert, consulting discreetly with his colleague about the best way to approach the possible perp. Unfortunately, there was a big hitch with that strategy: the perp in question *was* David's colleague, which made things very tricky indeed.

His fellow air marshal did not outrank David, but the combination of his natural authority combined with his grim demeanour meant that David was having a damn hard time asking, as tactfully as possible, what the hell was up. What he really wanted to say was that Gerhardt was freaking the shit out of him and needed to get a damn grip pronto, but somehow, despite David's fifteen years in the LAPD regularly taking down gang members and drug dealers, he was floundering when it came to confronting Gerhardt about why he was acting so weird.

It had started even before they boarded the plane. Gerhardt, who was normally so self-controlled and composed that a mere few weeks into air marshal training he'd been nicknamed the 'Iceman', had been acting like he had ants in his pants as soon as they reported for duty at Heathrow. Gerhardt had been unable to sit still, pacing constantly, even going AWOL for a while after they went airside. When he returned, just in time to board, David had been about to ask in his best casual tone: 'Hey, anything up?' But when he got a good look at the expression in Gerhardt's cold silver eyes, he closed his mouth without uttering a word. Gerhardt was back and good to go – that was what mattered.

Though now David was having to radically redefine his use of the words 'good to go'. It was common knowledge in the service that Gerhardt had dated his boss, Catalina, when he'd been working as her bodyguard. Lucky bastard. There wasn't a guy alive who didn't fantasize about getting a piece of that action – the video alone where she was in the cage, crawling around in just a leotard that went right up her crack, was enough to get anyone off. It was getting so you couldn't tell what was a porno and what wasn't. David was honestly amazed they could show that shit on primetime TV.

Before Gerhardt had joined, there had been endless joshing about the new recruit's recent conquest; strangely, however, as soon as Gerhardt had walked into the Los Angeles field office, all the jokes that his fellow air marshals had prepared had died, unspoken, on their lips. They'd heard the nickname the instructor on his federal law enforcement course had given him, and been prepared to mock that too, but it was a hell of a difference between hearing the name and actually meeting the Iceman in person. A couple of guys who had put up sexy posters of Catalina in the break room as a joke disappeared swiftly to take them down before the Iceman got royally pissed off by the sight of his former girlfriend sprawling on a shiny floor, her butt stuck high in the air, wearing only a leotard practically the same colour as her lightly tanned skin. Seriously, you really couldn't tell what was a porno any more. Maybe everything was.

So the posters had come down, way faster than they went up. No one wanted to fuck with the Iceman. David had taken some psych courses at college, so he knew that guys operated on a pack mentality much more than women did. Men sorted themselves into a hierarchy pretty damn quickly, and though the Iceman might be a newbie, his commanding presence and natural authority skyrocketed him right up to pack leader status.

Also, he'd made record shooting scores, and that was a big deal. They were all highly proficient marksmen, the best of the best; it was crucial in their job that you could take out a bad guy without hitting a civilian passenger or, even worse, some vital piece of hydraulics or electrical cable or fuel line that would send the whole plane plummeting if it were cut. It wasn't that you actually thought that Gerhardt would pull out his service weapon and start practising 'shoot to stop' on the first guy to make a dirty joke about Catalina: but still, you didn't want to get on the wrong side of a guy with that kind of aim.

Plus, look at his army background: the guy had been a drill sergeant, and he still had the air of a guy who expected everyone else to jump to his commands. And the accent didn't hurt either. German accents just sounded . . . well, authoritative. The guy didn't talk so much as bark. You'd never know he had an American dad, ex-military himself, who'd met a German girl while stationed over there and stayed on when his tour came to an end. Hence his eligibility for the Marshals Service: a non-US citizen would never have been allowed to join. The Marshals Service had been all over Gerhardt's application, fast-tracked it, in fact. Gerhardt was gold, someone no one would suspect of working for the federal government.

When he and David had been assigned to this flight, no one had been aware that Gerhardt's ex would be aboard; even if they had, it probably wouldn't have made any difference. But it didn't take a psych course for David to figure out that her presence was driving Gerhardt nuts. A couple of hours into the flight, he'd come striding down with a face like thunder to the back of the plane where David was sitting and insisted that David change seats with him immediately, no questions asked. Other guys, you'd have made them at least give you a quick heads-up as to why, but that drill sergeant thing of his was very effective: when Gerhardt said 'Jump', you did it first and then asked after if you'd gone high enough for him.

David had settled into Gerhardt's seat and muttered some lame excuse about his buddy who he worked with thinking the bulkhead was too draughty for him, but the guy in the window seat couldn't have given a shit about the change in occupancy of 14E. He was much too busy craning his neck over to the other side of the plane.

'Some chick just came in from the first-class cabin and made a hell of a scene,' he'd explained to David. 'Grabbed that other chick in 14A and started beating her head against the back of her seat. The steward had to pull her off. She was yelling for the girl to wake up. Pretty crazy stuff. Probably drunk out of her mind.'

David had glanced over, very curious as to what had triggered Gerhardt's sudden need to move, but all he could see was the outline of a sleeping young woman, mostly concealed by a white guy sitting next to her, playing a video game. He didn't have to ponder the mystery long, however; in a few minutes' time a very good-looking stewardess came through from Luxe Class, followed by two thin young women in those slouchy layered outfits that rich ladies wore to fly in. Legs like toothpicks in their skinny jeans, heads too big for their bodies. Chicks today were way too thin for David's taste; he kept telling his daughter that guys liked girls with a bit of meat on them, but would she listen? No, she ate like a bird and bitched for hours about him sabotaging her diet if he brought home pizza for dinner.

Shit. He realized that they were all looking over in his direction. Clearly Gerhardt had had a good reason to swap seats.

And then it dawned on him. Jesus, he was slow. But who would have thought that tiny little slip of a thing was *Catalina*?

He knew they hadn't realized he was checking them out. He was trained in covert observation and he could pick up more from a quick glance out of the corner of his eye than most people could with a direct stare. As far as they were concerned, he'd been gazing at his copy of *Forbes* magazine the whole time. But his seatmate had started to nudge him, and it would have been weird of him not to register the arrival of the group of women. He looked up to see Catalina pointing directly at him. David's eyes gave nothing away, but he was registering how pretty she was, much prettier without all that make-up she usually wore in her videos, and how miniature, like a little girl. Jesus, in that leotard she'd looked like she had curves that went on for days; the camera really did pile on the pounds. That must be why the girls starved themselves, he supposed.

He gave a little shrug, the reaction a businessman travelling for work might give to an odd event that had nothing to do with him. As if to say, *I have no idea why you're pointing at me, lady, but you look kind of nuts, and I have better things to do than have a staring match with a crazy lady*. He dropped his gaze once again. Out of the corner of his eye he watched the rest of the scene, a steward coming up to the little cluster of women, being asked about him, the steward covering for him and Gerhardt switching seats, Catalina collapsing and being hauled back to Luxe Class by the other woman and the drop-dead-gorgeous flight attendant.

That had been hours ago, and Catalina hadn't been back, which was a good thing. Last thing they wanted was any questions that might blow his and Gerhardt's cover. David had sat there for a good while; then he had strolled back to the tail of the plane like he was just stretching his legs and tried to corral Gerhardt back to the crew area for a confab. But Gerhardt had pretty much blanked him, and David hadn't dared to push things for fear that people would start figuring out who they were. Gerhardt had David over a barrel: if he didn't want to talk, David couldn't make him.

Dammit, this was a mess. David had gone back to 14E, hoping to hell that this would be the end of it. Catalina had clearly been as freaked out at seeing Gerhardt as he had been to see her, and then she'd lost it at his apparent transformation from big white German to stocky black American. For security reasons, naturally, the crew couldn't tell her what was going on, so she was very unlikely to start searching the plane for him.

She hadn't looked good; she was high, probably. Rock stars, what did you expect? So she'd probably think she'd hallucinated the sight of her ex because of whatever pills she was popping. Meanwhile, Gerhardt was back in the tail of the plane, sitting like he was literally carved of ice, not saying a damn word to anyone, which at least meant no trouble. All the two marshals had to do was keep their heads down for the rest of the flight and hope no one started anything.

But Gerhardt hadn't stayed in his seat. That was the problem with which David was currently wrestling. He had got up, seeming like a man on a mission, and what he was doing right now was causing David, a tough, hard-nosed LAPD veteran, to fidget as uneasily as if he were a kid halfway through Sunday church service who'd lied to his mom that he'd peed before they left the house and now badly needed to go.

His seatmate, thank God, was now snoozing and unaware of David's agitation; the excitement caused by Catalina's irruptions into the business-class cabin had faded, the flight attendants had been generous with the alcoholic beverages, dinner had been served and cleared, the lights had been dimmed, and most people were now sleeping off the free booze.

Which, thank God, meant that very few of them were awake to notice what Gerhardt was up to. No one seemed to have registered it yet, no one but David. He was seriously worried that Gerhardt had lost it, big time. What he was doing was . . . David couldn't even find the words to summarize how inappropriately Gerhardt was acting right now. It was light years away from air marshal protocol. And yet, once they deplaned, David would be obliged to sum up Gerhardt's actions on-board: it was standard requirement for each marshal to file post-flight reports for every assignment. How the hell was he going to write this up? But there was no way he could leave it out!

David had tried to intervene already, and been barked at so harshly to go back to his seat, that this was private business and no one was getting hurt, that he had obeyed the order. What was he supposed to do? He couldn't take the guy down – Gerhardt was ten years younger and way bigger than him – and he sure as hell couldn't shoot him.

So David had two pressing concerns. One was to make sure his colleague didn't go as apeshit crazy as his ex-girlfriend, which frankly was looking more and more likely, and the other one was to cover his own ass. David took a deep breath, brought every ounce of his extensive experience in ass-covering to bear on the pressing dilemma, and tried, as best he could, to block out for a few minutes his screaming anxiety about what the Iceman was doing to that woman in the galley . . .

Chapter Twenty-Four

Four months ago

By ten thirty the next morning, Catalina's nerves were so shot that she jumped every time she heard the slightest noise that might be Latisha returning from her appointment with the tech guy in the Valley. As Catalina had predicted, Gerhardt hadn't noticed the disappearance of his laptop; she had been ready to distract him by any means necessary should he mention needing to check his email, but he had shown no sign of going to retrieve his computer.

What if he really only used the laptop to create Photoshopped pictures of you? asked a nasty, untrusting little voice in her head. *If that were the case, once he'd done that and got what he wanted – you – the laptop wouldn't be much more use to him. So he wouldn't need to check it any more, would he?*

The voice had been talking to her almost non-stop since Latisha's visit to the house yesterday. Catalina actually felt like pressing her hands to her ears and pantomiming a scream, like a heroine in a silent movie. She'd played one in a music video years ago. Dressed up in a beaded 1920s vintage dress and a Louise Brooks bobbed black wig, she'd run through a ballroom full of costumed dancers doing the Charleston, chased by a man in the costume of a mad scientist. She'd fled down a wide stone staircase into a formal garden, been cornered against a hedge, and then the topiary statues had come to life to save her. The director's inspiration had been *Alice in Wonderland* meets a flapper in a horror film. Catalina had spent most of the shoot either running as slowly as she could, because beads fell off the dress almost every time she moved, or putting her hands over her ears while stretching her eyes and mouth into wide silent-scream Os.

The video had cost a fortune but, to be fair, it looked wonderful. And every time she wanted to scream now, or press her hands to her head, she called up the image of herself doing exactly that, and it did help to stop the impulse, made her realize how theatrical she was being; but instead, she was rocking back and forward and picking at her cuticles, an awful habit in which she hadn't indulged for years. When the manicurist came for her next appointment she would click her tongue in vexation and lecture Catalina disapprovingly.

Catalina could at least see the irony in fretting about that.

Honestly, if that's my biggest problem by the day after tomorrow – having Anastasia bitch at me because my cuticles are messed up – I'll kiss the ground with thanks! she thought, ducking her head to use her sharp little teeth on a particularly stubborn nub of skin clinging to the side of her thumbnail. She worried at it so furiously, channelling all her suppressed fears into the determined quest to bite it off, that she tugged too forcefully. Instead of severing it neatly, she pulled it at an angle that ripped the skin and made her wince in pain. Blood welled up from the crease.

Cursing, she sucked on it hard, digging her teeth in to distract her from the throbbing of her thumbnail. It was amazing how much such a little thing could hurt. All she had achieved was to drag the nub further out, making it even more obvious. She would have to trim it with clippers or it would catch on everything and keep drawing blood again.

Something to do: go up to her bathroom, get the nail clippers. Ridiculous how relieved she was to have a task. Ever since Gerhardt had gone to the gym at nine thirty prompt – he was a true creature of routine, she was learning, which seemed charming now, but she was intelligent enough to realize might pose problems further down the line – she had been unable to settle to anything, not even watching reality TV. She had flicked through magazines without even seeing the pictures, let alone reading the words; she had tried to listen to music, scribble down some lyrics, but her ability to concentrate was non-existent.

Exercise would have helped, but her stomach was churning too much for her to contemplate it, and besides, she would have felt too naked, too exposed in her workout gear. She was curled up in one of the oversized, American-proportioned armchairs that the decorator had bought to go in the over-sized, American-proportioned den. Reaching back, she pulled a big pillow from behind her back and hugged it to her narrow chest. It helped. Only a little, but it helped.

And then, at last, came the sound she'd been waiting for. Latisha's key, turning the lock of the front door. It had to be Tish: no one else was expected today. Catalina was on her feet, the pillow thrown to the floor, running across the den to the hallway. She'd meant to be cool about it, wait in her armchair, have Tish come to her, demonstrate that she didn't have any doubts about Gerhardt's innocence. Because, of course, she didn't. Tish would walk in with a rueful smile, apologizing for having made such a fuss about nothing; Catalina would forgive her but tick her off sternly; Tish would apologize some more, they'd hug, and Catalina would hurry to the gym to stop Gerhardt in the middle of his workout, just briefly, to kiss him and tell him how much she loved him, and he would stare at her, baffled but smiling indulgently at women and their inexplicable surges of emotion.

She had pictured it all. This was exactly how it would go. As she dashed into the atrium, the front door was closing behind Latisha, and the bright daylight behind her assistant meant that Catalina couldn't see her face at all. It was only when the door closed and Catalina's pupils adjusted that she could take in Tish's expression, and as she did, she felt as if all the air had been sucked out of her lungs.

'I'm so sorry, Cat,' Latisha almost whispered. 'I'm so sorry.'

These were the words Catalina had imagined her saying, but not like this. Not in that tone, not with that expression of guilt mingled with grief for what Catalina was about to experience. Latisha looked positively ashamed.

Catalina couldn't say a word. She stared at the laptop case Latisha was holding, fighting the impulse to grab it and dash it to the ground, jumping on it, smashing its contents.

'Let's go in there?'

Latisha nodded to the den. Like a zombie obeying a necromancer, Catalina turned and walked slowly back inside the room, returning to her armchair, retrieving the pillow on the way and hugging it again as she sat down. Latisha perched on the coffee table, unzipping the case, extracting the laptop, opening it and turning it on.

'I don't want to see,' Catalina said to the pillow.

Latisha's high forehead creased in dismay.

'I think you should, Cat,' she said. 'Just in case . . . I mean, you might think later I made it up. I think you need to see it with your own eyes . . .'

The laptop was loading. Latisha tapped some keys and put it on the table beside her. Images started to scroll across the screen, the Photoshopped pictures of Catalina's head on the naked, porn-star posing bodies. Catalina hadn't seen these for months, but they were as horribly familiar to her as if it had been yesterday. The one where 'she' had her hand between her splayed legs, the one where 'she' was fondling the boobs that were considerably larger than what Catalina ruefully called her own 'mosquito bites', the one where 'she' was on all fours, in a horrible parody of Catalina's 'Chasing Midnight' video, her naked behind thrust into the air, Catalina's face smiling back at the viewer as innocently as if she were fully dressed and posing with a group of fans rather than exposing her most private parts to the camera lens.

They were obscene. There was no other word that would fit those images. And seen close up like this, rather than scattered over the floor of a dressing room, it was obvious how much work had gone into creating them. The Photoshopper had not simply copied and pasted Catalina's head onto the porn-star bodies like an old-fashioned collage where you cut round an image in a magazine and glued it onto another. They had spent a great deal of time finding the right angle of her face, the tilt of her chin and fall of her hair, to match the original and make the pose seem as plausible as possible. The join was barely visible, the lighting on her face digitally filtered to match the rest of the picture. It was an almost professional job.

'No one who loved you could do this,' Latisha said after a while. 'I mean, no one who loved you . . . in the right way.'

It was undeniably true. All Catalina's wishful justifications fell away as she saw them for the smoke and mirrors they were. This was the truth, these disgusting, explicit, unjustifiable images of her. Catalina spared herself nothing, because she had been in denial, and now she had to face the truth. Merely picturing Gerhardt sitting in front of his computer for hours, carefully, meticulously, *lovingly* creating one after another – probably getting off on each one as he made it – made her want to vomit.

Latisha was absolutely right. This wasn't the kind of love anyone wanted in their life. It was the ugliest version imaginable: controlling, violent, degrading. Latisha had been right, too, when she insisted that Catalina look at the pictures. Without forcing herself to see them, Catalina would simply not have been able to take in the magnitude of Gerhardt's manipulation of her emotions, the betrayal that he had perpetrated by presenting himself as her saviour, the rock for her to cling to, when all along the reality had been that he was capable of this kind of nasty, dirty, vicious behaviour.

This wasn't just one brief, possibly drunken moment of impulse that would be bitterly regretted the next morning;

it was a long, deliberately planned campaign. No excuse was possible.

'How do you want to handle this?' Latisha eventually asked.

Catalina reached out over the cushion and pushed the laptop shut.

'We should go upstairs and pack all his things,' she said, her voice surprisingly steady. 'It won't take long. He doesn't have much.'

He really didn't. Just a big suitcase and a duffel bag, all he had taken on tour. Gerhardt lived in his unofficial uniform of black T-shirts and trousers, a couple of pairs of jeans and jogging bottoms for his downtime, and a tattered selection of old T-shirts plus shorts for exercise. As befitted a straight man, his toiletry selection was pitiful: toothbrush, mouth-wash, deodorant, two-in-one shampoo and conditioner, shaving cream and razor; it took Catalina barely a minute in the bathroom to sweep his gear into his battered old washbag.

She had been planning to get him a really good leather one for his birthday; actually, she had been planning to get him a great many things for his birthday. Very aware of the financial gulf between them, she had refrained, much as she wanted to, from taking him out to Rodeo Drive and buying him nicer luggage, a whole new wardrobe, a watch, a Jeep . . . It would be more for her benefit than his, she knew perfectly well. She wanted to spoil him, to give him lovely things, to treat him to soft John Smedley Sea Island cotton against his skin rather than his stiff, cheap old generic-brand T-shirts. Gerhardt didn't care that his washbag was so ancient the leather had cracked at the seams, or that his watch strap was in equally bad shape, but she did. She *had* thought he might not have minded if she replaced the strap before his birthday came due . . .

Everything was painful. Everything was a reminder of all the dreams she had had, the ideas she had had for cosseting him, the red carpet of welcome she had wanted to lay out for him in return for the happiness he was giving her. Gerhardt, of course, had asked for nothing at all. Not a thing. Not even sushi delivered for dinner. As far as she could see, he would have been happy to live off protein shakes and tinned tuna in brine.

Latisha had crammed all his clothes into his suitcase and was zipping it up when Catalina came back into the bedroom, tears in her eyes, the washbag in her hand. Silently she dropped it into the duffel bag, which was filled with Gerhardt's shoes. They were really what took up the room: his feet were enormous. Two pairs of black leather dress shoes for work, one pair of trainers; he was wearing the other. He had solemnly explained to her that he rotated them every day to let them rest.

They loaded the luggage into the lift without saying a word. The doors opened at the back of the ground-floor atrium, and Latisha was pulling out the suitcase by its chipped plastic handle – Catalina had so longed to replace that! – when Gerhardt passed through on his way up to take a shower, wiping his sweaty face with a towel.

'Here, let me!' he said, seeing Latisha struggling with the big suitcase. 'I can take that for you. You should have asked me to help! That is too heavy for you.'

His words trailed off as he stared down at the suitcase that he had just courteously removed from Latisha's grasp.

'But this is *mine*,' he said, confused. His forehead furrowed as he looked over at Catalina and saw that she had his big duffel slung over her shoulder, practically dwarfing her.

'And that is mine too! . . .' He frowned even deeper. 'I don't understand. Are we moving? Going on a trip? I should be told, Catalina. I am still your bodyguard. I need to check that everything is safe for you.'

'She'll be safer when you're gone, buddy,' Latisha said, squaring her jaw as she stared up at him.

'*What?*'

He strode over to Catalina. Latisha screamed something, tried to get in the way, tugged at his arm, but Gerhardt was already by his girlfriend's side, taking the heavy duffel bag from her and setting it down.

'You should not carry that,' he said reprovingly. 'You will strain your back.'

He turned to stare at Latisha, who was dragging on his arm with all her might but failing to shift him by even a millimetre. It was like watching an ant try to budge an elephant.

'I don't understand,' he repeated. 'Latisha, what are you *doing*? Why are you talking like this?'

'We know what you've been up to,' Latisha said bravely. 'We know everything.'

'Have you been smoking something funny?' Gerhardt said, bending down to look at the state of her pupils.

'Cat, I think we should call the cops,' Latisha said, managing to get between him and her employer. 'You get back in the elevator and go upstairs and maybe lock yourself into the bathroom.'

'Gerhardt won't hurt me, Tish,' Catalina said quietly, tapping her assistant's shoulder to get her to move aside. 'Honestly. I know he won't.'

'*Hurt* you?' Gerhardt stared down his nose at her, looking exactly like the Easter Island statue that had been his army nickname: huge, imposing, stone-faced. 'Have you been smoking something too?'

Latisha had her phone out now.

'I should have thought this through,' she said, hitting 911. 'I should have had a plan. My bad. I'm sorry, Cat.'

'Tish!' Catalina grabbed the phone from her before she could press CALL. 'This is crazy! We don't need the cops!'

She swallowed as she tilted her head back to look at Gerhardt. The T-shirt he was wearing was damp with sweat, and the wide gaps where he had cut off the sleeves were showing so much of his chest muscles that it was positively distracting. They were as sculpted as if he were wearing body armour, the pectorals like hubcaps, his abdominals thick washboard ridges. Gerhardt was built on gladiatorial lines. If he had wanted to, he could have picked up both women, one in each hand, like a giant in a fairy tale. But even though Catalina had unequivocal proof that it had been he who had stalked her, she was absolutely sure that he would never do anything physical to hurt either her or Latisha.

And even through her misery and grief, she couldn't help noticing that the idea had not occurred to Latisha either. Here they were, going against all the advice given to women in potentially dangerous situations. Catalina sponsored a women's domestic violence charity, had recorded public service announcements, as they were called in the US, about the signs to watch out for and how to leave the abuser as safely as possible. You bided your time until you could put into place a plan of action: when they were out of the house, you changed the locks, put their stuff outside, had a friend with you to help, left a non-confrontational message designed not to inflame things further.

Latisha had been with Catalina through all of the recordings and the events: the charity sponsorship had been her suggestion. Which meant that two grown women, who knew much better than to be careless with their own safety, had completely ignored all the extremely sensible rules of which they were perfectly well aware, with the result that they found themselves now with Gerhardt looming over them, more than physically capable of smashing Latisha's phone so she couldn't call the police and doing whatever he wanted to them after that.

But they were in no danger. Catalina knew that, and she realized that Latisha must too. Latisha was the most sensible, efficient person Catalina had ever met; being a personal assistant to a famous pop star required not only superb organizational skills but the ability to plan ahead for multiple contingencies. So if Latisha, who had known ever since picking up the laptop that Gerhardt was guilty, hadn't spent the time driving from the Valley to the Hollywood Hills in working out the safest way to handle this, that must surely mean that she, too, was aware that Gerhardt wouldn't harm a fly.

That reflection gave Catalina a measure of much-needed relief. She wasn't *totally* crazy. She might have fallen head over heels for her stalker, but she had, at least, chosen a man whom both she and Latisha were sure wouldn't raise a hand to either one of them.

'Gerhardt,' she began.

It hurt just to say his name. He looked down at her with such pain in his eyes that she had to summon every image that she had just seen on his laptop not to run into his arms. Oh yes, Latisha had been quite right to insist she look at those pictures.

'It's over,' she managed to say.

This was the hardest thing she'd ever had to do. He was so close to her, and it really didn't help that he had just been working out, that his muscles were so pumped and veined, that she knew exactly what his fresh sweat would taste like, could just picture the cleft between his pectorals, which she had loved to lick after he came out of the gym, lapping up the salty drops there like a cat with the cream, kneeling over him as he lay sprawled beneath her, his hands behind his head, displaying for her benefit the magnificent swell of his biceps and triceps. Gerhardt just had to scratch the back of his neck to make Catalina feel faint with lust. The size of his arms, the stretch of his armpit with its dark shadow of hair, the paler skin there that so rarely saw the sun, like something secret, intimate, that was being revealed only to her . . .

There was a huge lump in her throat. She swallowed very hard and nearly choked on it.

'But . . . I don't understand!' Gerhardt repeated, utterly bewildered. Clearly he had no idea that Catalina might have found out about the stalking. He was like a bull in the ring, being skewered with the lances of the picadors, tiny beside his massive frame, but still able to wound him. He glanced down at his luggage, at Latisha watching him intently, and then back at the agonized face of his now ex-girlfriend.

'What have I done that is so bad?' he asked her, looking baffled. 'What could it be to make you want me to go?'

'You *know*, Gerhardt! You must know!' Catalina was close to tears. 'Don't make me say it, please! Just leave!'

He shook his head slowly.

'No, Catalina. You must say it. You must tell me. I insist,' he added, almost gently.

It was almost impossible to talk around the lump in her throat, which if anything had increased. She managed, 'You were the one that . . . that stalked me. You put the photos in my dressing room, sprayed the walls. You did it so I would get scared and be vulnerable . . .'

Her voice trailed off. The expression on Gerhardt's face was unbearable. A shield had come down like a protective wall. His features stiffened, his jaw was set. He looked like a mask of himself. She remembered the 'Easter Island' nickname he had told her he'd been given in the army; she had never really seen it until now, when he might have looked at Medusa and been turned instantly to stone.

'We have the evidence,' Latisha said, keeping her voice up very courageously, given how intimidating Gerhardt's granite countenance was. She held out his laptop to him. 'All the photos are on here, the ones you Photoshopped to print out and put in Cat's dressing rooms. You can't deny it.'

Gerhardt's great head turned to Latisha as ponderously as a slow-moving statue from an old animatronic film. He gazed at her for a long moment, reaching his hand out to take the laptop: it looked like a tablet in his big hand. Bending, he slid it into his duffel and tossed the bag over his shoulder as if it weighed nothing at all. Then, straightening up again, he took one last glance at Catalina.

'I do not deny it,' he said, and the women both gasped at this admission.

'I do not deny it,' he repeated very deliberately, 'because if you believe it, Catalina, it is useless for me to say anything to defend myself. If you think I can have done this thing, then you are right. It is over. You are right to make me go if you believe this.'

He took the handle of his suitcase, swivelled on one heel, and began to walk towards the front door. Both Catalina's hands were pressed to her mouth in shock. She had expected him to argue, to plead, to invent explanations for the presence of the photos on her laptop, maybe even to accuse Latisha of setting him up: wild accusations, protestations of love, the conventional response of someone accused of a crime.

She'd thought Gerhardt's attempts to defend himself, to plead his way out of a tight corner, would be heartbreaking. This reaction, however, was infinitely worse. He was the one who had betrayed her so terribly, but somehow he had managed to make her feel like the guilty one.

'Hey, let me call you a cab,' Latisha said, her voice uncertain. Clearly she, too, was so taken aback by this reaction that she was unsure how to handle it. 'Or . . . do you want to have a shower first? I mean, you just got out of the gym . . . we could call you a cab in twenty minutes, let you wash up and get changed . . .'

Gerhardt raised one hand briefly in dismissal of her

suggestions, his back to them as he crossed the hall. The end came so swiftly that Catalina had no time to take it in. One minute he was so close she could reach out and touch him, smell his sweat, hear the deep rumble of his voice; the next, he was opening the front door. Sunlight poured in for a second and then was blocked almost completely by his huge silhouette, his shoulders nearly spanning the door frame.

He paused for a moment on the threshold. Or did he? Maybe that was merely her fantasy, that he would turn around, say some magic words that would resolve everything, allow Catalina to hurtle towards him and jump up at him, as she had with such a miraculous result in Tokyo. She waited, breath caught in her chest, for another miracle to happen.

But it didn't. He stepped forward, out into the light, his looming shadow trailing him along the floor. The shadow disappeared, sunlight flooded in again; the door closed behind him automatically, swinging back into place, the lock clicking shut. Gerhardt was gone forever.

The two women stood in total silence, coming down from the adrenalin high of confrontation, stunned by how fast things had ended.

Eventually Latisha said almost timidly, 'Cat? Are you okay? I mean, sorry, what a dumb question . . .'

'I still love him,' Catalina said in a tiny, piteous voice.

'Oh honey, I know,' Latisha, who had had a bad break-up herself the year before, said compassionately. 'I know, I know . . .'

She enfolded her boss in a close embrace, patting Catalina's slender back comfortingly.

'There'll be someone else,' she said into Catalina's mass of hair. 'Someone even better, you'll see. And in the meantime, you have me. I know it's not the same, but I'm here for you whenever and wherever you need me. You're not alone.'

'I can't stay here,' Catalina said in a whisper to Latisha's collarbones. 'I can't be here, not without him. I'd go crazy.'

'Do you want me to move in for the next few weeks, hon?' Latisha asked gently. 'I could go get my stuff right now if you want.'

Catalina shook her head. 'I just can't be here at all,' she said, still not raising her head. 'It's too . . . too . . .'

She swallowed hard, trying not to cry: she didn't want to break down here. Once she started sobbing, she might not stop for days, and she needed to be in a safe place when she let go. Here, in the house where she had been so happy with Gerhardt, where everything would remind her of him so vividly, was no longer safe at all.

Latisha was quick to understand.

'Sure,' she said swiftly. 'I get it. No problem. Let me just throw some stuff in a bag for you. Then I'll make a couple of calls and get a nice hotel suite all sorted out.'

'You'll stay with me, won't you?' Catalina asked. 'Please? I'm sorry, Tish – I know you were going to have time off –'

'Oh honey, any time! There's nothing I love more than hotel suites with room and laundry service! And besides, I owe you – you were there for me last year when I had my break-up.'

384

Stroking Catalina's hair, Latisha let out a long sigh.

'Men. Jesus, the messes they make. Maybe we're just unlucky, but shit, it's enough to make you seriously think about going the other way.'

She pulled back a little so she could see Catalina's face, hoping that this remark would manage to raise even the tiniest smile. Her boss did lift the corners of her lips, but that was all; her smile so forlorn that Latisha was very glad that Catalina was not going to stay in the house alone. If that had been Catalina's plan, Latisha would have seriously considered taking all the sharp objects out of the house for fear that her boss would try to hurt herself.

'You've still got me,' Latisha repeated reassuringly, looking down at Catalina, her hands now on her boss's slender shoulders. 'I've got your back, honey, just like you have mine. Men may come and go, but we'll always have each other.'

Catalina's feeble attempt at a smile faded as she struggled very hard with herself not to blurt out that, however well meant, this was no consolation at all.

Chapter Twenty-Five

On-board

'Hi! Do you have a minute?'

Lucinda exited the galley to find Jane standing in the corridor, smiling cheerfully at her.

'Miss Browne! What can I do for you?' Lucinda asked very deferentially.

Lucinda's smile of greeting was entirely genuine, a rarity for her with the passengers. She thoroughly approved of Jane. Not only were her manners impeccable, she had been a great help with Catalina, and was perfectly sober to boot; on this flight especially, that won Jane even more points than it would usually have done. The businessmen at the bar were slurring and slipping from their stools, and the champagne that Danny Zasio had drunk with Lord Tony – he had finished the entire bottle on his own – had put him into another stupor. Karl had had to half carry Danny to his pod, where the chef was now passed out and snoring heavily. Karl had very sensibly propped Danny on his side in the recovery position and was checking in on him regularly to make sure he didn't choke on his own vomit.

'Wouldn't be the first one to do that,' he'd said darkly.

Passengers who did not abuse the bottomless bar on offer

in Luxe Class were always favoured by the cabin crew. Lucinda shuddered briefly at the recent incident a friend of hers on British Airways Club World had undergone, a drunk woman barricading herself into a toilet and banging around inside so loudly that the poor crew, seriously concerned that she might be hurting herself badly, had been forced to take the door off. When they finally managed that, the woman turned out to have wet herself. Unable to stand, she was carried back to her seat, and in the process she punched an air steward in the face while threatening to shoot him with what, thank goodness, had turned out to be an imaginary gun.

And she only got a suspended sentence! Lucinda thought angrily. *How is that a deterrent? They swear at us if we don't serve them drinks, then they attack us when they get drunk! Someone really needs to go to jail for a year to scare the rest of them into acting decently for a change.*

But Jane was exemplary, a perfectly behaved passenger, and when she requested that Lucinda take a couple of photographs of her in her pod for her Twitter account, Lucinda was more than happy to fulfill the request with great good nature.

'I know it seems a bit cheesy,' Jane said self-deprecatingly as the two women walked back to Jane's seat. 'But the publicists love it. I have to hashtag everything with Oscar and Academy Awards – it feels so showy-offy, but it's a part of my job nowadays. I've taken some selfies already, but I really wanted to get more of the pod into the photos. People love that kind of thing, apparently. Travel pictures.' She looked rueful. 'But it means I can never really relax when I'm on the road. I'm constantly thinking about what photos I should be taking and uploading, and I do get frustrated, because it's really nothing to do with the work itself.'

'I do understand,' Lucinda said sympathetically. 'We've had so much of that recently ourselves.' She lowered her voice conspiratorially. 'We're always told it's an honour to represent the company, but we don't actually get *paid* for the photo shoots, you know. And they can take up a lot of time.'

'How annoying!' Jane said sympathetically. 'I mean, for me at least, the whole social media thing does help me get put up for more jobs. People see me on the red carpet and at fashion launches and think of me when they're casting a film or TV series. It keeps me in the public eye.'

She pulled a very expressive grimace.

'I hate all the dressing up and going out, to be honest,' she added, 'but my agent's absolutely right when they tell me to go everywhere I'm invited. Casting directors want to have a recognizable name to help publicize the film, you see. It's not just about who's best for the part.'

She turned into the opening of her pod, picked up her phone and exclaimed in annoyance.

'Oh, damn, it's out of charge! I should have realized!'

'I can plug it in for you,' Lucinda offered. 'There's a full charging station in your desk area. And we have chargers, just in case you've forgotten yours.'

'No, I've got it . . . it's just that the wretched thing takes forever to charge, and the angle won't be right if you take some photos while it's still plugged in . . .' Jane clicked her tongue in frustration. 'And I wanted to do them now and then have a nice sleep until just before we land . . . and you'll be too busy then to take photos . . . God, what a nuisance!'

'I could use my phone,' Lucinda suggested helpfully, 'if you have a way to transfer them over?'

'Yes! Perfect! I can Bluetooth them to my laptop!' Jane perked up instantly. 'Thank you so much. That's very kind of you!'

'Oh, not at all. My pleasure,' Lucinda said, pulling her phone from her jacket pocket.

'Oh dear!' Jane's face fell. 'That's an iPhone – I'd need a cable to transfer the photos over, and I don't have one . . . oh *no*, it isn't going to work after all, and it's my own stupid fault for not charging it . . . the publicist is going to be so cross with me . .'

She was the picture of distress, her whole body slumping in disappointment. Lucinda thought quickly. They didn't have connecting cables on-board, just chargers. She could try to borrow one from another passenger; but then she realized that she had a simpler solution to hand.

'Great news! I've actually got another phone on me,' she said, producing Karl's. 'It's a Samsung. That should be all right, shouldn't it?'

'Fine! Brilliant!' Jane's face was wreathed in smiles. 'Mine's a Samsung too – it'll definitely have Bluetooth. You're a genius! Right, I'll sit back here with a happy grin and let you snap away! Take lots – I always think that's best.'

Effortlessly, she took up a series of poses, so accustomed to being photographed by now that she moved and smiled as easily as a model, Lucinda clicking away as fast as the phone would let her. After a few minutes, Jane reached out a hand for the phone, saying:

'Thank you so much! I'll just look through them and quickly send the best ones to my laptop.'

She started scrolling through the pictures. A call light went on further down the aisle; Lucinda glanced over to see if anyone was answering it.

'Don't let me keep you,' Jane said with the friendliest of smiles. 'I can just find you and give this back when I'm done – it won't take me long.'

'Oh, I wouldn't dream of making you come and find me!' Lucinda said, horrified by the mere idea. 'I'll come back for it in a little while.'

Lucinda gave Jane her best smile and whisked out of the pod to attend to the needs of the passenger who had pressed their call button. She was surprised to see that the person in question was Danny Zasio, since he was still passed out on his side and snoring away, reeking strongly of tequila. How he could have managed to press his call button was a mystery. Lucinda frowned, hoping that they weren't malfunctioning: that would be a total nightmare for the crew. Still, there was nothing she could do about it then and there.

She did a loop around the bar and far aisle, carrying out one of her routine patrols as she gave Jane time to select the photographs she wanted. Everything, mercifully, seemed quiet and under control. Lord Tony was in his pod, playing happily with the multiple gaming options on the entertainment console like the big child he was, while the hipster in 6B was eating lobster and watching a video of Catalina on his TV screen, its imagery risqué enough to make Lucinda's perfectly pencilled eyebrows raise.

She hadn't seen this one before, and it was very hard to associate the prowling, scantily clad woman onscreen, radiating confidence and sexuality, with the fragile, hysterical creature who had attacked her assistant, and was now collapsed in her pod, hopefully sleeping off whatever combination of pills she had doubtless taken in time for her to pull it together and do the press conference on arrival at LAX. Greg had informed Lucinda, in private, that the person Catalina had seen had been one of the air marshals, who had changed seats with the other, and that the marshal in question was indeed Catalina's ex: he and Lydia had verified that with a swift check on the Internet.

Lucinda could certainly understand Catalina's shock at her ex apparently turning into a completely different person. However, since that incident had been preceded by Catalina's violent shaking of her assistant, and her insistence on the existence of phantom photographs and notes in her pod, Lucinda couldn't put down Catalina's hysteria to the apparent identity switch of her ex-boyfriend. And then Catalina had tried to insist that he must have sneaked into Luxe Class, not once, but twice, which was simply impossible . . .

No, Catalina was crazy, there was no doubt about it. As crazy in real life as she was talented onscreen. Lucinda shrugged. In her job, she had seen that combination more times than she could possibly count.

She smiled at Michael Coggin-Carr as she passed the bar; he was standing there sipping a coffee and chatting quietly with Karl. Another perfectly behaved, self-restrained passenger. If only they could all be like this . . . she exchanged a glance with Karl and could tell he was thinking exactly the same thing. Thank God for Karl. He was always in synch with her, a hundred per cent reliable.

Unlike Brian, said a little voice in her head. *The only thing you can rely on Brian to do is to chat up the new-girl trolley dollies and go back to his wife.*

Lucinda paused in mid-step. *Where did that come from?*

The answer popped right back at her; it had been the sight of Michael Coggin-Carr, who had had to rescue Catalina from being pestered by an overenthusiastic Brian. *Ugh, that was mortifying. Only a few hours after trying to run his hands all over Angela, he was practically dragging our most VIP passenger into the cockpit with him so he could have a surreptitious little flirt and bum-grab with her, right in front of the two other pilots! Honestly, you have to hope he meant to take her to the cockpit – Brian can get so randy he might even have tried to snog her in the shower room . . .*

Brian had been so entirely selfish that he had completely ignored the state that Catalina was in: near-collapse, her eyes dazed with the effects of the pills she had been taking. To anyone but the most self-absorbed of men it should have been completely obvious that all Catalina was fit for was lying down and sleeping it off. She had been in no condition to go anywhere with anyone, let alone to conduct a flirtation.

But Brian's completely selfish, the voice said. *Always has been, always will be. You know that perfectly well, Lucinda. You've always known it.*

The voice was absolutely right. It made so much sense that, in order to absorb its words fully, Lucinda was still frozen in place halfway down the aisle, her body totally still, but her brain racing. Angela, coming towards her, hesitated, seeing the cabin service director blocking her path. She ducked her head submissively, moving sideways to give Lucinda room to pass, showing complete deference; she would clearly have remained there as long as Lucinda needed to remain in the middle of the aisle, lost in thought.

Seeing Angela standing there, shoulders hunched like a whipped dog cowering from an abusive owner, an emotion swept through Lucinda so unfamiliar that it took her a while to recognize it. Finally, after some considerable thought, she succeeded. And it came as a very unpleasant shock to realize that the sight of Angela with her eyes lowered, to avoid looking directly at Lucinda and possibly anger her boss still further – risk calling down yet another punishment on her head – was making Lucinda feel . . . guilty.

'Go ahead,' she said, stepping to one side, gesturing for Angela to pass her.

Angela actually looked frightened, as if she thought Lucinda was setting a trap for her.

'Oh no,' she muttered, head still ducked. 'You . . . *please*.'

'Angela . . .' Lucinda began.

But, having started, Lucinda had no idea how to finish the sentence. She was experiencing not just guilt, but shame. Karl was right; she *had* gone too far. He had been right, too, to point out that it had been Brian flirting with Angela, not the other way around. Flashing back to the incidents that had annoyed her, Lucinda forced herself to remember them as they had really been. Not Angela cooing up at Brian, but Brian leaning towards her, his hand outstretched to push back a lock of her hair as she tried to avoid his touch. Not Angela flirting with Brian, but him winking at her as she moved away from him, making her blush . . .

'Go ahead! Really!' Lucinda said brusquely to Angela, her anger at herself and Brian making it come out like a snapped command. The younger woman positively dashed past, her cheeks flaming in mortification. Lucinda bit her lip; as she walked into Jane's pod to retrieve Karl's phone, she had the sense that her own face was red with self-disgust. As soon as she got the phone back, she was going to wipe those photos from the memory. She had already put Angela through enough hell, and for what? Jealousy about a man who could barely keep it in his trousers for the duration of a long-haul flight? A man who wasn't even hers anyway?

'Here you go. All done,' Jane said, handing the phone back to her. 'Thanks so much.'

'I hope everything came out all right,' Lucinda said a little stiffly.

'Yes, fine.'

Jane hesitated, looking at the cabin service director. She had got to her feet when Lucinda entered the pod, and though they weren't eye-to-eye, Lucinda being considerably taller, it was a more even balance than if Jane had been seated.

'Um – I scrolled a bit too far on that phone, by accident,' she said, 'and I happened to come across some photos of one of the stewardesses with the chef guy on the plane just now. Obviously – ahem – doing things that were meant to be private.'

Jane dragged down the corners of her mouth into a clown smile of embarrassment.

'*Very* private! Of course, I assumed the photos were taken by mistake,' she continued, 'so I deleted them. The phone must have gone off by accident. You know how that can happen – I'm always taking ones of my thumb or the inside of my bag.'

Lucinda's years of keeping a perfectly neutral expression on her face, no matter what outrageous suggestion or request she was hearing from a passenger, had never stood her in better stead as she took in Jane's words. She managed to nod in agreement, signifying that, yes, she did know how that kind of thing could happen.

'That sounds like a very sensible idea,' she said. 'Thank you so much. We certainly don't encourage that sort of thing . . . either the behaviour or taking photographs of it . . . but as you say, I'm sure it was an accident. The photo-taking part. Well, no harm done! I'm glad you got some photos of yourself that you could use.'

'Yes, thanks!' Jane said brightly. She moved to sit down on the bed again. 'I'm just very glad I spotted those photos and deleted them,' she remarked casually. 'I mean, obviously the stewardess was an idiot to behave like that, but it would be so unfair to have one mistake count against her for her whole life! I know I've done stupid things I'd hate to be reminded of forever – I'm sure we all have.'

'Oh, of course,' Lucinda heard herself agree as she turned to leave the pod.

She was supposed never to leave a passenger without asking them if there was anything else they wanted, but she couldn't bring herself to look Jane in the eye. Shame was overwhelming Lucinda. Jane clearly knew what had been going on: she had seen those photographs and put two and two together, had realized that it would have been impossible, from the angle at which Danny and Angela's sexual encounter had been captured, for the pictures to have been taken anything less than deliberately. Jane had just informed Lucinda that she knew what she had done, but so tactfully that she had spared Lucinda complete humiliation, and somehow that felt even worse.

Lucinda took a deep breath, resolving to find Angela and apologize immediately. She would assure Angela that she had deleted those photographs herself, that they would never be circulated, and that she would personally make sure that no one at Pure Air spoke of the incident again. Angela's career at Pure Air was over – Lord Tony had fired her, after all – but Lucinda would also assure Angela that she would pull strings to make sure Angela found another job as a flight attendant. Lucinda was already racking her brains for sympathetic contacts, people in the airline industry who owed her favours, when a realization hit her like a speeding train.

Contrary to what Jane had claimed, she *hadn't* just stumbled across those photographs. She'd known about them already. The ploys to ask Lucinda to take photographs of Jane . . . the actress's convenient discovery that her own phone was out of charge – Lucinda had never seen Jane's phone, come to think of it – and then Jane's quick thinking in turning down the offer of Lucinda's iPhone in order to manoeuvre Lucinda into offering Karl's phone instead . . . the call bell ringing as Lucinda waited to take the phone back, serving as a perfect distraction, summoning her to the pod of a sleeping Danny Zasio, who couldn't possibly have rung it himself . . . Angela, coming back from the direction of Jane's pod as Lucinda returned, clearly having nipped in to see Jane and confirm that their plan had worked, that Jane had secured Karl's phone and deleted all the photographs of Angela and Danny in the shower room . . .

It all fell into place. Lucinda had not only been caught out behaving like a mean girl by an Oscar-nominated actress, she had been outwitted by her own victim. Now, even if she swore up and down to Angela that she would have deleted those photographs because she had come to the realization that it was the right thing to do, Angela would never believe her. And why should she? Lucinda had been a total bitch, and she'd been thoroughly caught out, exposed for the bully she was.

The stakes had been raised even higher. Suddenly it became of the utmost importance for Lucinda to not only do the right thing, but be seen to do it. With the same fervour with which she had set out to ruin Angela's career at Pure Air, she was now determined to save it.

She hurried back to the bar, almost bumping into Michael Coggin-Carr, who was returning to his pod; apologizing swiftly to him, she jerked her head at Karl, indicating that he needed to come out and have a conspiratorial word with her.

'What is it?' he said, looking frankly scared. 'What do I have to do *now*?'

It was the last straw. Lucinda's faithful henchman was so nervous of her evil schemes that he assumed that any private conversation she wanted to have with him would inevitably be a precursor to yet another mission to ruin someone's life. Lucinda was looking in a mirror, and what she saw there were not the elegant features she was used to contemplating with pleasure, but something considerably less attractive.

'Karl,' she said decisively, 'I want you to come with me to talk to Lord Tony. We both have to tell him how amazing Angela's been on this flight and that we both think that she shouldn't get the sack.'

Karl's mouth dropped open.

'You *what*?' he said inelegantly.

'You heard me! Come on.'

Lucinda marched off, knowing Karl would follow in her wake. Her word was law. She was determined that she was going to be less of a bully from now on. She wanted to be able to look in the mirror reflected by her underlings and see respect, appreciation for her skills and talents, not cowering fear.

But there was no way she was going to stop being bossy. That would be going *much* too far . . .

'Thank you so much!' Angela hissed at Jane from over the top of Jane's pod, not daring to go in; this way she could keep an eye out for any other crew members and dart away before she was spotted talking to Jane. Angela was terrified of Lucinda finding out that she had confided in Jane about the photographs. The story they had concocted, of Jane accidentally coming across them while Bluetoothing the ones of herself, had been intended to avoid any suspicion of a conspiracy between the two women.

'No problem!' Jane hissed back. 'I think she went for it. Fingers crossed! Anyway, the pics are gone.'

'I honestly can't thank you enough . . .'

Jane made a pushing-away movement with her hands, indicating that Angela should remove herself from the area before she got caught. Angela slipped away, and Jane settled back against the headboard of her bed, reflecting that there was so much drama on-board this flight that it made Jane's actual job look positively dull by comparison. And there were still several hours to go. God knew what else might happen before they reached LA – on this showing, half the cabin crew might indulge in an orgy while the other half looked on and held up scoring cards as if they were in a ballroom dance competition.

Well, the crew might be organizing an orgy right now to inaugurate the maiden voyage of Pure Air 111, but Jane had a plan of her own for the flight. Smaller, focused, targeted. And come hell or high water, she was going to carry it out.

She reached for her tablet, which was sitting on the built-in desk beside the inflight magazine, the latter lying face up so that the photograph of Catalina, smiling so prettily, was on display. Jane stared for a moment at the magazine, unable to resist the impulse to gaze, as she had been doing regularly during the flight, at Catalina's face.

The pale honey skin, the petite, lean build. The big dark eyes, the lovely smile brimming with humour and charm.

She was so very like Simone.

Chapter Twenty-Six

Los Angeles International Airport

With only a couple of hours to go before Pure Air 111 was due to land in Los Angeles, preparations were well underway for the various reception committees that were forming to greet the passengers on-board. Lord Tony, of course, had wanted a huge event in the arrivals hall, with a famous pop band, cheerleaders doing backflips while waving cobalt Pure Air pompoms, and cocktails made with blue curaçao; but space was limited at the terminal, security alerts were high, and airport security had refused to give authorization for anything more than a small stage that would be occupied as briefly as possible.

The main press conference would therefore be held in a VIP lounge down the hallway to which the final decorative touches were being put. A big Pure Air banner, identical to the one in London, had been set up to wrap around the interview area, which was festooned with blue and white balloons in the shape of the LuxeLiner. TV crews from various entertainment networks were setting up there, but many paparazzi were already stationed in front of the sliding doors that separated airside from landside, ready to capture the moment of arrival.

That was standard procedure, especially around the time of the Academy Awards, when film stars flooded into Los Angeles for the ceremony. Gossip magazines regularly ran pictures of celebrities in airports for their 'Stars! They're Just Like Us!' pages, knowing that their readers not only relished seeing what film stars wore to travel, but also hoped to catch their idols off guard, sneak a glimpse of what they looked like when they weren't dolled up for the red carpet.

Of course, what the public didn't realize was that the stylists to the stars worked just as hard on their off-duty looks as they did on the red-carpet dresses. Building an image for a film star was all-encompassing. It was no longer just about the parts that they could snag by getting great publicity; it was the endorsements, the perfume ads, the spokesmodel status, the businesses that they could launch on the basis of the image they had established. Gwyneth Paltrow and Blake Lively were both the faces of fragrances and ran websites selling lifestyle products; Jessica Alba hawked baby food and eco household cleaners. How these women looked every moment they were out in public was, as their websites would put it, extremely carefully curated.

And equally carefully curated was the very photogenic little family group that was assembling at their rented Hollywood Hills home in anticipation of greeting Danny Zasio. Mrs Danny Zasio had grand ambitions to build her own lifestyle brand. She had already set up a thriving children's clothes company and was very aware that her image depended on being perceived as a sweet and loving wife and mother, glamorous but wholesome. Unfortunately, Danny persisted in undercutting the happy family image with his antics, and Melanie, his wife, was all too well aware of the need for her and their four adorable blond children to be papped for the benefit of the world's media to counteract the latest batch of negative press.

Danny had been roistering all over London during his visit there, which should have been entirely devoted to shoring up his crumbling restaurant empire. A long-term mistress had sold a story to the tabloids, a tell-all that went into considerable detail about Danny's sexual tastes, and, judging by what he'd asked Angela to do to him in his LA bachelor pad, the mistress had been telling nothing but the truth.

So it was time to roll out the full counter-attack, the beautiful wife and the charming children kept up way past their bedtime so they could be dressed up and paraded out for a photo opportunity. Melanie Zasio had spent hours deciding on the children's co-ordinated outfits, laying them out in their rooms so that their nannies could dress them up and do their hair before the drive to the airport. She was very accustomed to this kind of damage control; it wasn't the first time she had had to stage this kind of scene in a crisis, and it wouldn't be the last.

Melanie had always known the nature of the man she was marrying. Danny couldn't keep it in his trousers, and he couldn't be discreet about it either. He had alienated her from her entire family, who couldn't understand why Melanie had made this kind of bargain with him; or rather, they *did* understand, and thoroughly disapproved of the fact that money and status were so important to her that she would not only put up with him humiliating her repeatedly, but use her own image to shore him up.

For Melanie, however, it was a deal that she had been more than willing to strike. Danny had already been successful when she met him, working as a hostess at one of his restaurants, but he had instantly seen that she would give him the class his image badly needed. With her dignified carriage, her long dark hair, her aristocratic bone structure and enviably slim figure, Melanie was the embodiment of sophistication and elegance. He fancied her, of course, but then Danny fancied pretty much anything. He had been aware that his reputation was becoming tarnished, that the press was talking more about his hell-raising than his cooking, and Melanie was the perfect solution. Marriage to her had transformed Danny's image from the wild man-about-town to a doting husband and father: much more relatable. The publicists for the Zasio brand were ecstatic.

You didn't want to buy food from a man who looked like he rarely ate because he was too busy partying and drinking, hanging out with glamour models and soap stars, his hair tousled and sweaty, his eyes too bright. You did, however, want to buy it from a family man and devoted husband who talked earnestly in interviews about how marriage to Melanie had changed his life, how he had taken one look at her and known that she was the girl for him, the one to tame the playboy and make him instantly ready for fatherhood. It was the classic narrative of romance novels, the hellraiser transformed through the love of a good woman, and it had brought him an avalanche of female fans ready to buy his pasta sauces and branded cookware.

And for good measure, the clever publicists had also given their pairing a fairy-tale twist. It was Cinderella and Prince

Charming, Melanie the penniless restaurant hostess raised to dizzying heights of fame and fortune by sheer good luck and a beautiful face. The women's magazines adored her at once for the narrative she provided and her willingness to pose for engagement and wedding photo spreads. The demand for interviews with her rose incrementally every time she popped out one miniature version of Danny after another in quick succession and got her figure back miraculously each time after just a couple of months.

It was then, realizing how much women with children seemed to love celebrity role models, that Melanie had decided to start a children's clothes company. Every time she was photographed out with the kids they were walking, talking advertisements, four at one go, like a living catalogue; it was genius. This evening, Ottoline, Cinnamon, Herbert and Eamonn were modelling clothes from the spring Zassy Kids collection, the girls in bright polka-dot dresses with contrasting Peter Pan collars and colour co-ordinated tights, the boys in knitted sweaters with quirky animal motifs and chinos. It was Boden Kids crossed with the White Company, packaged for America, where they had been based ever since Danny's series *Eat Me!* had launched on the Food Network.

Melanie herself was exquisitely maintained, her figure streamlined through Pilates, her face serene from her daily dose of Lexapro, her long hair straight, shiny and hand-painted with a wonderfully rich mix of chestnut and caramel highlights, expertly done by her colourist using a technique known as balayage. She wore Balmain slim jeans tucked into Tremp ankle boots and a Lucien Pellat-Finet cashmere sweater with the face of a monkey knitted in orange on the front that had cost three thousand dollars from Barneys LA.

As the nannies got her children ready for their photo call, braiding Ottoline and Cinnamon's hair into matching plaits, Melanie was fully occupied doing her own hair and make-up. The latter took a good forty minutes alone. There were no flaws to cover, but experience had taught Melanie that airport lighting could be extremely harsh, and her image required her to look as natural as possible. And as any make-up artist would tell you, faking natural in harsh lighting requires much more careful work than simply looking glamorous.

The photographers, who would snap away in the arrivals hall as she stroked her children's hair lovingly, her skin glowing, her eyes bright as she talked to the assembled journalists about how excited they were to see Daddy again, would capture the image of a woman who truly seemed like the perfect mother. Meanwhile, however, Mariangela and Guadelupe, the Columbian nannies who were actually raising the Zasio kids – Melanie barely spent any time with them when it wasn't a photo opportunity – would be hovering in the wings, poised and ready to dart out and grab any child if they misbehaved. Nannies to celebrity children were very aware of their duties, which were to be invisible in public, never photographed, but constantly on full alert. Like the SAS, they might have to parachute into any situation to perform an emergency rescue.

It was standard Hollywood procedure. The most calculating celebrities had children almost entirely to get extra publicity, snag the cover of *People* or *Us Magazine*, sell the baby photographs, talk about the children in interviews and bolster their images for Oscar campaigns by taking the kids to pick out a pumpkin from the Mr Bones Halloween Pumpkin Patch in Los Angeles. The entire set-up depended, however, on the public's belief that the famous people in question were bringing up the children themselves, rather than simply writing out the kids' schedules and handing them to the nannies every morning.

So it was crucial that the nannies were rarely, if ever, visible in the paparazzi shots. Parents would strike deals with the paps, calling them to inform them that they would be taking their children to the playground, or the Pumpkin Patch, and in return for the photo opportunity the paparazzi would agree to keep the help well out of shot, giving the impression that the parents had the entire responsibility for their own kids.

Mariangela and Guadelupe had done the Danny-greeting routine at LAX many times before: they knew the drill. Melanie would take up a prime position, surrounded by her children, in the best lighting possible and in prime view of the paparazzi, while the nannies would discreetly move aside, half-concealing themselves behind the curve of the Starbucks counter. It was close enough for them to keep an eye on proceedings, but far enough away for them not to be identified as part of the Zasio entourage. And they rarely needed, in this kind of situation, to parachute in and whisk a wailing child away for time out. Ottoline, Cinnamon, Herbert and Eamonn saw their father so rarely that they were always genuinely excited to welcome him home, so they could generally be relied upon to behave well under the threat from Melanie of being taken away by one of their nannies and not allowed to greet Danny as he appeared through the doors of the customs hall.

As Melanie checked that their driver was on his way and that the children were all dressed exactly as she had prescribed, a slim, well-groomed woman was consulting the calorie-count chart of the various drinks available from the very LAX Starbucks counter behind whose curve Mariangela and Guadelupe would soon be tucking themselves away. From a distance the woman looked in her early thirties; closer up it would have been hard to tell, due to the extreme smoothness and plumpness of her complexion. Her cheeks were oddly high and pillowy, pushed up high enough to give her cat's eyes, and below her wrinkle-free forehead her eyebrows were peaked at the centre, giving her a perpetual look of surprise. Blonde hair tumbled below her shoulders: women with faces like hers always favoured long hair, as they felt it made them look more youthful.

She was soft-voiced and polite to the Starbucks assistant, taking the cup and moving away from the counter to position herself close to the sliding glass doors that led to the baggage hall and customs desk, her eyes regularly flickering across to the arrivals board. Special Agent Herrera and Smithee, the FBI agents with a warrant to arrest a suspected killer on the flight, were already in place, posing as a couple, wanting to observe the people who were gathering by the arrival area. Herrera glanced at the woman and said something quietly to Smithee, who nodded in return.

Around the terminal a phalanx of FBI agents was positioned to blend in seamlessly with the rest of the crowd. Even if someone had known about their operation, it would have been impossible to pick them out from the civilians present. Were the two similar-looking males smoking e-cigarettes and checking something on a tablet computer they were passing back and forth brothers, partners, or a pair of special agents? Was the lone man desultorily pushing a mop further up the arrivals hall a sloppy LAX employee or did he have a concealed earpiece under his baseball cap? What about the short woman by the Java Java counter, her eyes also fixed on the arrivals board? Or the two women gossiping beside the magazine rack at Hudson News, seeming completely absorbed by the cover of the latest *InStyle*?

Herrera pulled out her phone and pretended to make a call. Just another person waiting to pick up a friend or relative; checking, maybe, on the kids back home, wanting to hear if they'd gone to sleep okay. As she did so she turned away, looking as if she was trying to find some privacy for the call. But her gaze was moving around the arrivals hall, making sure that her team was following instructions, had spread out far enough down so that they could observe their target fully before moving in to make the arrest. She nodded, and it looked as if she were agreeing with the person she was talking to. In fact, she was approving her own precautions. Everyone was where they ought to be. This should go as smooth as silk.

Herrera would have had significant cause to amend that opinion, however, if she had known that not one, but two passengers currently aboard Pure Air 111 would be arrested once the plane landed in Los Angeles in just a couple of hours' time.

Chapter Twenty-Seven

On-board

Catalina woke up slowly and groggily. The plane had been swaying gently in the Atlantic jet stream for the last hour or so, and sleep had been positively pleasant, like being in a cradle with a steady hand rocking it to an even rhythm. She had not dreamed at all, which for her was unprecedented, because she always dreamed: short stories, vivid images, snippets and ideas, sometimes entire songs. She jotted down what she could of those on waking, although so far she had never managed to transcribe an entire song, just snippets. Still, she had been composing and writing lyrics for so long that she had learnt that the rest would work its way to her conscious mind when it was ready to emerge.

Catalina was becoming more prolific as the years passed, writing songs for other artists as well as herself. Some critics had been surprised by the strength of her career, but that was because they had been judging her as a pretty little thing who was just a money-making puppet for her manager and record company, to be discarded after a few years as the latter picked up another fresh young girl who'd sign anything they put in front of her in the hope of becoming a star. Those observers had been too busy leering at her dancing in skimpy outfits to absorb the extent to which Catalina was in control of her own career.

Catalina didn't even think she was at the height of her writing powers yet. But that made sense: you pretty much always got better at your job the longer you did it. That was standard for professionals, and if surgeons and lawyers and politicians peaked in their forties and fifties, why shouldn't she? Yes, her voice might not be so strong by that time, and she wouldn't be able to throw herself around a stadium stage as athletically as she did now, but she could still perform – Kylie Minogue was going strong, wasn't she? And, more importantly, she could still write songs, which was where the real money was.

I'll be a mother by then, she thought. *Maybe even a grandmother. Living mostly in Argentina, lots of kids running around, all brown and happy in the sunshine. I won't be dieting all the time, I'll be able to eat pasta every now and then – mmm, spaghetti vongole! – and I'll have the love of my life by my side.*

Ugh, it always came back to that. The love of her life, with whom she was so obsessed that she had begun to have hallucinations of him. The memory of having seen Gerhardt on the plane – the *false* memory, clearly – was enough to make her kick back the sheet and coverlet, knuckle the sleep out of her eyes, sit up and draw a long deep breath.

It didn't help to get the image of Gerhardt out of her mind, however. All her songs since the break-up had been about him, and there had been a *lot* of songs. Her management team was beginning to become concerned about the prospect of a new Catalina album that consisted entirely of melancholy ballads; they had pointed out that Pink's break-up album, *Funhouse,* had featured not only an image of Pink laughing on the cover, riding a rocking horse, but plenty of fast-paced, half-angry, self-mocking songs, which prevented the album from being, as they put it brutally, a total dirge-fest downer.

Their suggestion had been that Catalina license to other recording artists some of the heartbreaking songs that had been pouring out of her ever since she finished the world tour. But Catalina couldn't bear the idea of someone else's voice singing her words, someone else's personality interpreting her most intimate descriptions of love and loss.

And they were very intimate, as poor Latisha could attest. She had had to listen to so many of them, multiple iterations of Catalina's misery, each one a miniature story of heartbreak set to exquisite, soaring tunes. Latisha usually considered that being the first person to listen to Catalina's new compositions was one of the huge perks of her job: she had been a hardcore fan of Catalina's years before she became her assistant. But recently, when Catalina had announced that she had a new song for Latisha to hear, her assistant was tending to find urgent paperwork she needed to complete, or reveal that she had a headache coming on . . .

Yet another song about Gerhardt was hovering on the edges of Catalina's subconscious, triggered by the recent experience of having been sure that she had seen him on the plane when, clearly, he had never been there at all. Latisha had bought her boss a novel a month ago called *Exes Anonymous*, thinking it might help her with her recovery: the story was about a heroine struggling with a break-up so painful that she had to form a support group, like

Alcoholics Anonymous, to help her to get over it. The heroine had repeatedly spotted her ex-boyfriend around town, even though she knew it couldn't be him, because she lived in London and he had moved to New York. Even the slightest resemblance would set her off, convincing her that he was sitting at the next table to her at a restaurant or passing her in a supermarket aisle.

Great, Catalina thought as she swung her legs over the edge of the bed and onto the floor, her feet fishing for the sheepskin-lined slippers. *I'm turning into that girl, seeing Gerhardt everywhere. Going batshit crazy.* She realized that her stomach felt weird. She hadn't had anything to eat for a while, but it didn't feel like hunger; she wasn't sure what it was, but she had the feeling that a visit to the toilet would not be the worst idea.

I just hope I don't bump into Gerhardt on the way to the toilet! she thought, trying to cheer herself up with some black humour. *I honestly don't think I could cope with anything more happening on this plane . . .*

The LuxeLiner was rocking more, back and forth, still like a cradle, but now one being pushed by an over-vigorous child with their doll inside rather than an adult soothing a baby to sleep. It didn't bother Catalina, who was very used not only to flying but to performing on wobbly high catwalks thrusting dizzyingly out over packed stadia or rigged over swimming pools. She had shot a whole video on a yacht, climbing agilely up into the rigging, miming her lyrics the whole time. A little mild turbulence, so low-grade that the captain hadn't even bothered to put on the 'Fasten Seat Belt' sign, didn't even register on her radar.

412

She did, however, pause as she emerged from her pod. She was moving much slower than usual; her stomach was feeling strange and her brain was woozy.

'Hey! Are you feeling better? Have a good rest?'

It was Michael Coggin-Carr, coming back down the aisle, a glass of water in his hand. She found herself looking at it longingly, and he instantly saw the direction of her glance and offered her the glass.

'Thank you,' she said gratefully as she took it, so used now to the luxury of having actual glassware on an airplane that she took for granted the pleasure of not having to drink out of a plastic cup. 'I always seem to be thanking you, don't I?'

'Oh, I really haven't done anything,' he demurred. 'All I've managed is to fend off an overeager suitor and give you a little water. It's not quite knight-in-shining-armour status yet. But feel free to give me a ring if you find yourself trapped in a tower fending off a dragon!'

Catalina couldn't help smiling. His self-deprecation combined with his very British sense of humour, and that clipped accent, were all extremely charming. He might not be stereotypically handsome, but he had a very pleasant, friendly face – *and God knows*, Catalina thought wistfully, *I haven't always gone for traditionally good-looking men* . . .

There she was, back to Gerhardt once again. But for a minute or so, she had almost flirted with another man without Gerhardt popping into her mind, and those brief moments had been very enjoyable.

'I won't say thank you again, then,' she said, holding out the glass to him, now half-full. The plane jerked beneath their feet, but he had surprisingly fast reflexes, stepping quickly towards her, taking the glass with one hand and steadying her arm with the other. Catalina realized with surprise that she was more unstable on her feet than she had thought; the effects of sleeping in a heavy, dreamless haze had clearly not yet worn off.

'Were you going somewhere?' he asked. 'Can I help you? You still look a bit zonked, to be honest.'

It was normally annoying when someone told you that you looked tired, but this British guy somehow managed to pull it off. He certainly had a way about him.

'Just, uh, to the toilet,' she said, smiling again. 'And it's right there. I'm sure I can manage—'

The plane lurched again, and so did she. He had just taken his hand away from her arm, but he grabbed her again, his forearm bracing hers, stabilizing her.

'I don't know why I'm so wobbly!' she exclaimed, cross with herself. 'Maybe it's the slippers – they're a bit big.'

'Let's just get you to the loo, shall we?' he said sensibly. 'By the feel of things, the captain might be putting the Fasten Seat Belt light on soon, so you'll want to get in there while you can.'

They turned towards the toilet, their arms linked.

'Catalina?'

Jane, behind them, was calling Catalina's name. She came quickly up the aisle towards them.

'Everything okay?' she asked in concern.

'Yes, fine.'

But as Catalina turned to look at Jane, she tripped in her slippers and would have fallen if Michael Coggin-Carr hadn't been holding her arm.

'I do feel a bit funny,' she admitted, as Jane took her other arm. 'I'm not sure why. I thought it was the slippers . . .'

'It's a bit bumpy, but . . .' Jane's voice trailed off as she took in Catalina's appearance. 'Look, are you off to the loo? Shall I give you a hand?' she continued.

'I was helping her—' Michael Coggin-Carr started, but Jane broke in.

'That's so nice of you,' she said with great warmth, turning on a professional charm offensive that was impossible to resist. 'Very kind. But you know, maybe a woman should do it? She looks awfully green – she might need a bit of a hand inside as well . . .'

It sounded like a suggestion, but Jane's words were such a clear instruction to Michael Coggin-Carr to back off that it would have been impossible for any man not closely related to the singer to have insisted on continuing to take responsibility for her. Jane was intimating that Catalina might need to throw up, require someone to hold back her hair and clean up after her, and to insist that he perform this office for a woman he didn't know would look entirely perverse. He had no choice, therefore, but to back away, smiling politely, as Jane replaced him by Catalina's side.

'I do like the way you guys say "loo",' Catalina said hazily. 'I wonder if I could put that in a song? What would it rhyme with?'

Michael Coggin-Carr's eyebrows shot up. 'Has she taken anything?' he asked Jane *sotto voce*.

'Buggered if I know,' Jane said. 'But yes, I wouldn't be surprised . . .'

The plane lurched again, the worst bump so far, listing

sideways and staying there for a good few seconds before it righted itself. All three of them leaned right into the wall of the pod to brace themselves. A loud ping was audible and, over every seat in a bright line reaching down the cabin, the Fasten Seat Belt sign finally came on.

'Come on,' Jane said urgently to Catalina. 'Let's get you into the loo before they make everyone go back to their seats. It really does look like you need to pop in there for a little bit.'

'Ladies and gentlemen,' Lucinda said over the intercom in the smoothest of professional tones, 'the captain has switched on the Fasten Seat Belt sign. Can you all please return to your seats . . .'

'What's going on?' came a crisp voice behind the little group in the aisle. Vanessa had emerged from her pod behind Michael Coggin-Carr's. 'Everyone should be back in their seats!'

'Catalina needs to use the loo . . .' Jane began.

'She's looking pretty delicate . . .' Michael Coggin-Carr started at the same time.

'Oh, for goodness' sake! Look at the two of you flapping around there instead of just getting the poor girl into the toilet when she needs it!'

Vanessa bustled towards them, her tone so perfectly that of a reproving teacher that both Jane and Michael hung their heads like naughty schoolchildren caught out smoking cigarettes behind the bike sheds.

'Back to your seats, both of you!' Vanessa instructed sharply. 'And seat belts on! I'll have her in and out and back to her pod in no time at all.'

Karl and Angela, coming to check that everyone was buckled in, entered the aisle just as Vanessa opened the door of the toilet and practically picked Catalina up off her feet, heaving her inside.

'Right, let's get this done, shall we?' she said cosily. 'Need a wee, dear?' She clicked her tongue. 'That Jane Browne,' she said disapprovingly. 'So pushy, acting as if she knows everything about everyone! Between you and me, I can't say I warm to her. The quiet ones are always the worst, aren't they?'

Catalina didn't know how to answer this, but it didn't seem as if Vanessa required a response. She was locking the door, turning to look at Catalina's reflection in the large mirror over the sink.

'Do you need to be sick?' she asked frankly. 'Tummy a bit funny?'

Catalina wasn't sure. But Jane had been right about the greenish tinge to her skin; even in the flattering, golden light of the toilet, Catalina could see that her face looked pale and drawn, her eyes puffy.

'I don't know,' she admitted. 'I slept really heavily and it knocked me out. I still feel . . . weird.'

'Never mind. If you need to be sick, go right ahead. Take your time,' Vanessa said comfortingly.

Catalina would have much preferred to be by herself if she were going to throw up, but she didn't know how to say so. Vanessa had been so kind already, sitting with her as she fell asleep so she didn't feel alone, making sure she had a calming tea . . .

'I don't know *how* I feel,' she repeated, hearing her words come out a little bit slurred.

'Probably because of that Jane trying to boss you around,' Vanessa said, adjusting the neckline of her blouse. 'She's gay, you know. She doesn't admit it, but it's common knowledge. No wonder she glommed onto you like that. She'll be wanting to get into your knickers.'

Catalina stared in surprise at Vanessa, these words taking her aback. But Vanessa looked as stolid and dependable as ever. She was leaning against the bathroom wall, her legs wide to steady herself against the now constant rocking of the plane. Catalina grasped the edge of the sink for balance.

'Maybe I should go back to my seat,' she said. 'It's getting really bumpy, and the Fasten Seat Belt sign's still on . . .'

'But if you feel sick, this is the best place for you, isn't it?' Vanessa pointed out. She pushed herself off the wall and crossed the toilet to stand behind Catalina.

'I'm right here,' she said cosily. 'I'll make sure you don't hurt yourself. Oh look, your hair's all messy! We don't want that, do we?'

Before Catalina could say anything, Vanessa had reached down – she loomed above the smaller woman – and started to pull the elastic off Catalina's bun, very carefully, not catching a single strand.

'I'll just tidy that up,' she said. 'You do need someone to look after you, don't you? All that talent and money and success, but you're really just a little girl who needs a big sister to look after her, aren't you? Make sure you're all taken care of, get enough rest, tie your hair back for you, brush it every night . . . a hundred strokes with a proper Denham brush, a nice boar's bristle one . . . oh, I know your hair looks nice enough now, but wait till you see the sheen you'll get on it with a regular brushing! And don't worry about it being extra trouble for me, not at all. I'll be happy to do it for you while you read a magazine or whatever you fancy . . .'

Catalina's body was stiff with tension as she absorbed the meaning of the words that Vanessa was speaking so easily, so reassuringly. Her tone was so soothing that it was only gradually that Catalina was able to take in what she was actually saying. She couldn't move her head, because Vanessa was holding her hair in a vice-like grip now, one hand firmly wound around it, the other stroking Catalina's scalp in a way that would have been very relaxing under entirely different circumstances.

'I need to go back to my seat now,' Catalina said, trying to sound as calm as she could. 'Thanks for helping with my hair, but I really think I should sit down and put my seat belt on—'

'Oh no, it's not that bad!' Vanessa said as the plane bounced in the air. 'I've known much worse than this, haven't you? Goodness, the flights we must have both been on, travelling so much for work! I wish I could spare you that, I really do. It must be so exhausting. And then having to perform afterwards, the way you tear around the stage non-stop! Dancing, singing, changing costumes so fast . . . the times I've watched you from backstage, just amazed at all your energy. Like a whirling dervish! That's why you need me, you see. I'm the only one who can really take care of you.'

It was a weirdly slow process for Catalina to come to the realization that the woman standing behind her, the large, buxom woman dressed in a dowdy suit, unflattering cardigan and floral top, the woman who was stroking her hair in such a motherly way, saying things that were pleasant and flattering and sympathetic, was also quite insane.

Catalina tilted her eyes up as far as she could to see Vanessa's face. Very surreally, Vanessa's expression had not changed at all. You would think that there would be some sign, some craziness in the eyes, some distortion of her features, but no: it was the same woman whom Catalina had met in the Marlborough Suite, the one with whom Latisha had organized this flight and reported as being very easy and straightforward to work with, the one who had presented herself as a sensible businesswoman at the height of her profession.

Catalina braced her hands against the sink surround and pushed back as hard as she could, trying to get some space between them. Vanessa was standing so close to Catalina's back that Catalina could feel the heat coming off her large body. If Catalina could manage to reach for the door, unlatch it, she might not make it outside – Vanessa could drag her back by her hair – but the banging of the open door would surely alert people that something was wrong, cause one of the flight attendants to come over to check—

'*Oh no you don't,*' Vanessa said sharply, barging Catalina back into the sink with such force that her hipbones banged into the surround and twin bruises started to form on the front of her narrow body. 'You're not going anywhere yet.'

Catalina opened her mouth to scream. One of Vanessa's hands shot round and clamped over the lower part of her face before she could get any sound out.

'Naughty!' Vanessa said reprovingly.

Still holding Catalina in place by the weight of her body, she reached inside her jacket and pulled out a piece of pre-cut duct tape that had been stuck there. Catalina's eyes widened in panic as Vanessa slammed her palm under Catalina's chin, forcing her lips together again, the other hand slapping the duct tape over her mouth. Catalina tried to push herself back again, using her legs, bracing them against the sink: her dancing meant that she was very strong for her size.

But tough as a flyweight in boxing may be, they are no match for a heavyweight, and Vanessa's big, solid frame, combined with the strategic advantage of having wedged her victim into a position where she could not easily strike out against her opponent, meant that Vanessa easily managed to block Catalina's attempt. Grabbing first one of her hands and then the other, she wrenched them free from their grip on the sink, dragging them behind Catalina's back and fastening them together with another piece of pre-cut duct tape.

Vanessa let out a long sigh of sheer happiness.

'It'll sound funny, but this is *just* how I imagined it!' she said, staring at Catalina in the mirror. 'I knew you'd make a fuss in the beginning, which is why I came prepared. Clever me! But once you get to know me – once you understand how good we'll be together – everything will be different. You wait! You'll see how happy I can make you, how well I'll look after you.'

Catalina's eyes, huge and dark with fear, slid up to the still-illuminated Fasten Seat Belt sign. The air stewards, checking on the unoccupied pods, would have been told by Michael and Jane that Catalina had been helped to the toilet by Vanessa. And they would much prefer that, if Catalina were throwing up, she do it in the toilet rather than all over the cabin. But surely after a while they would come to make sure she was okay. How long would that take? They wouldn't want to disturb the head of publicity for the airline, who was taking care of the highest-rated VIP on the flight, but eventually, surely, they would *have* to summon Vanessa and Catalina back to their seats . . .

Catalina suddenly realized that the plane hadn't bounced around for quite a few minutes. Vanessa had been able to restrain her, cover her mouth, tape her up, without any turbulence interfering with her actions. And in horror, even as she stared at the sign, she heard another loud ping and watched the light turn off, the message disappear.

'Perfect! No one will bother us now,' Vanessa said with great satisfaction. 'Oh, how cosy this is! Finally, you and me together! I had a dream of us on a plane, you see,' she added, settling her hips to wedge right against Catalina's bottom, her hands free now to bury themselves in Catalina's hair, pulling it out to spread over her shoulders like a cape.

'Oh, it's even softer than I thought it would be,' she said, closing her eyes for a moment in sheer bliss. 'So lovely! But it'll be shinier when I brush it every night . . . mmm, and it smells so good!'

To her horror, Catalina watched Vanessa lower her head, bury her face in her victim's hair, and take a long inhale of its scent.

'So fresh . . .' she sighed. 'So delicious! Just as I dreamed it would be! That's why it had to be like this, you see. Because of the dream. It had to be *exactly* like it – you standing in front of me, both of us looking in the mirror . . .'

Catalina ducked her head down to the sink, unable to watch this any more. Vanessa promptly yanked on her hair, pulling her back up again.

'Both of us *looking in the mirror*!' she repeated sharply. 'Me running my hands through your hair, smelling it, stroking it . . . Oh, I can't believe it's finally happening! All this planning! I had to get myself onto a plane with you, and how was I going to manage that? How would I know what flight you'd be on, and how would I make sure you didn't have that assistant with you to get in my way? I worked out that I was going to need complete control over the seating, the cabin, everything.'

The crocodile smile flashed widely.

'So I had to get myself a job at an airline, obviously. In publicity, of course – that's my job. Which is how I first saw you,' she explained to her silenced victim. 'Backstage, like I said, when I was doing PR for the Mobile Power stadiums. Oh, it was a revelation! I couldn't take my eyes off you! I hate to confess this, but I'd never heard your music before – not to recognize, anyway. But when I saw you onstage, dancing and singing so magically, like a tiny fairy come to life in your glittering little outfits . . . I couldn't take my eyes off you. And that night I dreamt about you – you and me together on a plane – and I knew that it was meant to be. If I could get you alone like this, I could show you how much I care, convince you that we're supposed to be together, me looking after you, caring for you, cuddling you, making you feel the best you've ever felt . . .'

She drew in a long, ecstatic breath.

'I knew I had to be patient until I could get this set-up

all sorted out,' she continued, her eyes bright with excitement. 'But I couldn't bear the idea of not saying a word about it. I had to let you know that there was someone out there who loved you more than anyone else could, to tell you to wait for me just like I was waiting for you. That's why I sent you the messages, the photographs – ooh, they were so much fun to make! – to show you how much I loved you.'

Vanessa licked her lips.

'And you realized, didn't you? You realized how much I must care about you, to be going to all that trouble! To have taken the time to make those saucy photos and risk getting caught when I sneaked into your dressing room – what a proof of love! And you were scared, I understand that, because you didn't know who I was – but now you do! And now you know that I tried to tell you the best way I could, to let you know that I'd be coming for you when the time was right, and everything would be perfect from this moment on, when you were mine . . .'

Vanessa twisted Catalina's hair more, winding it into a long rope, pushing it to one side so that her hands had full access to Catalina's neck.

'Such lovely skin,' she cooed. 'So soft. And it smells so good too, just as nice as your hair . . .'

Catalina closed her eyes as tight as she could to avoid seeing Vanessa lower her head to sniff her skin. Vanessa's hands were wrapped around Catalina's neck by now, her fingers extended, the tips almost meeting on Catalina's windpipe. It was a possessive, rather than threatening, gesture, but Catalina still cringed in terror as if she were trying to shrink herself down until she was tiny enough to slip out of Vanessa's grip and escape.

'Of course, I shouldn't tell you how easy it was to sneak into your dressing room!' Vanessa said on a laugh. 'Or you won't appreciate me properly! But it wasn't hard at all to make sure there weren't cameras focused on the area or people hovering around. I could walk around backstage wherever I wanted, send a security guy off on some made-up task, pick my time for popping in and leaving you my special message. It never took that long. There was a guard outside for a while at some of our stadiums, but I heard he was pulled off by the time you got to Tokyo so I flew over there specially.'

She preened.

'I was very high up at Mobile Power, you know. I'm fantastically good at my job. And all the while I was busy talking to headhunters, negotiating away, saying I fancied a change to airline PR. The perks are excellent in this job – it was a very believable request. And I had lots of offers! But as soon as I met Lord Tony, I knew Pure Air was exactly what I needed. God, how that man loves publicity! He'd go along with any stunt I suggested, the crazier the better! Timing this flight for the Oscars was perfect. He was agreeing before I even finished the pitch.'

She looked down fondly at Catalina.

'Such a bright little thing, to be singing at the Oscars! And with a song you've written, too! I couldn't be prouder of you! So creative! Who would have thought there was such a clever brain behind such a pretty face?'

All this time, Catalina had been trying to use her tongue

to pry free the tape over her mouth. Her hands were much too tightly bound behind her to be good for anything, and Vanessa's heavy body was crushing them so hard into her groin – Catalina was doing her best not to think about that proximity – that she couldn't even wiggle the fingers. She was sure her circulation was being cut off.

So she had concentrated on her lips, wriggling them, making her tongue into as pointed and as rigid a tool as she could manage, like a dagger that would force the sticky tape away from her skin. However, she was realizing why victims of kidnappings in films never managed to get the tape off their mouths. The adhesive was more than a match for Catalina's attempts. Duct tape was a terrifying thing, worse than a gag, worse than handcuffs.

'You're not feeling as energetic as usual, are you?' Vanessa asked almost sympathetically. 'That'll be the sleeping pill I mashed into your tea. Not all of it – I didn't want it to taste too bitter, and you're just a little slip of a thing! But it certainly knocked you out for a while, didn't it? And you still look groggy. Never mind, the clouds'll clear soon.'

She smiled.

'Like everything else! Like all the obstacles! One by one, I cleared them away! That bodyguard you started seeing – silly girl, as if he could ever have been worthy of you! But *he* couldn't possibly have been on this flight, could he now? We wouldn't want some big nasty man barging in and ruining everything! So I had to get rid of him. I had quite the time thinking about how to manage it, and I do pride myself on what I came up with.'

She winked.

'I knew Latisha, of course, from arranging so much with her about the LuxeLiner launch. So I arranged a meeting with her in LA when I was over for work, and we had a nice chat about all sorts of things . . . and I mentioned I'd been working for Mobile Power till recently – we met a few times backstage, and she remembered it, which wasn't ideal, but didn't seem to ring any warning bells . . . *Anyway*, I brought up all the fuss about the photographs and so on, and we agreed how awful it was that the person who did it never got caught, and I went all thoughtful and suggested that there might be a really simple reason for that.'

Tears started to form in Catalina's eyes.

'She wouldn't believe me at first,' Vanessa went on, 'but I'd thought about it very carefully and I made a very good case for it being that hulking German. Pretending, of course, that it was just occurring to me at that very moment. The timings worked out very nicely –_and I *may* have twisted the truth a little along the way, rearranged the order in which things happened, to make it seem even more likely that it was him. Of course Latisha believed my version of events if they contradicted hers – I was an executive for the stadia, I was bound to be right, wasn't I? And when she was beginning to think that my theory might, very sadly, be plausible, I suggested a way for her to verify it. Having, of course, paid a *lot* of money to that computer chap in advance to make sure that when the laptop came back, it was positively full of all those photographs.'

She sighed.

'I *did* resent giving that German credit for all my hard work!' she said rather crossly. 'I did such a fantastic job with those pictures! But still, it worked. The German was toast. And then all I had to do was make sure that Latisha was seated in business class so she couldn't get in the way. Easy enough, with the excuse that the demand for Luxe Class seats was so high on the maiden flight. But I put a sleeping pill in her champagne as well, just to be sure that she wouldn't interfere. Still, she's a nice girl. We should keep her around, shouldn't we? You're fond of her, and she's very good at her job. Of course, she'll have to understand that I'm the most important person in your life now.'

Vanessa grimaced, disgusted.

'Not like the nasty German, of course! Nothing like that! We're not *lesbians*! No one's going to be able to use that horrid word about us! We'll be best friends, travelling together, living together, sharing a room because we never want to be apart . . .'

Catalina was crying now, consumed by the realization that Gerhardt had been innocent. Her emotions were all over the place: fear of what Vanessa was planning to do to her was competing with the adrenalin rush of sheer happiness. She couldn't believe that for months she had been living without Gerhardt, had driven him away for nothing. Why hadn't she trusted him? Why hadn't she trusted *herself* not to be so completely wrong about the person she loved so much?

The questions kept coming in an unstoppable flood. Would Gerhardt understand and forgive her? Would he be okay when she tracked him down, found him, begged him to take her back, explained how badly they had both been tricked? Or would he tell her that he could never reconcile with someone who was capable of believing such an awful accusation about him?

Whatever it took, whatever she had to say, she would do it. She would jump through any hoop he held out for her, humble herself in every way possible, prove to him how utterly unhappy she had been without him, apologize profoundly for even listening for a moment to Latisha's suspicions . . .

Tears were pouring down her face, but Vanessa's words indicated that she didn't even notice.

'I know I can make you happy!' Vanessa was saying, with such conviction that her eyes glowed as if she were a devout Catholic seeing a vision of the Madonna. 'And *you* make *me* happy just by being yourself, so you never need to worry about that!'

She smiled happily.

'I knew you'd have to go to the toilet sooner rather than later,' she said. 'But I knew that when you did, you'd be all wobbly, and *then* all I needed to do was keep an eye out and offer to help you – goodness, how keen everyone else was to stick their nose in, weren't they? They all want you!'

Vanessa's mouth tightened.

'But they *can't have you*,' she said. 'You're *mine. Cat is mine.*'

The hands on Catalina's shoulders began to slide down. They reached her elbows, which were pressed tightly against her waist, twisted forward because her hands were taped in the small of her back. Vanessa's hands moved along, across, to the waistband of Catalina's jeans. Her head ducked again. Catalina felt Vanessa's mouth, wet and open, land in the crook of her neck as Vanessa's hands met at Catalina's belly-button, her fingers starting to unfasten Catalina's jeans.

'I'm going to make you so happy right now,' the wet mouth said to Catalina's neck. 'I'm going to make you happier than anyone else has ever done. Make you forget that nasty German, the polo player, everyone you've ever been with before. I'm going to make you feel so good that afterwards you'll realize I'm the only one you'll ever need, you'll turn to me and tell me so . . .'

Bile rose in Catalina's throat, sudden waves of it, surging up, making her panic that she would choke with her mouth taped shut. She drew in a deep breath through her nostrils even as she bucked wildly against Vanessa's invasive hands. Catalina had been fooling herself, lured in by Vanessa's talk about not being a lesbian, about them just being best friends. She had been planning to agree to anything Vanessa wanted just to get out of this bathroom, to be safe again, free from the smell of Vanessa's body and her breath, from hearing the horrible stream of words pouring out of her mouth.

But *this?* This she couldn't go along with, not even to escape afterwards. This was rape. Hands trapped, shoulders and wrists screaming in pain because of the way Vanessa had taped her up, torqueing her joints, Catalina blocked out any thought of using her arms and instead concentrated entirely on her lower body. Her thighs were trapped, too, but she could move her calves a little, and she started kicking against the sink surround in front of her. It was moulded plastic, like almost everything on the plane, and it made some noise when she banged against it, even with her slippered feet. She kicked at it again, gaining momentum, the noise audible enough so that, if she kept it up, people would hear it, would be concerned enough to start knocking on the door and asking if they were okay –

'Stop it!' Vanessa hissed.

Her hands, hot and damp, had been unzipping Catalina's jeans, but she pulled away to deal with this problem. Grabbing Catalina's hair, she bent over, dragging Catalina with her, down to the toilet. Catalina thrashed, thinking that Vanessa was going to push her face into it, but instead Vanessa reached round the bowl, retrieving something that had been cached behind it.

Behind the duct tape, Catalina moaned in terror. Because in Vanessa's hand was a small fire axe, the most frightening weapon imaginable, its blade gleaming in the yellow light. Breath coming heavy with the exertion, Vanessa pulled Catalina to her feet again, sweat now moist on her brow, beads beginning to trickle down her cheeks. Both the women's faces were wet now as they wrestled silently and desperately, Catalina frantically twisting and contorting her body to get as far away from the axe as possible, Vanessa using her weight advantage to shove Catalina slowly and surely back into the position in which she wanted her: against the sink, facing into the mirror, just as she had been standing in Vanessa's dream.

As Catalina's hips once again slammed painfully into the plastic sink surround, Vanessa took another twist around Catalina's heavy rope of hair, pulling it so agonizingly tight that Vanessa's sweaty knuckles were digging into Catalina's scalp. She was gripping the axe equally tightly with the other hand, and now she lifted it, placing it so close to Catalina's face that, behind the duct tape, Catalina let out a high, terrified scream.

Vanessa made a swift slicing gesture with the axe and a lock of hair, severed by the blade, fell into the sink before Catalina's horrified eyes. Her pupils were almost completely dilated with terror, black and huge.

'See how sharp it is?' Vanessa hissed. '*Don't! Be! Naughty!* Stay still like a good girl and I won't have to use it! It's for hacking through these walls if there's a fire – can you *imagine* what it would do to you? You know I don't want to hurt you – you know I wouldn't harm a hair on your head . . .'

The irony of these words, with the dark curly ringlet lying in the sink in front of them, was entirely lost on Vanessa.

'But I need to make you realize how important you are to me,' Vanessa babbled, 'the most important thing in the world, *how important it is to me to make you happy . . .*'

The hand twined in Catalina's hair loosened its grasp, Catalina's scalp sore and red now from the pressure. The relief was only momentary, however, as the hand slid right down, diving straight to Catalina's crotch, finding the edge of Catalina's lacy pants, the sweaty fingers fumbling their way underneath to bare skin.

Catalina screamed as hard as she could, the sound bouncing round inside her skull, unable to find release. Her chest was tight, and she tasted acid at the back of her throat, truly sure that this time she was going to throw up against the duct tape. Vanessa pressed the blade of the axe against Catalina's cheek, icy cold, so cold every molecule in Catalina's body froze to match it. Even the tears in her eyes seemed to freeze, as if nothing dared to move even a fraction for fear of what Vanessa might be about to do with the axe.

'Don't fight me,' Vanessa said, her mouth wet now on

Catalina's ear, like a huge invasive slug, her fingers wet and slug-like too. 'It's going to be so wonderful, you'll see. Soon you won't fight me any more – you'll feel so wonderful, you'll be crying with happiness and you'll turn to me and tell me you want us to be together forever . . .'

Catalina's lips were straining against the duct tape, frantically trying to loosen it, even slightly, make the smallest gap that would allow her scream out into the world, even as Vanessa's fingers slid right down and cupped Catalina's crotch.

And then the world exploded with a deafening bang. The toilet door flew towards them, the door like a missile, a thrown shield, coming right for the sink and the two women pressed against it. Vanessa shrieked, pulling back, trying to drag Catalina with her, the axe swinging away in an upwards arc. As soon as the blade left her face, however, Catalina wrenched herself away from Vanessa's grip, staggering forwards: she would rather get hit by the toilet door than be anywhere near that fire axe.

A split second after he had kicked down the door, Gerhardt's giant body blasted into the toilet cubicle. One hand slammed the flying door against the sink, pushing it away from Vanessa and Catalina, his reflexes lightning-fast. Grabbing Catalina off her feet, he turned, bundling her out of the door and into Latisha's waiting arms. Without pausing for a moment he spun right back on the balls of his feet to confront Vanessa. Her eyes finally reflected her deranged state of mind, blazing with madness as she lunged towards him with the axe.

Gerhardt sidestepped, brought his right arm round and

lifted Vanessa off her feet with a perfectly judged uppercut that sent her teeth slamming together. Her head smashed into the far wall, hard enough to temporarily knock her out, but not to break her neck. The axe fell from her hand; her eyes rolled up in their sockets and snapped shut.

'I got this,' Latisha said from the gaping doorway of the toilet, where she was stripping the duct tape off Catalina's mouth. 'I'll make sure Vanessa's dealt with. You get Cat out of here. You earned it, hero.'

'Oh, oh, oh . . .' Catalina sobbed as Gerhardt swung her round and ripped the duct tape from her hands.

Her mouth and wrists were red and burning, her face wet with tears. The strain on her shoulders from having her wrists twisted and taped up meant that lifting her arms to embrace Gerhardt was agonizing, but she didn't hesitate, fighting right through the pain to hug him, press into his shirt and cry out her terror and relief and love for him all mixed together.

'You're safe now,' he said, enfolding her in his arms. 'You're safe now.'

'I'm so sorry!' she said through her tears. 'I'm so sorry! I should never have believed it, not for a *moment* –'

Once again, Gerhardt picked her up and carried her away, deftly manoeuvring both of them into her pod. He drew the privacy curtain and sat down on the bed just as Lucinda and Karl, having heard the crash of the cubicle door being kicked in, came as swiftly up the aisle as they could without breaking into a run and panicking passengers still further; they were instructing everyone they passed in urgent voices to stay in their seats and let them deal with what was happening.

Meanwhile, cradled in Gerhardt's arms, a stream of apologies poured from Catalina. She was letting out all of her guilt at not having trusted him, her mortification at her own stupidity, her terror during her ordeal with Vanessa and the heart-stopping reaction when he and Latisha had rescued her. She told him everything that Vanessa had said; she needed to spill it all out, as if she'd been poisoned and she needed to purge herself before it infected her.

'Hey, hey,' he said eventually, when she had calmed down a little. 'Take a breath, okay? Take many breaths!'

'But I needed you to know . . . I needed you to understand . . .'

'Shh,' he said. 'It's okay. I understand everything. I promise.'

But Catalina was still vibrating with delayed reaction, so many emotions flooding through her that she would have found it difficult even to name them all; she felt as if she were about to burst, that her body was physically unable to contain everything she was feeling.

'Your mouth is really red and sore,' he said gently, looking down at her. 'Where is your cream?'

Catalina managed a giggle. Gerhardt knew very well that she never had fewer than three tins of Elizabeth Arden Eight Hour Cream lip moisturizer in her handbag or jeans pocket: she swore by it. It had always been a private joke between her and Gerhardt, one of those things that are ridiculous to outsiders but unite a couple in a shared moment that closes out the rest of the world. He called it a cream, because of the packaging, whereas Catalina would point out firmly that actually it was a lip balm.

She twisted to look for the tin on her desk, her spirits

rising. Surely Gerhardt's slipping back into one of their in-jokes could only be positive.

'Here,' he said, taking the tin from her, opening it, and starting to dab the balm around her mouth gently with his huge finger. 'I will talk, you will be quiet and rest your spirits. Okay? I will explain how I am here, how Latisha and I came to realize what was happening. You sit and calm yourself.'

Catalina nodded dutifully, so entranced by the touch of Gerhardt's finger on her upper lip, his arms around her, her bottom snugly cradled by his big thighs. It wasn't a sexual feeling, but one of being comforted: sex was the furthest thing from her mind. As soon as she got home she would be taking the longest shower she had ever had in her life, washing away every trace of Vanessa's sweaty touch from her body. She would have showered on the plane, but she couldn't bear the idea of getting naked in such close physical proximity to Vanessa.

Catalina remembered the slug-like fingers grabbing her crotch and shuddered from head to toe. But she was safe now, safe and secure with the man she loved, and she pushed the memory away, choosing instead to focus on her current state of sheer happiness.

'So, I did not know that you were on this flight until yesterday,' he began. The mere hint of a smile flickered across his straight mouth. 'I am not stalking you.'

Catalina opened her mouth to protest that she knew that, but his smile deepened even as he shh-ed her again.

'It is a shock to me,' he continued. 'I was not happy about it, not at all. Because, of course, I worry that this is what you will think, that I am the stalker. But of course, I know

436

I will be in business class, and you and Latisha are always in the front of the plane, so I know you will not see me and get worried.' He grimaced. 'Then Latisha comes into business class, and *I* get worried. But she looks tired, sleepy. She doesn't look around at all, she just sits down and stays in her seat, and very soon she goes to sleep. I hear her snoring.'

'Vanessa gave her a sleeping pill in a glass of champagne,' Catalina explained. 'That's why she was so out of it. Tish took her usual Zopiclone as well, so the combination must really have zonked her out.'

'Ah, that makes sense. I have never seen Latisha pass out so fast like that on a plane! So I think everything is okay. Unusual, but okay. Of course, you know what happens next. You come in and you are very upset, very agitated. I am worried, for you, but also that you will see me. I know I must move, but I decide I will wait until you are gone and then I will change seats with my colleague.'

'Your . . .?'

Gerhardt nodded.

'I am an air marshal,' he told her. 'That is why . . . my God!'

He moved her off his lap and jumped up.

'I must go to tell David! He should arrest her immediately! My God, Catalina, being with you again makes me crazy! I lose my brain! What was I *thinking*?'

'Don't leave me alone!' she said urgently. 'Please, *please*!'

She jumped up too, grabbing onto his shirtfront.

'I'll come with you. *Please*, I can't be alone. I'll only feel safe with you –'

Just then, all hell broke loose outside the pod. Gerhardt

pulled back the curtain to reveal a positive mass of people in the aisle, the blue uniforms of the flight attendants predominating. Passengers were screaming and ducking down inside their pods, all staring in the same direction: the broken-down door of the toilet, from which something terrifying was emerging.

As Gerhardt had just realized, in his haste to get Catalina away from the woman who had been attacking her, he had significantly failed to follow correct air marshal procedure, his instincts switching entirely to those of the bodyguard he had been before changing career. A bodyguard was supposed to focus completely on the safety of his client, get them to a place of safety as fast as possible, and that was what Gerhardt had done, leaving the very efficient Latisha in complete control of the situation.

Swiftly, Latisha had pushed the fire axe across to the far side of the room, far from Vanessa's reach, and then looked around for something with which she could tie Vanessa up. Her own rage was boiling hot, and she was trying her best to keep as calm as she could, but the knowledge of how she had been tricked by Vanessa was making her want to lift Vanessa's head off the floor and slam it back heavily more times than she could count.

Vanessa moaned faintly, which meant that she was starting to return to consciousness. Latisha reacted quickly, kneeling down to straddle Vanessa, sitting on top of her, starting to drag off her own belt to bind Vanessa's wrists together.

Unfortunately, then everything went very wrong indeed. Lucinda, taking point, as she had bravely insisted to Karl that, as the cabin service director, she should go first, reached the open doorway of the toilet and paused in disbelief with Karl just behind her. They were confronted with the sight of what clearly seemed to be a passenger who had knocked their head of publicity to the ground and was violently assaulting her. Not only that, it was a passenger who shouldn't have been in Luxe Class at all.

Angela had been stationed at the bar when Gerhardt had entered the Luxe Class cabin with Latisha. Knowing that he was an air marshal, she had said not a word about the fact that he was bringing in a business-class passenger; he must, she assumed, have a good reason for doing so. But neither Lucinda nor Karl had seen this. To them, Latisha was not only committing assault but trespassing to boot.

It wasn't even a choice. Without hesitating, they dashed into the toilet stall, grabbing Latisha's arms and dragging her up and off the prone body of Vanessa.

'No! No, let me go!' Latisha yelled, thrashing frantically in their grip. 'It's her! *She's* the one – she's been stalking Catalina!'

Lucinda and Karl, looking down at the half-stunned Vanessa, didn't believe this for a moment. Vanessa had obviously just suffered a senseless attack by the crazy pop star's crazy assistant, who had also clearly committed criminal damage by kicking down the toilet door for some psychotic reason of her own.

'You have to calm down, *now*,' Lucinda commanded, in the sharp, authoritative tone that succeeded in quieting all but the most rambunctious air travellers. 'Let's get you back to your seat.'

Where we'll secure you with restraints, was the unspoken subtext of this, understood very clearly by both Lucinda and Karl.

'No! No, don't leave her alone – she has an axe!' Latisha screamed, trying to lurch forward.

Even as they hauled her back, Lucinda and Karl exchanged a swift eye roll that said, *Just when you think you've heard it all . . .*

'We'll definitely keep an eye out for that, don't you worry,' Karl assured her smoothly. 'Let's give you a hand back to your seat, shall we?'

'I'm not crazy, for fuck's sake!' Latisha screeched, jerking her arms back and forward so strongly that Karl and Lucinda had to hold on for dear life. 'She's got a fucking *axe!*'

'Yes, we'll be sure to check for that,' Karl said in his most soothing voice. That was how he and Lucinda usually dealt with a troublesome passenger: Lucinda would bark orders and Karl would soothe, a two-pronged strategy that normally worked very successfully.

'Vanessa, are you okay?' Lucinda asked, very concerned.

'She came in and attacked me!' Vanessa groaned, holding her head. 'I have no idea why!'

'You liar! *Look!*' Latisha gestured desperately with her head towards the corner of the bathroom, where the axe was lying half-hidden behind the toilet. 'See? It's a damn *axe!* She brought that in; she was threatening Catalina with it! Where the hell would *I* get an axe from on a plane? How would I ever carry that thing on-board?'

'Bloody hell!' Karl blurted out, completely forgetting the high standards of language to which he was supposed to

440

conform at work. 'Lucinda, look! She's right, there's a fucking fire axe on the floor!'

'*She* brought it in here,' Vanessa said quickly, heaving herself up to sit. 'I never laid eyes on that before she started to attack me with it—'

'Liar! How did I carry it in here without anyone seeing?' Latisha interrupted furiously. 'Look at me! Where did I put it?'

Karl and Lucinda looked at Latisha, who was wearing a close-fitting sweater and jeans, a thin scarf wrapped around her throat. She was right: there was nowhere she could possibly have concealed an axe, even a small one, on her person.

'She probably had it under her jacket!' Latisha said, guessing half-right: that was where Vanessa had carried the axe when she retrieved it from its secure hiding place in the crew area at the back of the plane and carried it into the toilet cubicle to conceal it, wedged firmly, behind the toilet bowl. Vanessa had always planned to access the crew area and remove the axe, just in case Catalina needed any convincing to agree to let Vanessa 'make her happy'. The porn-star passengers had been the perfect excuse for her to enter the rest area, but she had been ready with several other cover stories to use if she had needed them.

Lucinda and Karl hesitated, their grips on Latisha's arms loosening a little as they processed this. The presence of the axe across the room had put them on high alert; they couldn't risk getting this wrong. Still, Vanessa was their boss, and Latisha's accusation, though logical, seemed completely ludicrous.

'Ask her why she has a piece of duct tape stuck on the

inside of her jacket!' Latisha said, jerking with her head now to the flap of Vanessa's jacket, hanging open. 'She tied Catalina up with it, that's why!'

'Vanessa,' Lucinda said, 'excuse me for asking, but why *do* you have a piece of duct tape stuck on the inside of your jacket?'

'For emergencies,' Vanessa said, as if it were the most obvious thing in the world. 'Of course. I always have a piece cut and ready just in case.'

'What kind of emergency would need *duct*—' Lucinda began.

'Oh shit,' Karl exclaimed, looking round the cubicle for any more clues as to what had really gone on in there, 'is that *hair* in the sink?'

'It's Catalina's!' Latisha cried. 'That crazy bitch must have cut it off with that damn axe! *Now* do you believe me?'

Vanessa looked from Karl to Lucinda and saw the doubt in their eyes. Karl was clearly creeped out by the lock of hair, his expression revolted, while Lucinda was frowning as she tried, and failed, to imagine why a publicity director would ever need something as rough and ready as duct tape in a crisis.

'You hold her,' Lucinda said to Karl. 'I'm just going to go and secure that axe.'

She looked at Latisha.

'Do you promise you'll be good and stay with Karl?' she asked, surveying Latisha's face to read her response.

'I swear. A hundred per cent,' Latisha said with obvious sincerity. 'I just want you to get that axe the hell away from her.'

Lucinda let go of Latisha's arm. And that was when Vanessa, up on her knees now, lunged across the room to grab the axe.

'Shit! Let me go!' Latisha yelled, wrestling herself free and throwing herself towards Vanessa in a desperate attempt to reach her before she got hold of the weapon. Still on her knees, Vanessa swivelled round, the axe now grasped in both hands, and drove the haft up into Latisha's midriff, winding her so thoroughly that all the air was driven out of her in one explosive gasp. Latisha staggered back and doubled over, making tiny, painful, hiccupping noises as her body spasmed for breath.

'Get the air marshals!' Lucinda said to Karl. 'Get them *now*!'

'No, you go! I'll take care of this!'

'*You!*' Lucinda screamed. 'That's an order!'

Karl turned and ran, pushing aside the passengers who had come out of their pods to see what on earth was going on, crashing past Angela, tearing down the plane to summon the cavalry from business class. Lucinda heroically threw herself on Vanessa while the publicity director was still getting to her feet, wrestling her for possession of the axe. Vanessa was heavier, but Lucinda was tall and in very good shape due to regular gym sessions, and she got her hands on the shaft. Giving it a powerful wrench, she almost managed to drag it out of Vanessa's grasp.

Vanessa promptly let go of the axe with one hand, sending Lucinda off balance. With the other, she punched Lucinda square in the face. Blood spurted from Lucinda's nose. Vanessa dragged the axe free and stood up, holding the weapon high as Lucinda tripped over Latisha's doubled-up body and fell against the wall, both hands pressed over her nose to try to staunch the flow of blood.

Any attempt at feigning normality had been discarded for good as soon as Vanessa went for the fire axe. Eyes gleaming, she looked psychotic, a serial killer from a horror film. The only thing that was missing from the scene was blood dripping from the axe, but since some of the gush of blood from Lucinda's nose had splashed onto the floor, that gave a sufficiently gory touch to the scene. Lucinda and Latisha were both moaning in pain, while Vanessa's breathing was loud and panting as she crossed the cubicle and emerged into the aisle. Axe held high, she looked as if she were fully prepared to cut her way through the crowd of people outside to get to Catalina.

Screams of fear greeted her appearance, the screams heard by Catalina and Gerhardt. Most of the passengers had taken refuge in their pods and were standing on their beds, watching the scene unfold in fascination, terror and sheer disbelief. Jane and Michael, however, in pods dangerously close to the action, ducked down, afraid even to stick their heads above the parapet in case they got cut off.

Behind Vanessa, Lucinda stumbled out of the toilet, a clump of pale blue hand towels pressed to her nose, blood pooling on them horrifically. More screams came from the watchers as Vanessa strode towards Catalina's pod, the axe held high, confronting Gerhardt, who had emerged from it and was standing there. Making a swift assessment of the situation, he pushed Catalina to hide behind him and stepped forward to tackle Vanessa.

But even as he did so, Angela, who had been crouching surreptitiously in the entrance of Michael Coggin-Carr's pod, stepped out, stood up and, in one fluid upward motion, smashed Vanessa square in the jaw with the fire extinguisher she was holding.

Vanessa went down with a mighty thud, accompanied by further screams as the axe flew backwards in an arc and hit the cockpit door. Gerhardt stopped dead as David Webber, holding his air marshal badge in hand to identify himself, tore up the aisle towards them, followed by Karl and Lord Tony, the latter with the disheveled hair and disoriented expression of someone who has only recently awoken from a nap.

'What the bloody hell is going on?' demanded Lord Tony, striding up behind David to stare in disbelief at Vanessa's prone body. His eyes rose to take in Lucinda, her face hidden by blood-soaked towels, and then Angela, the fire extinguisher still in her hands, gasping in the aftershock of having saved the day. Her blonde bun dangled at an angle from the back of her skull, pulled loose with the force of the blow she had just delivered.

'My God!' Lord Tony exclaimed. 'Lucinda! Are you all right? And *Vanessa*! Someone help her!'

His attempt to step forward was blocked by Gerhardt, who put one large hand on his sternum.

'We will handle this, sir,' he said, producing his own badge from his trouser pocket. 'We are both air marshals. Please return to your seat.'

'But why did Angela hit Vanessa with the fire extinguisher?' Lord Tony said helplessly. 'Did she hit Lucinda too? What on *earth* is going on?'

Latisha emerged from the toilet, moving slowly, her hand grasping the wall for support, her breathing stertorous.

'I don't *believe* it! Has half of Luxe Class been in a fight?' Lord Tony said in utter disbelief.

'Banessa went berserk,' Lucinda managed to say, her voice thick and bubbling with blood. 'She got an axe. She hit me, and her.' She pointed at Latisha. 'If Angela hadn't hit her, we could all be . . . I don't want to *think* what would've happened.'

'It's true,' Michael Coggin-Carr chimed in. 'I saw everything. That stewardess' – he nodded at Angela – 'was incredibly brave. She took the fire extinguisher from the wall, lay in wait and took the psycho down with it so no one else got hurt. Didn't even hesitate! She's an absolute heroine. Someone should give her a medal.'

'*Vanessa* went insane and started flailing around with an axe?' Lord Tony said in disbelief, running a hand through his thick golden hair. 'She seemed so . . . *sensible*! Feet on the ground . . . head screwed on right. Was she drunk? I just can't believe it!'

He shook his head in disbelief and turned to stare at Angela, who was setting down the fire extinguisher, visibly embarrassed by all the attention.

'How did you get up the pluck to do something like that, Angela?' he asked her, fascinated. 'Have you had martial arts training?'

Angela shook her head, realized that her bun was hanging loose and shot her hands up to pin it back into place.

'No, nothing like that. But you wouldn't believe how rough ReillyFly could get sometimes,' she said, pulling out kirby grips and pushing them back in to anchor her bun with the skill of long practice. 'Lots of drunk passengers kicking off. The late-night flight back from Magaluf . . . or Prague with stag dos on-board . . .'

She shuddered at the memories.

'You had to be ready for *anything*,' she said frankly. 'I mean, I never actually had to hit someone with a fire extinguisher, but there were a couple of times we had to threaten them with one.'

'Well, Angela, you're invaluable in a crisis,' Lord Tony said admiringly. 'Best instincts I've ever seen. You're rehired. With a bonus.'

'I thought she worked here already?' Michael Coggin-Carr said, confused. 'She's wearing the uniform.'

Angela burst into tears of happiness. Lucinda, stepping up to her, gingerly enfolded her in a hug of congratulations, keeping her own bloody face away from Angela's. Angela fell on Lucinda's shoulder, sobbing with utter relief. Lucinda patted her sympathetically as Gerhardt and David pushed past the two women to put the unconscious Vanessa in handcuffs and frisk her for concealed weapons.

'I will come back to look at your nose,' Gerhardt said to Lucinda as he and David lifted up Vanessa's limp body. 'I have a lot of experience with broken noses. I can set it for you.'

'Oh *God*,' Lucinda wailed quietly. 'Has adyone got painkillers?'

'Oh sweet baby Jesus!' Karl said, coming forward, his view of the scene having mostly been blocked by the large bodies of Lord Tony and Gerhardt. 'Lucinda, your *face*! And why is Angela crying?'

'She's been an absolute heroine! I've rehired her,' Lord Tony said.

'Well! Finally some good news,' Karl said happily. 'Well done, Angela! We put in a good word for you, you know, Lucinda and me.'

He looked at Lucinda's bloody face, at Vanessa, being secured in handcuffs, a gigantic bruise already forming on the lower part of her face, at the axe lying on the cabin floor . . .

'Just goes to show,' he said, managing to find a positive spin to the recent carnage, 'there really *is* a silver lining to every cloud!'

Chapter Twenty-Eight

'When I saw Vanessa walk past me, I recognized her at once,' Gerhardt explained some time later.

He and Catalina were sitting on the bed in Catalina's pod, with Latisha on the pull-down seat. Vanessa had been returned to her own pod and secured there, belted to her seat and handcuffed. Extension seat belts had been used to wrap around her chest and legs, and her feet were cable-tied to the legs of the chair, with David Webber stationed on the fold-down seat, keeping guard. Still, Catalina was too nervous to leave her seating area to go to the bar, where they would have had more space; she felt safest in her pod, with Gerhardt reassuringly positioned between her and the entrance.

'She didn't see me,' Gerhardt continued. 'She was looking straight ahead. Of course now we know that she was going to get the axe, so I imagine that she was thinking only of that.'

Catalina shivered at the mention of the axe.

'Drink a little more brandy, hon,' Latisha said, handing her a snifter glass. 'It'll help, trust me. I'm on my second and I feel a hell of a lot better.'

'So she did not notice me, which is very lucky,' Gerhardt said. 'But I saw her and I immediately thought, *That is the woman I saw a few times at the Mobile Power arenas. How strange that now I see her on the plane!* I am trained to recognize faces, you see,' he added. 'So I start to think, to try to remember when I see her backstage, and I realize that she is there both times that someone does the vandalism in the dressing room. And now she is on the plane with you. That it is a very big coincidence, and I am also trained to suspect coincidences.'

He paused.

'Also, she looks . . . very excited as she comes to the end of the aisle,' he said. 'I wonder why. People do not look excited on planes unless they are drunk, or maybe going to have sex. And I do not think she is drunk or going to have sex. So I decide I must talk to Latisha.' He pulled an unexpectedly comic face. 'That is very, very difficult. Much more difficult than kicking down a door to the toilet.'

'I was *out* of it,' Latisha said ruefully. 'Like, *drooling*. There was this hot guy sitting next to me – he must have been totally grossed out. Snoring, dribbling . . .'

She sighed in resignation.

'There's no way I can go back to my seat and explain to him that someone slipped me an extra sleeping pill and that usually I never act like this on planes, is there?' she asked gloomily.

'I get Latisha up, and I take her into the galley,' Gerhardt continued, frowning at Latisha's frivolity even as Catalina smiled ruefully at her assistant, knowing that Latisha's real aim was to cheer her boss up. 'I slap her round the face to wake her up. I put ice cubes on her neck, I give her coffee. A lot of coffee.'

'I need to pee soon, actually,' Latisha said. 'My kidneys are swimming.'

'Poor Tish,' Catalina said sympathetically. 'First you get me shaking you, then Gerhardt slapping you . . .'

'My face *is* pretty sore,' Latisha admitted, lifting a hand to cradle her cheek.

'You get an all-expenses-paid, five-star holiday on me when the Oscars are over,' Catalina promised. 'To Cabo.'

'Yay!' Latisha's face lit up.

'*So*,' Gerhardt said severely, annoyed by what he considered ill-timed feminine chit-chat, 'when I finally succeed to wake up Latisha fully, she tells me that it is Vanessa who has said that there is no room for Latisha in Luxe Class, it is Vanessa who suggests that I am the stalker, and Vanessa who gives Latisha the name of the computer man who puts the disgusting photos on my laptop, with fake dates. You will give me his name,' he said in an aside to Latisha. 'I will pay him a visit when we are back in LA tomorrow.'

'Poor guy,' Latisha said, grinning.

'*Poor guy?*' Catalina was incensed. 'What he did was terrible! I don't care what Gerhardt does to him – he deserves everything he gets!'

'I agree, hon,' Latisha said, reaching round Gerhardt to pat her employer's hand. 'Totally. But don't you feel even a *tiny* bit sorry for someone that's about to face the wrath of Gerhardt?'

Gerhardt ignored them masterfully.

'Instantly,' he said, 'I realize that Catalina is in danger. Vanessa must be the stalker, and she is on the plane. We go to look for you, but the lady in the next pod says you have been helped to go to the toilet by Vanessa.' His jaw tightened. 'So I run there and kick in the door,' he finished.

'That was *amazing*,' Latisha said enthusiastically. 'He did it with one kick, just like in the films!'

Gerhardt turned to look at her.

'The door is made of plastic, like the wall,' he said matter-of-factly. 'The lock also. You could have done it easily. And in films, it is all fake, not wood at all. In real life it is very, very hard to kick down a locked door unless the wood is very old and will splinter. That is why we use a battering ram instead of breaking our feet.'

'Well, it *looked* awesome,' Latisha said, undeterred. 'Gerhardt, I'm so sorry for believing Vanessa. I know she totally set me up, but I shouldn't have listened to her. I swear, though, she did it so well! It was like it was just occurring to her, and she was thinking through the dates as she went, working it all out in her head. She did such a good acting job. I was totally fooled.'

'She fooled everyone,' Gerhardt said. 'It is not a problem.'

'So we're good?' Latisha asked.

He nodded gravely.

'She fooled everyone until you, at the end,' Catalina said gratefully, winding her fingers through his. 'You spotted her and worked out that something was wrong. You saved me.' She shivered again. 'She was going to . . . ugh . . .'

'Drink more brandy,' Gerhardt said. 'Latisha is right about that.'

Catalina nodded, sipping the brandy. It burnt, but in a good way.

'Miss . . . um, Catalina?'

Lord Tony was looming over the pod, an awkward expression on his face. Catalina looked up at him.

'Please allow me to say, on behalf of the airline, that I'm *so very* sorry about what happened to you,' he said fervently. 'Needless to say, I had no idea – no one had any idea. The headhunters who recommended Vanessa gave her the most glowing write-up. Obviously, I don't mean to make excuses, but we absolutely couldn't have predicted her going completely psycho . . .'

'She fooled everyone,' Catalina repeated, echoing Gerhardt. 'Apart from him.'

She smiled lovingly up at her boyfriend.

'Obviously, I can offer lifetime free flights for the three of you,' Lord Tony said anxiously, clearly nervous that Catalina might file a lawsuit. 'Any time, anywhere. First class all the way.'

'Maybe we can go into space?' Gerhardt said, grinning: Lord Tony had recently announced plans for a fleet of spaceships that would orbit the earth, and Pure Planet had been immediately deluged with people putting down deposits on the three-hundred-thousand-dollar tickets to take a flight.

'Absolutely! All three of you!' Lord Tony said without a moment's hesitation. He had instantly calculated that, if they all decided to file lawsuits against Pure Air, they would receive millions each, far more than nine hundred thousand dollars; not to mention the incalculable cost of the negative publicity for Pure Air that would result from a trial for damages that would be reported worldwide.

'Not me,' Catalina said firmly. 'From now on, I'm only

making flights that are one hundred per cent necessary. You two can go.'

'Oh my God! This is amazing! I gotta say, this day is ending a *lot* better than it started,' Latisha said enthusiastically. She stared firmly at Lord Tony. 'Apology accepted, and we'll get the lawyers to draw up the paperwork. But Catalina won't be doing the press conference when we land, of course,' she said, now using her best managerial voice. 'She's still real shaken up.'

'Really?' Lord Tony said, looking disappointed. 'Not even a smile for the cameras? A couple of quick photo poses? She wouldn't have to say anything – we could explain she was saving her voice for the Oscars—'

'She was *assaulted*,' Latisha hissed furiously, not wanting anyone else to hear. 'You get that, right?'

'Yes, of course. So sorry.' Lord Tony looked abashed, but still hopeful. 'It's just that—'

'*Totally* not going to happen,' Latisha barked, earning, as far as Catalina was concerned, an upgrade to the best suite at the best resort in the whole of Cabo. 'She gets off the plane and goes straight home to rest. And we still get the lifetime flights and the space tickets.'

He nodded gloomily.

'But hey' – Latisha's tone softened now that she had carried her point – 'why don't you put that nice Angela girl front and centre at the press conference? You can spin the publicity fuck-up of having hired Catalina's stalker by showing what a heroine Angela was! And Lucinda too,' she added fairly. 'She was hella brave. She could have let Karl tackle Vanessa, but she sent him for reinforcements and went after her all on her own when I was out of commission.'

454

Lord Tony nodded.

'You're always safe on Pure Air,' he said, testing it out. 'Our staff will risk their lives – no, God no! – go to the absolute limit for you.'

'I mean, it's happened,' Latisha said. 'There'll be a trial. The whole stalking thing'll come out. You have no choice – you've got to get ahead of the story.'

'You don't want a job as the head of publicity at Pure Air, do you?' he asked, not entirely in jest.

Latisha flashed him a big, white smile.

'I'll think about it,' she assured him. 'Thanks for the offer.'

'Could I see Angela for a moment?' Catalina asked. 'I'd really like to thank her.'

'Of course!' Lord Tony said enthusiastically. 'Happy to oblige!'

He disappeared down the corridor, and soon Angela appeared, looking overwhelmed, exhausted and happy, as befitted a heroine after the execution of a dramatic deed.

'I just wanted to say how amazing you were, Angela,' Catalina said. 'Thank you so much! And Lucinda too. Latisha says she was really brave as well. If you give me your details, I'll get you both sent tickets for my next concert.'

'Oh, *really*?' Angela went pink. 'That would be fantastic! I'm such a fan of your music – thanks so much! Would it be really cheeky to ask for an autograph?'

'I can do better than that,' Latisha said, standing up. 'I have some of Cat's latest CDs in my hand luggage. I'll bring them here and she can sign them for you. And I'll get my day planner and take down your info as well.'

'Congratulations,' Gerhardt, his arm wrapped around

Catalina, said to Angela. 'This is the first time ever in my life that a woman not even trained in combat does a job as good as I could do.'

'We could have used you on the Knock to Stansted run on ReillyFly,' Angela said very seriously. 'Oh my God, that was bad. We'd do anything to get out of that one if we saw it on our roster. Once we had a whole planeload of drunken nuns and priests limbo-ing all over the shop – like Father Ted but with more tequila. Or Father Jack, I suppose.'

She saw her American/German audience was looking baffled.

'Knock's in western Ireland,' she explained. 'There's nothing to do there at all, so you get lots of clerics hitting the booze. I'm Irish myself, but that lot always scare the living daylights out of me.'

'I've always wanted to go to Ireland,' Catalina said to Gerhardt. 'It sounds fun, doesn't it?'

Gerhardt's smile was like sun on a glacier.

'Clearly,' he said, 'you cannot go there by yourself. I will need to be with you to protect you from the nuns and priests drinking tequila.'

'It's *really* hard to tell a nun who reminds you of your Sunday School teacher that she's had enough and needs to put the bottle down,' Angela said ruefully. 'Even when she's taking a swing at you with it.'

Latisha returned with the CDs and Jane Browne, whom she had collected from the bar on her way. Jane, like almost everyone in Luxe Class, had repaired there, directly after Vanessa had been removed from the scene, to discuss eagerly the dramatic events that had just taken place. The only Luxe

Class passenger missing was Danny Zasio, who was still passed out and snoring in his bed. When Danny went on a bender, it took more than a psychotic stalker running rampant with a fire axe to wake him from his drunken stupor.

Jane leaned over the partition to say, 'God, I feel so sorry for letting you go in there with her, Catalina! I can't apologize enough! But honestly, I had no idea.'

'No one had any idea. She fooled everyone,' Catalina repeated. 'Apart from Gerhardt.'

Lovingly, she picked up her lover's hand and kissed it.

'And I'm *also* really sorry for not believing you when you told us about the photos on your bed!' Jane continued, determined to make a full apology. 'Vanessa must have put them there, right? And then taken them away once you'd seen them. She was wandering around the cabin the whole time. But of course people just assumed that she was doing her job – you know, making sure that everything was going smoothly.'

'No, I'm sure I sounded totally crazy,' Catalina said. 'It's fine – I don't blame you for not believing a word I was saying. I was so confused! I thought it was Gerhardt who'd put the photos and the note there – it's a long story – but I couldn't see how he could have got into Luxe Class. I didn't realize he was an air marshal. So I thought he must have an accomplice, which *really* made me freak out—'

'Oh no!' Jane, an enthusiastic mystery fan, interrupted. 'It would be so disappointing if there were two of them! I hate that in detective novels and horror films, don't you? It's just not playing fair. You think someone's innocent because they have an alibi, like in *Scream*, but then it turns out that they're in a conspiracy with someone else, and I always think that's cheating when a writer does it.'

'Thank God there was only one of Vanessa,' Latisha said fervently. 'Can you *imagine*?'

Catalina, who didn't think she would ever be able to use an airline toilet again, shivered at the mere idea.

Gerhardt nodded, his huge head moving slowly and heavily.

'One,' he agreed, his deep voice rumbling, 'was more than enough.'

Chapter Twenty-Nine

Los Angeles International airport

It was five minutes to midnight in Los Angeles, and the arrivals hall of Terminal 2 was now full of international press waiting for the scheduled arrival of Pure Air 111, exactly on time. Outside the terminal, sirens blared as two police cars pulled up, red and blue rotating lights sweeping the glass walls as they came, turning the interior briefly into a garish multicoloured carnival. In LA, cop cars were so common that no one blinked an eye at their arrival, not even Special Agent Smithee, though he did glance over at Herrera; she nodded, and swiftly texted Evan Jennings, the head of LAX security, to ask whether the LAPD had any operation underway that would impede their ability to arrest their target. Meanwhile, a small group of Pure Air cabin crew, distinctive in their bright cobalt uniforms, bustled in from the publicity lounge, followed by news crews, and took up a stance on the small stage that had been set up at the far side of the arrivals hall.

'Hi, everyone! It's nearly midnight!' a woman with her blue hat at a particularly jaunty angle said brightly into the mike at the front of the stage. 'And that means something really exciting – the first-ever Pure Air direct service from London to LA is about to land right here, at LAX Terminal

2! Our state-of-the-art, brand-new LuxeLiner offers the perfect flight for business travellers – our patented deep recline seats mean that they're fresh and ready for work the next morning. Jet lag's a thing of the past with the Pure Air 111 LA route!'

Music swelled from a PA system behind the stage, and the spokeswoman did her best to lead the occupants of the arrivals hall in a spirited round of cheers. In Britain, at midnight, she would have had very little success, but Americans are much more open to the idea of spontaneously making noise in public than the British, and she managed to get a few ragged whoops and a smattering of applause to warm up for her countdown.

'Just a minute to go!' the woman said, sounding as excited as if she were announcing that Prince William was leaving Duchess Kate for her. 'And then our Pure Air 111 LuxeLiner will land for the first time ever in LA, with major celebrities on-board! Catalina, here to perform her song 'Forever is Now' at the Oscars! Danny Zasio, celebrity chef! Jane Browne, Academy Award nominee! They'll all be walking off our new Pure Air flight, the *only* airline choice for business travellers between London and LA!'

Genuine cheers and whoops greeted Catalina and Danny's names. And though Jane's name prompted no nods of recognition, an LA crowd can always be guaranteed to show great enthusiasm for the Academy Awards; enthusiastic claps followed the mention of the ceremony that made their city the centre of the world for a couple of weeks every year.

'Five!' the woman caroled. 'Four!'

Behind her, the rest of the Pure Air crew made sweeping

gestures with their arms, encouraging the crowd to join in even as they yelled along with the countdown.

'Three! Two! One!' the crowd duly shouted, their voices rising with every number.

The music on the PA switched to a carillon of bells, and from a net in the ceiling tumbled a dramatic fall of Pure Air blue confetti, cut in the shape of LuxeLiners. Lord Tony and Vanessa had wanted airplane-shaped balloons in the net instead, but Jennings, picturing mayhem as travellers with suitcases fell over them or burst them with their trolleys, had nixed that request, confining the balloons to the press room.

More applause, plus oohs and aahs of appreciative surprise, greeted the fall of confetti. The recorded bells merged into the opening bars of Catalina's song 'Forever is Now', and the Pure Air crew came down from the stage to hand out bottles of Pure Water with bright blue labels, airplane-shaped chocolates wrapped in blue and silver foil, and information leaflets about the new route. As had been planned, the exclamations of pleasure that greeted the offer of free swag, together with the consumption of the water and the chocolates, took up the next ten minutes or so, together with more eulogies over the PA system to the superior benefits of choosing to fly between LA and London with Pure Air and announcements asking people to recycle their water bottles responsibly in the designated containers.

The VIPs had been rushed through passport control and their luggage prioritized. In barely a quarter of an hour, the glass doors slid open to reveal the large frame of Lord Tony, looking fresh as a daisy, his arm around Danny Zasio, who was quite the opposite: red-eyed, puffy and almost visibly sweating out a skinful of booze.

'*Hello,* Los Angeles!' Lord Tony boomed out, waving at everyone with a bright white smile.

Lord Tony had the God-given ability to act as if a sparse crowd of tired people up past their bedtime, bulked out by photographers and camera crews, were a reception committee equal only to the inhabitants of Ancient Rome gathered on the steps of the Forum to welcome Julius Caesar's triumphant return from the Gallic Wars. It was a very important skill for publicity: it meant that, viewed on camera, the launch would look like a highly attended, raving success.

'*So* wonderful to be back here!' he continued, managing somehow to smile and talk simultaneously. 'This is one of my favourite cities in the world!'

Lord Tony always said this wherever he had just landed; it never failed to please.

'And I've brought you back one of our most famous exports, the incredibly charming and talented chef Danny Zasio!'

'Hey, Danny! Eat me!' someone yelled from the crowd.

'Funny, mate,' Danny muttered. 'Fucking original.'

But, very aware of which side his bread was buttered, he too managed a full-beam smile, his British teeth having been straightened and whitened for American TV many moons ago, and said loudly, 'I love Pure Air! Best food I've ever eaten on-board a plane!' and winked for the cameras.

'Daddy!' shrieked little Eamonn, and, prodded by his mother, he started to run towards Danny. Not to be outdone,

Herbert followed. The two boys were currently the most photogenic of the children, who were all sturdy little chips off the old block. Danny's stocky build and square face were much more suited to boys than girls, and, at ten and twelve, Ottoline and Cinnamon were, in Melanie's opinion, both homely. She had put the two of them on strict diets, and done her best to dress them in flatteringly loose outfits that disguised what she called their chunkiness, but she was already assuming that they would need major chin reduction surgery at the age of sixteen, for starters.

'Eamonn! My little man! And Bertie! Look at you both!' Danny cried happily.

To much cooing among the female spectators and gruff noises of approval from the male ones, Danny bent and swept both his sons up into his arms, kissing each of them with noisy theatrical smacks of his lips. Melanie stepped forward, positioning their daughters slightly behind her on either side to hide some of what she considered their bulk. Giving the cameras her best sweet, loving smile, she widened her eyes and flicked back her hair.

'Darling!' she said, pitching her voice so that the mikes would pick it up. 'Welcome home! The kids and I have missed you so much!'

Danny put down his squirming sons, threw his arms wide and embraced his wife, who accepted his kiss with great enthusiasm: no one, seeing Melanie hug and kiss her husband, would have guessed that he reeked of stale alcohol and sweat. She had had a great deal of practice at concealing her revulsion. After fifteen years of marriage, and hundreds of staged reunions, Melanie would have been genuinely amazed if Danny had emerged from a plane smelling of soap and freshly applied aftershave.

'The only good thing about going away is that I get to come back to you every time, love!' he said, to more coos.

'Lucky, lucky me!' Melanie said, her voice pitch-perfect, but with a brief narrowing of her eyes at Danny, signalling that she was speaking with more sarcasm that anyone else realized, her head, however, angled so that the cameras wouldn't pick it up.

'Otto, Cin, how are my two precious girls?' Danny said with genuine affection, kissing both his daughters.

Cinnamon, an emotional child, burst into tears and was promptly shushed by Melanie. Tears were definitely not in the script.

'Hey, guys, my kids are tired, it's past their bedtime,' Danny said to the press camera. 'They were just so keen to come and greet their old dad! I'll answer a few questions, and then I and my beautiful wife need to head home and get these rug rats to bed, okay?'

He linked his arm through Melanie's and, guided by an LAX security officer, strolled down the hall to the lounge that had been designated for the press conference.

'Happy, are you, you fucking bastard?' Melanie hissed at him as they walked. 'I had to drag the brats out of bed and get them dressed for this fucking stupid photo opportunity because you've been shagging your way through half of London and your publicists rang me and said they needed me to kill the rumours. We're all *exhausted*.'

'*You* got the kids up and dressed?' Danny retorted. 'That'd be a first! Sacked Mariangela and Guadelupe and looked after your own kids for a change, did you?'

'Fuck you, Danny!' she retorted. 'How many stewardesses did you get to blow you on the plane? Tell me you were at least discreet about it!'

'Define *discreet*,' Danny said incorrigibly.

'You're a fucking cunt!'

'Maybe I wouldn't have to go looking for it if I got it at home more.'

'When are you ever at home?' she snapped. 'And try smelling yourself! No one wants to fuck someone who stinks like you do!'

They moved into the press room, the children tagging along by their heels. Danny turned briefly to wave at his fans, many of whom waved back.

'You really can fool some of the people all of the time,' Melanie muttered bitterly.

'Let me present Jane Browne, Academy Award nominee, here to see if she's going to win an Oscar!' Lord Tony was saying from the podium, and the crowd clapped for the mention of an Academy Award nominee. Jane gave the cameras her best smile as Lord Tony, dwarfing her, threw his arm around her and posed for pictures.

Michael Coggin-Carr, who had offered to load her suitcase onto his trolley, waited to one side during this necessary process. He and Jane had sat together in the bar until it was time for the descent into Los Angeles, talking over the dramatic events they had witnessed on-board; being so close to the action had bonded them tremendously, and they had naturally resumed their chat as they deplaned together.

'Miss Browne, can we whip you along to the press room?' an aide said, motioning for Jane to follow her. 'Security's really fussing for some reason about people standing around for too long. I don't know why, but they're making us hustle this evening.'

'Would you like to share a cab into town afterwards?' Michael asked her as they walked along. 'I'm happy to wait until you finish the press conference.'

'Oh, thanks!' Jane said. 'But the film company will have sent me a limo. There he is.'

She gestured to the man in a black suit holding up a card with JANE BROWNE – COGNA FILMS on it. He fell in behind them.

'I could give you a lift somewhere, if you'd like,' she offered.

'Oh! Well, that would be very kind, thanks!' he said.

'Janey?' said a hesitant voice, as the small woman who had been standing by the Java Java stand stepped into Jane and Michael's path.

Jane stopped dead and let out a shriek of surprise. Michael, utterly taken aback by this reaction, swivelled his head between the two women, who were staring at each other as if each had thought until now that the other one was dead.

'I can't believe—' Jane started.

'I wanted to—' Simone said at exactly the same time.

They both stopped, paused and tried again, once more speaking simultaneously.

'How come you—'

'I flew over—'

Again, they stopped.

'Miss Browne, could we . . .' the aide tried, but with no

success. Jane's entire attention was riveted on the woman in front of her.

'I was going to ring you as soon as I landed,' she said very softly to Simone. 'I've been wanting to for ages, and I finally got the courage up to convince myself to do it. I was sitting on the plane working out everything I was going to say . . . I even wrote it all down on my tablet so I wouldn't lose my nerve! "Hey, I'm in LA, I'm halfway to Australia already – can I fly to Sydney after the Oscars and see you and try to make you see that we should be together – I've never stopped thinking about you" . . . but here you are!'

She caught herself, the words spilling out of her so fast that she had run out of breath.

'I can't believe you're here,' she said simply.

'Neither can I!' Simone said immediately. 'I got a really good deal on the ticket. Used my air miles. And I've got friends to crash with here, so . . .' She managed a smile. 'Hey, it's closer than coming to London! And I knew you'd be on this flight, so I'd be able to meet you off it – it was all over the papers. How weird, we both came to meet each other halfway . . .'

They were still staring at each other with such intensity that neither the aide nor Michael dared to say a word.

'I broke up with Rangi,' Simone said with great abruptness, as if it were extremely urgent to convey this piece of information.

'Oh,' Jane said faintly.

'I couldn't stop thinking about . . .'

'Oh.'

They took one step towards each other, and then one

more. The handle of Jane's small carry-on, which she had been pulling, fell from her grasp, the bag thudding onto the floor. The two of them snapped together like a pair of magnets, north pole and south pole attracting each other with great power: the same shape, the same size, the same weight, their mouths locking together, their arms wrapping around each other, the bond so tight it looked as if it would take tremendous force to pull them apart.

'Huh,' said the aide, her eyes flickering to Michael. 'I kinda assumed . . .'

'Oh no,' he said wistfully. 'That is, I hoped . . . but no. I mean –' he cleared his throat – 'obviously not.'

They both looked at Jane and Simone, entwined like two grass snakes in mating season. Meanwhile, Herrera started to speak discreetly into her mike, the FBI agents stationed around the arrivals hall giving single-word acknowledgements of her instruction.

'Uh, Miss Browne?'

The aide eventually summoned up the nerve to tap Jane on her shoulder.

'I'm sorry – we just have press waiting – I hate to break this up, but if I could just steal you for a few minutes . . .'

It took more than a few repetitions of the message before Jane finally came up for air. She was transformed: her face was pink and glowing, her eyes bright, and she could not stop smiling. Simone was equally blissful, her dark eyes huge as headlamps, an identical permasmile plastered to her face.

'I'll, um, probably just be heading off now,' Michael said.

Jane glanced at him as if she had no idea who he was or what he was talking about.

'I'll unload your suitcase, shall I?' he suggested.

He heaved it off his trolley. Jane's limo driver came forward swiftly to take it, retrieving the carry-on case that she had dropped. Behind them, Lord Tony was triumphantly announcing the arrival of Catalina, her arm wound tightly through Gerhardt's. The entertainment press, instantly recognizing Gerhardt as both Catalina's ex-bodyguard and her ex-boyfriend, started eagerly shouting questions.

'Catalina! Are you two back together?'

'Catalina! Is it true love this time?'

Lord Tony, delightedly realizing that this was a heaven-sent opportunity to spin the disaster of Vanessa's violent meltdown into something much more positive, said jovially, 'True love blossoms on Pure Air flights! We're all about romance on Pure Air! That's why we've introduced a system on our handsets which lets you message or buy drinks for people on-board who've caught your eye!'

'Um, that's a bit stalky,' Latisha muttered to him as she passed. 'You might want to dial that down for the time being.'

Latisha was accompanied by Justin, the long-suffering traveller who had been sitting next to her; she had apologized to him when she had finally returned to her seat, explaining that she had accidentally taken a double dose of sleeping pills and passed out so heavily that her employer and her employer's bodyguard had become increasingly concerned about her. Justin was very sympathetic and naturally asked her what it was like working for Catalina. The conversation had morphed into a discussion about music in general, and bands they both liked in particular, getting on so well that by the time they landed, Latisha had suggested that Justin join her in the VIP priority line for deplaning, passport control and customs.

Clinging to Gerhardt's arm, Catalina did not even pause momentarily for photos with Lord Tony. Not only was she exhausted, but she had also been advised by the wise Latisha that, with the coming trial of Vanessa and all its attendant publicity, any smiles or waves as she left the flight would be used by Vanessa's defence lawyer to suggest that Catalina had not been deeply upset by Vanessa's attack on her. Vanessa would be convicted, of that there was no doubt, but they not only wanted to ensure that she was given the maximum sentence, but lay the ground for obtaining iron-clad restraining orders when she was eventually released.

'Our star is resting her voice,' Lord Tony said, making the best of the fact that his major VIP was walking past him with barely any acknowledgement. 'We're so excited at Pure Air to have had the honour of bringing this superstar to LA to perform at the biggest award ceremony in the world – the Oscars! Ladies and gentlemen, here she is, one of the biggest pop stars in the world today – Catalina!'

Applause rang out again. Gerhardt's arm tightened protectively around his girlfriend, shielding her, as Latisha took up a position on her other side. A porter, following them, pushed a cart bearing stacks of Catalina and Latisha's luggage, plus Gerhardt's small carry-on, as Catalina's limo driver came forward to identify himself. They cleared the metal barriers behind which the paparazzi were stationed, Gerhardt shooing away autograph hunters politely but firmly as they started down the central aisle of the arrivals hall, heading for the exit as fast as they could go.

The aisle was blocked, however, by Jane and Simone, who were standing in the middle of the hall, holding hands. Jane was saying apologetically to Michael, 'It was very nice to meet you. Sorry I can't give you a lift after all . . .'

'Oh, not at all. And likewise – very nice to meet you,' Michael said ruefully. 'Well, I'll be heading out . . .'

A flurry of movement surged around them like a shoal of fish through water heading towards food. The ripples started low, but swiftly rose in intensity until the crowds that had formed around them, the people drawn by Jane and Simone's dramatic kiss, the journalists and fans following Catalina, began to part as FBI agents pushed their way through. The cleaner had discarded his mop; the two women by Hudson News had put back their magazines to converge on their target.

Herrera and Smithee were the pilot fish leading the shoal: Smithee deftly pulled the suspect's arms behind his back to handcuff him while Herrera said, 'Jason Woodson, also known as Jeffrey Alan Marks, Jarrett Smith and Justin Lanata, I have a warrant here for your arrest and extradition to the United Kingdom on the charges of murder and fraud by false representation . . .'

Gasps rose at the word 'murder'. Latisha, who had been elbowed aside by the agents, stood back, staring in amazement at the sight of 'Justin' being arrested and handcuffed. The woman with the over-youthful blonde hair and face full of fillers, who had been making her way forward to greet him, burst into tears.

'What's happening?' she wailed, as the two female agents promptly moved towards her. 'Justin? *Justin?* It can't be true!'

Jason Woodson cast her a brief annoyed glance over his shoulder.

'I've never seen that woman in my life,' he said firmly.

'Justin! How can you say that? Tell them! Tell them it's not true!' the woman who had been his latest target wept, even as the two agents who had been stationed by Hudson News gently grasped her upper arms, preventing her from getting any closer to him. 'Tell them you know me and this is all an awful mistake!'

'Ma'am, if you wouldn't mind just coming with us to fill us in about the contact you've been having with the suspect,' one of the agents said gently, successfully making this sound like a request rather than a demand. 'Was he expecting you to meet him at the airport?'

'No, it was a surprise,' the woman said, crying even harder. 'I drove here all the way from Vegas on impulse – I thought he'd be so happy to see me! I even got him a tea – he said he loved tea, being British and all –'

She waved the Starbucks cup she was holding, which contained a Teavana Oprah chai latte.

'I took *so* long picking it out!' she continued. 'It's a chai blend with black tea and rooibos – I thought it would be perfect to help him with the jet lag.' She looked wistfully over at Jason. 'Can I give it to him?'

'Sorry, that won't be possible. You should probably drink that yourself at this stage, ma'am,' said the agent.

'Yeah,' said her partner. 'It sounds calming.'

Forming a tight knot around Jason/Jeffrey/Jarrett/Justin,

the rest of the FBI agents escorted him from the terminal, the blonde woman, still clutching her oversized tea container, swept along securely behind him by her two minders.

'Are you *kidding*?' Latisha said in disbelief, staring after them. 'I was sitting next to a *murderer*?'

'You were getting along very nicely with a murderer,' Gerhardt observed. 'I think maybe you need to work on your judgement of men a bit.'

'Hey, fuck you,' Latisha said without acrimony. 'The shitty thing is that you kinda have a point there.'

Jane and Simone, oblivious to anything besides each other, allowed themselves to be guided into the press room, where Jane promptly, and to the great annoyance of her producers, came out as a lesbian. They couldn't argue that her announcement of her sexual orientation had influenced the Academy members to vote for someone else – the Oscar ballots were already in, and Jane had never stood a chance of winning – but the producers would much rather have not had her red-carpet appearances be dominated by the gleeful repetition of the word 'lesbian' by entertainment reporters.

Still, Jane and Simone made an adorable couple, and the publicity certainly didn't hurt the release of *Angel Rising* on DVD and Netflix.

Danny and Melanie were exiting the press room as Jane entered, trailed by their children and nannies.

'Can't wait to get home,' Danny was sighing. 'My own bed, my own wife . . .'

'As opposed to someone else's?' Melanie said sourly.

But Danny had poured on the charm in the press conference, singing Melanie's praises, calling attention repeatedly to her beauty and youthful appearance, even remembering to namecheck Zassy Kids not once, but twice; so Melanie softened towards him a little, her fingers wrapping around his.

'Just got to check the luggage,' he said, falling back ostensibly to count his suitcases, but actually to give a swift slap to Guadelupe's broad, flat buttocks. Guadelupe might not be a great beauty, but she was available, willing and conveniently on the spot, and for the priapic Danny, those were three very attractive qualities. He maintained his LA 'bachelor pad', as he called it, for a rotating series of temporary flings, and it was fully equipped with all sorts of toys, plus a stripper pole as well. However, like Arnold Schwarzenegger, who had notoriously conducted a long-term affair with his housekeeper, Danny also liked to have someone in the house to clean his pipes whenever he fancied at the snap of his fingers.

'*Hasta luego,*' he said in Spanish. See you later.

Guadelupe's dark eyes flickered in acknowledgement, while Mariangela pretended not to notice. They had both signed hardcore confidentiality agreements, and Danny always insisted to Melanie that the nannies got substantial Christmas bonuses.

The Zasios headed off for their Beverly Hills home, a little procession that passed in front of Catalina, Gerhardt and Latisha, who were waiting by the press conference room. Catalina had wanted to linger, just to make sure that everything was under control, and a few minutes later they were treated to the spectacle of a heavily sedated, glassy eyed Vanessa being pushed through the terminal in a wheelchair, the bruise on her chin from Angela's blow with the fire extinguisher now a spectacular firework burst of reds and purples. She was escorted by David Webber, the air marshal, a couple of paramedics and the LAPD officers who had just arrived at the airport; she would be taken to hospital, as an airport doctor had diagnosed that her jaw was fractured, to be held under arrest there.

'See?' Gerhardt said softly to Catalina. 'She is all done. All gone. No more worries. From now on, I will keep you safe.'

She squeezed his hand.

'Let's go home,' she said. 'It's been a very long night.'

They exited into the soft, dark, starry Los Angeles night. Back in the terminal, on the little stage, the crew and Lord Tony were smiling and posing for photographs – all but Lucinda, who had been whisked off the plane immediately on landing to be splinted up and treated by the airport medical team. Lord Tony didn't make his employees stay too long, however. They were exhausted, and he had no wish for them, overcome by weariness, to blurt out any information about the events on the flight. There could be no hushing up what had happened: Vanessa would be arraigned, and if she had any sense would plead not guilty by reason of insanity. However, Lord Tony wanted to consult the best publicist in town before the matter was openly discussed by Pure Air representatives.

'As a very special reward for my marvellous crew, who provided sterling service on this flight,' he announced, 'I'm sending them all to the Beverly Hills Hotel for their layover in Los Angeles!'

Screams rose from the assembled crew; Emma Louise and Kevin actually pogoed in excitement, clasping their hands to their breasts. They threw themselves on Lord Tony, the women kissing his cheek, the men pumping his hand in gratitude.

'Sir, on behalf of all of us at Pure Air, let me thank you and say what a pleasure it is to be working for you,' Brian said – as the captain, he was the natural spokesperson.

He adjusted his cap and flashed his best sexy smile at the cameras as he shook Lord Tony's hand, the last crew member to file off the stage. Outside were two stretch limousines, champagne chilling in their built-in bars: Lord Tony had rung the Pure Air LA office immediately on landing to set up this extra treat for the crew, one that would hopefully serve as a reminder of not only how much they were valued but as a clear incentive not to answer questions from any reporters that came snooping around.

Lucinda was sitting just inside the first limo, having already started on the champagne, her nose now padded with gauze, splinted and taped into place. The doctor had pronounced that Gerhardt had done an excellent job of resetting the cartilage on-board and applying a field dressing to hold it in place. American doctors were very generous with prescription drugs, and Lucinda was now the possessor of a large vial of Vicodin. Still, the pain relief hadn't fully kicked in yet, and the champagne was definitely helping to smooth out any remaining rough edges.

She waved at the crew as they came up. Karl immediately piled in next to her, stowing his case further down the limo, asking her how she was doing. She poured him a glass of champagne, and then, much to everyone's surprise, filled another one, leaning forward to hand it to Angela.

'Thangs,' she said, not able to speak much through her gauze-packed nose. 'Good job back there. You saved our bacon.'

'Oh, *thank you*!' Angela said, almost as gushingly as the blood that had streamed down Lucinda's face. 'I really admire you – honestly, you're like my role model –'

'Jesus, Angela, stop wittering on and get in the bloody limo so we can zoom off to the *Beverly Hills Hotel*!' Karl instructed, emphasizing the name of their destination in order to send everyone into fresh whoops of delight. 'Get in and drink your fizz, girl! You've earned it!'

Trying not to cry with sheer happiness at how well everything had turned out, Angela climbed in and shyly accepted the champagne glass from Lucinda.

'Room for one more?' Brian said jauntily, placing one foot on the limo step.

Karl glanced swiftly at Lucinda.

'No,' Lucinda snapped. 'Biss off.'

'But Luce—'

Brian looked completely taken aback. He had spent the last seven years with Lucinda as his girlfriend, a wife at home, and a rotating series of stewardesses and waitresses; Lucinda had cut up rough about his not leaving the former, and on finding out about the latter, but he had always been able to coax her back. This radical change of attitude was a complete surprise to him, as was her being disrespectful enough to swear at him in public.

'Luce!' he protested indignantly. 'Come on! You've got a whacking great piece of metal plastered to your face, you look like hell, and I *still* want to be with you! You're my girl!'

He flashed the smile that always worked with Lucinda, the one that melted her underwear away, the one that had never failed in the past to make her forgive and forget.

'Fug off, Brian,' Lucinda said, swivelling around to turn her back on him.

'You heard her!' Karl snapped to Brian, as always following Lucinda's lead. 'Apparently she just isn't grateful enough for your generous offer to screw her even though she's not looking her absolute best.'

'There's no need for that kind of language, Karl,' Brian said, looking thoroughly wounded. 'No need at all.'

He turned and walked over to the other limo.

'I'll come with you, Brian!' Emma Louise said, dashing to follow him. Usually the female flight attendants didn't dare to flirt with Brian for fear of Lucinda's wrath. Now, however, it was open season.

'Me too!' Lydia said. 'Ooh, did I tell you about those Ben Wa balls Kevin gave me for Christmas? I put them inside me and sat at Door 3 for the landing 'cause it's over the wheel, so it's jiggliest. Oh my God, it was amazing!'

She giggled madly.

'Well, you sound like a *very* naughty girl,' Brian said with his best faux-disapproving voice.

'We *both* are!' Emma Louise said, not to be outdone.

'Jesus, I thought I was a big slut,' Karl commented as the first limo pulled away, 'but those two run rings around me.'

Back in Terminal 2, the press were firing questions at Lord Tony. The FBI had arrested one of the LuxeLiner's passengers for murder, while another had been taken off in handcuffs and a wheelchair; naturally, this had spurred them to a frenzy of excitement to discover what on earth had been happening on-board the inaugural flight of Pure Air 111.

Lord Tony's smile was as beatific as the Pope's. He might have been blessing tens of thousands of congregants in Rome from the balcony of St Peter's Basilica.

'My crew are absolute stars, total heroes,' he said. 'I'm afraid my lips are sealed on matters of security, but I'm over the moon to be turning round and flying back to London on the second ever Pure Air LuxeLiner flight tomorrow with Luxe Class full of even more celebrities! We have Milly Gamble, the actress, Devon and Cesare, the celebrity cooking couple, plus Wayne Burns, the internationally famous footballer! Corks will be popping in the Luxe Class bar, champagne will be flowing the whole time . . .'

He paused for a moment, wondering whether to say aloud the line that had just entered his head. A PR handler would strictly have advised against it. Vanessa would have had a conniption.

But then, Vanessa had gone crazy and nearly slaughtered half of Luxe Class with an axe, and had just been wheeled out of Terminal 2 handcuffed to a wheelchair, looking like death warmed up. So frankly, who gave a shit about what Vanessa would have said?

In further unconscious imitation of the Holy Father, Lord Tony threw his arms wide.

'There's never a dull moment on Pure Air!' he declared.

'I just want to be boring for the rest of my life,' Catalina was saying in the limo at that very moment, snuggling up to

Gerhardt. 'You know? I don't want any more excitement for years and years. Maybe *ever*.'

'Can I be boring with you?' he asked, his arm tightening around her.

'Oh yes, *please*,' she said in heartfelt tones. 'You can be boring with me forever. I never want to get on a plane again. Let's just stay in LA for the rest of our lives and bore each other to death.'

'Like we did before when we were in LA,' he said, smiling down at her. 'We can be boring like that. We already know how to do it.'

Catalina managed her first fully happy smile since Vanessa had attacked her. The memories of her time with Gerhardt, holed up in the Oriole Way house, were so wonderful that they overrode her recent trauma.

'That was *so* boring,' she said, turning to kiss his arm.

'*Ridiculously* boring,' he agreed fondly, stroking her hair.

'Guys, I swear to God, I can't take much more of this,' Latisha said from the facing seat. 'I really can't. I know you're going to be doing this all through the next few days, but I warn you, I'm booking that flight to Cabo to leave straight after the Oscars ceremony, okay?'

'That sounds like a very good idea,' Gerhardt said. 'We are too boring for you to want to spend time with us.'

'Oh my God, kill me now,' Latisha said, pulling out her tablet and turning it on. 'I'm sorting out that Cabo booking *immediately*, on your credit card. A suite with an infinity pool and butler service.'

'Whatever you want,' Catalina said. 'Anything you want.'

Latisha, looking at her boss curled up in her boyfriend's

arms, thought that she wanted exactly what Catalina had. True love, someone to rely on, someone you could absolutely trust . . .

'We need to order some Mexican food tomorrow,' Gerhardt was saying to Catalina. 'You are so thin. Too thin. I can feel all your ribs.'

'Oh my God,' Latisha sighed. 'A man who wants you to put on weight! Cat, you're so lucky!'

'No more sad songs,' Catalina said dreamily. 'I wrote so many sad songs in the last few months.'

'She really did,' Latisha confirmed to him. '*So* many. All about you.'

'Really?' Gerhardt's voice went up. 'I would like to hear them *all*.'

'There are *so many*,' Latisha said. 'It'll take *days*.'

But nobody was listening to her any more. Catalina and Gerhardt were whispering sweet nothings to each other, his head bent low over hers, her hand raised to stroke his cheek. Latisha scrolled down through the available flights to Cabo, factored in recovery time from the post-Oscar afterparties, and chose one leaving at seven p.m. the day following the ceremony. She'd fly first class, get a private transfer to the hotel, and wake up the next day to dazzling Mexican sunshine glittering on the blue water of her private infinity pool.

'No more sad songs,' Catalina was repeating softly to Gerhardt. Latisha rolled her eyes and plugged in her headphones, already counting the days until she could escape to Cabo and maybe score herself a hot pool boy. Catalina and Gerhardt thought they were joking about being boring, but the truth was, Latisha reflected with an eye roll, that they actually were. Big time. There really was nothing as mind-numbingly tedious as a pair of reunited lovers.

Of course, Latisha's main emotion was jealousy. It was impossible for any single person to look at a couple can-oodling like that and not feel a surge of envy. However, Latisha decided to take the high road; she would, as her meditation teacher was constantly preaching, take the nega-tive energy and convert it into positivity. Cat had found true love, and Latisha chose to see that as an omen that she, too, would find her soulmate, preferably sooner rather than later.

Hey, she thought, perking up. *Maybe Gerhardt has a friend for me! I've always liked the macho ones. And if he's going to criticize my taste in men, he can damn well pick me out a good one.*

This idea cheered her up so much that she flashed a beaming smile of self-satisfaction, settled back in her extremely comfortable leather seat, and clicked on TripAdvisor to find the highest-rated hotel in the whole of Cabo San Lucas.

Acknowledgements

Huge thanks to:

The amazing team at Pan Macmillan – I'm over the moon to have landed here! I love Wayne Brookes, my brilliant and very clever editor; Louise Buckley and Eloise Wood, who have taken great care with the nuts and bolts of putting *Mile High* together; and Kate Green, my dedicated and really focused publicist! And Jeremy Trevathan, with whom I've giggled immoderately at many Polaris . . . HUGE thanks, too, to the design team who worked so hard and thoughtfully to get my cover as superb as it is!

Valerie Laws for coming up with the name for Danny's cooking show, *Eat Me!*.

Dan Evans at Plan 9 for my beautiful website and tons of online help.

Matt Bates, my book supplier and Tudor gossip buddy.

Zoe Bellucci, a very talented singer/songwriter, for coming up with the 'Chasing Midnight' lyrics in literally three minutes flat. Quite amazing.

Angela Stiven for bidding at the auction run by Angela Collings and Dawn Hamblett, on behalf of the charity Moodswings, to get her name in a book. Better late than never and now you're a heroine, Angela!

The fabulous Bernie Keith for coming up with 'Maliboobed' – describing the transformation the Pure Air stewardesses go through on the LAX route.

Mandy Baker for telling me why all the Brontës died – their water supply had been poisoned by seepage from bodies in the overfilled graveyard in nearby St Michael and All Angels Church, Haworth.

Jamie Ranieri, Travis Pagel and Marcos Malkmuth are my NYC cheer team and I love 'em to death.

Vina Jackson and Stella Knightley for their lovely quotes – fantastic writers and wonderful friends.

Dorcas Pelling, who gave me the hilarious anecdote about the flight attendant making a catastrophically wrong announcement.

The gorgeous team of McKenna Jordan and John Kwiatkowski, and everyone at Murder by the Book, for bringing my smut to Texas.

Wayne Herbert, Justin Lanata, Jason Woodson, Jarrett Smith, Jeffrey Alan Marks, and David Webber let me use their names for the book . . . and Greg Herren and Lydia 'English Rose' Laws, who didn't but found themselves in it anyway!

Bloggers Kevin/I Heart Chick Lit and Emma Louise are such huge Twitter supporters of my books that they found themselves in this one as the Terrible Twins.

Steen Albrechtsen spreads not only the Scandilove worldwide but also love for my books – thanks, darling!

Sue Welfare for the suggestion about the Knock flight route being filled with terrifyingly drunken nuns and priests.

I honestly don't think I could have written this book in an even shorter time than usual without the Rebecca Chance fanfriends on Facebook and Twitter cheering me up with delightful banter! Thanks, Angela Collings, Dawn Hamblett, Tim Hughes, Jason Ellis, Tony Wood, Melanie Hearse, Jen Sheehan, Helen Smith, Ilana Bergsagel, Katherine Everett,

Julian Corkle, Robin Greene, Diane Jolly, Adam Pietrowski, John Soper, Gary Jordan, Louise Bell, Lisa Respers France, Stella Duffy, Shelley Silas, Rowan Coleman, Serena Mackesy, Tim Daly, Joy T. Chance, Lori Smith Jennaway, Alex Marwood, Sallie Dorsett, Alice Taylor, Joanne Wade, Marjorie Tucker, Teresa Wilson, Ashley James Cardwell, Margery Flax, Clinton Reed, Valerie Laws, Kelly Butterworth, Kirsty Maclennan, Amanda Marie Fulton, Marie Causey, Shana Mehtaab, Tracy Hanson, Beverley Ann Hopper, Nancy Pace Koffman, Katrina Smith, Helen Lusher, Russ Fry, Gavin Robinson, Laura Ford, Mary Mulkeen, Eileen McAninly, Pamela Cardone, Barb McNaughton, Shannon Mitchell, Claire Chiswell, Paula Louise Standen, Dawn Turnbull, Fiona Morris, Michelle Heneghan and Bryan Quertermous, Derek Jones and Colin Butts, the very exclusive (i.e. tiny) club of my straight male readers. Plus, of course, Paul Burston and the loyal Polari crew – Alex Hopkins, Ange Chan, Sian Pepper, Enda Guinan, Belinda Davies, John Southgate, Paul Brown, James Watts, Ian Sinclair Romanis and Jon Clarke. And the handful of beloved relatives brave enough to read my books – Dalia Hartman Bergsagel, Ilana Bergsagel, Sandy Makarwicz and Jean Polito. If I've left anyone out, please do send me a message and I will correct it in the next book!

As always, thanks to the Board. We are so lucky to have each other.

Lastly, to the FLs of FB, to none of whom will I EVER say, 'Bye, Felicia.' Not even the Pixie.

Killer Affair

by
Rebecca Chance

A shocking betrayal deserves wicked revenge . . .

Stunning, charismatic Lexy O'Brien is the reigning queen of British reality TV. Her life in front of the camera is planned and manipulated as successfully as any military assault.

But success breeds jealousy. When you're on top, the only way is down – and there's always someone standing by to give you a shove . . .

Dowdy Caroline Evans, a part-time blogger and writer of erotic fiction, is brought in to chronicle Lexy's life. Being taken under Lexy's wing is a dream come true for Caroline. But sampling the star's lifestyle is like tasting the most addictive of drugs, and it's not long before she is craving what she can't possibly have – or can she?

As Caroline and Lexy's lives and loves become increasingly entwined, it's only a matter of time before the hidden rivalry becomes a powder keg waiting to explode . . .